SHAMAR

THE SENTINELS OF EDEN

BOOK FOUR

CAROLYN DENMAN

ODYSSEY
BOOKS

Published by Odyssey Books in 2019
www.odysseybooks.com.au

A Cataloguing-in-Publication entry is available from the National Library of Australia

ISBN: 978-1925652758 (pbk)
ISBN: 978-1925652765 (ebook)

Cover design by Elijah Toten and Rebekah White

For Brian and Miche

Because having the dedication to read with, and then pray with your daughter every night should have some recognition. Yes, it was worth it, and thank you.

Also in this series

Songlines (Book One)
Sanguine (Book Two)
Sympath (Book Three)

The fruit of the righteous is a tree of life,
and he who wins souls is wise.

—Proverbs 11:30 NKJ

But he who would be born again indeed,
Must wake his soul unnumbered times a day,
And urge himself to life with holy greed;
Now ope his bosom to the Wind's free play;
And now, with patience forceful, hard, lie still,
Submiss and ready to the making will,
Athirst and empty, for God's breath to fill.

George MacDonald
A Book of Strife, in the form of the Diary of an Old Soul—1880

Author's Note

The *Sentinels of Eden* series is set in a fictional town based on Jardwadjali Country. I would like to acknowledge the traditional owners of that place. I also express my deepest respect for all Aboriginal elders, both past and present, across this Great Southern Land.

This novel is a speculative fiction story that draws loosely upon the foundational beliefs of many religions and cultures, including Judeo-Christian and Indigenous traditions. However, I do not purport to represent or detract from either ontological perspective. What is known as 'The Dreaming' is the foundational belief system of Aboriginal communities in Australia and I value and acknowledge Indigenous ontologies and epistemologies. I present my narrative ever conscious that Australian Indigenous society is the oldest continuous living culture in the world.

My desire is that this fantasy tale reflects the co-existence and interconnectedness of belief systems and that you enjoy it, always conscious of my deep respect for Aboriginal country and Aboriginal society.

Chapter 1

Annie felt burdened by a memory that wasn't hers. It belonged to someone she'd never even met. The man responsible for her mother's murder, Mr Rosa, had died in jail. She remembered the day her partner Cherub, Harry, had raced up from the cottage to switch on the news report so she and Lucas could hear it for themselves. While Harry's face had been cast in a sturdy mask of passive contentment, his heart had been full of sorrow and longing. Was there anyone left who could see through that mask? No. Wait. Harry was gone now too. If only he'd listened that day when she'd tried to convince him to move to the Garden. Instead, he'd insisted on remaining in the place where rubies and diamonds were valued more than lives. A place where those whispers would continue to haunt her, even without Mr Rosa. Chills chased the memory of that voice around her mind and down her spine. It hunted for a clue. Hunted for her. Relentless.

I have a story worth investigating. A frightened jeweller to whisper to. And a town to search.

There had to be a reason the standing stones had revealed someone else's secret, and now she had to choose whether to allow Eden's perfection to soothe away her sense of urgency, or to follow the thread of her flawed recollections. After spending the night reliving her past she was exhausted, yet too afraid to sleep. Too afraid of her dreams, in case they forced her to remember even more. Why couldn't her story just have ended there? Why couldn't she have stayed locked away in those first few years after Lucas decided to stay in Nalong? That town was not timeless like Eden. Events kept ticking along, counting down from one disaster to the next.

Beside her, a silver tree dropped a ripe piece of Fruit that rolled gently to a stop within arm's reach. Its ambrosial fragrance made her mouth water and her fingertips twitch. One bite of the Living Fruit would dull her memories and cure both her tiredness and anxiety. Sadly, there were ramifications for her. She wasn't ready to unravel all the tangled emotions that were wrapped around her past. Enough shame still haunted her that eating from the Tree of Life would infect it with an illness it couldn't heal. Besides, she had work to do and couldn't afford to get lulled by the Garden's autumn somnolence. Nor could she continue to hide from her own memories. She turned from the Fruit with a sigh.

There was only one person in Eden who might understand, and she finally found him with a group of five others, grinding various coloured rocks to make paint. Nayn came over as soon as he noticed her waiting under a nearby tree. His unruly white curls were streaked with bright orange where he'd pushed it out of his face with dusty fingers.

You are not happy, he signed as he approached. As if she didn't know.

Just tired. I've been up all night. Remembering.

He gave a solemn nod. *The standing stones can hold many memories. They act like the planet's own consciousness. Stones, gems, some metals. The bones of the Earth have ways of keeping hold of memories, and what is consciousness if not memory with emotion?*

Annie grabbed hold of Nayn's wrist, inspecting the orange stains on his hand. *How much of this ochre have you been breathing in?*

Enough to give me heightened powers of deduction. You are not just tired. Dallmin has hurt your heart, and you are angry, he persisted. There was no sign for angry, but he used his facial expressions to convey what he meant. If she hadn't been feeling so miserable it would have been comical.

He is gone now, so how can I be angry at him?

As easily as breathing. You feel what you feel. That is the way we are built, even here.

Pressing her lips together, she looked across to the people mixing paint ingredients. They were laughing at Bungee, who'd tipped a wooden bowl of powdered lapis lazuli over himself and was now sneezing out blue dust. Their carefree laughter at the dog's antics only made her feel jealous. Her anger at herself and at Dallmin had no place in Eden, no matter what Nayn said.

I should have known better, she signed. *Have I lost all sense of rea-son? Have my memories of Nalong slipped so far away that I've lost touch completely? Lainie was so shocked when she discovered he had left, so why wasn't I? I've basically killed him, Nayn. By letting him leave the Garden I've doomed him to an early death. What will become of him? And what does that make me?*

Nayn wrapped a strong arm around her shoulders and gave her a quick squeeze. Then he picked a bunch of tiny yellow flowers and started to weave them together with some long grass strands. *Dallmin is not dead, Annie. He is alive and burdened by knowledge he should never have had to face. It is important you remember this. He still loves you. What that makes you … is a beloved one.*

And what use is it to be beloved if I cannot love back? He can never return here.

When Nayn frowned at her she realised how bitter her words were.

Perhaps you should get some rest, he suggested. *And we can talk later.*

Why bother talking more about this? The outcome won't change whether I'm rested or not. Dallmin is lost. No one ever returns once they have been outside.

Finishing the tiny floral crown, he placed it on her head. *Except us.*

Yeah. Except Cherubim.

And one other … that I know of.

Annie gaped at him. *Really? Who?*

He laughed and refused to answer, despite all her cues telling him how badly she needed to know. Instead, he jumped up and trotted away to join the paint-makers. Unless she wanted to make a scene in front of the innocent humans, she would have to wait for him to return.

Chapter 2

I was dying. Again.

'Can't breathe.'

My lungs were being crushed. I'd already been poisoned earlier that day, and then resurrected by my best friend, Noah, who'd confused me by telling me off for eating too much Fruit while simultaneously shoving a juicy piece of it into my mouth. Then I'd scaled a cliff face with numerous failed attempts, each time waking up to the sight of Beltana's patient smile and the taste of more Living Fruit on my lips. And now I couldn't breathe. Enough was enough.

I sucked in a shallow sip of air and craned my neck to look at Bane. He wasn't going to be of any use. His smile was all roses and chocolates as he leaned back against the bench with his ankles crossed and did nothing.

Since I'd climbed my way out of Eden at sunset, Bane had worn an expression that kept switching between thrilled and guilty—like someone who'd come in second but won the Cattleman's Cup on a minor technicality. He was so happy he'd even let me drive us down the mountain on my dirt bike without a single argument. Or perhaps that had something to do with the bandage and grazes on his forearms. He'd ignored my question when I'd asked about them, just like he'd evaded my demand for my ring, mumbling something about waiting until we were alone. I hadn't argued, secretly relieved at the thought of a proper proposal. After all, neither of us had actually mentioned the word 'marriage', so maybe the ring his mother had sneakily passed to him was an ordinary gift and I'd misunderstood. Things in this world always seemed to be more complicated than I expected. There was no way I was going to mention it again, just in case. I would look like a right drongo. A drongo who might need him to heal me if I didn't get out of this bear hug soon. Tessa and Aunt Lily were too busy sterilising baby equipment to even notice my predicament, and Noah was stretching to reach the bag of chips he'd hidden on the top shelf of the pantry he thought no one else could get to, which he apparently thought was far more of a priority.

'Please,' I croaked. 'I like air.'

Senior Sergeant Mick Loxwood wiped tears from his eyes as he finally loosened his grip. Holding me at arms' length, he looked me over as if checking to see I hadn't accidentally left any body parts in the realm of the dead.

'Incredible, Lainie. Absolutely incredible. It really is all really real, isn't it?'

I hoped he didn't babble this unprofessionally when he was working.

'Sergeant, you can't tell anyone,' I reminded him. Far too many people knew the truth about the Garden of Eden already and it was getting way out of hand. Noah had some explaining to do as to why he'd allowed Tim to come up the ridge with them. He'd been *right there* when I'd emerged from across the boundary, alive and well, making it impossible to explain away the day's events with anything other than the truth. Just because Tim had earned Bane's trust during their time with the Army Reserves didn't mean it was fine to tell him about the world's most holy secret.

Out of the corner of my eye, I could see Tim staring at me from the far end of the kitchen. He hadn't spoken a word since my resurrection. What would he think if we told him it wasn't my first? I wasn't sure what I could do to help him so I'd been trying to give him space, only he kept following me, staring at me with those great big brown eyes.

Sergeant Loxwood stood straighter. 'I know how to remain discreet. You can trust me. And please, Lainie, I think it's time you called me Mick. Most adults around here do. Besides, I'm fairly certain that in the grand scheme of things you outrank me by a long way.' He took a step back and lifted his chin. 'You're a holy creature. I mean, a higher being. Should I be genuflecting or something?'

'Genu ... what? No! No kneeling or bowing or anything, please.

Could you imagine what Noah would be like if people started doing that to him? He's insufferable enough as it is.'

Noah paused his salt and vinegar chip feast and smiled at the policeman. *That* smile. Full of confidence and mischief. It made Mick roll his eyes. 'I see your point.'

'Seriously, I'm still just *me*,' I insisted, catching Tim's eye in the hope that he understood too. As if on cue, Aunt Lily grabbed me from behind and peppered me with kisses like I was five years old again. It was a much more welcome way of showing me affection than the policeman's suggestion, but she'd been doing it on and off since I'd walked in the door and it was getting sticky, so I wriggled around and hugged her back, relieved beyond words that I hadn't left her alone again. She was my rock, and I'd abandoned her for too long already. I had no intention of leaving her to clean up my messes anymore.

Reminded of messes, I turned back to the burly officer.

'Um, Mick, what happens now? Who thinks I'm dead? What did I miss and what do I need to do?'

The sudden silence in the room was very disconcerting.

The sergeant gave a little cough and brushed his fingers across the badge on his shoulder, as if it might help him switch back to reality. 'Well, there are really only the two ambos who worked on you, I think. They declared you as deceased. What would you like us to tell them? I mean, do you want to stay officially dead? We could do it if you like because Noah, well, he … made a copy of your … corpse.'

My eyebrows rose about as much as Noah's eyes suddenly lowered. It was hard to stay focused. What exactly did I want? My first thought was of my mother. I'd grown up thinking she was dead, and all the logical reasons in the world would never make up for what that had cost me.

'I don't want to be dead,' I decided. 'It's not as exciting as it sounds— at least, I don't think so, it's a bit hard to remember … My point is that I want to live, properly, with my family and friends. No way am I going to hide away for the rest of my life.' Bane's smile began to slip, so I kept talking before he could argue. 'Listen, my job is to protect Eden so, presumably, the reason Jake's compelled to kill me is to prevent me from doing that. So clearly I need to be alive. End of discussion.'

Tessa handed me a glass of water. 'Can we tell the paramedics Noah revived her after they left? They did see him insist on continuing the CPR. It'll freak them out a lot, but it's still the most logical explanation there is—not to mention it's actually the truth.'

The senior sergeant peered at me, considering. 'They'll expect you to still be very sick though, with traces of cyanide still in your system. They'll insist on running all sorts of tests in hospital. Will you be able to fool them?'

I winked, but Bane cleared his throat. His hands gripped the bench so hard that a spot of blood blossomed through the bandage on his forearm.

'Traces of cyanide? *How* will you fool them, exactly?' And just like that his elusive smile was gone again.

It was a fair question. How *was* I going to fool the doctors? Dose myself with a small amount of poison and let Bane heal me once the hospital was satisfied? That didn't sound like fun, even though I couldn't remember much about my last experience of it. The details seemed too irrelevant to dwell on, but it felt as if I had died in a game and then re-spawned and kept going. It made me wonder how many lives I had left and whether I could collect some little spare-life hearts somewhere in case I ran out. Perhaps it would be best to avoid recontaminating my body with cyanide after all.

'Well, maybe I could avoid the issue altogether. I'll tell them I'm going to Melbourne for a "proper" check-up and disappear for a while. Maybe that will make it harder for Jake to track me.'

Across the table, Tessa opened her mouth to say something, but Bane glared at her so icily she snapped her mouth shut again. There was more going on than anyone had been game to tell me. I decided to be patient until I could pester each of them individually. Much better chance of getting the whole truth that way.

Once again Mick Loxwood came to our aid. 'Leave the paramedics to me. The coroner was never called so you were never legally dead. I'll write in my report that you were revived and if anyone asks, I'll make sure they leave you alone and stay quiet about everything that's happened.' He sounded overly confident, like he was trying to suck up to one of his superiors. It felt weird to have him sound so deferential.

'What about the Ashbrees?' Aunt Lily asked as she rummaged

around the fridge for some leftovers to heat up. 'They've been calling all afternoon. I avoided telling them about the poison, but they know something's up. It might be worth letting Liam swing by to reassure him you're okay.'

I nodded. 'And also let him know you can all stop patrolling. I assume Jake did a runner once he realised I was dead?'

Bane nodded, looking grim. No one else met my eyes and the room became even quieter. I prudently suppressed my curiosity and instead tried to cover the awkward moment by reaching for a piece of fruit, only the fruit bowl was gone. Feeling rather embarrassed, I hopped up on a clear section of the bench and sat on my hands. Time to switch topics.

'Should I change into other clothes? I'm not sure I can explain to Liam why I would be wearing this,' I said, regretfully poking at a tear in the diaphanous red dress Beltana had given me, which I'd ruined by spending the afternoon rock-climbing in it.

'Why *are* you wearing it?' my aunt asked.

Images of bright trees and curious animals flashed through my mind as I remembered what I'd been feeling after I'd read Bane's stupid letter. Everything there had been so simple, so obvious. Bane had been miserable. So had I. We wanted to be with each other, and in Eden there was simply no point in trying to come to terms with why we shouldn't be. My desire had been very strong, and so I'd needed to let him know. Simple.

'I wanted to be clear about what I wanted,' I explained, throwing Bane a slinky smile. Then I remembered. 'Oh, I gave my other clothes away. I don't even have any spare jeans anymore.'

'Um, I made some more for you, if you don't mind wearing some-thing that's been on a fake corpse,' Noah mumbled, letting his pale hair fall forward to avoid meeting my eyes.

Everyone else in the room looked queasy, but I was incredibly curi-ous to see what he'd done. Darting out of the kitchen, I started searching each of the bedrooms for my body and soon discovered they'd left it on the floor in the lounge room, lying on a stretcher. By the time I found it Bane was there waiting for me, looking like he'd been asked to give a speech in assembly. He was very pale. Almost as pale as my dead body.

'Woah, it's exactly like me. Man, that is *creepy*.' I picked up my dead hand and waved it at myself cheerily. 'Typical. Noah made my boobs too big. Hey, do you think he could do it again? You know, to me?'

'Lainie, do you have to joke about this?' Bane asked, tight-lipped.

'*Of course I do.* I'm looking at my own fake dead body! How long do you think it will keep? Maybe we can preserve it somehow, or stuff it or something,' I suggested, peeling back my lips to see my teeth.

Groaning, my Guardian slumped down onto the couch and buried his head in his arms so he didn't have to watch. 'We can't keep it. Someone might see it,' he mumbled from underneath his elbows. 'Please, Lainie, can you just get on with it? I was going to help you undress it, but I honestly don't think I can now. Can't you find something else to wear?'

'Oooh, tough soldier you are. Can't even undress a corpse. Your training must have been pretty slack,' I teased as I sat on the floor and started to tug my jeans down. Were my ankles really this bony?

'I must have missed that demo. They probably had it right after the lecture on how to stop your girlfriend from climbing up a cliff with no safety equipment. Bad day to pull a sickie, in hindsight.' He still refused to stop hiding.

'Safety equipment? You still haven't grasped the whole Tree of Life concept yet, have you?'

His head snapped up. 'How many times did you need it today?'

'I don't remember,' I evaded.

He rubbed his eyebrow and groaned like he had a whopper of a headache. Then he took a calming breath. 'Why are you always so stubborn?'

I let the dead leg drop awkwardly to the floor and gave him my full attention. 'Because I know what you went through last time I left. It wasn't fair on you. You were introduced to a whole new reality when you found out about Eden, and about the role you were born for, and I cut you off from it because I arrogantly decided that was in your best interest. That wasn't my choice to make. Just like it isn't your choice to decide where I should live. So tell me the truth. Do you really wish I hadn't come back?' I tried to sort through the tangle of complex motivations that were part of this world. It was no good. The conflicts were not so much 'tangled' as 'dreadlocked'.

He met my eyes with a sigh. 'No,' he said. 'Seeing you return today—so vibrant and alive—was one of the happiest moments of my life. I don't deserve it and I'm being incredibly selfish. Maybe I should be stronger and somehow force you to stay safe in Eden. I made that choice for you earlier today when you were … when you couldn't speak for yourself. I guess I hoped you would wake up in the Garden and forget all the terrible things that had happened here. Slide peacefully back into the life you'd built and move on.' He gave a self-deprecating smile. 'I arrogantly decided it was in your best interest. I'm sorry. And besides, I can't make myself let go of you again. I can't.'

We stared at each other, both wanting more and both too afraid to be the one to move. I was still freshly Eden-prejudiced and our 'wants' matched all too well, so I was having all sorts of electric feelings flooding my system. I didn't know what his excuse was, but eventually he buried his head back in his arms again with a soft whimper.

Resolutely, I finished pulling off the jeans and then stripped the body of the t-shirt Noah had conjured.

'Noah!' I roared. 'Get in here *now*.'

Panicked by my tone, he and everyone else rushed over from the kitchen. To his credit, Tim didn't actually faint. He did, however, take one fraught look at me sitting on the floor next to my cloned body before bolting for the bathroom, hand on mouth.

I turned back to Noah. My best friend didn't even bother to look ashamed as I pointed to the flimsy scrap of red lace he'd conjured for my undergarments. 'What was the point of the sexy lingerie, exactly?'

Bane exhaled and buried his head again, refusing to look.

'Dunno any other sort,' Noah mumbled around a mouthful of chips.

The sergeant, Aunt Lily, and I all turned to Tessa, who looked for a moment like she was scrambling for something to say. After a moment she simply grinned and winked at me.

Noah started throwing chips at Bane's head to make him open his eyes. 'I can try to conjure up a matching set for Bane to wear if it's equality you're concerned about.'

Emerging from his elbow cave like an angry dragon, Bane whacked him squarely in the face with a cushion. 'I don't know whose honour I suddenly feel the need to defend, or even why. I just know you need to be brought down a peg or two, Cherub,' Bane declared, chasing him out of the room. The frivolity ended, however, when a disturbing thump came from the hall where Noah had fled.

'Ah, Lainie?' I heard Noah call from the hallway. 'I think I broke him.' This time he actually sounded contrite.

Rushing out, all I could see was Bane's motionless form slumped against a wall, as if he'd run straight into it without even trying to stop.

'He was right behind me and then … I didn't do it,' Noah insisted, shaking his blond hair away from his eyes to look at me. His emerald gaze glowed with innocence, no less powerful for the fact I knew it stemmed from his supernatural gifting.

Aunt Lily kneeled down to check over Bane's fallen jumble of limbs while I stood frozen, feeling confused and terrified. Had Jake somehow poisoned him, too? I couldn't lose him …

'He shouldn't have tried to run so soon after a concussion,' she rebuked. 'Tim was right; we should have had him checked out properly.'

'Concussion?' I asked, trying without much success to piece together my scattered memories. Being resurrected with Living Fruit—multiple times—had really messed with my recollection of the day's events. None of what I remembered explained the bandage on my Guardian's forearm or the raw grazes on both his wrists, but until now I'd assumed it wasn't anything too serious because he hadn't paid them any attention at all. So much for waiting until we were alone for an explanation. 'What happened while I was dead?' I demanded. 'What did I miss?'

The awkward silence in the hall was broken after a few moments by a groan from Bane as he began to wake.

'I'll get some ice,' Tessa and Noah said simultaneously as they escaped back to the kitchen.

The sergeant kneeled and checked Bane's pupils and then stood back, looking reassuringly calm, so I took that to mean he wasn't dying. Kneeling down, I cradled Bane's head on my lap and it was then I felt the large lump behind his ear. No wonder he'd let me drive us down the ridge. He shouldn't even be out of bed, let alone riding dirt bikes or chasing rogue Cherubim around the house.

'What happened?' he mumbled as I checked his scalp for more wounds.

'You ran up a wall and forgot to flip over and land on your feet,' I explained. 'I thought I taught you better than that. Perhaps it had something to do with the concussion you neglected to mention to me?'

'Oh, sorry. You were dead at the time so I didn't think to tell you. Everyone else knew.'

Just then Tim's pasty-looking face appeared from around the bathroom door. 'I'm sorry, Lainie, I tried to make him rest. He wouldn't listen to me. Dallmin gave him one heck of a whack with that frypan. He really should have gone straight to hospital.'

This place was so weird. I gave a little snort at Tim's joke, but when I looked back at Bane his eyes were sad.

'Where *is* Dallmin? I assumed you didn't get as far as finding him before you had to come back for me. What on Earth makes Tim think he would ever hurt someone? He couldn't. Any more than you could hurt me. It would be impossible. Tell me what really happened, and don't be embarrassed to admit you tripped in a rabbit hole or something. I know how reckless you get when I'm ...' My voice trailed off as every muscle in Bane's face tensed up. A small shudder went through his frame, as if he was remembering the danger I'd been in.

'Dallmin's changed, Lainie. He betrayed us and kept me away from you on purpose while you were dying. He also tried to kill Noah.' His voice was slurred and he was struggling to focus on my face.

'Okay, I've changed my mind. Don't talk. Rest. You're not making any sense anyhow. I'll get someone else to explain.' Since Noah and Tessa had bailed, my narrowed gaze rested on my aunt's face.

She nodded in tacit affirmation of his story. 'Jake lied to Dallmin and tricked him into telling him about Eden. Dallmin lured Bane out to the state park and helped Jake to capture him so he could keep you both from the cave, hoping to get back home without you preventing him. Noah, Tess, and your mum stopped him, but Jake ran off with the sword. I can't tell you much more—I don't get given details.'

'There's a sword?' Tim gasped from the doorway. His lanky frame grew a few inches and the sudden glint in his eyes reminded me of a child in a lolly shop.

'Not anymore, apparently. Why are we all still here? Why hasn't anyone gone after them?' My voice was climbing higher by the second.

Noah's head, which had appeared from around the kitchen door, hastily disappeared again.

Luckily Tessa wasn't such a chicken. 'Jake saw Noah wielding the sword. He's aware now that Noah is a Cherub too. I don't want Noah going after that idiot, at least not without me. Although at the rate I've been going, Noah might be better off without me around at all,' she admitted as she handed my aunt a bag of frozen peas.

'Jake knows about Noah?' I wailed. 'Wait, did you say "wielded" the sword?'

She ignored me because Noah had re-emerged from the kitchen and had baled her up against the wall with only his freaky charming eyes.

'Tessa. How can you say that? You saved my life. If you hadn't tackled Dallmin, his knife would have gone straight through my heart. He has excellent aim, even if he's never tried to hit a living creature before. Not to mention that you healed my punctured lung. How can you possibly think I'd be better off without you?'

'You would have killed Jake if I hadn't intervened,' she replied. 'I'm still struggling to decide if I did the right thing in preventing you. He'll come for you. Both of you. And I don't know if I can stop him. If Bane with all his army training can't keep him from Lainie, then what chance do I have?' She crumpled into his arms and clung to him as if she was trying to heal him in advance of all the wounds she imagined him receiving.

How could this have happened? I was more confused than ever. Dallmin threw a knife at Noah? Tessa tackled him? Was that why her left eye looked swollen? And how the hokey had Jake stolen a sword that incinerated anyone who got too close to it?

'I guess it's a good thing I came back,' I pointed out, leaning back against the wall. 'Clearly, I'm needed here. One lousy afternoon off duty and the whole world craps itself.'

Everyone started shoe-gazing. Except for Tim.

'There's really a sword?' he asked again.

From the end of the hall came the sound of an infant's hungry wail.

Chapter 3

'Once when you were away, I ate half a can of condensed milk for lunch. That tin of chickpeas is much healthier. It'll be fine.'

'Ew, Lainie, I didn't want to know that,' Aunt Lily said as she reached into the scary back corner of the fridge to find something to go with the chickpeas.

Now that things had settled down, everyone was starving. Nathaniel, Noah, and I were the only ones who had eaten anything since lunchtime, and all my snacks had resulted in either a death or a resurrection. I kind of wanted to eat something boring for a change.

'I don't get it,' she said. 'I did the groceries a couple of days ago. All we have left is dog food. Speaking of which, Lainie, have you fed Wendy yet?'

Ah. Right. Wendy. Last time I'd seen her she'd been running around Eden with Bungee. 'She's in Neverland.'

Noah groaned and turned to Tessa. 'I thought you were watching her?'

'I got distracted,' she defended. 'Besides, you're the one who locked her in the Garden. Can't we hoist her up the cliff in a sling or something?'

'No,' Noah and I said simultaneously. Forcing anyone to leave Eden against their will—even a dog—was not something we could stomach even talking about. Not once they'd been allowed in.

Aunt Lily took the hint and wisely changed the subject as she pulled some end-of-season tomatoes from the windowsill. They didn't look very ripe. 'So what are we going to do for dinner?'

'We still have plenty of fruit hampers left,' I said with a grin.

'No, we don't. Mick just took them all away to be analysed. Would you really want to risk anyone eating them?'

Everyone seemed to have lost what little sense of humour they once had. In fact, they were all looking far too grumpy, given what a special day it was. Nathaniel's first day at home. A rough one, maybe, but he was safe and sleepy and full of milky goodness and surrounded by family. How sweet were those tiny fingers? Clasped around my pinkie. One day those fingers would be clasped around the bar of a hang glider, and I would be right there with him, giving him an aerial view of the Garden. Well, maybe not. Taking a hang glider into Eden where the locals could see it hadn't worked out so well last time.

Tessa gave me a tired smile as she scooped her son out of my arms and left the room to put him back to bed. The bruise on her face was starting to swell, and she looked about ready to collapse. It had been a long and eventful day for us all, although I felt great. Eden Fruit was amazing stuff.

The phone rang and Aunt Lily snatched it up before I could. It was David Ashbree. 'Tell him to send Liam for some pizza,' Tim suggested as she reassured our neighbour that everything was fine.

Great idea, I signed to her before remembering to speak out loud— or at least, in a loud whisper. 'It'll take ages, which will give us time to get our stories straight and dispose of the body, and give him an excuse to come over,' I said. Then I grinned at Tim. 'Did you hear that? I got to use the phrase "dispose of the body".'

Tim nearly smiled.

My aunt nodded to me and then started to explain to Noah's dad what Dallmin and Jake had done to Bane. I leaned across so I could listen in. Like the rest of us, he sounded incredulous at the thought of the gentle man turning on us. My aunt couldn't explain why and so didn't try. As she hung up, she rubbed her eyes.

'Liam's on his way. It'll take an hour and a half for him to get to town and back. I hope you appreciate what it takes to pop out for pizza here,' she admonished Tim.

Satisfied, I skipped to the lounge room to check on Bane. We weren't really supposed to let him sleep for too long without checking he could wake up. So I checked. Fairy-tale style.

Fascinated, and more than a little bit regretful, I watched my body dissolve into thin air. No one had agreed with me that it might be wise to keep a spare one around in case I broke mine again, although I suspected Tim was imagining all sorts of possible scenarios in which we could use it to lure Jake into a trap. Unfortunately, he was still too intimidated to speak up.

'Shameful waste of perfectly good lingerie,' Noah mumbled as his soft powerful phrases trailed away. I stomped on his foot and Tessa didn't even complain. On the couch, Bane stirred again so I shooed everyone back into the kitchen.

We'd spent the last half hour sharing each of our versions of the day's events, although I was restricted on most of mine, either unable to speak or unable to remember. Tim was given a badly structured lecture on the truth behind Eden, Cherubim, and Guardians pieced together from what each of us could force ourselves to explain, and tidied up a little by Aunt Lily.

What the others had told me was overwhelming. The ancient revolving sword had been stolen by a violent drug-addict who was compelled to kill me and my best friend, and potentially his infant son. Dallmin had turned against us and then run away, and was now exiled from his home and alone out in the world with no idea how to look after himself. Jake knew about Eden and knew where it was—my mind still reeled when I thought about that—but at least Noah and Bane had partially addressed that issue by blocking up the cavern with rocks again. All in all, things were looking disastrous. It was time for comfort food. The mood in the house lifted considerably when Liam finally arrived with an armload of pizzas, even if we all shushed him the moment he entered so he wouldn't wake Bane.

'What was Jake hoping to achieve?' Liam asked a little while later as he picked another mushroom off his pizza and flicked it at his brother. 'Why lure Bane away from her and then run away?' Confusion darkened his friendly Ashbree-green eyes.

'He tried to poison me. Tim called an ambulance and I'm fine,' I admitted vaguely. The deception felt like a ball of string tangling my insides, but it was a much smaller ball of string than the one I would have had if I'd tried to tell him the whole truth. 'Sorry we didn't tell you everything straight away,' I continued. 'Sergeant Loxwood wanted us to keep things quiet for a while.' I'd spent the last half an hour practising the lie and it didn't come out easily, so I watched Liam's reaction rather nervously.

Liam's slice of pizza slid back into the box while he stared at the table looking angrier by the second. 'Mick gave good advice. If I'd known what was happening I would have rallied everyone to go after that moron, and I can tell you now the Victorian Police Force wouldn't have approved of my actions if I'd caught up with him. Are we sure he's really gone? What if he comes back? I can't believe Mick didn't leave someone here to keep an eye on things.'

'He's coming back himself later tonight. And he's offered me somewhere safe to stay for a while,' I said, which was true. I just didn't tell Liam I'd refused. 'Bane and I will leave Nalong tomorrow. I won't have that lunatic anywhere near my family if I can avoid it. If he comes looking for me here, he'll be out of luck.'

Liam stood and swept me up into yet another crushing embrace. Given Aunt Lily was my only living blood relative—that he was aware of—it was obvious to everyone I was including all the Ashbrees when I talked of family. Of course, what he didn't know was that Noah was also a target now. Somehow I needed to track down Jake before he could come after my best friend. I glanced his way, and he met my gaze with barely contained frustration. Conflicted between wanting to help me retrieve the sword and needing to stay to care for his new baby and defend Eden, I could tell he was struggling to stay calm.

'Bane shouldn't drive for a few days at least,' Liam pointed out. 'Or has Mick arranged someone to take you?'

Tim interrupted so fast he almost choked on his mouthful of Meat-lovers. 'I'm driving them,' he announced, possibly to save me from having to lie again. Was I that bad at it? Or was he worried we'd leave him behind?

Liam looked Tim over as if assessing his trustworthiness and then nodded, apparently satisfied. Then he peered around the doorway to where Bane was asleep on the couch. 'Even so, you might want to wait a day or so for him to recover,' he advised. 'I remember the aftermath of the last concussion I had. A long car trip would have been torture.'

He was right. And besides, I had no idea where to start looking for either Jake or Dallmin. Perhaps some planning would be wise.

As Liam gathered himself up to leave, Aunt Lily gasped. 'Oh! That spare fruit hamper I brought over yesterday? Don't let anyone eat any of it.'

Looking both pale and cross, Liam nodded, gave my shoulder one last squeeze and then headed out the door.

A thick fog stifled the morning air, blocking my view no matter how hard I squinted out through the lounge room window. Our old floral curtains outlined the view like a tacky ornate frame around a blank canvas.

I turned away from the window to watch Bane sleeping with Inara curled around his elbow. A faded bruise coloured the corner of his jaw, so minor compared with his other injuries that even he probably hadn't noticed it, and his long dark eyelashes twitched in time with some dark dream. Even so, his face still looked more serene than I had seen him for a long time. As gently as possible, I stretched out my back, hoping my stiffness wasn't enough to disrupt his sleep. I'd spent an uncomfortable night on a blow-up mattress while he'd slept on the couch. After much arguing with my aunt, I'd convinced her to move back into her cottage and let me take the floor, as I hadn't wanted to move my Guardian anyway once he was finally allowed to sleep properly.

Shivering in my recently conjured jeans and t-shirt, I considered finding some socks and shoes. The fire was out, even though I could have easily fed it during the night. It hadn't occurred to me to bother, and now I felt bad because Bane was unwell and should probably be kept as warm as possible. Trying hard not to disturb him, I draped my own discarded blanket over his hips. Inara looked up at me, her tail twitching, but a quick scratch under her chin was payment enough to settle her back to sleep with her chosen companion before I turned to leave.

Despite feeling tired from waking every couple of hours overnight to check if Bane was okay, I still relished the idea of going outside to do normal morning chores like feeding the chickens and tossing out hay to the horses. Foggy mornings were my favourite, when cobwebs glistened like jewels strung between fence rails, all noises were muffled, and the farm was shrouded with mystery. Unfortunately, the mystery of what was hiding in the fog usually just ended up being unexpected sheep poo. Common sense overcame my laziness as I thought it through and turned in search of my boots.

'Morning, miracle girl,' Bane mumbled as he grabbed my hand on my way past the couch.

'Good morning, Lance Corporal Millard. Did you sleep well?'

'Not really. Some crazy angel kept waking me up every time I closed my eyes. I hated every moment,' he teased. Given the number of kisses he'd stolen each time I'd woken him, I highly doubted that.

'Well then, perhaps you should get a couple more hours now. I'm going out to do some chores. I won't be long.'

He closed his eyes and tilted his head, assessing the level of danger I was in to see if it was safe enough for me to go alone.

'Honestly, Bane. You can't follow me everywhere.'

'Don't I know it. If I could, we'd both be safely tucked away in paradise playing harps or something. Never mind, I'll just have to settle for a kiss before you go outside.' Pulling me closer, he started to sit up and then winced.

'Slowly!' I scolded. 'I don't want Tim on my case. He's even worse than Aunt Lily.'

'Yeah, except I don't think he would dare try to tell you off for anything. Not after yesterday.' He lay back down and tentatively touched the lump behind his ear. Although it had gone down a lot, it still looked very painful.

'What do I do about him, Bane? I can't have him treating me like some kind of superhero. People will notice.' I checked the bandage on his forearm. It needed changing again, but I wasn't confident I could do it well enough for Tim's approval.

'Lainie, you *are* a superhero. The things you and Noah can do seem limitless, and it always comes so naturally and easily to you. I think that's what freaks us all out the most. It would be easier to deal with if it looked like you were putting in some effort, at least.'

I thought it over, picking at his bandage. 'So your suggestion for putting Tim at ease is to look constipated as I speak the sacred language?'

Laughing, he pulled me down and wrapped me in his warm arms, deposing of the cranky cat in the process. The chickens were going to be hungry for a while longer.

⮬

Tim tied off the bandage. 'I've only tidied up the outer dressing for now because I don't want to disturb the steri-strips again. It should be fine for a while longer so long as you stop picking at it and *keep it dry*,' he commanded. He sounded scarily like Bane's mum Beth, and she was a music teacher.

'Lainie fiddled with it, not me,' Bane dobbed, and Tim's face went from stern to sheepish in a heartbeat. I shook my head at Bane in silent admonition. He ignored me, reaching over to serve up some of the hot breakfast I'd prepared. He took a tiny bite of scrambled egg, chickpeas, and soggy cooked tomato before sliding the same plate over to me.

'Do you always eat off other people's plates?' I objected, sliding it back to his side of the table.

'I do now,' he said with a shrug, taking a bite of my toast then pushing it back to me again. 'Don't worry. If you catch any germs from me I'll heal you. And I'll leave you plenty.' He was completely unapologetic.

'I cooked this myself,' I argued. 'I promise I didn't poison it.'

'The ingredients could have been compromised.'

'Compromised? You make it sound like the wild rabbits have been blackmailing the chickens to lay poisonous eggs. Are you seriously going to do this with everything I eat?'

'And drink.'

'Can't you just heal me if I'm poisoned?'

'Apparently not.'

I winced at my thoughtless lack of tact.

He set his jaw. 'Some poisons are fast-acting. I'd rather not risk it,' he said.

'So you'd rather be killed yourself and leave me unprotected?' I countered, feeling smug.

He pondered that for a moment and then pushed my plate over to Tim. 'Fine. Tim can do it.'

Shocked beyond words, I stared at them both as Tim happily took a second bite of my toast before sliding the plate back to me with a flourish of his hands.

'I can't believe you did that! How can you be so prepared to risk Tim's life without even talking to him about it?'

He shrugged. 'We have talked about it. Two years ago, when we were in the same fireteam. We have each other's backs. End of story,' he explained. Tim nodded in confirmation.

'I'm not part of your fireteam. He never agreed to risk his life for me,' I argued.

'You're basically family. Same thing.'

I had thought farmers were good at looking out for one another. This took the meaning of loyalty to a whole new level.

'Would you do the same thing for Tim's partner?' I challenged again, wondering if such a creature existed.

'Of course,' he declared, looking at his friend. 'Except maybe Fiona. She was annoying.'

Tim opened his mouth to protest, thought for a second, and then nodded again.

I took a deep breath. 'Bane. Seriously. Testing my food doesn't make any sense. You told me only the apple cores were poisoned anyway, so how would tasting it first have helped?' Surely he could see how ridiculous he was being.

'All right, just until we leave here, then,' he conceded, tucking into his own breakfast.

'Speaking of which,' I said as I pushed around my violated scrambled eggs, 'can you please do whatever it is you need to do to track down Dallmin's phone? He could be anywhere by now, and I'd like to bring him back as soon as possible so I know he's safe here before we go after Jake.'

A chickpea fell off his fork as he stared at me.

I glanced at Tim for a clue as to what I'd missed. He was biting his lip and watching Bane warily.

'Tell me you can track him, Bane, please.' We didn't have time to go searching each nearby town like when he'd first arrived.

'Of course I can. It's easy. But why would we want to?'

Horrified, I took a moment to read his body language, to check he wasn't joking. He wasn't.

'Because he's basically family,' I threw back at him. 'We have each other's backs.'

He slammed his fork down onto the table. 'He threw a knife at Noah's back. *At his back.* He chose *not* to be a part of this family, Lainie, when he let you die!'

'He didn't understand what he was doing! It wasn't his fault. You have no idea what he's going through, being exiled from his home.'

Noah peered around the corner, drawn by the sound of an argument. 'What's going on in here? We just got Nathaniel to sleep and Tessa's gone back to bed. Are you two actually *arguing*? I thought you both ran out of insults after high school.'

'Sorry, Noah. Bane doesn't think we should go after Dallmin. I won't leave him to fend for himself!'

'What? Of course not. Should we try the youth centre again?'

'Bane could track his phone if he stopped being such an arse,' I growled, realising I probably *had* run out of good insults.

Without pausing, Noah snatched Bane's phone from the bench behind us and typed in the passcode. Swapping phones around so often in the last few weeks did have some advantages.

'I've found the app. Which one of these codes is Dallmin's phone? Can't you use names like normal people do?'

Bane let out a gravelly sigh. 'Give it here, I'll find him,' he conceded.

A few minutes later we were studying a map on Tessa's laptop, trying to work out how far away Dallmin was. We'd tried to call Dallmin's phone a few times too, but there was no answer.

'It's the middle of nowhere. How on Earth did he get there?' Tim asked.

'By avoiding using roads wherever possible, by the looks of it. As if he wants to stay away from people. He probably walked straight through people's paddocks not realising he shouldn't,' Noah replied around a mouthful of my scrambled eggs. I gave up. Why *not* let him have it? Everyone else had eaten from my plate except me.

'My guess is he's following the river, more or less,' I pointed out. 'He

must have walked all night to get that far. He'll be exhausted and freezing. We need to go *now.*' I grabbed Tim's hand and pulled him up, picking up Bane's car keys at the same time. Tim threw an apologetic glance
Bane's way but didn't resist. If he was going to hero-worship me, I might
as well make use of it while it lasted.

'Bring the first-aid kit,' I instructed my Guardian.

Bane leaned back in his chair, arms crossed. 'You're overreacting. He
can take care of himself. Have you forgotten how old he is?'

Instead of replying, I grabbed the kit and led Tim toward the front
door, silently daring Bane to try to stay behind. Of course I won.

It took ages to get anywhere near the coordinates we had pinpointed.
Too many unmarked roads changed direction on us. In the end, the
closest we could get by car was the overgrown end of a fire access track
that led from a corrugated dirt road down to a river choked by willow
trees. There wasn't a discernible path to follow downstream and we
had to fight our way through some swampy terrain. We lost phone
reception when the river cut past a steep hill covered in red gums and
blackberries, and it didn't come back again on the other side. Somehow
I wasn't at all surprised that three years hadn't fixed all the problems
around getting reception in rural areas. We could only hope that if
Dallmin had moved, Tim's tracking skills would be able to take over
where the phones had let us down.

After nearly an hour of swamp-hopping, the river coursed back
into open pasture and Tim finally plucked up the courage to ask me to
stop for a while. I'd forgotten Bane was supposed to take it easy, and he
would probably have rather passed out than complained. I made him
rest under a tree while I went to refill the drink bottle from the river.
Thankfully he let me go on my own without comment, because I'd been
beginning to worry that I'd tipped him over the edge from Guardian to
snarling guard dog. I understood why, and I kept reminding myself that
any risks I took had unfair consequences for him. Problem was, three
years of recklessness in Eden was a hard habit to break. I missed racing
the leaping mirror fish down the river.

Precariously balanced on a slippery rock so I could reach the freshest flowing water, I had to discipline myself not to think too much about how dingy the water was here compared to the silver river back home. Startled, I realised I was still thinking of Eden as home. But how could I not? It was everyone's home, or at least it was supposed to be. Eden was like a safe nurturing nest built for beloved children and I had no doubt that every human would feel immediately at home there in a far more profound way than anywhere else. I wasn't human. Each time I'd died had brought me a slightly better understanding of what that meant as I'd glimpsed half-remembered snippets of my eternal future. That didn't change the fact that Eden was part of who I was, and it always would be no matter where I chose to live.

Murky river water churned about the rocks the same way my untrustworthy thoughts swirled around my brain. My Eden mindset warred with the mundane, making my perspectives on life feel all wrong. Or perhaps they were right, for the first time ever. Dallmin was now irreversibly severed from the Garden. The appalling reality of what that meant shocked me like a slap in the face. Never seeing home again? *Ever?* No more crystal caves with their hidden thermal pools. No hanging swing-nets laden with playful tiptoe monkeys. No honey-juice cocktails or spiral ice cascades. No more friendly faces laughing and running to catch him as he fell from a sleeping tree with his foot caught in a vine. Friends lost, never knowing where he'd gone, severed from family and loved ones who had known him and cherished him for hundreds of years …

The overwhelming truth of how much Dallmin had lost hit me so hard I literally threw up. Even my body rejected the concept—like poison. To know Eden and then be barred from it would be intolerable. How had I not seen it before? Part of his soul had been ripped away while I'd been busy pondering how nice it was that he'd learned to use a mobile phone. He would not be fine here. Not even a little bit. The trauma of exile would be more than enough to drive him insane, or worse. No wonder he'd done whatever he could think of to return. Without hesitation, I would have torn down the rockfall pebble by pebble if it was the only way for me to get back. Would I have tried to kill someone? Perhaps, if I'd expected death to not be permanent. Both

Noah and I were Cherubim, with access to the Living Fruit, and Dallmin was all too aware of that. Dying would only have been a minor inconvenience for us as far as he was concerned. From his point of view, he hadn't betrayed us at all. He had hurt Bane, though, and revealed Noah's identity to Jake. Those things were serious. Did he comprehend what he'd done? Up until the last few days he'd been incapable of harming another person, or lying, and never in his long life had he ever been deceived. How could he possibly have understood what it all meant?

Fighting down grief-tremors, I cleaned myself up in the river and then spent a full minute trying to compose myself. The human heart was never designed to go through what Dallmin was going through. Neither was mine.

My shaky path back to the riverbank felt treacherous and cruel, each slippery rock like a deliberate attempt to make me stumble and fall. This river was vindictive …

No. It was just a river. It wasn't out to get me. That wasn't how either world worked. If I fell, it would be my own fault. With deliberate movements, I made my way back across the wobbly stepping stones and then hauled myself up the embankment using fistfuls of tangled weeds. Somehow I had to pull myself together. I breathed in deeply, as if I could suck the sadness right out of the world, and then clutched the drink bottle to my chest and headed back to where Tim and Bane were waiting. No more time for resting; I had to know if Dallmin was even still alive.

Chapter 4

'How much would it be worth to you?' Jake asked as he swirled the dregs of his beer around his glass. He probably should have spent the last of his money on something else like food or a bus ticket, but he craved something that could silence the whispers and beer was all he could afford. The pub was starting to look busier, with people beginning to head away from the pokie machines to find something to eat. He'd tried his luck there too—unfortunately his charming personality didn't win over the machines.

The woman drinking next to him had straight black hair, which she left loose to frame her gaunt face. She was pretty except for the pinched look around her eyes. Tattoos of Asian symbols lined her arms. She probably thought they said lovely spiritual things like 'peace' and 'luck' and 'eating organic foods will make you live forever'. More likely they were Chinese slang for 'bicycle' and 'brick' and 'sucker'. In her late twenties and already weary of life, she'd found her way to the backwaters of rural Victoria to hide, although she claimed she was 'expanding her locational and cultural boundaries'. *Yeah, right. In Mildura. Tell yourself whatever you want. You're still hiding*, he thought as he watched her consider his question.

'A secret that will change the way I see the world? Let me think. I had two of those last week. It didn't last. The world is still crap and I can still see it,' she replied, running a finger around the top of her glass. 'Tell me more about your shoulder. Did you really get stabbed or are you bullshitting me?'

'Stabbed by a guy who once saved me from school detention by owning up to something he didn't do. I guess people change. I'd rather not talk about it. I have a more interesting question for you.' He tried hard to keep the slur from his voice. 'Have you ever heard of the Garden of Eden?' He leaned toward her, searching her eyes for a connection.

'Oh, no,' she wailed. 'Tell me you're not one of those. Give me a break. Just because I have a few tats and smoke some weird stuff doesn't mean I need you to save me. My soul is fine and feisty, thanks anyway. Save your speech for someone who hasn't seen the things I've seen.'

Then she was gone, leaving her barely touched drink behind. Jake was stunned. It had been a long time since anyone had walked away from him when he really paid them attention. She must have been determined to avoid anything that sounded remotely Christian. So much for being open-minded. Perhaps he should have coaxed her into coming back to the hostel with him and shown her the sword. That would have opened her mind a bit. Only, every time he thought about showing it to someone else, he felt reluctant. No, not reluctant. Afraid. He was afraid of letting anyone else see it. How was he supposed to sell it if he refused to let anyone even see it? Maybe for the right price he would overcome his fear— once he found the right buyer. The girl had been a waste of time.

He sculled her abandoned beer, ignoring the scowl from the bartender when he tried to put the glass down and missed the table. Damn shoulder wound. Somehow he had to track down the right sort of customer, someone who would appreciate what he was offering. It was unlikely he would find that person in a bar in Mildura. Maybe he could send out some feelers on the internet. Find someone who dealt in rare antiquities, perhaps. That could be done from almost anywhere and could result in a nice quick response. All he needed was access to a computer.

Antiquities? His foggy brain couldn't even fathom where that word had come from. Seemed like a good plan, though. Funny how all his best plans seemed to emerge when he was off his face. He looked at the cluster of empty glasses that had obediently stayed on the table where he'd left them and then frowned into his empty wallet. He couldn't even buy more beer, let alone a computer. Did libraries still let you use them without paying? Did libraries even still exist? He had no clue. Either way, it was time to do something about his money situation. Something that wouldn't attract the attention of the police department. Something … charming.

Chapter 5

Glossy winter sunshine sparkled across the water and reflected its gentle rhythms onto the motionless body of my friend.

Far too terrified to move a single muscle, I watched in horror as Tim and Bane waded *too slowly* across the thigh-deep river to where Dallmin was wedged against some rocks by the force of the current. His head was well above the waterline, but his eyes were closed and his dark skin looked sickly pale. I'd seen Dallmin die numerous times before, and in far more gruesome ways, but he'd never looked so ... defeated. In desperation I tried to feel for the echoes of life around me, searching for some sense of him, only this was not the same river that had sung me to sleep all my life. We were too far east. There was no way of feeling whether or not he was still here.

Tim's body blocked my view as he checked for a pulse and I held my breath and the grimy river didn't care. He shook his head once, slowly, and my heart forgot how to beat. Then Bane took hold of Dallmin's other wrist and closed his eyes. The river was slow and wide where it cut through the flat plains all around us, but still loud enough that I couldn't hear what it was Bane said, which made Tim straighten his shoulders and give a firm nod. They gripped Dallmin under his arms and hauled him out of the water. Did they look like they were hurrying? They wouldn't hurry if he was dead, would they? A small sob escaped my lips as I watched Tim lay him on his side, arranging his limbs the way you were supposed to for first aid, then gently shook his shoulder to try to rouse him. He must still be alive, or he wouldn't have bothered. I was halfway across the river before I even realised I'd moved. Splashing my way recklessly, I fell into Bane's waiting arms with a weird cry.

'He's breathing … sporadically,' he told me. 'We have no idea how long he's been unconscious for. It's not good. We can barely find his pulse. Lainie, I'm so sorry. I should have listened to you.'

I kneeled down on the gravelly bank and took Dallmin's icy hand in my own, rubbing it in a pitiful attempt to warm him up. On the left side of his jaw, I noticed a bruise, bright and puffy despite the cold, and I wondered if that was where Tessa had punched him.

'Dallmin! Wake up. Please. You don't want to go yet, not really,' I begged, ignoring the pain from the uneven river rocks that dug into my knees. 'I can help you. Please wake up. I don't want to have to tell Annie I lost you.'

'Tim, support his head and shoulders. Try not to jostle him too much,' Bane instructed as he ripped the buttons off Dallmin's wet shirt and peeled it off him.

'*Please*, Dallmin, don't give up now. I have so much to show you of this world and it's not as bad as you think. Please. I don't want you to die.' My voice sounded strange, cracked, like my heart.

Behind me, Bane was pulling things out of his backpack. I moved aside as he unfolded a shiny silver blanket and wrapped it around my friend's torso and head, while Tim started shaking heat packs to activate them. Both their faces were grim.

I gripped Dallmin's hand, searching for some sign that he even wanted to come back. Edenites had a way of knowing. All I felt was a deep sense of loneliness.

'No!' I yelled at him. 'You are not alone here. I don't *want* you to go. Please, please try!'

A frozen minute of agonised tension dragged, while I begged and whispered and challenged and yelled his name at him over and over, calling him back. Tim held his other wrist and kept glancing silent, semi-hopeful messages to Bane that he thought I wouldn't understand, until finally Dallmin's breathing began to deepen. Uneven, bouncy breaths, but at least I could see his chest move. He stirred, and then flinched as Tim placed another heat pack against his chest. With a sob of relief, I sat back and let Bane and Tim rearrange the space blanket so they could warm him better. When he opened his eyes, he took one hazy look at me and then squeezed them shut again like a frightened child.

'Should we call an ambulance?' I asked, wondering what would happen if the same paramedic crew turned up. There were only so many medical emergencies that could happen to our family before people started asking awkward questions. As it was we were relying heavily on Sergeant Loxwood's assistance.

Dallmin's eyes flew open in horror, unfocused, and vivid with panic. 'No ambulance,' he slurred. 'They take people to the hospital and I don't ...' He drifted out of lucidity for a few seconds before his head snapped up again. He looked as if he would have tried to bolt like a rabbit if Bane hadn't been pinning his shoulders down.

'Don't want to go to the hospital. People there are hurt and dying. Even you were dead when you were there don't make me go there I won't go there I won't be dead there I ...' He slipped into a different language and continued to mutter on, fighting to make his limbs move. The terror in his ungainly body language was heartrending; all traces of the joyful elf-like creature had gone and all that was left in his expression was fear and shame.

'Okay! No ambulance,' I soothed. 'Relax. Rest for a while. Maybe we can find a way to bring the car down here so we can take you back to the farm. We'll think of something.'

He shook his head in firm denial, but it took a few more long seconds for him to make his voice heard again. 'I won't ... return to the farm. I need to make ... things right,' he mumbled, trying to focus on my face. 'I lost him, Lainie. I followed him to the road, but it holds no trail at all and I ... searched everywhere along it. He was gone. I d ... d ... don't know how to follow a car. They leave no trace and they go so fast ...'

As I opened my mouth to console him, Bane got in first with stark practicality. 'When you got to the road, could you tell which way he walked along it?' His terse voice was so much like the Bane I'd known all through high school that I winced. Tim didn't seem to notice; he was busy checking Dallmin's pulse and frowning a lot.

Dallmin answered slowly and painfully as he sucked in weak breaths. 'He was heading toward the town where you found me when I first came here. It was the same road I took when I first saw a car. He must have done the same thing and stopped someone. I tried to do that too, but there were no cars until it was dark and then I saw a truck with many lights on and it was so fast, I was … afraid.' His eyes were full of shame. 'I ran into the trees and ran and ran until I was far away from any people.' He averted his gaze with such childlike fear that I had to blink away fresh tears. Ragged and frail, his voice tore up the air like a muted cyclone, devastating in its quiet anguish. 'What if I hurt someone again? What if they hurt me? I would rather die from my own choice than die from someone else's, and I would rather die here than hurt anyone again. Why didn't you let me die? I can't be near you anymore. What if I hurt you again?' His velvet brown eyes kept flinching away from Bane as he rambled, like a dog with his tail between his legs.

I lifted his chin and forced him to look at me. 'I won't let you. Until you understand a bit more about how things work here I'll make sure you don't hurt anyone. You just have to trust me and do what I tell you, and all will be well,' I promised him.

At last, he was beginning to shiver from the cold, which was a very good sign. We needed to get him indoors and warm as soon as possible.

'Tim, do you think you could get the car to this side of the river? We passed a bridge right before that canola farm down the road. You should be able to find the road leading back up to that house up there,' I said, pointing to an old weatherboard peeking at us from behind the line of trees at the top of the hill. 'Knock on the door of the farmhouse first and explain what's happened. You'll probably need to do some paddock bashing.'

'I don't care. It's Bane's car, remember?'

Without another word he took off upstream again, back toward where we'd parked, setting a cracking pace. Wordlessly, Bane forced Dallmin to drink some water, then continued to strip off the rest of his wet clothing. We had nothing dry to replace it with so we wrapped him as best we could with the silver blanket, tucking heat packs against his neck and chest.

By the time Tim found his way back to us, Dallmin had slipped into a deep sleep, but his heart rate had thankfully steadied. Once again I marvelled at the professional way in which Bane had taken control of the situation. He'd been trained for this and knew exactly what to do, only I couldn't tell how pleased he really was to be doing it. It was clear from his body language he had a long way to go before he would forgive Dallmin for what he'd done. Given the size of the lump he still had on his skull, I could hardly blame him. How was I going to make him understand why Dallmin had turned on us?

While the guys carried my friend's limp body up the bank and laid him across the back seat of the car, I retrieved Dallmin's pack from where he'd dumped it under a bush. As I threw it into the boot I winced at how light it was. Even if he had wanted to live, I shuddered to think how he would have managed to get by with so little. He had a long way to go before I was going to let him out of my sight again. We were going to be stuck together like frozen lamb chops.

Once Dallmin was settled into bed with a mug of tea and the electric blanket up high, all it took to melt the metaphorical chops and convince me to leave his side was the tantalising scent of a lavender bath. Aunt Lily offered to stay with him, and the bath was blissful even if I was too restless to stay in it for more than a few minutes. When I returned to the kitchen, towelling dry my hair, Tim had only just had time to emerge from his room in fresh clothes as well. He smiled at me before noticing Bane, still in his damp jeans, repacking things into the first-aid kit and making a list of what needed replacing.

'Right,' Tim declared, pushing Bane firmly onto a kitchen chair. 'If you get that bandage wet one more time I'm going on strike.'

Tessa sat down opposite Bane with a disturbingly eager expression, grinning around her mouthful of toast. I studied her closely. Her left eye was no longer swollen, and while the bruise had blossomed in an impressive selection of colours, somehow it was already quite faded. I hadn't seen her that morning, so maybe it simply wasn't as bad as I'd thought the day before. Then as Tim gently peeled away the dressing on Bane's arm, I suddenly understood.

'No way!' Tim exclaimed. The cut on Bane's arm had sealed up nicely and didn't look red at all. In fact, it was a perfect example of a week-old wound—except he'd only had it for a day.

Bane looked back at him placidly. 'Nice work, Tim, thanks. I don't think you need to bandage it again.'

'Guardian thing?' Tim asked in a fascinated tone, prodding at the skin surrounding the scar tissue.

'Yeah. I hate faking injuries I no longer have. How did you never notice before?'

'That you heal quickly? We all thought you were being stoic. You know, sore as the rest of us, only too macho to complain.' Sitting back, he lifted his chin rather haughtily. 'To be honest, I'm kind of gratified. You're not as tough as you seem. You were just cheating all this time.'

I laughed at the look of consternation on my Guardian's face as he opened his mouth to protest. Tim didn't let him. He pushed Bane's head down with a smidge more force than required, so he could examine his skull wound.

'There's still a lump, but it's much better than I expected. Does it hurt when I do this?'

'Ah, yeah!' Bane complained, ducking away. 'We still feel pain, you know.'

Noah, who had come into the kitchen with his infant son draped snugly over his shoulder, looked miserable at the reminder. He leaned down and kissed Tessa on the cheek with a feather-light touch. 'It's not fair that we can't heal you. How is it we can do pretty much everything else except that?'

'I think it's because we need to be reminded that there are consequences,' I said. 'We can't go around doing whatever we want, even to protect Eden, because others will still feel the effects. We're not invincible.' I glared pointedly at Bane's over-enthusiastic friend, hoping he'd get the message.

'You might as well be,' Tim said in a reverential tone. Although he was busy gathering the soiled dressings together, most of his attention seemed to be on searching Noah's head for a halo. I nearly snorted in derision—until I noticed how Noah looked. He had his pale curls tucked behind one ear and his lips pressed against Nathaniel's tiny fingers in a soft kiss, like a holy blessing. The baby looked so, so tiny and perfect, snuggled into his dad's neck. Of course, then Noah ruined the scene by filching the hot chocolate Bane had made for me.

Tim shook off the spell. 'And for the record, Bane, I'm never sparring with you again. You have an unfair advantage. It's just mean.'

'What advantage? I told you I still feel pain. Quick healing would only help if you ever actually managed to injure me,' he pointed out with a falsely bland expression, betrayed only by the mischievous glint behind his eyes.

'Well, who knows what other freaky traits you have that you neglected to mention? How do I know you don't have super-fast reflexes or Hulk-strength or something? It would explain a lot.'

'Like how I got knocked out and tied to a tree?'

'Well, even superheroes get caught by surprise sometimes,' Tim hedged. 'You were unlucky, that's all.'

The playful glint flipped into fury so suddenly it was clear it had been there all along—hidden and crystallising.

'Luck had nothing to do with it. I trusted the wrong man. Poor judgment will kill you quicker than any weapon.' His frosty tone sounded like he was quoting someone.

We all went silent, not knowing how to react to the abrupt change in mood, until we heard someone open the front gate.

'It's Nicole,' Noah told us, leaning his head around the corner to peer through the lounge room window. 'Looks like she's brought in the mail. Another parcel delivery. It doesn't look like another fruit basket, thank goodness.'

I moved to put the kettle on and prise the lid off the Milo tin, humming under my breath. Things were still awkward between me and the youngest of the Ashbrees, and I had no idea what to do about it. In my head, I'd come to terms with my involvement in her mum's death, but my heart still broke every time I saw her. Bane moved behind me and steadied me with a warm hand on my shoulder. He'd probably heard me humming. So much for thinking I'd broken the habit while I was in Eden.

Closing my eyes, I took a deep breath to compose myself, drawing strength from his closeness. It was just as well because as soon as Nicole saw me she dumped the huge parcel box onto the table and threw her arms around me, shoving Bane aside. Stunned, I looked over at Noah, whose jaw had fallen open. As far as I knew Nicole hadn't hugged anybody since she was six years old. My Eden instincts quickly kicked in where my logic faltered, and I embraced her back whole-heartedly.

For a long minute, she clung to me as if she wanted to make up for all the years of being so stand-offish, until she looked up at me with an apologetic expression and glistening jade-coloured eyes.

'Jake poisoned you? Liam told me. Are you okay? I'm so sorry! I bailed on my duty and he got through. I never dreamed he'd try anything so … so *evil*. You could have died!'

'Not your fault, Nic. He posted the poisoned apples in a hamper. You couldn't have—'

She cut me off, typically uninterested in the details. 'Tim called an ambulance, right? He saved your *life*,' she said, turning and hugging him as well. The last time I'd seen her so demonstrative was on her twelfth birthday when she'd been given her first stud ram.

Completely flustered, Tim looked like he wanted to crawl into a hole and hide. I glared at him from behind Nicole's back and mimed to him that he should smile. He obediently tried to grin at her, which kind of looked like he'd swallowed a goldfish.

Luckily Nicole was distracted by something else. 'Tessa, what happened to your eye?'

Tessa smoothly adopted a look of embarrassment. 'I got up to feed Nathaniel during the night and walked straight into the door. Combination of insufficient lighting and lack of quality sleep. Am I at least colouring up well?' she asked, proudly displaying her injury for Nicole to inspect. 'If I'm going to be so careless I might as well have a good shiner to show for it.'

Beside her, Noah no longer looked amused. In fact, he looked ill.

'Mmm, I've had worse. Remember that time I tried to jump off the back of the ute when Noah was driving me to school? He was going a bit faster than I thought.'

It had been one of the many times she'd tried to run away and ditch school. Their mum had given Noah a loud lecture about driving too fast over bumpy ground, assuming she'd fallen off by accident. Triumphantly, I realised I'd just remembered something from my childhood I'd assumed was lost from my flimsy brain forever. If that could come back, maybe I could piece together the rest of my earlier life.

'What's in the package?' Noah asked, steering the conversation away from black eyes altogether.

Nicole shrugged. 'The postie left it sitting on the ground down at the front gate. I think he must be getting sick of delivering packages here because he used to bring them right to the door if they wouldn't fit in the letterbox. Or maybe he was just trying to prevent those fruit hampers getting nicked by possums.'

Apparently, whatever was inside the mysterious package wasn't a threat to me because Bane wasn't careful with it at all. Tim nearly jumped out of his skin as Bane stabbed it with a large kitchen knife, slicing it open in a vicious fit of redirected aggression. Probably a good thing the postie hadn't come up to the house this time. My Guardian's face began to relax as he pulled out various bits of technical equipment. Security cameras and small solar panels nested in a bed of wiring and polystyrene.

We all crowded around to check out the new toys, and Bane didn't waste any time in putting them together. He sent Tim out to fit three of the cameras, while he gathered up the other three himself.

'Just six?' I asked sarcastically. 'Are you sure that's enough?'

'No, this was all they had in stock. There's another six on back order.'

'*Twelve?* Are you serious? We won't be able to scratch ourselves without someone watching. Are you going to put one in the chook pen too? In case one of the hens decides to build a bomb out of its poo?'

Rolling his eyes at me, he grabbed an armful of equipment and headed out the door while Noah followed him out to go and put Nathaniel to bed. Left awkwardly with just Tessa and Nicole, I poured them each a coffee and then sat down with my Milo to read the instruction manual for the cameras. Someone had to.

Within the hour, Bane and Tim had all the cameras installed, and ten minutes after they finally asked me for help we had them running and sending high-resolution video footage wirelessly to four separate devices. After that, I checked on Dallmin. He was still asleep, resting comfortably and looking much healthier already, so I coaxed my aunt into coming out to eat some toast. She wolfed it down so she could head into town to get more groceries before the shops closed. I paced around the house looking for jobs to do or someone to talk to. Nicole had glued herself to Tim and I could tell she wanted me to stay away. She had picked up on his new attentiveness toward me and it was clearly annoying her. Noah was out doing a hay run and Bane was teaching Tessa how to work the surveillance system. I was alone for the first time since my return, which was making me feel edgy and I didn't know why.

The TV helped for all of five minutes. Having three years of my favourite shows to catch up on felt far too overwhelming and I couldn't concentrate. After one too many adverts for stupid things like tile squeegees, and shampoo containing Pro-Vitamin-Hydroxy-Silicate-Shinex-Organic-Glitter-Honey, I gave up and went outside to split firewood. Exercise sounded like a good idea and it was nice to feel like I was doing something useful.

Thunk. Aim better. Thunk. Readjust my grip. Thunk. Swing cleaner. Thunk. Reposition the log …

I swung the splitter gently while I got used to it again. My shoulder muscles ached a little.

Thunk. Crack. Nice.

Swing. Ouch. Nice ouch. Stretchy ouch. Thunk.

The climb up the cliff had been arduous and I'd only eaten the Living Fruit when I'd really needed to, so there were a few leftover aches. It made sense. If Bane or the Fruit completely healed even sore muscles, how would I ever strengthen them? The physiological implications of healing were fascinating and comprehensive. Dallmin was testament to that. He was hundreds of years old and fit as a Mallee bull—at least when he wasn't suffering from severe hypothermia. Why hadn't I realised earlier what effect his exile would have on him?

I readjusted the block of wood and swung again. Thunk.

Had I been so deluded by Eden's 'everything would be all right' philosophy that I had become blind to his pain?

Thunk. Hit the edge nicely. I spread my hands further apart along the haft and heaved it again. Harder.

Perhaps I should have plucked up the courage to explore what the sword could really do. Had my cowardice stopped me from trying to find a way to get him home?

Wrenching the splitter out of the stubborn block of wood, I thought about how Dallmin must have felt in the cave, being so close to home, but not being allowed to try to get in.

I swung the heavy tool over my shoulder again as hard as I could and heard the satisfying sound of a large crack forming, and like a sudden bolt of lightning Dallmin's rage shot through me with the sound. Rage at being denied a chance to see Eden again, to taste its fragrant air and breathe in its vibrant colours. Rage at losing the only chance he had to leave this cold dead world, and frustration at being denied the opportunity to return to Annie's gentle arms. Screaming out the emotions that weren't entirely mine, I swung the splitter as brutally as I could at the block and was grimly satisfied when I saw the two halves flying in opposite directions. The iron edge of the splitter was wedged firmly into the support block below. It took a couple of tries to free it, and the moment I did, the scene around me changed.

I was there. In the cave. Watching the arrogant way Noah barred the way back home, holding the sacred sword that filled me with this new feeling of terror. I'd never been frightened of its pretty flames before. Noah's face was filled with determination as he whipped the weapon around and swung it toward Jake. The concept of one person aiming to kill another was overwhelming. Unthinkable. So I did the only thing I could think of to stop him. Noah couldn't be … allowed … to do this. And I had to somehow make him let go of the sword so I could get past it. Get past them both.

I felt myself aim the small knife Bane had given me. It would stop Noah's swing. It would also injure him.

No time to do anything else.

I was about to throw and then pain exploded in my jaw and everything went dark.

Hands of fire clutched my arms, searching for a wound that didn't exist. The pain was all in my mind and yet Bane had felt it too and had come for me.

'Dallmin's awake,' I sobbed. 'I can see what he saw.'

Steel eyes searched mine, frantic.

'I felt it, Bane. He had all these emotions he didn't understand and he was so close to home. He feels so lost …'

Powerful emotions were still ripping through me, echoes of my insight into Dallmin's psyche, amplified by my own longing for home.

'Let go, Lainie.'

'I can't! He's in my mind.'

'I mean let go of the splitter. Please? It isn't a safe thing to throw.'

Throw? In my mind I'd been throwing my little pocket knife, aiming for my best friend. I looked down at the splitter, gripped tightly in my hands. It was drawn back, ready to be hurled at whoever was in my way. Bane's grip on my arm was the only thing preventing me from launching it straight at his head. It slipped from my shaky grip and landed on the grass.

Bane gathered me into his arms to try to ease my trembling. 'I thought you had to be touching someone to do that,' he soothed, his hands tangling in my still-damp hair.

'Apparently not,' I hiccupped, trying to stop the flow of tears. 'I was thinking about him, and what he must have been feeling. I guess his emotions were so strong when he woke that I connected with him anyway.' They were still so strong, and I clutched at Bane's shoulder to distract myself from them. 'He needs help, Bane. He's not coping and I'm afraid of what he might do. You don't have to come, but I need to help him. Please don't try to stop me.'

'Of course not. I would never do that, but …'

I pulled away, wary. If he could feel what Dallmin was going through, he wouldn't be so hard on him.

Bane set his jaw. 'He's a danger to everyone right now, Lainie, not just himself. I don't trust him, and you shouldn't either.'

Instead of replying, I headed for the guest bedroom at the end of the hall with my stressed-out Guardian trailing behind me. It was a relief to find Dallmin still there. He was huddled in the corner of the room on the floor, looking like a frightened toddler. At least he hadn't run away again.

'Dallmin, can I get you something? Are you thirsty?' He refused to even look at me, so I sat down next to him. If he was going to become childlike then I might as well do the same. When I tried to put my arm around him he flinched away, which was so unlike him that I nearly burst into tears again. In bleak sorrow, I clasped my arms around my knees and waited.

For almost an hour we sat there in silence. I had no idea how to comfort him, so I waited for him to let me know what he wanted. Eventually, Noah came in and sat down on the other side of him while Bane left to get us something to eat and drink. When he returned we silently shared around the scrambled eggs, spoon-feeding them into Dallmin's mouth. Noah looked like he was really enjoying them. They tasted like dirt to me. That was when I realised I was still resonating with Dallmin's point of view. I liked eggs, and Bane was a pretty good cook, but Dallmin's mind was dwelling on memories of home, and no chef on the planet could match even the simplest snack from across the Skin of the World. I shifted the food around my plate, trying to remember why I was supposed to eat it.

Bane frowned at me. 'Okay, Lainie. I think you need a break. Why don't we go for a walk while Noah sits with him for a while?'

I couldn't even be bothered answering him. My earlier restlessness had dissolved into complete apathy. Walking anywhere seemed way too hard.

'Oh no, you don't,' he admonished, rescuing the plate as it slid from my lap. 'Linking with him to gain insight into how you can help is one thing, but getting hooked into his depression is not healthy for either of you. Let him go, Lainie.'

He led me out of the house and I was too exhausted to protest. Sadness hit me anew as I looked up at the sky outside and saw how few birds there were. The air was cold and smelled of wet wool and rust, and the trees were all grumpy. I hated this place. Why had I fought so hard to come back?

My feet shuffled toward the track that led to the state park gate, heading for home. If I could climb up a cliff, surely I could climb back down. Bane followed, hanging back a little as if he was unsure of what I was doing, even though it had been his idea to go for a walk. Ignoring him altogether, I began to anticipate the things I would do when I got back to my shelter tree. First I would swim, then eat, then sing, then find the foal and her mother. There would be no sadness, no grumpy trees, and no biting ants. No cameras or cars or phones. No babies born sick, no thieves, no kidnappers, no poison. No weapons of any sort. Nothing designed to hurt or kill. No angry people. When I felt a hand grip my elbow I flinched and wrenched myself away, backing up in fear. Who was hurting me now?

'Lainie, what's wrong? What are you so afraid of?' Bane had a hurt expression on his face. 'Where are you going?'

'Home. While I still can. I hate this place. Let me go!'

I left him standing in the middle of the track as I bolted toward the gate. I was so scared. I didn't trust people here, and I didn't understand who I was. All I wanted to do was run and run and never stop. My foot caught on a fallen branch and I stumbled, breaking my fall with shaky hands. Feeling my heart thudding in my chest, I forced my sluggish legs to keep moving and tripped again almost immediately. My limbs felt so mismatched. As if they weren't even mine. Who was I? The track was covered in wet gravel, which made me skid and this time I fell hard. Arms like steel closed around my waist and I screamed, fighting like a cornered animal. I was going to die! I knew he had a knife. A great big steel sharp jagged weapon. He was going to murder me in cold blood if I didn't get free, and he was so strong. Full-blown panic sent the world spinning out of control and my vision became red-hazed and dim. Crying out in fear and despair, I wrenched myself in every direction to try to escape my attacker and finally managed to get free, tasting blood on my lips, which frightened me even more. I ran again, but it was no use. Within seconds I felt my legs go from under me as I was bowled over and pinned down. Gasping out a breathless scream, I struggled with everything I had. It was hopeless. He was going to hurt me. He was going to *kill* me.

'Lainie, please, listen to me. These aren't your thoughts—they're Dallmin's. You have to let him go. You have to trust me. I love you and I would never hurt you, *you know that*. Please try to remember!'

Elbowing him in the gut, I tried to throw him off. I might as well have been wrestling a truck. I heard his words, yet they didn't make the slightest bit of sense to me. Blurred images of trees and sky didn't match what I was seeing in my mind, which made me panic more and I felt as though the monster pinning me down was going to push me right into the earth below. Once I was underground, I would be buried, trapped, suffocated. I couldn't move, couldn't breathe. The best I could manage was a pitiful, useless sort of yowl. My wrists hurt, in the same way they had when Jake had bound them. Twisting and pushing, I punched and kicked with every bit of strength I possessed, which achieved nothing. I'd never felt so helpless.

The weight lifted as I was rolled on to my side. A warm hand cradled my head against a broad chest and I could feel a rapid heartbeat, racing, matching the pounding in my own ears.

'Breathe, Lainie, just breathe. You're safe, you're safe, I promise. I'll never let anything hurt you. You're safe.'

Stroking my hair, he made soothing sounds, threaded with a soft melody I couldn't quite catch. I forced myself to keep still so I could listen. It sounded like a lullaby.

'Let him go,' the musical voice pleaded. 'Please, you have to let him go. You need to break the link to him before it breaks you. I know you want to help him, but this isn't going to work. Please trust me.' His soft words conflicted starkly with the way he was restraining me like a vice against his body.

'Let me go!'

'The second I stop feeling that you're about to hurt yourself, I will. I promise. You need to calm down.'

'I want to go *home.*'

He tilted my chin up to meet his eyes. 'No, you don't,' he whispered in an agonised voice. 'It's incredibly tempting to use this as an excuse and let you go back to where you'll be safe, only I know that the second you crossed the threshold you'd regret it. And I know you, Lainie. You'd be furious with me. I have no intention of making you angry ever again.' Irises like cracked ice pierced through my fear.

Stupidly bewildered, I stared into the beauty hidden there, behind the ice, and I was unable to frame any coherent thoughts at all.

His skin was hot against my own where he gripped my shoulder. 'Are you back?' he asked. 'Or are you still linked to Dallmin? Come back to me, Lainie,' he entreated with a chocolatey voice full of soothing.

My mind felt like jelly. I didn't know who I was or what I wanted, and I was still so frightened. Gentle fingertips traced along my jawline and brushed my mouth with a feather touch.

'Come back to me,' he repeated. 'Because I'd like to kiss you now, and I have no intention of kissing anyone other than you. Let me remind you who you are.'

I closed my eyes, confused by the delicious feel of his breath on my face. A moment later all my confusion dissolved like mist in the winter sun as his lips found mine. His kiss told me all I needed to know. I was Lainie Gracewood. I was safe, and I was cherished.

Chapter 6

Annie's exhaustion overtook her while she waited for Nayn to finish mixing the exact paint colour he'd been after, which she supposed was the whole reason he'd refused to answer her straight away. He wanted her to get some rest. Yet her sleep was not restful. Her dreams were full of memories too mashed together to be of any use. There was a guy stealing a sword, whose emotions lied, like he'd been riding a horse with its head obediently turned right, but its legs moving left. She was certain she'd met someone like that years ago. A man in a pale suit, dangling a ruby necklace from his fingers and grinning at her like she was something tasty to eat. Lucas had been there too. His fiercely protective stance had frightened her. Frightened for him. She had no way of distinguishing her dreams from her lost memories.

She woke with the feel of Lucas's arms around her waist, only to find Bungee nestled against her chest and a young black and tan kelpie snuggled behind her. She sat up and tried to wipe the wet lapis lazuli dog hair off, which only smeared the colour more. Nayn and the others had disappeared, leaving multi-coloured rivulets of paint leftovers swirling out from under the tree line. It seemed the rain had put a hold on the colour mixing.

The two dogs followed her to the food shelter where people were gathering for a hot meal, which was very welcome given she'd been too fretful to eat all day. As she cleaned her bowl and asked around, someone mentioned that Nayn had already left. It didn't take her long to find the elder Cherub sitting by the butterfly pools, leaning against a sandalwood tree to watch the sunset. The young kelpie and the blue-stained blue heeler trotted ahead to sit with him, each pushing to be the first in line for a belly scratch. The surface of the water rippled with hot pink fire, while silhouetted ducks swam lazily around the maze of reeds as if trying to drink the sun reflected there.

All right. I've slept and I'm not so grouchy. Will you tell me about this person who has been outside and returned, or was their trip to Nalong a past trauma that should be left alone? I will not make this person remember if they have chosen to forget.

Nayn beckoned for her to sit down next to him. *There is a time for forgetting, and a time for remembering. I think you already know which this is. And she forgets nothing.*

So who is it?

That's not my place to reveal. Her story is her own. She can choose whether or not to share it with you.

Annie drew her knees up. *Fair enough. Only, there are things going on out there. Dangerous things. I wish I could simply gather everyone I love into the Garden where they would be safe.*

Do you feel that's your task? Nayn asked.

I thought my task was done, she signed with a groan.

Nayn rubbed Bungee's belly with his big toe and said nothing.

She leaned against him affectionately. *Isn't this where you're supposed to give me some deep mystic riddle that involves the sunset, the ducks, and how they all relate to a great cosmic plan for my destiny?*

Destiny? Isn't immortality in Eden enough of a destiny for you? I could probably come up with a riddle, though. Ducks and a sunset …

Or you could simply tell me what it is you want me to do. You must believe this mystery person's story is important in our current situation or you wouldn't have mentioned her at all.

Did you bring anything to eat? he asked, rummaging around in the cloth bag she'd dumped on the ground.

For the first time in years, Annie felt a flare of impatience for his evasions. *A little bread. And some of Karinya's sweet-nut dumplings,* she replied as he began to toss things out onto the grass.

Discarding the bread, he opened a woven reed box and proceeded to stuff his mouth with fresh dumpling. His fingers flicked puffs of sweet-flour everywhere as he signed. *The person I'm thinking of has never been to Nalong. She came here before Eden was moved.*

She gaped at him. *Came here?*

She wasn't born in Eden. She was over a thousand summers old when she was brought here, completely free from the stain of sadness.

What? How did she live that long outside of Eden? Was she born without the stain or cured of it somehow? Who brought her? How long ago did she arrive? What happened to … Her questions were cut short as he pushed a dumpling into her hand to shut her up.

Do I look like an expert in ancient history? No, don't answer that. Stop pestering me with questions, child. Go ask her yourself if you want to know.

I would if I knew who it was.

Good point. I'll check with her first.

Annie took a moment to savour the treat, licking the sweet dust from her lips. *Are you certain it won't upset her?*

I told you. She is … unstained. I don't know what word you use for that. There is no part of her identity she is unhappy about. Her spirit matters have long since been resolved, unlike yours. His signs held no trace of criticism, only acknowledgment.

Nayn, I don't think now is the time for me to dwell on my problems. She sat up straighter. *There's something more important going on. The standing stones showed me something. A memory that didn't come from anyone I'd ever met. I don't know much about the spirit world, but I'm sure that means something. The memory felt … dangerous. I believe it was a warning. There are events occurring out there and Lainie and Noah are right in the thick of it. Lainie was murdered, Nayn. Killed.* There was no word for murder in the language of Eden, but from the disturbed look on Nayn's face the English one seemed to do fine.

Are you thinking of going back? he asked. His tone was gentle, his eyes piercing.

A shudder racked her body as memories long suppressed rose like ugly scars on her mind. *I … I would try. I could …*

What, pick up your old life again? Tell people you didn't really die all those years ago, and you were just playing a really long hiding game? No, Annie, it would not help anyone if you crossed back now. Your soul is no longer linked to that place. You would only make things more complicated for Noah and Lainie if they had to care for you also. I feel your task is to find answers they can't. Answers that our friend might have.

Our friend? You mean it's someone I know?

He somehow extricated his legs from under the two overly affectionate dogs so he could stand, then he grabbed her wrist and helped her up. She really was very tired.

His gaze settled her many questions with patience as deep as the winter moon. *Get some sleep, Annie. We'll find her in the morning,* he said, giving her a shove back toward the river.

As Annie stumbled back to her sleeping tree, it occurred to her that Harry may well have inherited his soothing gift from Nayn. When she finally shut her eyes, she felt a deep sense that all would be well. Somehow.

❧

The kitchen was so familiar and warm that Annie knew immediately it wasn't real. Cool water from the kitchen tap splashed over her fingers as she rinsed a bunch of fresh herbs, and the smell of roast lamb made her wish she could cry—only how could she cry in a memory? Such a physical response would surely dissolve the dream like sugar crystals, leaving her with the sweetest taste of her past and no coherent memories. For so long she had chosen to let them dissolve, yet that bitter-sweetness held no real nourishment and the memories had never stopped calling to her.

'Annie, did you remember to bring over some eggs? I think our hens are protesting the change in ownership—they've barely laid a thing for nearly two weeks.' Sarah's voice sounded far too buoyant for someone who'd spent most of the night comforting two teething babies. David was sprawled out on Uncle Willie's old leather armchair, snoring loudly. He'd taken the four until eight am shift.

Lily piped up on cue. 'They probably miss having Lucas tuck them into bed each night. Maybe you should try singing them a lullaby?'

'No more lullabies,' Sarah groaned, spreading the cutlery across the table in a loud clatter that still did nothing to rouse her partner. 'They never work anyway. The only ones that seem to settle the boys are Dave's renditions of the Hawthorn theme song. I'd rather do without the eggs, thanks.'

Annie shivered at the sound of Lucas's chuckle from behind her in the corner of the kitchen. If she turned her head slightly, she could just see his left shoulder. He was cutting up potatoes because he wouldn't let her use the knife—not that he didn't trust her, it was simply an ongoing joke between them.

'The chooks are moulting,' she heard herself say. 'They'll start laying again soon enough. I brought over a dozen eggs. They're on the bench next to the kettle.' Why couldn't she turn to look at him? She missed him so much. Was it because she was locked into reliving the memory exactly how it had occurred? Or was it because she was too afraid? He was *right there*. She could hear the rhythmic thunk of the knife hitting the chopping board. She could hear him breathing. If she turned to look, would he vanish?

She heard the back door closing as Harry returned with the firewood. He could never visit his childhood home without stocking up the pile next to the wood heater, no matter the weather. Although she couldn't see him from where she was, his presence felt as soothing as his smile always did. Somehow she hadn't missed him in the same breathless way. She would always be able to find Harry if she wanted to. No matter how far away he went.

'Um, Sarah?' Lily asked. 'Do you want me to take those?' She relieved Sarah of the two glasses hanging precariously from her limp fingers.

The young mother was staring vacantly into space, but Annie knew her attention was locked on the Cherub in the other room. She would have to learn to hide her reactions much better than that. Or else make a hard decision.

Lucas brought Sarah's attention back with a neat change of topic. 'When do the builders start on the new house? David mentioned wanting to get the slab down before the autumn rains start. Knowing his luck, the drought will finally break on the day the concreters arrive.'

His husky voice, so rich, so cherished, filled Annie with a longing that nearly broke her, but the words that came unbidden from her mouth were obscenely lighthearted. 'I keep telling you, Lucas, summers here are always this hot. Besides, how would breaking a drought be in any way unlucky? You're such a city boy.' She turned to pass him a handful of freshly washed chives to chop up.

And there he was. All blue eyes and pale curls, with his smile of shared secrets that was only ever for her. His emotions tasted like clear crystal, resonating with her own like a sharp tap on an expensive wineglass.

Sarah reached past her for the egg carton, breaking the moment. 'Um, I think there's still a heap of digging to be done. We've cleared the scrub from the new site so next we need to get it level,' she said.

'Are you going to invite us over for a roast every week now you've bought Harry's farm?' Lily asked, opening the oven to prod at the meat, and as usual including herself as an undisputed member of Annie's household. Lucas's sister seemed to be under the impression that if she spoke as if she lived with them on a permanent basis, then one day they might simply forget to send her home at the end of the holidays.

'Sure, why not?' Sarah replied distractedly. 'If you'll come.'

'Of course we'll come. Why wouldn't … we?' Lily replied, her voice petering out. Even she'd noticed the subtly raised tension in the room as Harry came into the kitchen to wash the wood dirt from his hands. 'Harry, you love a roast, I'm sure you'll come every week—won't you?'

The room went silent as they all waited for him to answer. With deliberate care, Harry dried his fingers on the hand towel and then folded it neatly back onto the handle of the oven. When he finally answered, his voice was gentle but as unyielding as steel. 'No, Lily. I won't.'

Lily pouted. 'Why not?'

Harry looked up and locked his eyes on Sarah's. 'You know why,' came the heartbroken whisper. He slipped out of the house so fluidly it seemed he'd never been there at all.

Poor Lily looked utterly shame-faced. 'I'm sorry,' she said. 'I didn't think. This was his family's home …'

Tears welled in Annie's eyes at the dual sorrow her best friend had to bear.

And as she knew they would, her remembered tears became a river of grief. A sacred river, calling her home.

Her eyes opened to fragrant darkness and although the night-time sounds of the Garden did their best to calm her, it still took her a long time to find the courage to go back to sleep.

Chapter 7

'I'll do what I can to help him,' my Guardian declared as we lay on the muddy grass so I could kiss all the places I'd tried to bite him a few minutes earlier. Luckily Bane was a trained fighter so I'd only drawn blood twice. I still felt terrible about it.

'Because if you don't help him, he'll suffer, and if he suffers, I suffer.' It wasn't supposed to have sounded like an accusation.

Looking up at the sky, he exhaled. 'No. I'll help him because you've forced me to see what he's going through, and I wouldn't wish that on my worst enemy … maybe. Anyhow, I know how complicated depression can be. I was lucky enough to have a supernatural answer to my mental health issues, both times. I don't think that's likely for Dallmin this time, do you?'

I shook my head, miserably reminded that I'd been the cause of Bane's problems as a young teenager and also when I'd abandoned him for three years. I'd learned from my mistakes. Trying to release him from the bond to live his own life had cost him. I hadn't given him the freedom to choose what it was *he* wanted. That was unfair of me. With the lightest of touches I traced around the two scars on his forearm. One had been given to him by Sarah Ashbree the day she died, the other by Jake, yet both were indirectly my fault. He shivered at the feel of my fingers on his skin.

'Poor Bane. One minute I'm scratching and biting and the next I'm kissing you. How did you end up stuck with such a difficult person to look after? I'm sorry I'm so messed up.'

'You don't need looking after. You just need people to stop trying to kill you. And as for being messed up, it's been a tough couple of days.

Don't be so hard on yourself.' He kissed my knuckles. 'How many times *did* you die yesterday?'

I knew better than to trust his light tone. 'Even if I could remember, I would never tell you.'

His face went blank and I could almost see his imagination spinning images of me falling and breaking, over and over. I blew gently in his ear to dispel them until he shivered and gave me a wan smile.

'Yeah, probably best that I don't know.'

I kissed the corner of his jaw and a dimple magically appeared on his cheek. Good trick.

'I have to say, the kissing *almost* makes up for the scratching and biting. And kicking and elbowing, I might add.' He tentatively prodded a spot on his ribcage.

Pouting in shame was dreadfully unbecoming so I made myself stop it. Instead, I lifted his shirt and kissed him where my elbow had connected with his ribs. His skin was smooth and the muscles beneath were tense. And strong, and …

'Ah, Lainie, what are you doing to me?' His voice was tight, yet when I looked up, his eyes were glowing with a hunger that defied restraint. A hunger that dared me to unleash the desire I felt and see how high we could fly together.

I pulled away, trying to piece together my ability to reason with my out-of-control emotions. 'Sorry,' I said, wriggling away a bit further and trying to lie as still as I could. Cold mud soaked into my hair, which was a helpful distraction. Somehow I had to get my body back under control, but my brain was just so fried. 'I didn't mean to rush you. I guess you're a bit young to start thinking about having children. I'm okay, I can wait as long as you need.' Something about what I was saying wasn't quite right. The words sounded blunt to my Nalong ears, and complicated to my Eden ears. And it was hard to think straight when he was looking at me like that.

He sat up and his eyebrows made a shape I hadn't seen before. 'You think *I'm* not ready?'

I shrugged my shoulders, at a loss as to how to respond.

He opened his mouth to speak, and then closed it again, not really breathing. Then he started playing with the golden bracelet on my wrist with the tips of his fingers, and I wondered if it would somehow give him the courage to say what he wanted.

'Lainie, I've thought about nothing else for three years,' he finally blurted. He paused as if to test my reaction, and then threw me a sideways smile when I kept staring at him. Lowering his gaze, he continued. 'I used to have this recurring dream where I'd be holding our little girl. Her face was like yours, only she had my mum's eyes, and her laugh was like pure innocence even though she'd just poured cold water down my back. She was so real, so vividly alive that I could remember the smell of her hair when I woke.' Remembered grief coloured his expression. 'Losing the feel of you both when I came back to reality used to reduce me to tears. Ask Tim, he'll remember, not that I ever told him what I'd been dreaming about, of course.'

Little girl? Wow. She'd better not be anything like me.

I would be someone's mum …

No way.

I knew absolutely nothing about motherhood. I'd only met my own mother a few years ago, and I was pretty certain she hadn't given me the best example of how to be one.

The idea seemed absurd—that I could *ever* consider having a baby, but in the next moment it felt like the most natural thing in the world. Which it was.

Children were the most precious of blessings.

Bane's daughter.

A little female version of Bane, with black hair and grouchy toddler tantrums and silver eyes and his exquisite tingling smile …

'Lainie? Are you all right?' He waved his hand in front of my eyes and I blinked, startled. 'I shouldn't have told you that. They were just my stupid dreams, I didn't mean to—'

'Can I have my ring now?'

'What?'

Had I misinterpreted things again? Did he want to marry me or not? Why couldn't he come out and say what he meant for once? I glared at him in consternation.

He shook his head ruefully and laughed. 'You're not going to let me do this right, are you?'

I rolled my eyes at him and sat up. Stupid social conventions. Stupid cultural expectations. Stupid ideas of romance. 'Bane, can't you see that everything you do *must* be "right"? Because you are you and I'm me and we're us. Have you learned nothing from all our previous mistakes?'

Leaning over to me and tucking a wayward strand of muddy hair behind my ear, his smile was shy, yet his gaze locked on mine with glorious determination. He breathed huskily, torturing me with his patient silence until finally he spoke. 'Marry me then, Lainie Gracewood. I dare you to bind yourself to me as tightly as I'm bound to you. I promise I will love you forever and protect you no matter what it takes. I'm already yours, heart and soul. I have been since the day you danced with me.'

A single fugitive tear slid down my cheek. What he wanted was abundantly clear in every line of his body and my spirit sang in tune with his devotion. Breathless, I struggled to get my words out of my heart and past my lips. It took me a few choked up seconds to do more than make weepy, mumbly noises.

'I know you, Bane,' I finally managed. 'I've known you when you were my most devoted and loyal enemy and when you became my most devoted and loyal friend and I've loved you through every bit of it. I don't know why I waited so long to say it. I love you, and I won't leave you again, with or without a marriage vow. Please don't feel you have to marry me to bind me to you, because I'm not going anywhere.'

Marriage. An unnecessary concept in Eden. If we'd been there, we would have been in the natural state of 'marriage' long ago. Commitments there were simpler, and profoundly unshakable. It was difficult to remember all the ramifications that marriage entailed in this complex world, and I was suddenly worried I might have manipulated him into this somehow by bringing it up. But the joy in his expression couldn't lie. Not to me.

Nor could his words, gently and insistently seeking a real answer.

'Will you marry me, Lainie?' he asked again.

'I'll marry you if you're sure it's what you want.'

Reaching under the collar of his grass-stained shirt, he pulled out a long chain from around his neck, the sort of chain that had once held army tags. Now it only carried a delicate gold and diamond ring.

'I've never wanted *anything* more than I want this,' he breathed.

Tessa was waiting for us when we returned to the house a little while later. She was grinning from ear to ear as she crushed us together in a tearful embrace.

'Why didn't you buy cameras with audio?' she scolded, reaching straight for my hand to examine the ring. Bane must have cut short my kisses for more than one reason.

'How much could you see?' I asked, feeling my cheeks warm. Not the biting. Please say you didn't see me biting him.

'You aren't much of a fighter, are you?' she remarked, confirming my fear. 'Not that I could see much. You were right on the edge of range of the view from the house and the next camera is miles away at the park gate. I tried to zoom in, but it was too far.' She was unrepentant. 'Was this your mother's ring?' she asked Bane.

'My grandmother's. Mum threw her ring in the river when Dad left. My grandparents were married for over fifty years before Pa died of a heart attack. After that, Nan always talked about him as if he'd popped out for milk and bread and would be home any minute. They had a wonderful partnership.'

'It's gorgeous! And it fits her perfectly,' she gushed.

'It's a pretty plain one. They couldn't afford anything too fancy. I could have it altered if you want something different,' he told me, looking almost bashful.

Snatching my hand away, I scowled. 'No way! It's perfect how it is, and it matches my bracelet nicely. You're not having it back, not even to alter it.'

A muffled crash from inside the house brought us all back down to Earth. We rushed to the guest room to find Dallmin standing on top of the chest of drawers, cringing away from Noah who was picking up pieces of a broken vase.

'Sorry, Lainie, I didn't expect him to do that. He's frightened of me, but I haven't done anything to him, I promise.' Awkwardly holding the broken china, Noah looked baffled, as if he'd never had to deal with anyone being scared of him before. For good reason.

'He's terrified,' I explained, remembering my earlier fear. 'Of us and of himself. Can you charm him down from there?'

Noah looked at me as if I was crazy, still not convinced his charisma was anything special, then he moved to stand in front of Dallmin and looked him directly in the eyes.

'No one's going to hurt you, mate. We want to help. Please climb down? You can sit in the corner again if you want. I promise I'll keep my distance.' His dazzling smile was so infectious that Dallmin's face began to relax and he glanced at me as if for support, so I smiled as confidently as I could.

From the doorway, Bane was watching me with narrowed eyes, worried I might slip back into Dallmin's mind again. No wonder my mother had always sounded so apathetic about her natural gifting. My own gift linked me to people's memories, to their point of view. And usually only when I touched them. Annie's made her feel all the emotions others were feeling—all the time. She'd once told me that knowing how someone feels should be enough to help. *Feeling* the same things they did was going a giant step too far. Now I understood why.

I worked to keep my attention firmly on my own current mood, which actually wasn't too difficult to do while fiddling with my ring.

Dallmin slid down from the furniture and slunk back into the corner in a huddle with his back to us, his arms wrapped around his knees.

'Noah, do you have any headphones we could borrow?' Bane asked, getting out his phone. 'I have a playlist he might like to listen to. It used to help me a lot when I didn't want to think too hard about things. It might help to settle him down.'

Full of gratitude, I hugged my fiancé as Noah left in search of what we needed.

⌒

'Right, so I've been gone almost three hours from this madhouse,' Aunt Lily huffed as she dumped an armload of shopping bags on the kitchen table. 'What's happened?'

Tim followed her in carrying even more bags, having just said a prolonged goodbye to Nicole. 'I haven't told her anything,' he assured me. 'Yet.'

'Anything about what?' my aunt asked. 'And why has Noah been crying? He wouldn't say a word as I came in. He gave me a stupid-looking grin and then practically ran away when I tried to ask him about it. What have I missed?'

As I began to unpack the groceries, I tried to get my head around the events of the last few hours. 'Well, let's see. Right before you left, Tim found out that Bane's been cheating in army training because of his super-quick healing abilities. Nicole came around and hugged me and I have witnesses who will verify that she does, in fact, know how to utter the word "sorry", even if it was for something she had no need to apologise for. Bane and Tim prepared the farm to become the set for a reality TV show, so we can't go wandering around the place in only our bras anymore without the rest of the world seeing. Then, while you were in town I split an astounding total of one piece of wood before turning mildly insane, I bit Bane and then we got engaged. And Dallmin broke a vase.'

Five whole seconds of stunned silence was followed by a very girly sounding shriek as my aunt squished Bane and me and the box of Weet-Bix I was holding into a massive head-locking hug. In the past twenty-four hours, I had been hugged almost as often as I had in a whole week in Eden, and that was saying something. Tears flowed. Again.

'I knew it would work out this time. I just knew it! I'm so happy for you both,' she congratulated.

'Really?' I asked a little wistfully. 'No lecture about how young we are? I'm not even twenty-one yet, and Bane isn't much older.' I'd spent considerable effort trying to see things from a non-Eden point of view and our ages were the biggest issue I could think of. I peered at Aunt Lily, genuinely curious to see whether she thought it was a problem, while I tried to pop the box of cereal back into shape.

She blinked at me. 'So what? Do you want me to suggest waiting, in case someone better comes along? Or delay things so you can both be certain about how you really feel? Come on, Lainie, I knew this was coming the day you first told me his name.' Grinning, she pulled out a bottle of wine from one of the shopping bags and began to open it. 'I even bought some red wine to celebrate, since I know how much you hate the sparkly stuff. I *knew* this had to happen sometime soon!'

Tim tilted his head to read the label. 'Huh. What are the chances?' he mumbled. Bane laughed. I looked from one to the other, waiting for an explanation. 'It's from my family's estate,' Tim said. 'We do quite a nice Cab Sav, but I like the Merlot better. You chose a good one,' he said approvingly.

Aunt Lily's jaw dropped as she looked again at the label. It was a *very* well-known brand. My heart smiled, gratified that Tim was now comfortable enough with us to reveal his background of hidden riches.

Sipping on the wine a few minutes later, I listened to the sound of my family celebrating a wonderful event, while inside I began to feel anxious again. Tomorrow we would have to leave in search of Jake and I was terrified of what would happen to Dallmin when I was gone. It was so tempting to 'peek' into how he was feeling, only I was scared I would lose myself again. His emotions right now were way too powerful for me to cope with, so I tried hard not to think about him. Eventually, Bane noticed my discomfort and drew me aside.

'You're tired. Can I help?' he asked, giving my shoulders a rub. Trust him to know exactly where my muscles were sorest. Heat flowed from his fingertips in a very scrumptious way as I leaned back into his touch. 'You didn't sleep much last night,' he continued. 'Were you worried about my concussion or was something else keeping you awake?'

'Just transitioning again,' I assured him. 'It'll pass soon. Plus, I wasn't really that tired, given I'd spent most of the afternoon dead. What about you? How's your head feeling?'

Sweet breath caressed my ear. 'Euphoric. I'm getting married!' he whispered. 'I have so much I want to show you, Lainie. There's so much more in this world to see. I know it won't compare to Eden, but there's beauty in its imperfection all the same.'

Warm fingers traced the curve of my neck and I quivered, indulging in his closeness. How could I concentrate on anything when he did that?

'There are so many things we can explore together,' Bane crooned, practically purring.

I bit my lower lip in an effort to gather my thoughts again. 'First we need to find Jake,' I reminded him. 'It's bad that he's on the loose with the sword. We have no idea what it's capable of. Perhaps my restlessness has more to do with him than anything else. I'm sorry if I seem less than euphoric right now.'

My Guardian straightened, and that lovely moment of playfulness dissolved. Damn stupid evil idiot Jake. He had a lot to answer for.

'You don't need to apologise,' Bane said. 'I understand completely. Jake is still a threat to you and Noah. I've learned to hide the tension pretty well, and Tessa's holding up great, but I can see the strain behind her eyes.'

I glanced over to where Tessa was sipping her wine, smiling at something Aunt Lily was saying. Her hand was gripping Noah's.

'Is that why she's so clingy?

'She's actually doing pretty well. If she's feeling anything like I am, her instincts are probably screaming at her to bale him up into a corner with her back to him and growl at anyone who comes within shouting distance. I guess she spent most of high school learning to control her impulses too.'

As if she could sense us talking about her, Tessa flicked a guilty glance at Bane.

'She knows we'll be leaving soon, and she's feeling bad because you'll be getting closer to danger while Noah stays here.'

Poor Tessa. If Noah felt the same compulsion to retrieve the sword as I did, he was going to be painful to live with for a while. On the other hand, I also felt tied to the farm by the usual undeniable need to stand guard against intruders, and that hadn't lessened one bit since Noah had blocked the path with rocks. One of us had to stay, and with a baby to care for, our roles were obvious.

'I'm going to check on Dallmin,' I said, abandoning my barely touched wine. 'Somehow I have to get him to talk to me before we go, and we can't delay leaving any longer.'

⌒

Apparently, baroque classical music was an effective tool for helping to stabilise depressive and fearful emotions, particularly for someone already fascinated with experiencing new musical genres. Dallmin had his hands over his headphones, his knees drawn up, and his eyes closed when we slipped into the room. Lost as he was in Vivaldi's *The Four Seasons*, I was afraid to disturb him, particularly if he hadn't been able to hear us come in, so I sat down on the floor to wait, trying to look as unthreatening as possible. Bane sat too, looking ready to react in an instant if Dallmin so much as looked at me the wrong way. Being willing to help him did not mean Bane was willing to trust him.

For six minutes I waited patiently for the concerto to end, staring at the revolting lilac walls and mint-green architraves Aunt Lily had always stubbornly refused to let me paint over. And then I waited less patiently for another three. And watched. And fidgeted. And studied my ring. And plaited my dirty hair. Far out, these classical pieces could drag on. Outside, the sun was turning the sky into a pinkish-orange night-light and I silently sang myself a happy birthday. It had been exactly one whole day since I had been reborn into this world. And I was already engaged. Who knew what would happen to me in the next twenty-four hours? Idly picking at bits of purple carpet fluff and rolling them into little balls, I began to play miniature lawn bowls with them until I noticed Bane watching me. He had the patience of bedrock. I stuck my tongue out at him. Smiling, he did it back, so I screwed up my face and showed him how I could touch the tip of my nose with my tongue. *Copy this,* I dared silently. That was when I noticed Dallmin staring at us both. He'd turned the music off and seemed to be trying to decide whether to be frightened or not. It must have been hard to be frightened of someone trying to stick their tongue in their nostril though, because he took a deep breath and sat up.

'I need to make things right,' he declared. 'Somehow I must do something that will make things right again, only I don't know how. It is not possible to have the same time again and do things differently.' With his slender fingers he placed the headphones on the floor with precise movements, and then leaned toward me in supplication. His fine-boned face looked too delicate for this world. It made me sad.

'What do people here do to make things right when they have acted like an animal? I am a *man*. I have been changed by this place, but I'm still able to think and to feel and to choose. Jake told me of a word, only I don't know if anything he told me is real. Is an "apology" real, or was it a lie? I want it to be real because I want to apology to you. Is that a way

I can make things balanced again?' His large brown eyes held no trace of insincerity.

'Um, well, it's a start,' I told him, relieved that he was brave enough to talk about it.

'How do I apology?'

This was going to be tricky. 'Hmm. I'll try to break it down for you.' I fiddled with my ring as I thought about it. 'When someone hurts you, what you want most is for them to know you're hurting, and acknowledge that they caused it. It can be difficult to heal the wounds of the heart if the other person doesn't do this. Saying the word "sorry" shows us you know that what you did caused us pain, and you wish you hadn't done it. Without this declaration, it's harder for any of us to find healing.'

Nodding, Dallmin crawled over and sat cross-legged in front of us. Taking my hand, he turned my palm up and kissed me formally on the wrist in the Eden way of greeting, offering me as much of his attention as I might want. 'Lainie-Shamar, Watcher of Eden, I am sorry.'

Shaw-mar? What the hokey was a Shaw-mar? I opened my mouth to ask, but Dallmin was on a mission to articulate a full-blown apology.

'I am sorry for keeping Bane from you when you needed him,' he continued. 'I am sorry for allowing Jake to find out about Eden and about Noah. I am sorry I hurt the people you are bonded to the most tightly.' The genuine appeal in his phrasing evoked compelling forgiveness … and I melted.

Turning to Bane, he reached for his hand too, but my Guardian flinched and pulled back. I glowered at him until he capitulated and reluctantly held out his hand. His other fist and his jaw remained clenched. Instead of kissing his wrist, Dallmin brushed his lips over the fresh scar forming. 'Guardian-Bane, keeper of the Creator's heart, I am sorry. I am sorry for telling you one thing when I believed another so I could control your actions. I am sorry for hitting you with a cooking tool and helping Jake to weave you to a tree. I am sorry I stopped you from healing Lainie. I am sorry I used the knife-gift you gave me to hurt your friend. I am sorry that because of me you chose to say goodbye to your love partner so she would stay safe.'

Bane said nothing.

The exiled child of Eden turned to me again. 'Why did you not stay at home? Bane wanted you to stay there. Now you are here again. I don't understand.'

'My want was stronger,' I explained simply.

Dallmin turned incredulous eyes to Bane, his graceful fingers clutching at the worn carpet. 'She loves you with all the songs in her heart if she chose to leave the Garden for you. Love so strong is special, even in Eden. It took me a very long time to …' He took a shaky breath and then shook his head as if dispelling an unwanted train of thought. 'I have no words to tell you how I feel about myself for causing you to choose to leave her. Everything I have left, I give to you to help keep her safe from Jake. I *will not* do wrong again.'

Pressing his lips together, Bane glowered at him. 'Yeah, you will. You'll make more mistakes because there's too much about this world you don't understand. I can't risk having you mess up again, Dallmin, you're too dangerous. I'm sorry. We're leaving in the morning with Tim to try to find Jake and get the sword back. Maybe Noah can teach you some wisdom before we get home, and then we'll talk again. You need time to adjust and heal, and time is something we don't have for you right now.' His heartbreaking words were firm, his eyes as cold as snow at dawn.

For a long minute, Dallmin looked like a broken toy as he considered his words, then he knitted his brows together. 'Because of what I did, Jake has the sword that burns,' he said, head bowed as he peered up at us like a submissive child. 'Because of what I said, he knows about Eden, and where it is. Because of what I have done, he might tell others and they might come looking for the road to my home. If too many people know of Eden, Noah and Lainie may not be able to keep it safe. My home and my family are in danger because of me. I will not stay here and take time to adjust, or to heal. I will find Jake, and I will stop him. No healing can happen for me while my home is threatened because of what I did. You *will* let me come and you *will* do whatever you need to, to make sure I do not make more mistakes.'

For someone who had been so meekly apologetic a moment before, he was suddenly incredibly forceful. Looking from one pair of righteously angry flashing eyes to the other, I watched the staring competition unfold until finally Bane must have seen something he needed to see.

'Okay,' Bane relented. 'We leave at dawn.'

Chapter 8

'Dawn? Why dawn?' My bleary voice sounded too whiney for a Shamar—or whatever it was Dallmin had called me. 'I know we need to track down Jake urgently, but surely an hour or so won't make too much difference.'

It had taken me a long time to get to sleep, and knowing I was keeping Bane awake when he needed to recover had only made it harder to relax. Crazy images and emotions had swirled in my brain for hours on end until I went back to my old solution of playing loud music through headphones to drown out all other thoughts. Even so, I'd only managed a few hours' restless tossing.

'And by "dawn", you know he means nautical dawn, right? That's six-thirty-five, by the way, for all you civvies,' Tim clarified. 'Seven minutes to go.'

As I sat by the last embers glowing in the wood heater, nursing my mug of tea, I tried to ignore the way the rest of the household buzzed in a mad frenzy of activity. Seven minutes to go. Honestly. You couldn't get further from an Eden outlook on life than working to a countdown. Besides, I was ready to go, except Aunt Lily had taken one look inside my overnight bag and proceeded to run around the house in a panic searching for all sorts of things she insisted I needed. I'd been pretty proud of myself for remembering to pack a toothbrush. What else could I possibly need?

'You can sleep in the car,' Tim suggested, cuddling three bags of chips and two bottles of soft drink. 'Oi!' he protested as Noah relieved him of two of the bags and promptly took them back to the kitchen.

On her way past, Tessa deftly swapped my mug for her adorable son and then followed Noah out of the room. Fumbling with the baby blanket, I realised she was hinting at something. Now that we were engaged, she evidently had no qualms about pushing Bane and I ahead to what she considered 'the next stage'. Tessa was trying to make me clucky. I snuggled my best friend's son against the crisp morning air and looked into eyes far more vivid green than any newborn had a right to. Let alone one with Asian genetics. A fine velvet cap of dark hair crowned the baby Cherub, who looked back at me way too seriously. Breathing in the scent of total innocence, I allowed myself to become a little bit lost in his point of view. It wasn't like the emotional memories I usually got from people; it was simply a sense that all was well with the world, and he was patiently waiting to see what other amazing things life would show him. I wondered how long his patience would last. Not long if he was anything like his dad, who'd already returned from the kitchen with a bag of apples for me to take. His body language was screaming at us all to get on with it and leave.

'Goodbye, Nathaniel. I'll be back as soon as I can. Don't let your daddy eat all the chocolate bikkies the way he usually does, because people might expect to see him get fat and he would have to live up to their expectations then, wouldn't he?'

A tiny frown creased his perfect brow and I laughed.

Noah pursed his lips and tried to swap his son for a bunch of paperwork and a pen. Something about wedding preparations. Whatever. I managed to scribble my name next to Bane's without relinquishing my hold on the sweet Cherub in my arms. If I had to leave, then I wanted as many last-minute cuddles as I could get.

'Come on, Aunty Lainie, you need to catch the bad guy before he lets the whole world know about Eden,' Noah chided, taking the paperwork from me. 'It's hardly fair that we can't talk about it and everyone else can.'

I caught my breath and we both froze, staring at each other.

'How thick am I?' I wailed. 'Noah, why did you let me be so stupid? I could have stopped all this from happening if I'd been paying attention. My stupid brain must be fried. I'm so sorry.' Bitter self-loathing engulfed me as I handed Nathaniel back to his dad, who promptly dropped all the papers on the floor.

'Dallmin,' I called. 'Come here for a minute. Please?'

The despondent man came and stood before me as if waiting for orders. And I gave them. Gripping his shoulder to help me focus, I gave a series of clipped commands. While the Words flowed as effortlessly as spilled water from my lips, the force of them slammed something shut with a deep reverberation that shook my spine. Dallmin watched me with a puzzled expression. Noah gave a satisfied grunt. Everyone else in the room threw each other furtive, anxious looks.

'Whatever you tried to do didn't work?' Tim guessed, dropping the chips and drinks onto the couch.

'Of course it worked. Why wouldn't it? It would have worked even better if I'd thought to do it weeks ago. I'm such an idiot,' I grouched, turning to him next with my hands outstretched.

He took an uneasy step back. 'Wait, shouldn't we kneel in a circle and hold hands or something?'

'Go ahead, if it makes you feel better,' I told him, but I didn't wait. He flinched as I grabbed both his shoulders and spoke the same lyrical Words over him. Backlash slammed into me in a very satisfying way and Noah smiled.

'Let me do Jake,' Noah said through gritted teeth as he passed Nathaniel over to Tessa. 'I'm going to stop him from speaking altogether.'

'Bad idea,' I warned him. 'That might make him even more noticeable, and as much as I appreciate Mick's help, I'm not really sure I want the police to find him before we do. It will complicate things an awful lot if they get hold of the sword,' I explained.

In the doorway, I could see my aunt shrugging her shoulders at Tessa's silent query.

'Fine,' he agreed. 'The same embargo we have, then. I'll do Jake if you do Mick. What about your aunt?'

'What about me?' Aunt Lily asked, her eyes flicking between us while her fingers twisted the strap of my bag.

'I think we should leave her be. She's done pretty well over the years. Imagine if she hadn't been able to tell me anything when Uncle first disappeared? That would have been disastrous,' I replied.

'I'm right here, you know. And I'd appreciate an explanation before you put a whammy on me, thanks.'

At the word 'whammy', Tim whipped his head back toward me, eyes wide.

'We won't do anything to you, Aunt Lily. And Tim, stop worrying. You didn't even feel it, did you?' I was still feeling furious with myself.

'Tim, tell me where Lainie went yesterday,' Noah asked eagerly, testing it out.

'The Garden of Eden?' he replied, clearly wondering if it was a trick question.

Noah glared at me in consternation and I rolled my eyes. 'Well, of course he can still tell *us*,' I reminded him.

Tim blinked. 'But no one else. Is that what you did to me? You didn't need to do that. I would never tell anyone, I swear,' he insisted, looking hurt.

'It's not a matter of being able to trust you, Tim. Even we have the same restriction, remember? It's an extra safeguard, that's all,' I said, trying hard not to sound sulky.

Beside me, Dallmin looked devastated, as he realised that his mistakes could have been easily prevented if I'd simply thought to do it earlier. If Dallmin had been unable to speak about Eden, Jake would never have used him to betray us. He probably still would have murdered me, but at least he wouldn't have found out about the cave or the sword or that Noah was a Cherub.

I gave Dallmin a feeble wave of my hands—there were no signs for what I had to say. 'I'm so sorry, Dallmin. I'm not as clever as I need to be for this job. I've let you down. You and everyone else,' I said, glancing at Bane. All that pain and anguish he'd been through because I hadn't used the brains I was born with.

Noah placed a comforting hand on my shoulder. 'Lainie, no one else thought of it either, so stop being so hard on yourself. Everything looks obvious in hindsight. What matters is what we do now. Please stop beating yourself up so I can concentrate.'

As I felt the corners of my mouth rise in relief, I narrowed my eyes suspiciously. Had he just used his charm to make me feel better? As I started to protest, he closed his eyes and lifted his chin, trying to slap a speech embargo on Jake, so I had to shut my mouth and settle for giving in and feeling better.

Taking a deep breath, I closed my eyes as well and tried to feel for Sergeant Loxwood.

Nothing happened.

He wasn't a Cherub so I had no way of locating him unless he happened to be encroaching on our territory, which he wasn't. I chewed on my lower lip and tried again, not bothering to locate him this time, only concentrating on the need to protect Eden from any inadvertent words the sergeant might let slip. Whispered Words of molten intent slipped off my tongue, but I felt nothing else. Had it worked? Opening my eyes again, I waited impatiently for Noah to finish. He always did like to embellish things.

'Done. I think,' he announced a few seconds later. 'Jake can't tell anyone about Eden, or us, or the sword.'

'Did you feel any backlash?' I asked.

'No. Was I supposed to?'

'I'm not sure. I felt it from Dallmin and Tim, but that could be because they're so close. I didn't feel it with Mick either. The Words felt right though, so I guess we'll have to hope for the best.'

'Um, guys?' Tim interrupted. 'I hate to be the one to point out the obvious, but if you can do that, then can't you just sort of … summon the sword back here or something?'

Noah shook his head, dispelling the sudden hope that had filled the room. 'I already tried that, not long after he left. He's running *away*, so Eden's not under enough of a threat. I couldn't even find him once he moved far enough away from the cave. I've tried and tried to concentrate on the fact that the sword itself is a danger. Nothing's worked so far. Maybe I'm messing up the logic somehow. I'll keep at it.'

'I don't think you're messing it up,' I told him. 'My guess is that the sword is a servant of Eden like we are. We can't use our authority to protect it or each other. And to make things worse in a twisted sort of way, we just took away even more of the threat by stopping Jake from revealing anything, so we can't even use that logic to work with. The bottom line is that Eden is currently pretty safe, so if we want to find him we'll have to do it the hard way.'

A tiny sigh emerged from the bundle of blankets Tessa was rocking, as if Nathaniel was as frustrated as the rest of us.

His mother looked up at me. 'Does that mean you don't have to go? After all, it'll only be a matter of time before he's compelled to make his way back here. Maybe we should stay here and wait for him,' she suggested.

'And what?' Noah asked. 'Patrol again? For how long? It could take months or even years for him to return, Tess. I won't risk having him come after any of us again, let alone Nathaniel.'

Dallmin shuddered.

'And who knows what he could do in the meantime? I mean, we all had the speech embargo and yet Lily, Mick, and Tim all found out about Eden. It's not reliable enough,' Noah continued.

All good reasons to go, yet they were overshadowed by my insatiable need to get the sword back as soon as possible. I knew Noah felt the same, even if he was trying hard to contain his agitation. We were intrinsically linked to the mysterious weapon and I felt deeply uncomfortable that it was out with some stranger, exploring the planet. I needed to have it tucked safely back where it belonged. After what it had done to Sarah, I both hated it and was completely awed by it, which felt very confusing, but it didn't diminish the craving I had for it to be returned to its spinning glory. Somehow there had to be a way to link the compulsion I felt with a logic that would convince me that finding it would protect Eden. I just needed to be smarter.

'I guess we should get moving then,' Tim suggested, gathering up the snacks again and heading to the door with Bane and Aunt Lily moving to follow.

I narrowed my eyes at him. 'You look way too bouncy for this time of the morning, Tim. It's not like you. Do you have any idea of what it is you're getting yourself into here? Jake Evans is on the run from the police. He's compelled to kill me on sight. He has a sacred sword whose powers even we don't understand, and we have no idea where to look. And we have to take a depressed, possibly psychotic elf along for the ride.'

Practically bouncing on his feet, Tim threw the chips and drinks at Bane, who was on his way past. 'Lainie, my friend,' he said, wrapping his arm around my shoulder and herding me toward the door. 'Do you have any idea how many gamers would sell their own grandmother to be allowed to come on the quest you just described?'

Chapter 9

Currawongs called to each other from the tree line that separated the park from the footy oval, while a family of galahs played somersaulting games on the grassy slope. By ten o'clock on Saturday morning, the local kids were split into three groups: the footy players warming up for their game, their younger siblings left to entertain themselves together in the park, and the inevitable spattering of kids who refused to join in with anything but had been dragged along anyway, their faces bathed in phone light. Over by the rubbish bin, the old homeless guy who always hung around the park was tossing bread to the ducks. Good to know the bakery still gave him the previous day's leftovers for breakfast.

Wet grass clippings stuck to my boots as I headed back to where Bane and Tim were waiting for me near the picnic tables. Dallmin was standing quietly, watching the little ones chase each other around the swings.

'You could have mentioned that the reason we had to leave so early was to visit your mum before she started teaching,' Tim complained to Bane as I approached. 'I would have asked Noah to drive me into town to meet up with you after a nice long sleep in.'

'And miss Mum's French toast?' Bane countered. 'Besides, she specifically asked to see you.'

'That was before she knew you'd proposed to Lainie. I honestly don't think she even noticed Dallmin and I were there.'

'She still would have been furious if you'd left town without saying goodbye. And I know Mum. There's no way we could have dropped in for a quick cuppa, told her our news, and then skipped town. We had to give her the morning. And now I can focus on what needs to be done.'

'Can you, though? You don't look quest-ready. You're too happy.'

'Why shouldn't I be happy? My fiancée will use her special skill-set to locate the thief, I'll take him apart piece by piece, and then we can all go back to eating French toast at Mum's.' Bane reached out a hand behind him and took hold of mine without needing so much as a glance back to know exactly where I was. His hand was nice and warm.

'Unfortunately, your fiancée is not a miracle worker,' I said.

'Yes, she is,' Bane and Tim said together.

'Well, okay, I am. But this time it didn't help. Firstly, I looked pretty weird going up to Jake's dad and shaking his hand with some lame excuse about what a great job he's doing coaching the Under 10s, just so I could read him. Secondly, it turns out that if someone really doesn't want to think about a painful topic, it kind of hurts when I ask them about it. Felt like I'd jumped off a cliff expecting to land in water and hit ice instead.'

'I'm hoping you're using that example as a metaphor, and not because you've done it,' Bane said.

I chose not to reply to that.

'Did you specifically ask him if he'd heard from Jake?' Tim asked.

'I did. He hasn't. Not since the court hearing last week. Which means the only lead we have is that Dallmin thinks he may have hitched a lift toward Horsham. We'd better head there now and hope there's a trail to follow. Let me know if any of you have any miraculous ideas, because I'm all out of them.' I started for the car park until I noticed Dallmin wasn't following.

'Dallmin, what's wrong? You look worried.'

'Will Bane really take him apart piece by piece? I don't understand. I hope I don't understand.'

Tim placed a comforting hand on his elbow. 'Oh, Dallmin, no. He won't do that. It's another of those idioms I told you about.'

'So he won't hurt him?'

'Erm … Bane, you have to be more careful with your words. Hey, look, is that homeless guy dumpster diving?'

I peered around Bane's shoulder to see Mr D pulling a paper bag out of the bin. The bag was from Nalongest Yard Fish and Chippery so it probably had most of a hamburger inside it. No one ever managed more than a bite or two of those.

Bane shrugged. 'He does it every day, Tim. Always has. He isn't quite right in the head and he's never listened to anyone who tries to stop him.'

'He listens to me,' I remembered suddenly. 'He likes me. Calls me Pudding-Kitten, and then he runs away.'

'Pudding-Kitten? Wish I'd known about when you were calling me Baney-Rabbit.'

'Mr D, that isn't very hygienic,' I called. 'What are you looking for? Your lost treasure? Let's get you cleaned up. Come on. There's a tap over by the barbecue.' I took a step toward him, but someone was holding my sleeve. 'Bane, come on. Look at him. He's got tomato sauce on his elbow. Who knows when that bin was last emptied? It's not like he's a threat to me, is he?'

My Guardian narrowed his eyes for a moment, and then shook his head. 'Not a threat, no. Just unpleasant. The last time I tried to speak to him he literally growled at me. Like a dog.'

'And when was that?'

'Back in high school.'

'Bane, everyone growled at you back in high school.'

'Well, I've never liked him.'

I sighed and kept walking. 'Mr D, there's no treasure in there. I promise.'

The man snapped up straight, like something had bitten him. He straightened his pale grey suit jacket and then wiped his hands on the blue t-shirt underneath. 'Pudding-Kitten?'

Behind me, I heard Tim try to stifle a laugh.

'Baby girl, I thought I'd lost you. I kept looking, though. Never stopped looking for my treasure.'

'I can see that. Perhaps it's over here, near the tap. Should we look together?'

The man looked like he was about to cry. 'I couldn't hold him any longer. I tried to, Pudding, I really tried even though it hurt. He got stronger every year, like you did. I'm sorry. I should have tried to drown him again. I thought about it. Many times. He wouldn't let me go anywhere near the river.'

Bane tugged on my sleeve again. I ignored him. 'Who wouldn't let you?'

Mr D leaned toward me and hissed in my ear. He smelled like old tomato sauce. 'The whispers are gone. The dog bites. I couldn't hold on. I'm sorry.'

'Lainie, you can't help everyone,' Bane admonished, drawing me back and stepping between us.

'Sure I can. I'm a mir—' Of course, my words became choked in guilt and got stuck in my teeth.

'I'm certain the treasure is in the river, but I was never allowed to look there. The treasure is in the river,' the homeless man mumbled. 'In the river.'

'Let's go there now and clean you up,' I said, reaching for his hand. He flinched so fast he tripped over the bin and nearly fell. Then he ran away, surprisingly fast.

We watched him go and then Tim and Bane turned to me with questioning faces.

'See? Like I said. Calls me Pudding-Kitten and then runs away. Every time.'

A two-hour drive doesn't sound like very long unless you happen to be sharing a ride with an overexcited spec-fiction fan on a quest, a potentially suicidal exiled Edenite, and a highly strung soldier. The soldier kept flipping between suppressed anger, unbridled joy whenever I cheekily flashed my ring at him, and overprotective fear. It made for some interesting music choices.

'Lainie, are you all right?' Bane asked in a rusty whisper.

I looked down in confusion at the way he was gripping and shaking my wrist to get my attention. 'Of course I am. You should know. What's the problem?' I asked, entwining my fingers in his.

'You've been staring out the window for twenty minutes straight without so much as a fidget. You look like you're on guard duty,' he said, smiling. 'You even managed to stay focused when I tried to ask you a question. My commanding officers would be impressed with your dedication.'

'Oh, sorry. What did you want to ask me?'

'Whether you think we should start by visiting each of the pubs to see if anyone's seen Jake, or if it's worth trying to track down some of the local drug dealers in case he's tried to charm some merchandise out of any of them.'

Impressed by his practical outlook, I tried to anticipate what Jake would do. I really had no clue. After three years of being surrounded by perfect innocence I simply had no idea how to get my head around what Jake's mindset would be like. The insight into his character I'd gained when I'd seen him last was all centred around his attitude toward me. It wasn't very helpful. Nice of Bane to try to let me lead though.

'Honestly? I have no idea. How would we even go about tracking down a dealer? It's not really my area of expertise. Perhaps we should start with the pubs. Maybe my gift can trace whether anyone's seen him lately, but it's a long shot. I'm happy to go with whatever you recommend.'

He tilted his head in concern. 'You are? Are you sure you're okay? What were you thinking about, anyway?'

I paused—a bit embarrassed—and fiddled with the button on my cuff. 'Oh, you know. Death. Humanity. Whether we're defined by the thoughts in our heads and what that means for the after-life. Just the usual.'

He watched me with curious expectation.

'I'm not human, Bane,' I tried to explain, 'and the more often I die, the more I realise how different I am. It turns out it's a tricky concept to come to terms with.'

He seemed unsure of how to respond. Silence stretched awkwardly as I drifted back into grasping at half-remembered feelings from beyond the grave. It was like trying to catch bubbles; you had to follow them without grabbing at them so tightly they disappeared.

Eventually we reached the outskirts of Horsham and began to look for the nearest watering hole. Giant adjustable billboards advertising counter meal specials and pokie machines made the search easy. A woman with long dark hair and Asian tattoos down her arm held the door open for us on her way out. Unfortunately, that was about the most meaningful interaction we had all afternoon. We showed around an old school photo of Jake that Bane had stored in his phone, but even I hardly recognised him as the same man who'd abducted Tessa. Nobody remembered seeing him.

⮜

'She spent half the rent money on an x-ray for her son and a third course of antibiotics for her daughter who has tonsillitis,' I muttered to Bane as I stepped out of the café. The brisk air blew away the last traces of the mental images that weren't my own. 'That's the only reason she sounded so snippy. There was no need to snap back at her.'

Wandering around talking to people at random really wasn't working. After nearly two full days of it I was emotionally exhausted and well beyond frustrated. Surely someone must have noticed a man fitting Jake's description with a fresh shoulder wound, unless he'd bypassed Horsham altogether. It made sense. If I were him I would have run as far away as I could get, particularly if I knew the police were after me. The problem was, we had no clue as to which direction he would have gone. He probably went wherever his ride had been willing to take him, which could have been anywhere. If he'd found the right truck he could be in far north Queensland by now for all we knew. I had tried hard to find even a hint that he might have passed through town by 'reading' as many people as I could find an excuse to touch. Chances were he'd never even stopped here.

I glanced back through the café window at the woman who was chasing after her young son. The three-year-old had wriggled out of his arm sling and was bolting toward us. As the last one out, Tim barely managed to close the door behind him before he could escape. I waved a quick goodbye to the kid as he pressed his face up against the glass door and then turned to scan the street to see who else was around that I could read. Bane was in my way.

'No more readings. Your heart is too compassionate to cope with everyone else's problems. I'm putting my foot down this time. It's not good for you and it's not getting us anywhere. We've asked at every pub, bottle shop, café, and hotel in town. He didn't stop here. Until we find a new lead, I suggest we go home for a while.'

'If you need a rest, Lainie, I could keep asking around,' Tim suggested. 'I'm full of energy.'

His enthusiasm was getting on my nerves. 'No, you aren't. You don't even know how tired you are because you've never felt completely well.'

Dallmin's eyes flicked toward me and I mentally kicked myself for being so tactless. To both of them.

'I'm sorry. Forget I said that. Bane's right, this is getting us nowhere, but I can't go home yet. Give me some time to think of another way to track him.'

'What's rent money?' Dallmin asked quietly. 'Is it different to normal money?' His depression hadn't lifted and yet his inherent curiosity had still somehow managed to reassert itself.

Tim answered him before I could—probably glad to change the subject. 'No, not different. It's money that's been set aside to pay to stay in someone else's house. Sometimes people buy more than one house, so they live in one and rent out the other to people who can't afford to buy a house of their own,' he explained.

Tim was the only one of us who still had the patience to answer Dallmin's millions of questions. As grateful as I was that my friend was talking and engaging with us again, I simply couldn't keep up with all the explanations.

'What is an x-ray? And antibiotics?' he asked. 'What's tonsillitis?'

Even Tim sighed. He took a box of Nerds out of his pocket and shook some into Dallmin's waiting palm to distract him—the man was as obsessed with lollies as he was with learning.

'Lainie?' Tim asked plaintively. 'Surely it's important for Dallmin to blend in and not attract the wrong sorts of questions from people? Can't you sort of … whammy him into knowing everything?'

Without waiting for the answer he knew I would give, he proceeded to answer each of Dallmin's questions in turn. He should have been knighted for his valour. Or sainted for his patience. Or else shot and put out of his misery.

Bane looked disturbingly thoughtful. 'He does have a point. We can't keep doing this. He does need to know more, but it's wearing us all out.'

'So what do you suggest? Use Words of power to mentally upload him with the history of the world?' Now I was the one sounding snippy.

Bane smiled his dimpled smile at me as he led us down the street toward the main shopping strip.

An hour later we sat in the local park eating soggy hot chips drowned in vinegar, while Dallmin sat cross-legged on the grass, figuring out how to use his new touchscreen tablet to access an app on how to read English. Although it was a wonderful solution, it got me thinking. As I crafted my leftover chips into little stick figures using toothpicks, I considered the best way to broach the subject. Eventually I decided to ask Bane outright and be done with it.

'What are we going to do about money? You can't keep buying us everything. Dallmin's phone and now this tablet—he'll need to pay you back at some point. Somehow we'll both need to find a way to support ourselves here. I can't expect any income from the farm since Noah, Tess, and Aunt Lily have done all the work for the last three years. Perhaps I should try to find a job somewhere. I'd love to study, only I can't plan that far ahead until Jake has been dealt with. Who knows how long that will take?' Unwilling to face the truth, I hedged around my fear of going to uni. I could hardly remember which subjects I'd taken at school, let alone any of their content. What if I had to repeat some of them? I remembered enough to know I would hate that.

'You already have a job,' Tim said in a horrified voice. 'A divinely appointed job to protect the Gar..gghh ...' he choked, spluttering chips everywhere.

Bane laughed and patted him on the back as we watched an old man with a Zimmer frame amble past us.

'I'm so sorry. I didn't mean it,' Tim cried, nearly in tears. Perhaps I'd overdone it a little on the guilt factor when I'd muzzled him.

'It's all right, Tim. I understand,' I said. 'But I'm still going to have to find a way to pay the bills. Unfortunately I can't just conjure up money whenever I want. Trust me, I've tried. Besides, I'll need something to put on my tax return that I can actually write down.'

'What's a tax return?' came the inevitable question from the eager student at my feet, who was gracefully playing the touchscreen like it was a musical instrument.

'Look it up later,' I said as patiently as I could. He still picked up on my lack of enthusiasm.

'I'm sorry to pester you,' he apologised. 'This world is so complex and ...' His language limitation hit another bump.

'Confusing? Frustrating? Dangerous?'

'Symmetrical,' he supplied.

Not what I had been expecting.

He gave me a wistful smile. 'Everything here is balanced. If you smile at someone, they smile back at you. If you ignore someone, they ignore you. If you do not care for your body, it will not care for you. If you break the rules, you suffer. And if you want something, you need to give something of equal value in return. We must give something in order to get money, Lainie, and we need to get money in order to get other things we need. It is important I gain as much knowledge as I can so I can keep things symmetrical.'

I blinked at him.

Completely at ease, Bane took two of my chip people and joined their hands together as if they were a bride and groom on a wedding cake. 'Don't worry about it, Lainie. We have plenty of time to get your career back on track whenever you're ready. Until then, we'll make do. I have a bit of money set aside. Besides, you might yet decide you don't want to work *too* hard for the next few months. I expect there's only so much I can do to heal … natural processes.' He peered at me through his long eyelashes. It was a gentle test to see whether I still felt the same way about our plans.

So far he'd nearly always been the one to reluctantly pull away from a kiss and remind me that we needed to find Jake and the sword before we took things too far. It was getting harder and harder to remember that, for both of us. Even the implications of his words sent my heart thumping wildly. Tim heard them somewhat differently. Standing bolt upright, he stared at me, opening and closing his mouth in a futile attempt to speak.

It took a moment for me to work out what his problem was. 'I'm not pregnant,' I reassured him, stomping on Bane's foot under the picnic table.

'Yet,' my naughty fiancée mumbled under his breath.

Dallmin looked up sombrely from his study. 'It could take years for them to be blessed with a baby, Tim. Most couples are together for hundreds of years before they sing awake a new life,' he explained, using much the same slightly condescending tone Tim often used with him.

'Hundreds of years?' I croaked. Waiting even a few weeks seemed unbearable. Bane chuckled at my reaction and I belatedly remembered that our situation was completely different to the people Dallmin was describing.

'Are you two really in such a hurry to have kids?' Tim asked in a strangled voice.

'Yes,' I declared, full of anticipation for the future. Bane tilted his head, studying me, and I studied him back. 'Why aren't you saying yes?' I asked him. 'Are you having second thoughts?'

He slid his arms around my waist and pulled me close. 'Not at all. I just don't want you to feel you're being rushed into anything. Especially if you're still … how did you put it? Transitioning?'

'Ah. Fair point. Ask me how I feel about it again next week then, just in case.'

Bane kissed me on the cheek. 'We'll wait until you're absolutely certain. Take as much time as you want.'

'All things will happen at the best time,' Dallmin said sagely, still sitting with his legs crossed and poring over the words on the screen in front of him.

Shaking his head in disbelief, Tim sat down again. 'Well, at least you seem more relaxed today, Bane. I don't think I've seen you this happy since the day we first arrived in Nalong.'

Shocked, Bane and I looked at each other. A series of mixed emotions flicked across his face before he settled into a grin. 'He must be a long way from here. I still feel the danger to you, but it's much less than before. More like occasional shivers down my spine than a burning need to protect you. I guess it's been a gradual change so I didn't notice. You're safe right now.'

'That's terrible!' I wailed. All three men glared at me. 'Oh, come on. I'm not the only one of us who wants to get all this over with. We need to catch up to Jake, danger or no danger. Bane, is there a particular direction that feels more risky than any other?'

He glanced around and then shook his head. 'It doesn't really work that way. My compulsion isn't designed to head off danger in advance. It's more about getting to you in time to protect you. It isn't directional.'

'Well then, does the threat level change when I move around?' I asked, walking backward away from him.

'Only if you count the fact that in seven more steps you'll trip over the edge of the garden bed,' he replied. 'I don't think it's a significant enough distance to make a difference.'

'So we drive her,' Tim concluded, brushing the last of the salt from his fingers. 'We'll take each of the highways in turn and when you start acting like your normal grouchy self again, we'll know we're heading the right way.'

Sadly, it was the best option we had.

Chapter 10

A single friendly bark warned Annie that a car was on its way up the driveway long before she heard its engine or the crunch of the tyres on the dusty gravel. It had taken nearly ten months, but Bo had finally accepted his role as custodian of the farm and hardly ever turned up at his old home anymore. Of course, that meant Sarah no longer had such a convenient excuse to come over, Annie reflected as she pulled back the curtain to watch the red Gemini pull up. So what lame excuse would she find instead?

She'd had that thought before. Just as she'd pulled back the curtain before. In fact, Annie had *lived* this before. More than once. Was she ever going to be able to sleep normally again? After two whole decades, these memories should have faded, slotted neatly into the background buzz of her mind, nestled with thousands of others as a part of her character and experience. Instead, that natural process had been disrupted, her memories shielded when she'd hurled them away in fright and grief and guilt. The Living Fruit had protected her fragile psyche from having to relive the things that tormented her, yet the memories were not lost. They had simply been held for her in safekeeping until she was ready to deal with them. Until she was ready to heal and to learn. If the other world hadn't intruded on her so brutally again, would she have ever made herself face the past? Trapped in her dream by her own longing to see Lucas again, Annie let herself be taken back to the late November afternoon when both everything and nothing had changed.

Sarah's car settled to a reluctant halt in front of the house, as if it was still trying to decide if it wanted to be there at all. The engine kept running for nearly a full minute before its driver finished wrestling with her conscience and switched it off. There had been plenty of times when Sarah had made it that far and then turned around and gone home again. This time she chose to stay. Annie was getting heartily tired of her indecision. It was hard on everyone.

Behind her, she could sense Harry enter the room. He'd been helping Lucas to repaint the spare bedroom—the last of the rooms to be finished since the fire had made such a mess of the back of the house—and he was adorned with lilac speckles. The room would be a nice surprise for Lily's inevitable return once school finished in another couple of weeks.

Annie turned to give him a sympathetic smile. She could feel the surge of anticipation and affection that ran through him when he glimpsed the car through the window ... and a second later she felt the bleak determination with which he suppressed it. As usual, he said nothing. If he kept up that method of controlling his emotions, she was sure he was eventually going to forget how to talk at all. She already missed his jokes.

'Do you want me to leave?' Annie asked.

Harry shook his head, wiping his hands on an old towel. 'Please stay. It makes her uncomfortable when we're alone. She doesn't want anyone to think we might ...' His voice trailed away as if he'd already forgotten how to use it.

'Oh, for goodness sake. It's us! We already know, so what difference does it make?'

'Her integrity is at stake, Annie. Even if she doesn't actually do the wrong thing, it's important to her to be seen to be doing the *right* thing. People could get hurt otherwise.'

'People *are* getting hurt. And I'm still not convinced she *is* doing the right thing.'

'Me either,' came a soft voice from the hallway.

Annie jumped a mile and cursed the ridiculous Guardian stealth that had enabled Sarah to come inside so quickly and quietly.

Her neighbour stepped into the lounge room carrying a smooth oval rock slightly longer than her hand. Certainly not an excuse to visit they'd seen before. Perhaps she needed to get away from the twins for a while. The boys had both started walking and were like an unstoppable force of nature. Even her Guardian advantages didn't seem to be enough to help her cope. She looked like a bit of a train wreck. Her hair was tied in a messy knot at the base of her neck and the way she kept rubbing her eyes gave the impression she hadn't slept properly for at least a week. Both Cherubim waited patiently for her to speak.

Sarah licked her lips and tucked a wayward strand of her pale hair behind her ear. 'It will be David's birthday soon. I thought maybe Lucas could give me an idea about what to get him.'

As if any of us would be fooled into thinking that was why she'd come.

'How about a pocket knife?' Annie suggested. 'So he can cut some ties.'

'Stop it, Annie,' Harry said. 'And, Sarah, please get to the point. Why are you really here?'

Perhaps her tiredness was the reason her next words weren't tactful ones.

'We've finished demolishing your house.'

Annie glared at her, but didn't sense the grief from Harry that she expected.

Sarah continued blithely. 'We found something in the rubble. It was set into the foundations as if it had been placed there deliberately. I thought you'd better have it.'

She handed Harry the flattened stone. It was carved with some odd markings—symbols or perhaps letters of some sort. He flipped it over and they both blinked in surprise at the simple diagram of a familiar gem that Harry had chosen to give to a museum months earlier. Heart-shaped and cradled by a pair of wings, the carving only lacked the blood-red colour of the rare diamond.

'It can't be,' Harry said. 'My dad only had the setting made when he got married. The house was built before he was born.'

Annie peered more closely. 'Maybe he was told about this, or saw a copy and designed the setting to match. Our families aren't always reliable at passing information from one generation to the next.' She smoothed her fingers over the picture. It felt powerfully alive, somehow. She could feel it like a tiny ocean crashing around in her chest.

Harry looked up at her, clearly feeling it too and wanting answers.

All she had were questions. 'Which one is it referring to? The original diamond or the ruby lookalike I made?'

'If it's important, then I'm hoping it's the ruby because I threw the diamond off a cliff at the southern end of the valley not long after your mum's funeral. That bloody diamond should never have left Eden in the first place, so I made certain it will stay there.'

The stone felt cool in her hands as she flipped it over again. They'd have to take it Next Door to see if anyone recognised the markings.

'I hope it's okay that I touched it,' Sarah said. 'I read somewhere that some objects are only supposed to be seen by certain people who have earned the right. I'm sorry if I did the wrong thing, but I wanted to get it to you as soon as I could.'

'I honestly don't know what this is, so I can't say,' Harry replied. 'Other than the marked tree near the lake, the closest thing to a sacred object I know of was the giant gum-nut my uncle carried everywhere. And I don't think it was sacred, just personal. It was the biggest I'd ever seen. He used to keep odd stuff in it—a pinch of dirt, or a pebble, or a leaf. The bits would always fall out before long and get lost, but he said that didn't matter. He'd simply collect more. He said the treasures of the Earth helped to ground him. When we buried him with it, it had a butterfly wing, a twig, and a dead Christmas beetle in it.'

It was about the longest speech Annie had heard him make in nearly a year, and it was utterly irrelevant. As if he wanted to make friendly conversation and had forgotten how to do it.

'I gave him the beetle,' Lucas said, having snuck up behind her. 'I knew he liked them. It was shiny blue and gold and he said it looked too pretty for this world.' He wrapped his arms around Annie's waist and whispered in her ear, 'just like you'. His hands were clean, but he had mint-green paint on his cheek so she cringed away. He grinned and rubbed his face against hers on purpose, making her roll her eyes. 'I have a sacred object too, you know,' he mumbled, and she smiled at the thought of the seashell he still carried around in his pocket. If she'd known it was going to become some special token she would have taken the time to find him a prettier one.

Sarah heard and frowned at him. 'I don't think it's appropriate for outsiders to hijack their traditions, Lucas,' she admonished.

Harry and Annie exchanged glances.

'He isn't an outsider,' Harry explained. 'Neither are you. Guardians are recognised as part of our community, although not everyone is permitted to know why that is. The connections in our mob are a bit unusual. I can explain the dynamics to you … if you want to know.'

Sarah obviously didn't know how to respond to that challenge.

In the awkwardness that followed, the kitchen clock was the only one who spoke, ticking away in steadfast ritual. Annie waited, knowing they were at the point in the conversation when normally Sarah would rattle off a list of all the urgent jobs she had to get done and rush away. When she didn't, Annie's curiosity got the better of her and she began to focus on what Sarah was feeling. It made her wish she was anywhere but in that room. When she cleared her throat and tried to think of an excuse to leave, Harry caught her eye and signed at her to stay. Although he'd never spent enough time in Eden to properly learn the language, some signs were easy to pick up. Still, for him to use it now meant it was important to him. So she stayed put, gripping Lucas's fingers behind her back.

When it was clear no one was leaving, Sarah gave in and told them all what was really going on.

'David wants me to marry him.'

That was not news. David had been hedging around asking her for over a year. He knew as well as the rest of them did that Sarah was not likely to say yes, so he'd been biding his time.

'He's going to ask me on Sunday night.'

Annie gaped at her. 'You mean he warned you ahead of time that he's about to pop the question?'

'Not in so many words, but I know him. He's taken the boys to visit his parents in Melbourne for the weekend,' she explained in a shaky voice. 'He told me I should …' Her hand covered her mouth as a small sob escaped. She took a deep breath and continued. 'He told me to come here. He … he broke up with me.'

Lucas gasped so suddenly he nearly choked. '*He what?* I thought you said—'

'I know what I said!' she snapped. 'He's not stupid, Lucas. He knows why I'm so frustratingly erratic all the time. He *wants* me to spend the weekend with Harry so I can make a proper decision. Don't you get it? He's made it very clear that we have no official commitment to each other—I'm technically free to do whatever I want. As if breaking up with me really changes anything!'

In the stunned moment of silence that followed, poor Harry looked like he'd been punched in the gut while being told he'd won Tattslotto.

'So what will you do?' Lucas asked bluntly. There was a hint of a challenge in his voice. David had been his best friend since they were five, but he also understood all too well the intense power of the bond between a Cherub and Guardian.

Sarah answered Lucas's question while looking Harry right in the eye. 'I'll do what I should have done at the start. I'll make a decision so I can finally stop torturing the people I love.'

The way she baled Harry up against the wall with her fierce kiss left no room for further discussion. She practically raised steam as her healing hands sought out every minor graze and bruise he had. His shoulder, his neck, his wrist, and then her hands scrambled to lift his shirt to slide around to the small of his back. Super-quick Guardian reflexes was the only reason Lucas managed to catch the carved rock as it slipped from Harry's fingers.

Even if Harry had been capable of giving any more hand signals, Annie still wouldn't have hung around a moment longer. She stormed out of the house and down to the river. Lucas only caught up to her once she'd plunged into the cool current. The icy water tugged at her clothes.

'Don't be mad at them, Annie, please. Just because we've decided to wait doesn't mean they have to make the same choice.'

He was missing the point.

'Come on, Annie. This was what you wanted, wasn't it? Dave will be crushed, but I think it's for the best. I mean, they're *bonded*. It couldn't have ended any other way.'

Fire burned in Annie's chest, unquenched by the river. 'Sarah knows full well what the consequences are, Lucas—all of them.'

He paused, halfway into the river. 'She'll fall pregnant,' he said. 'I haven't forgotten.'

Water tugged at Annie's fingertips, calling her home like always.

'Was that ever really in doubt, Annie? We're supposed to continue the line. You can't be mad at them for doing what we're destined to do. So what if they aren't officially married yet?'

'Yet,' Annie said. 'You make it sound like it's a done deal.' She looked up toward the house as if she could see right through the walls and into Sarah's head. Not that she wanted to. She'd already felt what was in her heart and that was more than enough.

Lucas grabbed her hand and kissed her knuckles. 'Give Harry this one weekend. She won't have a hope of resisting her true feelings once he's had a chance to have his say.' His smile was full of misplaced confidence. 'And I know this sounds terrible, but she won't be so held back by guilt over the twins if she's carrying Harry's baby.'

'Make a bet?'

His smile faded. 'You felt something from her?'

Annie blinked away tears and couldn't speak.

'No. That makes no sense,' Lucas said. 'Why would she come here at all then? Just to torture Harry? Or for one forbidden taste of what she could have had?' He lowered his gaze. 'Actually, that does sound possible. I'd fall for that temptation, for sure.'

'That isn't the only reason.' A new feeling began to take seed inside her. Something that went beyond guilt. Something that would prevent her from facing her memories of this moment. Unlike guilt, shame was not a healthy emotion. 'I couldn't keep the truth from her, Lucas. I had to make certain she knew *all* the consequences of her decisions. You said it yourself. We're supposed to continue the line.'

She turned away from her Guardian, hiding behind as strong a shield as she could make. She couldn't bear to feel his condemnation.

For far too long, neither of them said anything and when Annie finally turned back to him, Lucas was scrubbing tears from his eyes. His mouth was set and she could feel his anger leaking in through her shield.

'She believes she's doing the right thing,' Lucas said. 'Harry's only human. What chance does he have of resisting her? His own Guardian? He's never going to forgive himself for this.'

'He's not only human,' Annie corrected him. 'And for us, there are consequences for not being able to forgive yourself.'

Chapter 11

The glow of the morning sun tried to cast an enchantment on my eyelids to prise them open, only they were too heavy. What finally coaxed me to wake up was the sound of someone breathing, right in front of my face. I smiled at Bane's silhouetted outline as he leaned down to kiss me. And then I yelped as he shifted enough for the light to show his features. It wasn't Bane.

A close-up of Jake's eyebrow ring and stubble was not something I wanted to see so soon after waking. Let alone his sharp gaze that seemed to want to cut and slash and stab at whatever he looked at. His laugh was a study in arrogance.

'It's not the response I usually get. Still, I think I like it,' he remarked as I scrambled away and promptly fell out of the bed in a tangle of blankets.

'What the hell?' I frantically tried to free my legs while searching the room for my Guardian. There was no sign of him. We'd prudently decided not to share the same hotel room at night in order to prevent things from getting out of hand, much to Tim's astonishment. It had helped a little. Why hadn't Bane already barged his way in if Jake was here?

'What have you done to Bane? How did you get in here?'

'Relax,' Jake replied, peering around the edge of the curtain to look out the window. 'I haven't done anything to him. You're not in any danger so he's probably sleeping and totally oblivious. Let's try to keep it that way. Telling him anything about this little visit would only upset him. And as for the other question, I didn't.'

'Didn't what?'

'Didn't get in here.'

I blinked at him in confusion while he looked me over.

'Well. You look like a human, as far as I can tell. I'd been wondering about that,' he said. Abruptly I realised that I was only wearing knickers. And I was damn lucky I'd gone to bed in that much. While nakedness hadn't bothered me for years, the sleazy expression on Jake's face made me feel ill, so I snatched up my blanket and drew it around myself as best I could.

'How much did Dallmin tell you?' I asked warily, not wanting to risk revealing anything he didn't already know.

'That you're a fraud,' he accused. 'Posing as a broken human all these years, pretending to be one of them, when really you're a monster who has no right to even set foot in this realm. Go home, Cherub! This is *our* time to rule.' No longer placid, he crouched down as if to pounce at me like an animal and his face took on a feral sneer that sent chills up my spine.

'Our time? How many of you are there?' I asked, glancing at the door and trying to decide if it was worth making a run for it. 'I take it you don't count yourself as a "broken human" then. That's somewhat ironic, don't you think?' I was fishing for information, although I didn't think it would work.

He narrowed his eyes. 'I am not one of those pathetic creatures who have infested this sad world. They *belong* to us. You can't even protect the ones you already have hidden away.'

That stark truth made my chest hurt. He was right. Dallmin was now as broken as everyone else on this side of the boundary. More so. I didn't know how to respond and now Jake had gotten between me and the door.

'What is it you want from me?' I asked, trying to keep him talking. Bane should at least know I was awake, and despite Jake's assurance that I wasn't in any danger, I was struggling to believe it. He'd already killed me once. Any moment now Bane would burst in and we would have to pay for another broken hotel room door. I backed a little further into the corner and hugged the blanket.

Jake faced me like a predator, fingers curling. 'Want from you? I want you to go back to where you belong. Leave your cumbersome bones and flesh and fly back to your own realm. Leave the humans to choose their own path without you interfering with your pseudo-Heaven trickery. This is *our time*.' He launched himself at me so I scrambled backward and jumped onto the bed.

'Hey! Who are you calling cumbersome?' I protested as I threw the bedside lamp at him. Somehow I missed and it thudded harmlessly to the floor, not even making the useful noise of smashing glass. My foot tangled in my blanket just as Jake lunged for my ankle … and his hand passed straight through me. With a howl of rage, he swung his fist at my stomach and I ducked sideways, badly, trying to concentrate on making the right Words come, but of course I had nothing. Again his hand passed right through me as if I was a ghost. Panicking, I wondered if maybe I was. Had I died again without noticing? If I had, then why was he still trying to kill me?

Swearing like a trooper, Jake raised his hands as if preparing to throw lightning at me—which at that point wouldn't have surprised me much. Instead, he clapped his hands together and disappeared into thin air. For a moment, I could almost sense how he'd done it. How he'd been somewhere and not been there at the same time. If I could find him that way, follow him back to wherever he was holed up …

I squeezed my eyes shut and concentrated on the fading sense of his presence. I was used to feeling for Noah, but I had no such connection to Jake. And yet the further I stretched my senses, the more I felt I could let go of everything holding me back from searching for him. A flicker of movement ahead gave the impression he was taunting me, daring me to follow. In frustration, I struggled to shake free of the weight holding me down, but all I managed was to shake away every thought in my head. I felt my legs give way and then the whole world disappeared.

Chapter 12

What finally coaxed me to wake up was the sound of someone breathing, right in front of my face. I took one look at the man's silhouetted outline and screamed.

'Woah!' Bane said, scrambling back. 'Sorry, I didn't mean to startle you.'

Gasping in a few panicked breaths, I tried to relax. It really was Bane, this time. My eyes searched the room while the rest of my body remained frozen. I couldn't see much because I'd fallen off the bed for the second time that morning.

'Are you okay? What are you doing on the floor?' he asked. He seemed unsure whether or not to keep his distance.

'B … b … bad dream, I guess.' I peered under the bed. Nope. Definitely no Jake-shaped demons hiding under there. Grabbing the front of Bane's shirt, I pulled him toward me and buried myself in his chest, wishing I could hide there forever. He held me while I took the time to align my mind with the waking world. After a minute or so he became restless and I realised I could feel his heart racing.

'Lainie. You forgot your pyjamas again.'

I would have given him a saucy wink, except his eyes were squeezed shut. 'Yeah. Let's go with "forgot". Stay here. I'll get dressed.' I stood up, wrapping myself in the blanket as I stepped away … and nearly tripped. He was holding the corner in his fist, grinning. With a firm tug, I yanked it from his grasp and then ducked into the bathroom before either of us could change our minds.

Staring at myself in the mirror, I tried to work out what had happened that morning. Had Jake's visit been a dream? Surely not. Only, why hadn't Bane known anything was wrong? *When* exactly had it happened? I remembered that the sun had been shining through the curtain—how long had I passed out for? And had I actually passed out, or was I simply sleeping the whole time?

'What time is it, Bane? Did I sleep in?' I called out, poking at my face to check if my body was real. The vivid memory of Jake's fist passing through my stomach haunted me.

'Yeah, you did. It's after ten. I didn't want to disturb you because I know you haven't been sleeping well. Mind you, by the looks of things I'm not sure you got the best sleep last night anyway. What did you do to the poor lamp?'

'Uh, not sure. I think I threw it at someone in my sleep. Is it damaged?'

'Nope. Still works fine. I'll have to teach you to throw better.'

'It would help if the person I was throwing it at wasn't a figment of my imagination,' I replied with mixed feelings. A real-life encounter wouldn't have been all that helpful either, but that was what we were trying to arrange, after all.

Cold tiles. Squeaky shower taps. Long wait for hot water. When it came through I let it melt away all my tension, if not my confusion. Real or not, some of what Jake had said was messing with my mind big time. Pseudo-Heaven trickery? Was that what he thought Eden was? *You can't even protect the ones you already have hidden away.* I made myself unclench my fists. Punching the tiles would only make Bane start banging on the bathroom door.

And what was the deal with Jake? He hadn't always been like this. If he really was possessed, then what sort of creature was responsible? The word *demon* seemed ridiculous, laughable even. Until I put it up against the idea that I was a Cherub in a human body. Groaning, I decided not to think about it until I had at least eaten breakfast. Or brunch, given how late it was. I simply wasn't capable of unravelling the mysteries of the universe on an empty stomach.

Once I was clean and clothed, I felt composed enough to act as if it had never happened. The last thing I needed was for Commando Bane to reappear just because I'd had a bad dream.

When I emerged from the bathroom he was lounging on the bed, flipping through a tourist magazine. In jeans and a collarless shirt, he looked ready to go except for his bare feet, which he'd tucked under the edge of the bedspread for warmth. He seemed utterly relaxed, and I loved it.

'I'll be ready to leave in a minute, once I've brushed my hair. Sorry if we have to pay extra for a late check-out,' I apologised.

'When has brushing your hair ever taken only a minute?' he teased.

I tilted my head in reluctant acknowledgment. 'Okay, so I'll finish it in the car. It should be almost done by the time we get to Warrnambool,' I admitted, throwing my few belongings haphazardly into my bag.

'Let's stay here today, Lainie. We've been on the move for nearly a week now. That lead Mick told us about in Warrnambool is the most tenuous one yet. I'm not sure it's worth following up, and we need a break.'

I narrowed my eyes. This must be a trick. Jake had somehow made himself look like my Guardian. Since when did Bane ever suggest taking a break? From anything?

He laughed. 'Don't look at me like that. Surely you must be getting sick of spending hours on end in a small car with three grown men. Even army officers understand what cramped conditions can do to a person. A break is appropriate.' He stretched his hand out, inviting me to come and sit with him.

'Ah, no. I don't think I'll be sitting on the bed with you right now if you don't mind. You look way too hot in that white shirt. I didn't know you even owned a white shirt. I thought everything you had was either black or army green.'

He raised his eyebrows at my frail attempt to distance myself by chattering, and when I tried to move past him he somehow snagged me around the waist, and then I was sprawled across the mattress and he was grinning smugly with his face above mine. He was gracefully *fast*, and sneaky. And I wished I'd thought to convince both him and Tessa to play footy with us at school. We would have beaten the Catholic college for sure. Maybe. So long as they hadn't bitten anyone.

My attempt to hide my smile was pointless. 'Bane, I'm not sure I can be trusted—'

The way he kissed my neck deleted the rest of that thought altogether, but less than a minute later he was letting go of me again and pulling my hand out from under his shirt. Something in his shoulders changed as he sat back and grabbed an over-starched pillow to strangle.

'I tried to warn you,' I sulked. 'Wait, are you nervous?' I was good at reading body language and there was a tension in him that seemed different.

'Nervous. Yes. Or terrified. At least conflicted. Take your pick.'

This was new. I waited for him to explain.

'You talk about having two wants?' he attempted. 'I have about five. I want to prove to you how disciplined and trustworthy I am now, compared with when we were in high school. Then there's the reflexive want that refuses to do anything that might compromise your physical ability to avoid danger.' His words were tripping over each other like startled chickens.

'You mean I can't run or fight as easily if I'm pregnant?'

He gave a sharp nod. 'Then there's the want that can't decide whether to lock you safely away in a nuclear bunker or take you skydiving so I can show you my world.'

I rescued the pillow, but it would never be rectangular again. Ever.

Suddenly bereft, he clasped his fingers behind his neck and buried his face in his elbows so his voice came out muffled. 'Then there's the primal desire that involves actual cloth-ripping and breaking furniture and holding you so close that—'

'Okay, maybe this one should stay in your head for now,' I suggested quickly. A silent moment passed. Then I had to know. 'Are you worried you'll hurt me?'

His head was still buried when he answered. 'Sometimes,' he admitted. 'Until I remember that I won't.' Without even opening his eyes he reached out and took my elbow. There was a faint red mark on it, a bruise just starting to form. I must have hit it on something when I'd fallen out of bed that morning. It should have hurt as he pressed his thumb into it, yet all I felt was tingling warmth. He pulled me gently into his chest with a deep sigh. 'I won't hurt you, Lainie. I can't. Not even by accident. When we finally do this, it will be incredible.'

❧

The others were waiting for us in the cafeteria. Dallmin, as usual, was glued to his computer tablet and didn't look up. He'd gone down the

Wikipedia rabbit hole two days earlier and had yet to emerge back into the real world. It was as if he thought that the more information he gathered about this world, the more chance he had of finding a way out of it. Learning to read and type had been no problem given that he'd known how to read and write in other languages for hundreds of years already. Some of the other knowledge he'd revealed astounded us. In all my time in Eden, I had never once considered that someone might want to spend some of their infinitely long life crunching numbers for fun. He said he'd learned it in a city called Siyyan. There was a city? That revelation alone had been enough to render me speechless. I would have to find another opportunity to talk to him alone to find out more about that. It would be more than irritating if the embargo I'd imposed on him stopped him from talking to me about Eden too.

Tim pulled a chair out for me. 'Morning, Lainie. Did you sleep well? I found you some fruit salad for breakfast. To go with your muddy river water, of course,' he said, handing me my water bottle.

He'd gradually become more comfortable around me, although he still seemed over-eager to see to my every whim. Or maybe that was how he always was with everyone. It was hard to tell.

'Thanks, Tim. Sorry I slept so late. I guess all that sitting doing nothing in the car for hours on end really tired me out.'

'Me too,' Dallmin muttered, not picking up at all on my sarcasm. Was there a wiki page for sarcasm?

As usual, Bane ignored him and sat down opposite Tim. 'We're thinking of taking a break for a day or two. Lainie's safe enough for the moment and we all need some time to catch up on a few things,' he said, sipping the scorching black coffee Tim had handed him.

'Oh, thank God,' Tim said. 'But couldn't you have decided this last night and let us *all* sleep in?'

'Sorry, you can go back to bed now if you want,' he replied.

Tim stared at his friend as if he had no idea who he was. Bane didn't react, so he licked his lips and tried for more. 'Um, actually, I was thinking of going for a run. I could use a stretch. I know. Shut up, mate, you don't have to say it. Is Lainie safe enough for you to come with me?'

We all watched Bane as he assessed my current danger level. His face stayed relaxed. 'She is,' he replied.

Had everyone forgotten that me being safe meant we were failing our quest?

'Seriously, Bane. We can't really stop,' I said. 'We must have been close the other day because you were positively stroppy near Bendigo and you were pretty confident Jake was somewhere to the southwest. If he's moving, we need to follow his trail. As you said, we just have to be methodical about it. Or maybe we should try to get ahead of him somehow.'

His eyebrows said no and his words followed. 'Bad idea. What if he somehow loops back toward home and we're too far away to help? Maybe Tess was right. Maybe we should go home and wait for him to come to us.'

A shiver ran down my spine as I considered the possibility that he already had in some freaky, non-corporeal way.

'All right,' I countered, 'we'll stay for a day and I'll think about it. So long as I get to look at wedding dresses.'

His smile was dazzling.

'No, you weren't supposed to smile at that! Dress shopping was supposed to put you off hanging around.'

'But shopping with you is so much fun. I'd love to see you take a wedding gown for a spin.'

'You can't,' Tim said. 'It's bad luck. No way.'

Bane snorted. 'You think we believe in bad luck? After everything you've seen?'

'I don't care. It's tradition, then. I won't let you. If Lainie wants to shop, I'll take her. You take Dallmin to see a movie or something. Try to cheer him up. And get him away from the tablet before his eyes go square.'

Looking up at me in panic, Dallmin opened his mouth to ask the inevitable question so I hurried to reassure him. 'No, they won't, it's just an expression. But they can get weak if you spend too long looking at things close up and never look far away. It would probably be a good idea to leave it switched off today.'

Nodding compliantly, he turned it off and tucked it into his bag and then sat waiting for his next instruction. How long was he going to be like this? Since we'd left Nalong he'd been wholeheartedly obedient to every instruction, suggestion, and unspoken thought any of us had had. While I was grateful that it gave Bane no excuse to doubt him further, it still made me incredibly sad. He'd always been eager to please—as was everyone in Eden—in a carefree and natural way. Now, however, complying with our wishes no longer filled him with delight. It was simply a way of avoiding fear and pain. It did seem to keep him from the worst of his depression, though.

Tim's attitude was another matter. Turning to him, I decided it was high time I put his awe of me back into perspective. 'All right, Tim, I'm yours for the day. Find me a wedding gown fit for my status,' I challenged in my snobbiest voice. 'I want to shine like an angel.'

Chapter 13

'Well, that didn't take as long as I expected,' I muttered, trying not to pout.

'Don't worry, we'll find something. There are still a few more shops to try,' Tim reassured me.

'No, please, no more today. It's torture.'

'Then we'll check out the boutique stores when we reach Melbourne. It's hardly my area of expertise, but I'm sure it's not unusual to want to visit more than three stores before choosing The Dress,' he said. 'Besides, everything you tried on looked stunning to me. I liked the one with the slinky thingy at the back. And the one with no back. And the one with the poofy curtain thingys on the skirt was pretty nice and I'm not really helping, am I?'

'Not at all, no. And I'm afraid it won't matter how many shops I try, none of those dresses suit who I am anymore.'

Tim looked around unsubtly to check if anyone was close by. 'Well then, let me ask you this: if you were having the wedding … you know, over there, what sort of dress would they make for you?'

I stopped and glared at him with my hands on my hips. 'I'd be in the nuddy, Tim. Unless it was chilly. Like everyone else.'

His shoulders slumped in embarrassed defeat.

As we ambled listlessly down the street, I tried to put my finger on why I felt so disappointed. 'I'm sorry I dragged you along with me. I thought it would be simpler than this. Somehow I thought that when I got married I'd have all my friends helping me to narrow down my choice from ten gorgeously adorable gowns to one and now it turns out I don't like any. I spent a good chunk of my childhood dreaming about my wedding day. I guess it's like discovering that the remote-controlled helicopter you always wanted only flies properly in the shopping centre. I crashed mine into a tree within five minutes. Smashed to smithereens along with yet another childhood dream. It simply didn't live up to my expectations.'

'I crashed mine into Dad's car. Scratched all down the passenger door as it crumbled. Didn't get any pocket money for months after that. And when I did, I saved up and bought a genuine gold *Lord of The Rings* "One Ring". It turned out normal fire did melt it after all.' With his hands in his pockets and head hanging, he still looked like a little boy flattened with disappointment.

'Oh, Tim, I'm so sorry,' I sympathised. 'I still have mine. Hey, maybe I can give it to Bane for a wedding ring. It's not like I have any money to buy him a proper one. And I can't exactly ask him to pay for one.'

Tim stopped and pulled me around to face him. 'Lainie, you shouldn't have to worry about normal things like money.' He leaned in and said softly, 'What you're doing is way too important to have to spend time earning cash. Leave it with me. I'll sort out that side of things for you.'

The sound that came out of my throat was somewhere between a cat with a hairball and a stepped-on cane toad. 'No, you will not,' I spluttered. 'You don't even have a job anymore because of me. Bane told me you quit. There's no way I'm going to let you pay for *anything*.'

His face twitched as he tried to articulate something that was out of bounds in such a busy street, so he swallowed his reply and kept walking. After a few moments, I noticed a small smile creep onto his face. 'I can't believe you have a One Ring.'

'And I can't believe you were stupid enough to melt yours,' I countered. 'What else did you have?'

'Well, in grade six I got a sonic screwdriver.'

'I got a fob watch.'

'Countless pop vinyls. Please don't tell Bane.'

'He wouldn't care. He has his own. I saw them when we visited his mum the other week. That man has hidden depths.'

'I don't believe you. He would have mentioned it.'

'*Hidden* depths, Tim.'

'Fair point. He didn't even tell me he played guitar. What other good stuff do you have?'

'A time-turner necklace,' I said, trying to remember where I'd put it. 'And Noah bought me Han Solo-in-carbonite chocolate moulds for my eleventh birthday.'

'Nice. Do you still have them?' he asked.

'I expect they're in the bottom of a kitchen drawer somewhere, unless Tessa chucked them out. Remind me to check when we get back there.'

'Not good enough. I'm hungry now. How about we find something to eat before we go back?'

'Fish fingers and custard?'

He laughed, looking more like the fun-loving Tim I'd come to adore. 'Tried it. Don't recommend it. And you have a lot to catch up on. How about we try for a plain but hearty stew, coarse bread, and some ale from the local tavern?'

'Now you're talking. Only one problem. You know how a minute ago I was adamant I wasn't going to let you pay for anything?'

'Ha! Give in or starve, my friend. You can't escape my evil payment plan this time.'

It then became abundantly clear just how many well-spent hours he'd taken to perfect his evil laugh.

⸜

Half an hour later we sat at a picnic table by a picturesque lake enjoying the rare June sunshine. A toddler kindly offered me his fistful of squashed bread so I could help him feed the ducks. The seagulls got most of it.

Not one café had sold hearty stew so we'd had to settle for buying a whole loaf of fresh bread and a wedge of cheese. The ale came in a can, which didn't seem to bother Tim. He offered me some, but I stuck to my supply of Nalong river water. Tiredness was rapidly becoming an issue for me. I didn't know if it was due to being away from Nalong, post-death adjustments, or simply boredom from driving around Victoria day after day. I figured I'd better dose up on the river water as much as possible, either way.

'Okay,' Tim murmured as the toddler's dad strapped him into his bike trailer, preparing to leave. 'There's no one else around. I've been dying to get you alone so I can ask without bursting into tears. That spell you put on me is really effective. I feel sick every time I try to talk about things I shouldn't.'

'It wasn't a spell,' I grumbled.

He shrugged and passed me the bread loaf.

'Ask me what?' I prompted, tearing off a chunk as if I was a traveller in medieval times.

'What's its name?'

'What's what's name?'

'You know. The thing we're looking for.'

'Jake. Its name is Jake.'

'Not him. The thing he stole. The … sword,' he whispered.

Laughing at the irritated look on his face, I relented. 'I knew what you meant. I just wanted to see if you could say it. It doesn't have a name, as far as I know.'

'Oh, Lainie, come on. All the great swords have names. And this one is *real*. It must have one.' His earnest face reminded me of Noah when he wanted me to keep a secret.

The moment Nathaniel was born, the sword's flames had paused long enough to reveal a silvery script along its blade. There was so much we didn't understand. If it did have a name, it was in a language I could sometimes speak but never properly remember afterward—or have a hope of pronouncing once the moment passed.

I took a bite of the cheese Tim handed me. 'Maybe you can help me choose one. At least until we find out what it really is. What classic names can we pick from?'

Crossing his long legs in front of him, he stretched out in the sun with his hands behind his head. 'Anduril, Flame of the West,' was his first suggestion.

'Glamdring,' I added. 'Or the Sword of Gryffindor.'

'How about Excalibur? Or, I know, The Sword of Truth,' he said seriously.

'Keep thinking, Tim. You can do better.'

'Can I name you too?' he asked. 'Tongue-Binder. Mother-of-Storms. Sword-Seeker.' His eyes lit up. 'How about My Lady of the Garden?' He grinned at the sour expression on my face. 'I'm just trying to help.'

'How is naming me supposed to help? The idea is for no one to know about me, or about any of it. The last thing we need is a legend for people to get curious about. All I want is to get the sword back to where it's meant to be and then hide it from the world forever.'

'Hiding things is easy.'

'Yeah. My family have been great at it, until I came along.'

'Can't you just put a new whammy over everything?'

'Such as?'

He stood up and started pacing around, so full of enthusiasm that I started feeling uncomfortable. A cave. A sword. Miracles and supernatural beings. In ages past, people would have run screaming from such things, but not now. Even a whiff of the Tongue-Binder and her Sword of Flames could knock all cat videos from the internet rankings within hours. We'd be stuffed.

'Come on, Lainie. There are heaps of ways to hide things. You could make the cave invisible.'

'Noah tried it already. There is actually no such thing. Even camouflaging it creates a weird light distortion that's really noticeable. Kind of has the opposite effect.'

'All right, so that cuts out chameleon circuits, Romulan cloaking, and a Room of Requirement,' he said, ticking them off each finger. 'But there are plenty more options. How about making it Somebody Else's Problem? Put an automatic spell on anyone who sees it. Or a time-lock. Relativity should be real enough to give you something to work with.'

He was too obsessed to even notice me throw my last bit of bread at his head, and I didn't miss.

'Wormhole?' he continued. 'Or, I know, Mary Poppins' bag. Do you think you could make an inter-dimensional pocket?'

'I think you should go back to naming things.'

'I'll let you name me as well if I get to be your sidekick,' he offered.

'Sidekick?' I spluttered. 'Why would you even consider hanging around us crazies for a moment longer than necessary?'

He gaped at me. 'Are you kidding? Lainie, you can do mag—' He almost swallowed his tongue, even though no magic was ever involved in what Noah and I did. He tried again quickly to cover his lapse. 'Okay, how about because Bane is my best friend? And someone has to be around to comfort all the other girls when they finally give up trying to snag his attention.' As soon as the words left his mouth, he flinched, realising he'd said too much.

To make a point, I took hold of his hand in both of mine. 'Have you forgotten my other talent already, Tim?' I asked. 'I don't always need skin contact to read people, and I've known Nicole her whole life. Bane's the only one who's oblivious to how she feels about him. So how's your plan working out? I'm on your side in this, after all. Go for the rebound, mate. If it works, everyone wins.'

He gave a soft laugh. 'I'm doing my best,' he said, pulling away from my grip looking embarrassed. He had no reason to be. If only I could make Nicole see in him what I saw. Maybe she would, with enough time.

'In the meantime,' he said, 'I don't suppose you could extend my speech embargo to include anything I shouldn't be opening my fat mouth to say?'

'Now *that* would be a superpower worth having,' I said, right when his phone buzzed.

We both looked down at it with apprehension. Poor Bane had been lumped with Dallmin all morning and I wasn't at all certain it would have been a positive move for either of them. The man's unexpected betrayal had hurt Bane far more profoundly than the hit with the fry-pan had. The text Tim received confirmed my fears.

Come get this drongo out of my sight before I kill him, was all it said.

❧

'Breathe, Dallmin. In and out. You know how, you've been doing it for centuries. Just keep breathing.' I tried to look him in the eye the way Noah would have, but of course it didn't make the slightest bit of difference. He was cowering in the corner of his hotel room, every muscle tense and shuddering as if he was having a fit. I couldn't even touch him without him flinching. It was awful to watch.

When we'd arrived back at the hotel, we found that Bane had locked Dallmin in his room and was standing guard outside the door with a grim expression on his face. I hated to think what any passers-by must have assumed. At first he tried to talk me out of going in, apparently worried that Dallmin was so worked up I was at risk of getting tangled with his psyche again. Too impatient to argue, I bent my own pinkie finger back with increasing force until he relented. He followed Tim and me in and then stood with his arms crossed in the corner like a night club bouncer. As I watched Dallmin's body curl back into foetal position again, I wondered what Bane would do if I did link with him. It was hard to help when I didn't know what the problem was and I was kind of scared to ask my cranky Guardian. Even Tim looked averse to saying anything.

'Dallmin, I need you to calm down. No one's going to hurt you. Relax. Do you want some music?' He shook his head, but his shuddering subsided as he forced himself to obey me. I waited for him to settle down, wondering how many times I would have to sit on the floor with him before he would learn to cope in our society. Eventually, he met my eyes, with an expression like a calf that had touched an electric fence and couldn't figure out what had bitten him. I waited for him to pluck up the courage to tell me what hideous thing he had done to make Bane so angry.

'I met someone, Lainie. A woman. Her name is Britt. She has golden hair.'

My jaw dropped. That was not what I'd been expecting.

'We were running. Bane said it wasn't a race so I slowed down to look at everything.'

And Bane wouldn't have been inclined to wait for him to catch up, I surmised.

'Britt was running too, along the same path, so I ran with her. At first she didn't want to talk until I asked her why she had wires sticking out of her ears. She laughed and explained they were for music, like Noah's headphones.' He glanced at Bane's disapproving stare and snapped his mouth shut again, so I shifted over to block his view of my grumpy Guardian.

'Then what happened?' I prompted.

'We stopped running and she let me listen for a while and told me I should keep singing along. Then I gave her one ear-wire back and danced with her.'

Inside I was struggling to work out if I was amused, or annoyed at Bane for overreacting, which at least enabled me to keep my expression bland. I nodded for him to continue and he threw me a puzzled, pleading look.

'My body reacted to her, Lainie. I never thought I would feel that here. My bond with Annie must be broken now. She can let go and so can I. I can't believe I have found a new love partner already. Perhaps it's because there are so many people here. I found her, Lainie, I found her … I found … her.' His words were slowing as he struggled with his confused emotions.

Three years in Eden had developed in me a strong empathy for what others wanted and it was clear to me he was not as ecstatic about his news as he thought he should be. Wincing, I could only imagine too well what must have happened next.

'Did you kiss her without permission?' I groaned, slumping down against the wall next to him. 'Did she get angry?'

'No,' he replied. 'I asked her first and she wasn't angry, but Bane was. Then she got angry at Bane. She used words I have never heard before. I stayed quiet and then she became angry at me too. Our bodies were linking, Lainie. She wanted me to kiss her and I wanted it too, so I did, so why was she angry?'

For a few moments, I simply sat and tried to absorb the scene. How on Earth did he get a complete stranger to want to kiss him within minutes of meeting him? Either Britt was a very confident woman or Dallmin had charm enough to rival Noah.

'You said your bond to Annie must be broken, so you can let her go. Is that what you want?'

The sudden grief in his eyes was all I needed to know the answer.

'When I watched Britt run my body reacted, so she *must* be my new partner. How could that happen unless my bond with Annie is broken?'

Three times I opened my mouth to answer. I couldn't think of what to say.

'My body would not react to someone unless that person is the one my heart wants to be with. Only, how could that happen so soon after meeting her?'

Oh. Right. Now I knew what I had to tell him. Just not *how* to tell him.

So I chickened out and beckoned Tim over. I needed his help to clarify things to Dallmin, so I tried to think of a way to explain to Tim about the way partnerships worked in Eden without choking on my words.

'Dallmin, tell Tim how many love partners you have been bonded to in the hundreds of years you've been alive.'

'Three … Or four. T'iel, Jilana, and then Annie. Does Britt count?'

'No. I'm afraid she doesn't. Three, then.'

'Three. I have been blessed more than most.'

A sudden disturbing thought occurred to me. My face grew hot as I forced the words out. 'Dallmin, did you have sex with Annie?' I was certain I didn't want to know about my mother's love life, but that didn't change the fact I needed to. Tim looked at me as if I was out of my mind.

'No. Annie was still … sad. I didn't know that's what it was when I was with her, but now I know what sadness is. It must be difficult to fully accept love when you are very sad in that way.'

I let out a relieved breath and at the same time felt a surge of sympathy toward my mother. She was so messed up already and now things would be even worse for her. Still, at least it meant I wasn't expecting a baby brother or sister. Noah's mum had explained to him once that our Cherubim super-fertility traits switched into reverse after the first baby was born, but how much trust could we put in that? Noah did have a younger sister, after all. So it was a massive relief not to have to tell Dallmin that he might have left a child behind.

I turned to Tim. 'Tim, my friend, would you mind telling Dallmin how many people you've seriously considered partnering with in the mere twenty years you've been alive?'

All the respect I'd earned from him flew away like helium balloons from a car window with that single blunt question. It couldn't be helped.

'Yes. I would mind. It's none of your business.' So much for the superhero worship.

Dallmin brushed my elbow to get my attention. 'Lainie, Tim is only a child. It will be many years until he is ready for a love partner. He does not want to answer you. Is it because he's lonely? Is that what happens here?'

'Hey! None of your business either, mate,' Tim complained. 'And what do you mean I'm only a child?'

'Your body will not respond to a love partner until you are much older and you find someone who wants you. It will take many decades.'

'Decades? Until someone wants me?' He crossed his arms. 'Five. All right? Five. Four women and one guy have communicated quite clearly that they were interested in me. That doesn't mean I always felt the same way, Dallmin. And there may well be more. Not everyone is comfortable enough to come right out and say how they feel. And … oh, forget it. I'm not saying another word.'

Dallmin looked stunned, so I figured it was only fair to balance things and shock Tim too.

'Dallmin, how long has it been since Jilana moved across? I mean, until you met Annie, how long had it been since your body responded to a woman?'

A flash of something like annoyance crossed his expression. It bugged him to have to think about measuring time.

'Almost seven hundred years, I think.'

Even I nearly choked.

Tim went white as a newborn lamb. 'Holy crap,' he said. 'No wonder you're so depressed.'

Despite the silent, desperately pleading looks he threw me, I left poor Tim to have a man-to-elf talk with Dallmin. The Edenite's ancient body was changing in ways he didn't understand. Whether it was a result of his new experiences in this fallen world, or because he no longer had access to the Trees of Life, I had no idea. All I knew was that after living for hundreds of years, he was suddenly faced with a whole new range of physical and emotional changes that altered the very foundations of who he was. Talk about puberty blues. I owed Tim, big time.

Bane still hadn't spoken a word, so I took his hand and led him from the hotel. It was Friday afternoon and there were enough people around that I knew it would be difficult to speak openly. I tried anyway.

'He didn't understand what he was doing. He has no idea of the consequences of his actions. We can't hold him responsible.'

Pulling me to a stop, Bane turned me to face him. 'You have to stop treating him like a child, Lainie. He has to understand that he *is* responsible for his actions. The things he does out of ignorance can still hurt people.'

The way he ran his hands through his short hair reminded me of Sergeant Loxwood when he was stressed.

'Less than seven minutes, Lainie. That's how long I let him out of my sight for and next thing I know he's snogging some stranger in the middle of the bike path! It's like he was waiting for an opportunity to do whatever he wanted. What would have happened if I hadn't come back for him straight away? What if he'd … forced her?'

'He didn't! And he wouldn't have … would he?' Yet even as I spoke I wasn't so sure. A couple of weeks ago no one could have conceived that he would ever physically attack anyone, but he could easily have killed both Bane and Noah, and his actions had indirectly caused my death. Even Dallmin himself had no idea what he was capable of now.

Bane rubbed his face. 'I don't know. Either way, we can't risk it. He needs to know the rules here before someone else gets hurt and I think it would be best if you were the one who taught him.'

This time I did pout. Giving Dallmin more rules was the last thing I wanted to do. It went against everything Eden meant to me, but I was no longer in Eden.

'Fine. I'll try to teach him, although I feel like I hardly know them myself,' I said as we resumed walking.

'You know enough to stay out of trouble,' he assured me. 'More or less,' he qualified a moment later as he steered me away from a broken glass bottle on the footpath. Looking down, I realised I must have slipped off my shoes when I got down onto the floor with Dallmin earlier and had forgotten to put them back on again. At least, I hoped that was when I'd slipped them off, otherwise they were probably on the floor of a bridal shop somewhere.

'If we have to give him rules though, could we at least try to balance it by letting him have a little fun sometimes?' I pleaded. 'He's still so depressed. And confused. Adjusting to this world is hard enough without thinking it's all about rules and fear and anger. There are good things too. Occasionally.'

Once again he stopped and turned me toward him, looking serious. 'Are you still talking about Dallmin, or yourself?'

Ah. Oops. He was almost more in tune with how I was feeling than I was.

'Both, I guess,' I admitted. 'This world is harsh, and complicated. Every minute I seem to have to stop myself from acting on crazy impulses and I get frustrated.'

'Such as?' he asked with a quirk to his eyebrows.

'Not just the obvious,' I said, smiling. 'There are other things I want to do. Every tree I pass begs for attention. Every sound I hear wants me to mimic it, just to see if I can. Every river wants me to dive in and play. Every hill wants me to slide down it head first in the mud. Every time I pass a shop playing music I start to dance. It's exhausting trying to stay normal.'

'So don't. As long as you're not upsetting anyone else, what's the problem?'

'The problem is I'm trying not to be noticed. I feel like I have a great big sign around my neck saying "Alien! Not human! Prone to sudden fits of dying. Steer clear." I need to blend in.'

'Well, don't bother because I can tell you now it's not working. *Everyone* notices you. You're glorious and no one can work out why. Everyone is drawn to you. Especially children,' he said, tilting his head toward a woman who was struggling to make her daughter stay in her stroller. The little girl was pointing at me.

'Oh terrific,' I groaned. 'As if I don't feel bad enough for forcing you to follow me around everywhere, then I get Jake the Terminator and now everyone else too. What next? Will I wake up one morning with rabbits and bluebirds gathered outside my bedroom door?' I looked up to check for bird paparazzi. There was only a magpie watching from a tree. 'Does Noah have this problem too?' I asked as we prudently crossed the road.

'I expect so. He was pretty charismatic at school and that was before his Cherub traits were triggered by Kolsom's mining activities. I don't think you need to see it as a problem though. Not until the animals start showing up, anyway.'

'No wonder my family has always liked to stay secluded. Between this and the homesickness it would be unbearable to spend too much time away from home. So much for trying to stay inconspicuous.'

'Exactly. So you might as well do whatever you want. Maybe your bizarre behaviour might even put people off a little,' he suggested with inappropriate cheerfulness. 'What do you feel like doing right now?'

Without a second's hesitation, I wrapped my arms around his neck and kissed him soundly. Warmth spread through me as our skin touched and I wondered what I had needed to be healed from this time.

'Better?' he asked with a relaxed smile, many languid moments later.

Taking stock, I decided I did feel more energetic than I had in a while. 'Actually, yes. What was wrong with me? Was I getting sick?'

'No, only tired. I think it's getting worse. I'm not sure how much longer we can stay away from Nalong. The river water isn't enough for you.'

'I don't mind if you keep healing me,' I said with a grin, but I knew he was right. Although we'd been away for less than a week, my joints were getting heavier by the minute, as if they were a heartbeat behind the rest of my body and slowing further.

'I'll heal you with a kiss anytime you like. With or without people staring at us. I told you. You draw people's attention.'

I followed his gaze to where an old woman with rainbow hair was watching us with a soft expression. She quickly turned to the pet shop window where she probably looked at the kittens exactly the same way.

'Honestly, I'm just me. Plain old Lanky Lainie. Have you considered it might be you they're staring at?'

Cradling my cheek, he pinned me with his adoring gaze and ridiculously exquisite eyelashes. 'You've never been plain old anything. You should have heard what the other guys at school used to say about you. Surprisingly, it wasn't even the smutty trash talk so many of them usually used around each other. They were mostly quite respectful. Mostly.'

I vaguely remembered that Noah had once tried to tell me something similar. I hadn't believed him. 'Bane, none of the other guys even noticed me unless I was playing sport with them.'

'None of them wanted to risk getting on Noah's bad side. You know how much they all adored him. As far as the school community were concerned, you and Noah might as well have been married since the first day of grade six. No one was ever going to mess with that. Or didn't you notice their jaws drop when you danced with me at graduation?'

Of course I had, but I'd assumed it was because of his dangerous reputation. 'Noah and I were never together-together. Noah dated lots of times, and I sort of dated Minh for a few weeks when he first came to our school.'

'Minh was a legend, asking you out on his second day when everyone else had spent years talking about doing it and never followed through. He got hooked in by you before he had a chance to figure out the class dynamics. It took ages for the guys to forgive him. And Noah only dated other girls when you'd done something to piss him off. Everyone knew that. No one took it seriously.'

I blinked, reassessing my entire perspective of Noah's infuriating behaviour over the years.

'Why would any girl agree to go out with him if that's what they believed?'

Bane snorted. 'For the same reason they still flirted with him. There's something enchanting about both of you that goes way beyond physical beauty. It's irresistible.'

'Enchanting? I'm not Cinderella.'

'Nope. Certainly not. What you have is far more profound. Angelic. Sacred. Too precious for the likes of us mere mortals.'

Now I knew he was crazy. No one would have ever thought of Noah and me as *angelic.* Not after the time we stored twenty yabbies in the drinking troughs and they all escaped before we could prank Mr Benson with them.

'Well, I guess I remember things differently to how you remember them, although at this point I'm grateful I remember at all. Did you know I've had the style of wedding dress I wanted planned since I was ten? Don't ask me what it was though—I have no idea and nothing I saw today triggered any memories of it either. At this rate, I'll be getting married in Beltana's torn red gown. Held together with safety pins.'

'Off-the-shoulder, lace bodice, chiffon skirt,' Bane mumbled, looking down. I goggled my eyes at him until he explained. 'You used to doodle it in your notebooks. I stole enough of them to know. The details changed a little over the years, but the basic design stayed the same. The last incarnation had a chiffon skirt and short train. I never kept any of them, sorry.'

'You're serious! You really stole my notebooks? Why?'

He took a deep breath. 'Because I was a sick bastard with a frequently desperate urge to know what you were thinking and doing. Probably triggered every time you planned something risky. At least stealing notepads was marginally better than spying on you. Sometimes I got so angry at myself for being tempted to stalk you that I wanted to scream at you instead. I promise I never stalked you. I used to watch you play footy at lunchtimes, but I never stalked you.'

His eyes became shadowed with a guilt we'd already resolved.

'The truth is,' he continued, 'I always knew where you were, so it felt like stalking anyway. I felt so ashamed of it that I did everything I could to push you away. I refused to get to know you, or even let myself like you.'

Time to snap him out of it.

'You were such a pest. Remember when you poured water in my lunchbox so I locked you in the toilet block and you got detention for being late to class?'

'Let's call it what it is. You bullied me, Lainie.'

'Yes, I did. And I'm sorry. We were hideous to each other. Wait. What else did I doodle in those notebooks? Did I say anything mean about you?'

'Only on every second page. Mostly you drew pictures of horses, Star Trek logos, and strange-looking trees. And you practised signing your name as Lainie Ashbree a lot in Year Eight.' He gave me a wry grin. 'I think I set those ones on fire.'

There was a time when I would have snapped out some hasty insult to hide my embarrassment at that. Now I just laughed. Which made the elderly lady smile at us again.

By the time we made it back to the hotel I was feeling tired again, but much happier. Bane was calm—right until he saw Mick pacing around the lobby.

'Where have you been?' he asked. 'I have news.'

Chapter 14

Sergeant Mick Loxwood stood in the lobby of the hotel attracting curious glances from the other guests. No matter how innocent people were, they nearly always felt intimidated by an officer in uniform. Which might have been why I received such shocked glances when I threw myself into his arms in a traditional Eden hello. Slightly chagrined, I remembered to refrain from the kisses just in time. Mick laughed and hugged me back.

'Lainie, how are you?' he greeted.

'Still alive!' He gave me a high five for that. 'And you?'

'Fine, unless you count the way I turn into a sobbing cry-baby at unexpected times. Your aunt suggested I have you to blame for that. I tried to call her yesterday and burst into tears before I could tell her anything useful. She advised me to try to catch you in person instead.'

'Oh, good, it worked then. I wasn't sure.'

'She said it was some sort of speech embargo to stop me saying the wrong thing in front of people.' He narrowed his eyes at a group of six who had just entered the lobby, as if worried they might trigger a teary breakdown. The expression on his face was so grim they turned and walked straight out again without a word.

'The same embargo we have, which is only fair. Tim, Dallmin, and Jake have it too.'

He turned to Bane and clapped him on the shoulder. 'Then I owe you both a huge apology. If I'd known how bad it felt to try to talk, I never would have interrogated you the way I did when Tessa went missing.'

'Yeah, you would,' Bane said.

He thought for a second. 'To get her back safely? You're probably right, I would have done anything. I'm still sorry though. I tell you, if we could do this to some of the people I have to work with, we could wipe out crime syndicates within a week. I don't suppose you can make people feel this bad about *not* talking?'

'Of course. I can do anything,' I replied cheekily. 'Under the right circumstances.'

He grimaced. 'Well, I'm afraid the circumstances might be aligning themselves for you to act again. Is there somewhere we can talk without me blubbering like a toddler in front of the whole town?'

A few minutes later, we were all crammed into Bane's tiny room again. Tim was perched on the corner of the bed while I bounced around on it, trying to get comfy. Bane stood guard near the door and Mick took the only chair. Dallmin sat on the floor in the corner looking miserable. I'd even told him it was okay to use his tablet again, until the sergeant took it from him and used it to look something up.

'There's talk on the net of a relic for sale,' he began while he waited for a page to load. 'The dealers are all in an uproar because whoever it is that's selling, they haven't gone through the usual channels. Most people think it's a hoax, but enough are curious. The thing that has everyone's attention is a symbol at the bottom of the advert, which I'm currently having trouble loading. A few clever people have figured out that it's a complex brainteaser and have posted a solution that's apparently only the first level of the puzzle. Also, they seem to love the fact that the seller has provided no way to be contacted. The instructions say that if anyone wants to bid for the relic they are to "call him by name" and "dream about it". Verification of the item's authenticity will be provided to those who are serious about wanting it. The implication is that you have to solve the puzzle to be considered serious enough. It has the fantasy and gaming communities in a spin. You know how easily these things can do the rounds.'

'Seriously?' Bane grumbled. 'Call him by name and dream about it? Who would fall for that?'

Tim and I both put up our hands. My Guardian rolled his eyes.

'Well, what have you got to lose?' I defended. 'You don't even have to make a fool of yourself. Do it before you go to sleep and see what happens.' I turned back to Mick. 'Does anyone know it's a sword?'

'Not yet, but I'm guessing that's what the puzzle will lead them to … damn, the webpage has crashed again, so I can't show you. It's getting that much traffic. Anyway, Jake has used every possible hint without actually saying the words to explain himself. Good work, Lainie, except the riddles have only added to the mystery. People can't seem to help proving how clever they are. Cleverness is valued more highly in our society than anything else. If there's a riddle, they have to solve it. He's exploiting a fundamental weakness.'

Groaning, I leaned back against Tim's chest, who patted me on the shoulder.

'So what's he planning to do?' Tim queried. 'Dream-walk over to potential buyers? Can he do that?'

A shiver ran down my spine as I realised he could. He already had— to me.

'What name did he tell people to call him?' Dallmin asked seriously. He seemed to accept that nothing was impossible in this place and he had ceased to be amazed by every new concept we talked about.

Mick took a deep breath, as if disciplining himself to spit the words out. 'Rabisu. He calls himself Rabisu.'

'Why would he name himself after a role-playing game character?' Tim queried. 'Is he into gaming?'

I shook my head. 'Jake? Not those sorts of games. No way. He wouldn't have the first clue about role-playing characters.' I slid off the bed to look over Dallmin's shoulder as he searched up the name on his reclaimed tablet. A quick read of the result had me even more confused. I read it to the others. 'Rabisu was a demon in ancient Mesopotamia. Also known as the Vagabond, he was supposed to be an evil creature that lurked in doorways waiting to pounce on his prey. How would someone like Jake know the first thing about ancient Mesopotamian demons?'

The answer, so obvious, made us all shudder.

As the discussions continued, the mood in our little group became even more sombre and so Bane came to sit down with Dallmin and me on the floor. We were stuck and we all knew it. I'd been hoping for a tip from Mick to help us narrow down our search, but so far Jake had done an excellent job of laying low. Despite my assurance to Bane that we must have been close the other day, using his level of crankiness as a gauge wasn't very reliable. I had known him all through high school, after all. Driving endlessly around Victoria hoping for either a new police lead or a miracle was starting to feel ridiculous.

Mick's research into the source of the advert hadn't yielded much either. At school, Jake had been the go-to guy for all our computer problems, but I wouldn't have credited him with hacker-level skills. Perhaps he'd charmed someone into helping him.

'You need an excuse to get your colleagues to delete the advert,' I surmised, interrupting the sergeant's rant about procedures and protocols.

Mick tilted his head. 'Not delete it, no. At the moment it's our best option of tracking him down. What I need is a better reason for them to investigate further. If I tell them the relic has something to do with our search for Jake, they're going to ask how much more I know that I'm not disclosing. I'm already getting some uncomfortable looks.'

I hated that we might be jeopardising his reputation.

'Okay, then what if I do something to the webpage that makes it clear it's a scam?' I suggested.

The policeman grinned. 'Shouldn't be too hard. There are so many ways to do that.'

The Word I used to add a mild virus to a webpage seemed even weirder than usual. Something about the concept of combining the sacred language with malware made it feel sort of ... ticklish. Adding a dodgy request for payment for a solution to the puzzle was less complicated.

Speculation as to what Jake was planning took over the conversation for far longer than it should have. I was pretty sure he just wanted to keep the sword away from Nalong so he could get past us into the Garden. Bane was convinced he was going to try to use the sword as proof the Garden was real. Mick argued that the demon would have done more to spread stories of Eden long before now if that was its motivation, and most crimes really did come down to money. Tim seemed to think the creature was attempting to gather some sort of army, which I quickly laughed off before one of Bane's heart valves ruptured. Although ... Jake had mentioned there were more of his kind. Perhaps he really was gathering allies. Not that I could explain this to the others without telling them about my argument with Jake, so I kept quiet and listened to the conversation circle around. Despite my best efforts, I drifted off to sleep against Bane's shoulder while the others discussed possible courses of action. I should have been in on that. It was extremely important. Being away from Nalong for so long was exhausting me and messing with my ability to focus.

As I slept I dreamed of Jake, snarling like an animal the way he had that morning, but this time I was completely unafraid of him, just really sad. He looked nothing like the guy I went to school with—my friend who had once taken the rap for the whole class that time Mrs Tierley was late and we unscrewed the whiteboard from the wall and hid it.

The Jake in my dream was more like a vile slobbery beast, a fusion of creatures from the wide selection of sci-fi shows I'd grown up watching. He prowled around the farm—my nightmares nearly always ended up located around the farm—silently watching me with his piercing blue eyes. They were the same blue eyes I knew so well, in a face contorted and twisted by hate and fear. The combination gave me a queasy feeling. That was probably why I was unafraid. This dream was way too clichéd to be anything other than a figment of my imagination, except that when I looked down at my own body, the winged creature I saw was freakily familiar. In fact, it weirded me out so much I woke up with a squeaky yelp.

'Lainie, what's wrong?' Bane asked, sitting up straighter and shaking some feeling back into his arm. He must have let me lean on it to the point of pins and needles rather than disturb me. Dallmin's tablet was on his lap.

'Nothing,' I croaked. 'I must have drifted off. What were we saying? Something about regrouping?' I shook my head to clear away the memory of Jake's predatory gaze.

He looked amused. 'That was almost two hours ago. We've kind of moved on from there. Mick's taken Dallmin out for a walk to give him a proper father-son lecture and Tim's gone for a run.'

I blinked stupidly and tried to gather my bearings, belatedly realising we were alone. Then I checked my chin for drool. Luckily I'd kept my mouth shut for once.

'What were you dreaming about?' he asked, trying unsuccessfully to sound like he didn't really care.

I yawned. 'Jake, again. But he looked like some sort of alien.'

'Again? So it *was* Jake you threw the lamp at. And another nightmare about him now? No wonder you're so jumpy.'

'Jake wasn't what frightened me this time though,' I admitted. 'It was the fact that I looked like a monster too. I was huge and kind of … shape-shifty.'

How could I explain to him that what disturbed me most was the way I'd felt more natural in that form than I did now when I was awake? Nothing from the times when I was dead remained in my memory and yet sometimes I felt such a strong sense of déjà vu I could hardly deny that some fragments must have filtered through. Was that really my true form?

My shoulder was being shaken gently. 'Lainie? Are you all right?'

'Hmm? What? Of course I am. Why?'

'You zoned out again. If your eyes were any glassier they'd shatter.' His own eyes narrowed. 'Is it because you died?'

The bluntness of the question made me flinch.

He gave a short sigh. 'I wish I knew what I could do to help you. I can't relate at all. It scares me, Lainie.'

'I'm getting better though, aren't I? I'm sleeping better, at least.'

'At all the wrong times. Would it help if you talked about it? I mean, can you? If you can only tell Noah I'll understand. You should talk to *someone.*'

Tucking my knees up to my chest, I considered his suggestion. He looked so anxious for me that I wanted to prove to him I wasn't trying to shut him out.

'It's not that I'm not allowed to speak,' I explained. 'It's just I can't remember anything.' Twisting my fingers together and resting my chin on my knees, I attempted to piece together what little I had. 'When I die, I go somewhere else. Somewhere warm and peaceful and very real, if that makes sense. It's not like a dream. In fact, it feels so real that coming back to life feels more like falling asleep.'

By the baffled look on his face, I knew I was doing a terrible job of explaining.

I tried again.

'There are other souls there, all travelling somewhere, purposefully.

Each time I go I'm filled with curiosity about where they're heading, but they get pulled across so fast I never get a chance to find out. I'm different, Bane. For some reason I … linger. Kind of pathetically really. I feel like a kid who got left off the school bus. It's almost embarrassing. Especially since …'

His tilted head begged, unspoken, for more.

So I exhaled and gathered my courage. 'Especially since I look completely different to everyone else. I'm like a great big flying duck, only weirder. It's hard to remember because it keeps changing.' My heart fluttered and I could feel my cheeks colouring in a way that made no sense to me. Why should I feel self-conscious about how I looked when I was dead?

Of course, he noticed my discomfort and his flirtatious smile unravelled the feeling quite effectively.

'I expect you were still unbelievably beautiful.'

He pulled me toward him and snuggled me against his chest. Instead of arguing, I listened to his heartbeat, using its consistent rhythm to steady my own. It was almost as if I had forgotten how to keep my own heart pumping properly and needed to be reminded of what it should feel like. My body was becoming a foreign thing to me and that scared me. How easy it would be to leave the cumbersome thing behind and fly away …

'Bastard!' I yelled, pushing myself away and standing up. My thoughts had matched Jake's snide suggestion that morning. If I hadn't grown up accustomed to Noah's charming ways, I might never have even noticed.

Bane looked stricken. 'What have I done?'

'Not you. Jake. He tried to charm me.'

The intense focus that hardened his features almost made me waver, but he had to be told.

'When I dreamed of him this morning, I don't think it was really a dream. More like a visitation. He was in my room with me, or at least, the demon part of him was.'

'No way. I would have known in an instant if he was anywhere near.'

'Not if he couldn't hurt me. He was sort of … intangible.'

My Guardian looked dubious.

I smiled indulgently. 'Ah, Bane, if only you had the benefits Tim and

I do from reading all the best sorts of cheesy books. Dream-walking-mind-controlling attacks are pretty standard for the bad guys. Usually it takes the victim a long time to break through the compulsion not to tell anyone.'

'He compelled you not to tell me?' Compulsion was something he did believe in and took very seriously.

'Ha! He wishes he had that much power. No, he only has his charm and I guess I've had years of practice at resisting because I'm too stubborn to let Noah have his way all the time.' Despite my confident tone, I could feel my distress rising like a lump in my throat.

Pulling his phone from his pocket, Bane sent a quick text to call the others back again. Then he called Noah and handed me the phone. I described the morning's creepy episode in as much detail as I could, wincing as I watched Bane's expression harden. Noah assured me he hadn't experienced anything like it, which helped me breathe easier. As I hung up the phone I turned my mind to how I was going to pacify my overprotective bodyguard, but as I opened my mouth to speak he laid a gentle kiss on my lips and smiled.

'Shhh, it's okay, Lainie. You don't have to say anything. So long as you agree, I think we should go home tomorrow.'

And with those words something inside me released, as if my soul had been holding its breath and could finally exhale.

It was a relief to acknowledge that our quest had been an abysmal failure. It was time to go home, regroup, and rest.

～

Failed quests don't pay well and the only one of us currently employed was Mick, so when we invited him to stay and share our usual dinner of supermarket deli salads, he offered to shout us all dinner at a restaurant instead. He promised us one with tablecloths that weren't made of paper. He even bought some popping candy for Dallmin, which fascinated the Edenite so much he stuck his tongue out to show everyone we passed on the walk to the restaurant.

On the way I explained to the others what had happened with Jake, forcing myself to talk through all of it, even the uncomfortable parts of the afternoon's dream that made me sound like some sort of weird flying bunyip. When I repeated Jake's comment about me being unable to protect the humans who were hidden away in Eden, Dallmin's face fell and he put the rest of his candy away in his pocket. It felt like another slice of his innocence was being put away with it.

When our meals arrived, Tim forbade Bane to join in the who-could-eat-the-spiciest-dish challenge due to his unfair advantage and declared that he was owed a reimbursement from a previous similar bet. Quick healing had more advantages than I'd realised.

'How many more bets did you win unfairly?' Mick mumbled to Bane as he pushed his Vindaloo around reluctantly with his fork.

'All of them, until Tim stopped pressuring me into his little games,' he declared, as if daring Tim to complain. Which he did.

'We're *mates*. Mates trust each other. I trusted you, yet still you cheated.'

Dallmin frowned. 'Mick, you told me many things this afternoon. I thought I understood. Now I'm confused again. Tim and Bane are mated?'

Luckily Mick was mature enough to explain the double meaning of the word 'mate'.

'So it can mean love partner or friend? Doesn't that get confusing?' Dallmin asked. I could tell he thought English was a bit stupid.

'Not usually. And a mate is more than just a friend,' Tim replied, glaring at Bane. 'A mate is someone you trust with your life. You don't expect them to cheat you.'

Bane shrugged. 'You were a pest. You once challenged me to see who could take the most paintballs without flinching, remember?'

'I was *trying* to lighten you up a little. Nothing else was working,' Tim grumbled, idly rubbing his ribs as if still remembering the pain.

It was a relief to realise someone had been looking out for Bane. Icy fingers of guilt began to creep into my chest as I thought about the three years in which I'd abandoned everyone while I'd frolicked around in paradise. Bane, of course, noticed my reaction.

'I was serious about my training, that's all,' he said a bit too quickly.

When was he going to learn it wasn't his job to protect me from the consequences of my own bad choices? Aside from the physical ones, anyway. I tried to change the topic by reaching across and stealing a giant forkful of Tim's meal. My competitive nature was hard to control, in either world. It tasted amazing.

'It's only fair,' I said as I went for a second piece of beef and all four of my companions frowned in disapproval. 'He ate food off my plate back in Nalong.' I realised my error as Bane's eyes widened and he held his breath. It wasn't the lack of table manners they were complaining about. Feeling the spices sear my mouth, my eyes sent a silent apology to him. I hadn't expected spice burns to trigger his healing compulsion the way a real burn would. So, he was sensitive to my pain rather than my injuries. Or maybe both?

'Interesting,' Tim murmured, as fascinated as I was. Bane glared at him. 'Ah, I mean … Lainie, are you okay?'

Good question. As I braced myself for the pain, I wondered where we could get to that would give us some privacy before Bane insisted on healing me. Only, the pain never came. I could feel the sensation; it just didn't bother me. The fact that it didn't bother me really bothered me though. I slurped up a big spoonful of coconut cream as the conversation around the table crashed.

'I propose a toast!' Mick announced into the awkward quiet. 'To the newly engaged couple. May you both live happily ever after.' He clinked his glass with each of ours. 'Now kiss the girl already, will you?'

Bane practically threw himself at me and as our lips touched I felt heat flow through me, soothing the triggered pain receptors in my mouth. Healing a false pain I couldn't even feel. Yet Bane's relief was obvious.

Mick was a genius; no one around us was likely to stare too hard as we kissed, so hopefully our little bit of supernatural byplay would go unnoticed. Within moments, however, I didn't care at all who was noticing what, because I suddenly realised I could *feel* again. I felt everything: the burns, the tingling as they healed, the double thump my heart made and the way my body thrummed in response to the feel of Bane's fingertips on my neck. Everything became clearer and sharper. Including the sound of Mick clearing his throat. Agonisingly, I allowed Bane to pull away, shutting my eyes against the longing reflected in his gaze. My blood sang a raunchy tune with lyrics that would never be allowed on commercial radio.

Once we finished our meals and gratefully allowed Mick to settle the bill, we headed out to explore the city centre. Geelong was the largest town we'd visited all week. It was Friday night and the streets were full of people making the most of the clear and cold June weather. A few brave buskers even filled the air with music and I wished I had something to offer them.

One busker, snuggled in a thick puffer jacket and wearing a hand-knitted beanie in loyal Geelong blue and white, was playing a saxophone and doing a marvellous job of not looking like he wanted to be home in front of the telly watching the game with the heater up full blast. He had a brood cap at his feet with a few coins in it. As we passed by, Bane glanced at me, his expression revealing that ephemeral trace of playfulness I loved. Tuned to my every unspoken desire, he knew even better than I did what I wanted. He grabbed my hand and swung me around, daring me with his dreamy silver eyes. I laughed as he began to lead me in the same dance I'd taught him on my first day back from Eden, and as the saxophonist picked up his pace to match our enthusiasm I saw Dallmin's expression light up. I shot Tim a warning glance, but it was too late. Dallmin smoothly grabbed the hand of the nearest passing woman and gently kissed her on the inside of her wrist. By the shocked look on the elderly lady's face, I assumed she was expecting to have her handbag snatched. Instead, Dallmin gave her a graceful bow, staring earnestly into her eyes to determine what she wanted him to do. I had no idea when he'd picked up on the bowing convention, yet it certainly seemed to have the desired effect because the lady practically threw her handbag at the younger woman she was with and allowed the handsome young stranger to lead her in a jaunty quick-step.

From the corner of my eye, I could see Tim almost wet himself laughing. He gallantly offered his hand to the younger woman, who was still staring in shocked amazement at her aged mother. She shyly refused until Mick flashed his badge and offered to mind their belongings. That must have gone a long way to set her mind at ease because only a few moments later she and Tim were swinging around as if they'd danced together all their lives. The saxophonist looked ecstatic as people stopped to stare, throwing money into his cap just to feel they were a part of it all.

After that, it was difficult to focus on what anyone else was doing because all I could feel was the way my body responded to Bane's. He led me faster and wilder with each passing note, challenging me to keep up, which after three years of being trained by the Edenites was no problem. His silver eyes were locked on mine the whole time, both of us revelling in the way we could connect with each other without having to worry about going too far. All too soon the song ended.

Panic flared.

I *needed* this. I needed to *feel*. In his arms my body worked right, I understood it, and it felt real and natural. It was only then that I truly grasped how disjointed I'd become over course of the last week and it frightened me. I clung to him, afraid to lose contact now the music had ended. Why hadn't the busker started a new song yet? Couldn't he see he had an audience? Did we need to pay him first before he would play any more? My frantic eyes sought him and I realised what the delay was. Dallmin had released his entranced partner, who was beaming like a child and blowing him a kiss as she and her daughter retrieved their bags, and he was now talking to the musician about the instrument, inspecting the mouthpiece critically.

'Play something else,' I pleaded, sending all my feeling toward Dallmin in the hope he would sense how much I wanted more. The busker shook his head in response to something Dallmin asked.

'Sorry, mate, no one touches the sax. You can play my guitar if you know how,' he offered.

'He knows how. I'll vouch for him,' Tim assured the man as Dallmin lovingly lifted the guitar from its case.

Still looking unsure, the musician cleared his throat. 'Well, what songs do you know? Play something you're familiar with and I'll follow you,' he suggested.

'You name one and I'll see if I have heard it,' Dallmin countered.

Well, this should be interesting. Dallmin had been completely unexposed to any of our music until a few weeks ago.

'Okay then, how about we start with "Khe San"? Or is that too old for you?'

I smiled. Too old? Probably not the biggest issue.

'How does it go?' Dallmin asked simply.

The man shook his head in disbelief before playing the opening bars. A dozen heads that had turned to leave paused and swung back around.

'Oh, yes, I know that one. It was playing in one of the pubs in Sale. I may not remember all of the lyrics though. I only learned English recently.' Then, without hesitation, he launched into a perfect rendition of the classic Australian rock anthem, with only a couple of lyrical alterations, where he substituted words he didn't know with ones he did. The surprising thing was that even those were seamless and barely noticeable. How on Earth had he picked up the entire song after one hearing? Money poured into the hat from the gathering bystanders.

It became a challenge after that, with passing strangers suggesting songs they were certain he'd never heard. He joined in quickly every time and transformed each song into a masterpiece. Plenty of dancing gradually eased my panic, until I was content just to be held and listen. When someone requested John Lennon's 'Imagine', hearing the lyrics flow from the exiled Edenite's torn heart made even our stoic police sergeant lose his composure.

It took less than twenty minutes for the busker to dare Dallmin to try his sax, well-convinced by then of his ability. His mouth literally hung open when, after only a couple of minutes to learn how to blow into it correctly, the talented stranger did a perfect repeat of their previous song. The gathered crowd applauded wildly.

'It is a beautiful instrument. Who crafted such a thing?' Dallmin asked, studying the structure and feel of the metal.

'It's a Keilwerth. My baby. She's my most precious possession.'

Dallmin looked intensely at the man's face, as if trying to read what he was not saying. 'If she is as precious to you as a child, then you must really love it. But a child is far more precious than an instrument,' he corrected, suddenly sounding more like his real age.

Tears welled in the musician's eyes. 'I know. I had a child once,' he rasped, 'but she died at birth. My wife and I never … we were never blessed with another.' The whole street mall went suddenly silent in shared grief.

Dallmin handed the saxophone back reverently. 'I am deeply sorry this happened to you and your family.' He took a few deep breaths, struggling with the concept of losing a child. 'Marcus, may I ask you how it is you are not always sad? How have you continued to hold your soul together after such a terrible event?' I could see his body tremble as he fought to remain composed. The desperation in his brown eyes reflected an honesty and innocence that denied a cynical response.

The whole street seemed to hold its breath, each person afraid of the reaction to such a personal question, but at the same time, all wanting to know the answer.

'I'm not sure my soul *is* held together. Not very well, anyway. I guess I've patched it with a bit of duct tape. It's not as durable as it used to be.'

'Duct tape?'

'Music. Music is my duct tape. And my wife. I hold on to her with everything I have.'

'Music? Even if you don't feel like dancing or singing?' Dallmin's craving for answers was plain. 'How do you play when you're sad?'

'I pick music that suits my mood and if there isn't any, I make some up. Surely you've done it yourself. I can't really believe you have all that talent and don't write your own music.'

'I've only made joyful music for my friends to dance to.'

'Then maybe it's time you played something for yourself,' Marcus suggested, handing him back the guitar.

A few numb moments passed before Dallmin nodded, acceding to his suggestion. What flowed then—so easily from fingers that had harvested from the Tree of Life, from a voice that had sung to the stars in paradise, from a heart that had known complete joy and lost it—was a melody so poignant and fragile people actually sat down where they were so they could listen more attentively. Never had I heard Dallmin pour such longing and sadness into a melody. As his fingers plucked at the strings, I heard the life-filled echoes of the River thread their way in and out of the lilting harmonics. Perfected mastery forged anguish into sound until the air itself seemed to hum in resonant empathy with his torn soul. His lyrical cry, in a language long lost to the race he was now singing to, didn't fail to evoke understanding from all who dared to really listen. His torment was inescapable and tears flowed freely.

As his song reached out, pleading for healing from someone … anyone … my gift began to drift out with it.

Sadness was reflected in the elderly lady's eyes as she remembered her husband, lost years ago to a heart attack. Another grieved for a loss of faith, as his heart had been hardened by religion that had little to do with a loving God. Yet another was struggling in a relationship with her sister, torn apart by destructive criticism that could not be easily reconciled. A part of me knew that the empathic link Dallmin's music was forging was not entirely healthy for me, but I couldn't seem to care. Their needs went so much deeper than my own. Captivated by the depth of pain and loss each person was clothed in, I listened as Dallmin played them back all the distress he read in their eyes, echoing his own sorrow. Unbidden, my heart cried out, begging for surcease and comfort.

Words answered.

Voice fused with power, and the sheer force of my sung supplication melded with Dallmin's tune until he was drawn into the new progression. As his voice made way for mine, melodies folded and layered until his grief was softly undercut by my understanding, his pain woven through with my compassion. Vibrant healing infused itself into heartache. Tenderness softened angst. Fear and shame were shattered by love.

Finally, the Words of grace played themselves out until the last notes faded into the frosted air. Tears had completed their flowing course and run dry. No one spoke or clapped. Some of the people hugged, others fled, unable to face the vulnerability they'd felt. I simply hung, drained and limp in Bane's supporting embrace.

Joy-giver needs a new game, I signed to my friend, fumbling it a little.

Dallmin smiled and placed the guitar back in its case. 'Perhaps this *is* my new game.'

Marcus swallowed hard and spoke in a hushed voice, as if reluctant to break the spell. 'What language was that? Those words …'

When I couldn't answer, Dallmin simply said, 'It's a new song.'

The busker hugged the strange young man who had gifted him with compassion and healing, then turned to me with a grateful nod, picked up his instruments and folded chair, and walked away.

Leaving us with his cap, stuffed full of cash.

Chapter 15

'Go away, Jake. I'm too tired tonight. Come back tomorrow if you must.' I opened one gluey eyelid, knowing full well who was snarling like a dog in my hotel room. Sure enough, the shabby form of my high school friend stood by the window in a narrow sliver of moonlight, pacing back and forth. Illogical relief flooded through me as I saw him in his human form. Even though it meant this was probably an actual visitation, I still preferred it to the dream I'd had of the demon itself and the image of my own alien shape.

'Brave of you to still sleep alone. Or have you two had a fight? Did Bane finally let slip how jealous he is of your new boyfriend?'

I sat up and watched as he passed his fingers back and forth through the curtain, concentrating hard. He grasped it between two careful fingertips and pulled it back so he could look outside. His lips twitched in a triumphant smirk that was somehow also angry.

So he could touch things sometimes. Terrific.

'New boyfriend … you mean Dallmin? Aren't you a bit old for playground taunts?' I asked as I double-checked I had my t-shirt on. 'How old are you, anyway?'

Instead of answering he gave me a condescending look. Well, it was worth a shot.

'What do you want, Jake?' I asked, yawning. 'You apparently can't hurt me, so did you come to talk? Negotiate, maybe? Or charm me into submission? Whatever it is, get on with it. I'm tired and I want to go back to sleep.'

'Why are you still in Geelong? You normally move every day.' His eyes were resting on the tourist brochure on the bedside table.

'You've been tracking our movements all week,' I accused. Damn. No wonder he'd evaded us. And how many times had he been in my room?

'I haven't needed to.' He leaned toward me with a hungry look in his blue eyes. 'Didn't Bane tell you? I can feel you, Lainie. I can always feel where you are.'

Oh now, come on. No way. Did I have some sort of psychic stench? And if Bane knew, why hadn't he mentioned something that important? This entire trip had been a complete waste of time.

'How much are you asking for my sword?' I challenged, wanting to change the topic.

'*Your* sword? You have no right to it. Your internet tricks won't hide it forever. It's an important artefact, Cherub. The humans have a right to know what's going on around them. I don't really care what price I get for it, so long as it goes to a kind, forever home,' he said in a falsely sweet tone. 'I might even let your friend Jake keep the money.'

My friend Jake? That I was talking directly to the demon itself was disturbing. My mind raced with a hundred more questions I couldn't ask without revealing things I didn't want him to know. Like, for example, my total ignorance of demonic matters.

'So you'll find a way to tell the world about it, then what? What are you hoping to achieve?'

He let out a laugh that made my untainted hands want to slap him, then took a coin out of his pocket and flicked it around, the same way Jake used to do in class when he was bored.

'As if I would tell the humans anything about us. We *own* them. They will learn what I let them learn and nothing more. As soon as I find a buyer with the right resources, I'll make them destroy that wretched sword once and for all. The technology is around now and I have a few ideas about what might work. There won't be a thing you can do about it because you can't even find me.'

So much for the humans having the right to know. He didn't seem to know what he wanted. It was time for a bluff.

Trying hard to look unflustered, I climbed out of bed and poured myself a glass of water. I hoped I was better at lying than I had been a few weeks ago.

'We don't need to find you and we don't really need the sword either. Do what you want with it. After all these years did you really think we wouldn't have come up with more than one weapon to use against your kind? Eventually, you'll have to come and face us, you know. You can't lurk in doorways forever. I dare you to come in person, with or without a sword of your own.'

'You're a terrible liar, Lainie. There's only one sword, and I know for a fact you don't have the amulet either.'

I nearly choked on the water. There was an amulet? Neither Annie nor Harry had ever mentioned anything about an amulet. Perhaps it was a sacred artefact lost through the ages because of our embargo against the written word. Noah and I had grown up without even knowing what we were. How many other times had that happened? How many secrets had failed to get passed down? Maybe this amulet was hidden in some forgotten location on the farm. Despite the danger I was probably in, I couldn't help feeling excited about a treasure hunt.

'—wouldn't let him search for it there.'

Oops. Shouldn't have let myself get distracted. Seriously, though. An *amulet*.

'Are you so certain we can't retrieve it any time we choose?' I asked, pretending I'd been paying attention. I gave him the most smug smile I could muster before taking another sip. He was wrong, I was a great liar. My lying muscle might be out of shape, but it was like riding a horse; you never forgot how to do it. Still, I put the glass down before he noticed my hands trembling. What was I risking here? Did I really think all those fantasy stories I'd read would actually help me outsmart an actual demon? Whatever I was doing, it certainly hit a nerve though, because he snarled and threw the coin angrily against the wall and then leaped toward me again. No matter how hard I tried to tell myself he couldn't touch me, I still couldn't make myself stand still. He had, after all, touched the curtain earlier. Ducking away, I suppressed a frightened yelp. Mostly. For some unknown reason, I reflexively grabbed the glass again as I moved and threw its contents at my adversary.

Unsurprisingly, he didn't melt.

In fact, he didn't even get wet. The water passed right through him the same way the lamp had. Somehow, I had to make sense of these new rules. I smashed the glass against the edge of the table and held its jagged remains out as a weapon.

He laughed. 'It won't do you any good. You can't hurt me any more than I can hurt you. And so of course your Guardian is sleeping peacefully through all the fun. You can try calling him, I guess, but most hotel walls are pretty soundproof these days. How does it work, Lainie? If I work out a way to slice you with that glass, will he sense it in time? Years ago, when I first watched him heal you, he knew you were in danger well before the incident began to unfold. So does that mean there is no chance for me to hurt you at all?'

With slow deliberation, he took another coin from his pocket and flicked it at me. I caught it without thinking. His resultant grin was definitely not Jake's. It was malicious and shrewd, like a hunter focused on his prey. I threw the coin back at his head and of course it passed harmlessly through his skull and hit the wall behind. So unfair. With a snarl, he reached for a piece of broken glass on the table, scrabbling to coax his fingers to pick it up. It shifted slightly.

That wasn't good.

'Thanks for the ethereal physics lesson, Jake. Or whoever you are. I think I have all I need now. You can go.'

With deliberate surgical precision, I used the glass I was clutching to slice the tip of my forefinger and breathed a sigh of relief as the door burst open behind me. Bane blew into the room like a mountain storm.

Snarling with rage, Jake swept the remaining glass shards off the table toward me in a burst of sparkles before throwing a look of sheer terror in Bane's direction and then vanishing in the blink of an eye.

Bane hit the wall behind where Jake had been standing with a very painful sounding thunk.

He was cranky with me. I wasn't terribly surprised, but that didn't mean I liked it. I wanted him to smile flirtatiously like he did whenever I begged him to play his guitar. Instead, his face was closed off and emotionless. He'd already healed the cut on my finger before calling for Tim and Mick, and now heat once again seared my skin as his power shot through me like a zap from an electric fence. He wasn't being gentle about it. It felt grumpy, like when Aunt Lily used to pin me down and swab my grazed knees with stingy antiseptic when I was well and truly old enough to know better. Fascinated, I watched the tiny fragments of glass tinkle off my skin and onto the floor. All the way down the inside of my arm, miniscule lacerations closed up like sleepy blossoms.

'Sorry, Bane. I tried to keep it small. I didn't know he would manage to throw the other bits at me too,' I mumbled as Tim and Mick came in and shut the door quietly behind them. 'Are you dizzy?'

'Damn it, Lainie. You don't get it. I'm not angry because your injuries make me uncomfortable. You were supposed to call out to me, not slice your finger off. Do you even feel pain anymore? You treat your body like it's a disposable toy.'

It was all I could do to hide my sudden fear as I snatched my hand away. He was entirely too close to the truth.

'You don't treat yours any better. Were you planning to get any sleep at all tonight?' I quickly countered, crossing my arms. 'It hasn't escaped my notice that you're still fully clothed … and *armed*,' I added, pointing to the obvious bulge under his jacket. He hadn't worn a knife since the day I'd died and I hadn't missed it one bit.

Clenching his teeth around a scream of frustration, he turned and stomped out of the room, slamming the door behind him in loud disregard of the fact that it was two am and the rest of the hotel patrons were asleep.

Feeling both embarrassed and grouchy, I began to collect all the bits of glass into a pile until Mick pulled my hands away from the mess.

'Don't, Lainie. If you cut yourself again he'll only get angrier. Let the housekeeping staff deal with it in the morning.'

Suddenly it was all too much. The emotional rollercoaster I'd been on for the last few weeks had taken one too many death-defying plunges and loop-de-loops. Mick's paternal hug absorbed my sobs and I was too exhausted to even pretend to care that I was crying again.

'What was I supposed to do?' I complained once my tears had slowed enough for me to get whiny instead. 'Scream the walls down? It's the middle of the night.'

He held me at arm's length and looked me sternly in the eye. 'Yes,

Lainie, as a commissioned police officer, I can confidently say that when there is an unwanted intruder in your room threatening to kill you, it is perfectly acceptable to scream as loud as you can no matter what time it is.' Behind him, Tim nodded his agreement. 'Why didn't you call out as soon as Jake appeared?' Mick asked, not unkindly.

'I needed to find out more, and he's terrified of Bane. Besides, I didn't think he could hurt me. If he could, then Bane would have barged in earlier.'

It had made sense in my head at the time, but now I realised the threat had only manifested once Jake had worked out how to throw things at me. Perhaps I hadn't needed to hurt myself after all. I flopped down onto the bed. 'Do I really look like I'm treating all this as a game? Because I'm not. I am taking it seriously.'

Tim shook his head, coming to sit next to me on the edge of the mattress. 'That's not what he said, Lainie. No one doubts that you're serious about wanting to find Jake. What he said was that you treat your body like it's a disposable toy. You don't look after yourself properly and he gets frustrated when you won't let him do it either. I wondered at first why it was you even needed a Guardian. I mean, the things you can do ...' His voice was quiet as he handed me a fresh glass of water, which I managed to drink without throwing it at anyone. 'But now I'm impressed that even he can keep you alive.'

I could feel a scowl forming on my face, so I put the glass down and made myself sit on my hands in case his next words triggered the slap I'd been saving for Jake.

'Woah, relax, Wind-Master. I'm not saying you're incapable of taking care of yourself ... okay, I guess I sort of am, but not because you're some useless Disney princess. It's just that you don't seem to have any natural sense of self-preservation. Dallmin is almost as bad, if that's any consolation,' he added quickly.

'How is that a consolation? He's barely hanging on by a thread, Tim. Are you suggesting I'm suffering from some sort of PTSD?'

'Only you can answer that, although that isn't what I meant. It's more ... well, do you remember the other day when Bane activated all the child locks on the car doors when we passed that wall mural you wanted to look at?'

Pouting a little, I nodded. He'd refused to let me out and deliberately distracted me instead with questions about where we should go on our honeymoon.

'Did you even realise the car was still travelling at eighty ks when you tried to open the door?'

'Was not.'

'And last weekend in Mildura when you and Dallmin nearly jumped off the bridge into the Murray?'

'Bane was probably right. It would have been pretty cold at that time of the morning.'

'Understatement, given it was eight o'clock in the morning and about six degrees. And yet still not the point. The Murray is huge, and deep, and fast. Really not all that safe, my flighty friend,' he pointed out.

Even Mick was frowning at me now.

'Bane didn't say anything about that,' I grumbled.

'Not to you. He knows how much you hate being lectured to.'

'Oh.' Poor Bane. He was far more patient than I gave him credit for. 'I've been a bit of a handful then,' I admitted.

'Like a toddler. With no road sense. For a while there, you barely even ate without being reminded.'

'Seriously?'

'We tested it. Twenty-four hours and you never even noticed. Put a plate in front of you and you wolfed it down, but if no one suggested eating …'

'I'm sure I'd have noticed eventually,' I protested. 'I love food.'

'Yeah, I know. And if it helps, Bane seemed to think you were improving. Until tonight, at least.' He tilted his head at me. 'So was it worth it? Did you learn anything useful?'

With a soft whimper, I rolled off the bed and picked up the two coins Jake had left behind. I gave them one each.

'I did. I learned that Jake can bring things with him. Real things that obey all the real laws of physics. Which means next time I go to sleep, there's a chance I could wake up staring at the yucky end of a gun.'

Chapter 16

Fresh sunlight warmed the tears on Annie's face as she opened her eyes. The branches of her sleeping tree swayed gently beneath her as if it was trying to soothe her back to sleep, but it was too late for that. Lucas was gone, and Sarah and Harry had moved across to find and forgive each other and had left her behind. Still, she was not to be pitied. She was home, and home was glorious. She sat up and breathed in the enticing scent of baking bread from the food shelter. She could hear Karinya's voice singing the alto harmony to someone else's song. She always sang as she baked, and not a day went by when she didn't bake something mouthwatering. The thought of pastries for breakfast was almost enough to dispel the lingering weight of her vivid dreams.

Nayn was waiting with a reed box of pastries and a warm mug of liquorice tea when Annie returned from her morning soak in the thermal mineral pools. *Are you certain you are ready for this, Annie?*

I am. You have made me very curious.

She sipped at her tea as they walked together to a bend in the river that embraced a stand of fir trees. A fine mist tickled her cheeks until they passed under the tree line to a sheltered area scattered with work benches and wooden stools. It was usually crowded when it rained, but today Beltana was the only one there, chiselling away at her limestone sculpture. Perhaps she could tell them where the others had gone.

Nayn gave the sculpture a cursory glance before greeting Beltana with a typical lack of tact. Tact was not an Eden requirement.

Is it a replica of some random bit of rock?

No, guess again.

A random bit of rock with horns.

Beltana laughed, enjoying the game.

'It's a goat,' Annie declared in English.

They both turned to her with eyebrows raised.

A grazing animal with horns. You can drink milk from the females and the males smell terrible, she signed. *I have never seen one in Eden.*

Me either. I miss the cheese, Beltana pouted.

Annie froze, astonished. Beltana was the friend born outside Eden? Impossible.

There it is, Nayn declared with a triumphant smile.

There what is? Beltana asked as she brushed dust from her knees.

The deep mystic riddle. I promised Annie I'd think of one. It has to do with missing the cheese.

Annie took another sip of tea, determined to stay calm. The last thing Beltana needed was to see her freak out. *I thought it was supposed to involve ducks and a sunset?* she signed.

Good point. Ducks, sunset, and missing the cheese. I'll keep working on it, Nayn said. *In the meantime, I have a question for you, Beltana.*

Annie took a deep breath.

Why are you wearing those strange clothes? They are too long for you.

Not the question Annie had been hoping for.

Beltana smiled and rolled up the bottom of her jeans a bit more. *Lainie gave them to me. The leg coverings are sturdy, if too warm. And long. Lainie is quite tall. Perhaps I'll give them to Dallmin to wear when he travels to the mountains next. He is taller than me. Where is he, Annie? I haven't seen him for some time,* she said before tapping away at her sculpture again.

Annie put her empty mug down on a bench so it wouldn't fall from her shaky hands.

Kindly, Nayn answered for her. *He's crossed the boundary. We are here to ask you if there is a way he can return. We know you lived there once and now live here, but you are not a Cherub. We have come to ask you about your past.*

The tools slipped from Beltana's fingers and clattered onto the table. *He's really gone?* She let out a long breath and clasped her hands together in a pointless effort to disguise her sadness. It made no differ-ence. Annie didn't need sign language to know what she was feeling, especially when Beltana's surge of grief matched her own far too well. Grief. From Beltana. Nothing about that was okay.

Is there any chance he can come home? Nayn asked.

Beltana shrugged. *That depends on what he sees out there, son of mine. Once something has been seen, it cannot be unseen. The land out there is not like where I came from, but—*

Annie grabbed her hand. *Wait, Beltana, sorry to interrupt. Did you just call Nayn your son?*

Well, great-great-grandson, with a few more greats thrown in. No idea how many. I've long since lost track. Both our families are very large.

Annie shook her head at the white-haired wrinkled man and the girl who looked not much older than she did. *No way. That makes no sense. He's Shamar.*

All the male Shamar come from my line, she clarified.

You're a Guardian? How did you come to be here? Her legs felt unsteady so she sat down on the stool Nayn dragged over for her and wrapped her fingers around her empty mug.

I was the first Guardian. That's why I came to be here, Beltana said as she selected a pastry from the box Nayn had opened. *You want to know about my past? The history of our people is not exactly a short story, but I'll try to outline the interesting bits.* She looked over to the grassy hill on the other side of the river, where three people were climbing a tree. They were well out of earshot but in plain sight. *It isn't the sort of tale that is good for others to know. How well do you know our spoken language?*

'Very well,' Annie replied. 'Dallmin loves teaching languages almost as much as he loves to learn.'

She thought she'd done well to keep the spike of sorrow from her voice, until Beltana gave her hand a comforting squeeze and said, 'Dallmin has been thinking of exploring for a very long time, Annie. The Shamar over the years have always demonstrated their discomfort with his interest in what lies beyond the cave, and he has always aligned his desires to match what they want, as is natural here. It doesn't surprise me that his curiosity finally outweighed your discomfort. When that happened, your desires aligned to his. There is no blame here.'

'Why him? What drew him there when no other Edenites show any interest at all?'

'He remembers others who left and he doesn't understand why they haven't returned. His fascination with you and your story will have added to the mystery.'

'Others who left? How many more do we have to rescue?'

Beltana shook her head. 'They left here long before I was born, Annie. They are gone. Let's sit and I'll tell you what I know of them, although their story will not bring you peace.

'My father was a travelling merchant. I don't remember ever having a home town. We would stay a season or two and then move on. We travelled so much that I started collecting small reminders of each place I'd been so I could keep them all straight in my head.' Her fingers drifted to her necklace, laden with its pretty tokens. 'You must understand, this way of life was not normal where we were. Perhaps my father originally came from one of the nomadic people, or maybe he was simply restless after my mother died. Perhaps he did it to keep me safer—it was a dangerous place for young girls and I had to learn to … play roughly … to protect myself. I never questioned his reasons. Either way, we used to visit villages that were very isolated. One of them was a small, nameless village I completely fell in love with. Not because it was at all pretty. In fact, as soon as you moved more than a short distance from the river, the landscape was dry and dull. What I loved about it were the people. So tall, so beautiful, and they had something new and precious. They had music. Not just the simple beats and whistles of the instruments my father traded. These people had bells and flutes made of silver. I had never seen silver before. My father bargained to bring the village food supplies for five whole summers in exchange for a single silver bell. It was a good trade. He sold it on for far more and after that the hunt for sources of silver really took off. The best part of the trade was that we were obligated to return every spring and autumn for the full five sun-cycles to fulfil our side of the bargain. We gained far more than the silver bell in that time. The villagers didn't seem to realise the value of their knowledge. They had ways of doing things we'd never seen. Ways of communicating complex messages with someone far away simply by carving some marks on a piece of wood and asking us to deliver it to them. I had heard of such things, but not with the complexity they did it.'

Nayn rubbed his arms, reflecting Annie's own discomfort. 'The villagers were from Eden,' he surmised. 'Were there no Shamar to keep them hidden? Keep them from revealing too much?'

Beltana looked dreamy. 'Shamar. Yes. The first. Dayana and Khané. To me, barely twenty summers old, all the tall villagers were like gods, but those two … they shone like that polished silver bell. And yes, they were secretive. The Shamar were never happy when we came. They only tolerated our visits because my father brought food supplies that were difficult to grow where they were. The villagers seemed afraid to travel far themselves and were grateful for our trades. The village had been there for a long time. They lived in rooms carved into the mountain itself, connected by a maze of tunnels. There were some we were barred from. So, naturally, my father sent me to try to discover what treasures were hidden in those secret caves. Only, no matter how stealthy I was, the Shamar always intercepted me. They were never angry with me; in fact, Khané seemed to enjoy the game. He was so confident I would never get past him. It made me very frustrated, which he thought was funny. My father was not so impressed. He was convinced there was truth to the stories that these villagers did not grow old. He believed the secret to their long lives was hidden in one of the caves and he … well, he instructed me to seduce Khané into revealing it.'

Annie blinked. This was better than *Neighbours*. 'And how did that go?' she asked.

Beltana laughed. 'Terrible! I'd already been utterly smitten by Khané since I'd first laid eyes on him and so I'd been flirting with him for years—with absolutely no success. Then the morning after my father's awkward little chat, Dayana took one look at me and said to Khané in front of everyone, "She's trying to seduce you to learn all our secrets." It was the most embarrassing moment of my life. I couldn't even look him in the eye after that. Not until the day I had to.'

And with those words, Beltana's whole demeanour changed. She didn't want to talk anymore. Nayn and Annie glanced at each other and waited. It was up to Beltana to decide, and it was hard to watch the way she wrestled with the decision. She'd always been so carefree.

After a few moments, she took a deep breath. 'I will not dwell on the details because these things are in my past and are done. Completed. I will tell you only the bones of what occurred, so you understand.'

Nayn kissed the inside of her wrist to acknowledge that he wanted whatever she wanted.

'Dayana and her love partner Muyae had been together for many summers. When she announced she was pregnant, the villagers all went a bit wild. I couldn't understand why. I do now. The exiled Edenites knew what Dayana and Khané were: shape-shifting Cherubim who had lived with them since the beginning of all things, who had been assigned as Shamar to guard the entrance to Eden when all the other Cherubim and Angels were sent home. Although they had been locked into human form and Dayana had taken on a human love partner, no one expected them to be capable of conceiving children. The reactions were mixed. It was then that I realised not all the exiles were entirely … stable. Most had left the village early on to try to live as best they could, far away from Eden. Some had returned in terror from what they'd seen in the new world. And some had returned to lie in wait for an opportunity to force their way back in. Their intentions had been veiled from the Shamar.'

'Veiled?' Nayn asked. 'How?'

'Khané said it all happened too fast. He knew they all wanted to return home. Of course they did. He had long since grown used to that feeling. By the time he felt their specific intent to implement their awful plan, it was too late to talk them out of it. He tried anyway, only he did not expect them to …' Beltana turned very pale and put her hand over her mouth as if she was about to be sick. It took her a while to be able to speak again. When she did, she kept her explanations clipped. 'They took the new baby and threatened to kill her if the Shamar refused to let them back into Eden. Dayana *could not* agree to that, and instead, she and her partner were both killed trying to take their baby back. They knew nothing of fighting. Nothing. Khané took the sword and tried to help. He would have been killed, too, if I hadn't taken up the weapon and protected him. I will not speak of what I did. It is a part of me that is finished and I do not need to go back there in my mind.'

Annie squeezed her hand. She understood completely.

'The ones who escaped ran away, and I taught the remaining villagers how to protect themselves. They set up a new village a half-day's travel away from the caves. From then on all trading was done there, in the tower. Outsiders were not permitted to even know about the cave system. Still, the tyrants kept trying. Khané and I raised the baby girl alongside our son, Tahuma, and I learned how to fight to protect them all. After many years I realised I was getting … assistance from somewhere. I was able to predict some of the threats to Khané and heal him. My reflexes became very fast and I was not growing old. The other villagers were suspicious of how fast I recovered from injuries.' She gave a wry smile. 'Some thought I had been allowed into Eden.'

'I expect that didn't go down well,' Nayn remarked.

'You could say that. It started *tahazu* … a game-for-all that ended in much blood and killing.'

'A war,' Annie breathed.

'A war,' Beltana nodded, testing out the new word. 'A war that lasted for hundreds of seasons, until the day Khané and I were trapped in the cave by a host of fighters. They … they killed him. I tried to take his body across before they could get to it. I burned, and they pulled him back, and I failed.'

Annie lowered her eyes, remembering the day her father had died trying to pass the boundary. 'The sword killed you,' Annie guessed. 'And yet you are here.'

'My adopted daughter, Zyndel, managed to pull my body through. I woke to the sound of her screaming my name over and over. Tahuma was beside me, groaning, with his eyes still glazed over. He'd died too. I can't tell you what happened because the Fruit took those memories away. All I know is they refused to let me return to find Khané's body. They told me it was too late. They had somehow woken the River and flooded the cave, washing the tyrants away. There was more to that story, but they wouldn't tell me. They said such things were not right for me to hear now I was in the Garden. All they would say was that the flood destroyed the tyrants once and for all.'

Something was not right. There was a flicker in her eyes that betrayed her discomfort. Using her gift, Annie tasted the emotions in the air. Nayn was curious. Beltana … frustrated. Her body language didn't display it. It felt like she'd learned to hide it, only Annie's gift saw right through her. 'You think they were lying to you.'

A tear fell from Beltana's cheek, testament to the truth of her origins.

Edenites did not cry. 'Not lying. Mistaken. The landscape had completely changed after the flood, so Zyndel and Tahuma took the opportunity to hide. They rebuilt the city on an island far away and used the same name for it to deflect any interest people had in the old stories about the Tree and flowing River that keeps you young. For almost fourteen hundred summers, Zyndel and Tahuma kept Eden a secret. Then one day Zyndel returned here, her happiness broken. Her love partner had been killed and Tahuma … she said he was lost to us. Unable to come home. He'd been stripped of his authority.'

Annie's heart stuttered. She glanced at Nayn, who gave a solemn nod.

'Beltana and I have discussed this before,' he said. 'When it happened to my partner Cherub. She killed someone in defence of our people and could no longer cross the Skin of the World. It can happen. That not-happy time was when Beltana first told me who she was. She told me about Tahuma. We think he must also have ended someone's life.'

The Guardian nodded. 'Zyndel implied he used his power in a way that was not good. I believe there had been another war and after it Zyndel did something powerful to make sure it could never happen again. She said she had moved the passageway to a place where the veiled ones wouldn't find it. The old records and stories would no longer be of use to anyone searching for Eden, so there would be no need to fight over them anymore. Soon after, she left the Garden for the last time. She said she didn't want me to watch her grow old. It had become too heartbreaking and too dangerous for Shamar and Guardians to remain young when no one else did. It was time for her to leave her history behind and begin again in this new place she'd found. She explained the people there had deep wisdom that fitted well with Eden.'

'These "veiled ones". Do you believe they are the same people who killed Dayana?' Annie asked.

She shook her head. 'Impossible. The exiles lived for hundreds of summers, so they seemed like gods to the rest of us, but without access to the Fruit they did grow old eventually. They were showing the signs back when Zyndel was born. It was what made them so desperate; they were running out of time. Even if they didn't perish in the flood they could not have still been alive by the time the second war occurred.'

Memories swirled in Annie's mind. Stories had a way of staying alive long after the original players were gone. The exiled Edenites may have been killed, and Zyndel may have hidden Eden away, yet someone was still searching for it. That whispering voice, ancient, cruel, and desperate. The emotion behind the whisper still felt like it was seeping through her skin, exploring every lead. It made her want to hide. She *had* hidden. With a hiss, she realised she had felt it before. Felt it watching her and she'd run from it. If only she could remember. She needed to remember.

She stood and gave Beltana a tight hug. 'You have been very helpful,' Annie choked out. 'And very brave to relive such painful memories for me. I believe it's my turn now.'

The first Guardian looked her in the eye. 'What will you do, Shamar?'

'I'll go back to the standing stones and face my past. And then I will finish what I should have done a long time ago, because I am *done* with hiding.'

Chapter 17

Fifteen minutes after he'd stormed off Bane returned from his time out. By that time Dallmin had come by to see what all the fuss was about, been sent back to his room to put some undies on, and had returned again fully dressed, including the busker's cap. All or nothing with him, apparently.

Bane scowled at him, still very agitated, and I assumed he would have stayed out longer if the danger to me hadn't drawn him back like an inescapable bungee cord. He nodded to Mick and Tim and then gathered me into an apologetic hug. I could feel the tension in his muscles.

'I'm sorry, Lainie. I never meant to imply that any of what happened was your fault,' he whispered. 'Jake's the one I'm angry with.'

'Tim explained what I've been doing. I'll try to be more attentive, I promise.'

I could feel his shivering ease as he held me in the safety in his arms. He was cold, I noticed proudly, which made sense given he'd been for a walk outside at two am in June. No wonder he'd been trembling. Temperature was important to take note of and I figured if I could start by noticing his, then it might be easier to keep track of my own.

'I wish I could relate to what it is you're going through,' he said, running the tip of his finger along the back of my hand.

How was I supposed to explain something I had barely even noticed until it was pointed out to me? A tiny blossom of heat unfolded under his touch and an infinitesimal fragment of glass caught the light as it erupted onto the surface of my skin, so small even a normal person wouldn't have felt enough pain to realise it was there. It was as if his sensitivity to me was heightened to balance out my own indifference to my body's needs.

I heard Mick exhale and when I glanced up at Tim, he was staring at Bane like he'd never seen him before. Knowing what Bane could do and seeing it in action were two different things. Even Dallmin peered at my hand curiously.

'I think it has to do with dying too many times,' I admitted. 'It seems to have done something to the connection I have with my body. It just doesn't feel all that essential to who I am anymore. Not disposable, exactly, and certainly not a toy, just … not essential. It's a useful tool and I know I need to care for it, but it doesn't define me. In fact, sometimes it's downright annoying, to be honest.' I could see him frowning, so I tried to think of a way to clarify what I meant before he got the wrong idea. 'Like shoes,' I suggested. 'Do you remember Kat? She left at the end of Year Ten. She used to love shoes. She had over forty pairs. I asked why she was so obsessed with them and she told me she needed a pair for each mood she was in. Those shoes defined her personality, or at least they helped her to express it.' Looking down at my feet, I curled my toes self-consciously. 'In case you haven't noticed, I tend to forget shoes these days. They annoy me.'

'Are you saying your body annoys you?'

'Sometimes, I guess. It's not like I'm suicidal, I just … can't really be bothered with it all the time.'

'I see. You mean it's a bit like owning a car. When it's shiny and new you tend to be a bit precious about it, but once it's been in a few too many accidents you don't care about driving it through the paddocks anymore.'

I grinned at his analogy. He was still such a townie. As if anyone who grew up on a farm ever cared about driving through paddocks.

With poignant delicacy, he tucked a strand of my crazy aprés-midnight hairdo back behind my ear, then leaned in and brushed my neck with his lips. Tiny bolts of lightning zapped through my veins at his touch.

'The thing is,' he whispered as a thrill of pleasure swept down my spine, 'I happen to adore your Ferrari. It's not damaged, or worn out, or even scratched. Its duco is polished to stunning perfection and its engine purrs like a kitten.'

He was right. I was purring a little.

'Hokaaaay,' Tim interrupted. 'I think she gets the point now. I think we all do, actually. I would tell you to get a room, but I guess you already did. Let's go, Dallmin.'

'No,' I protested, just as Bane said yes. He crossed his arms. 'I won't do that to you, or to me,' I insisted, hoping he understood.

Tim waited for a few seconds while neither of us spoke, and then frowned. 'Oh, come on, Lainie, this is Bane we're talking about. He's the very embodiment of self-control, if that's what you're worried about. You know he won't be able to sleep at all unless he's sure you're safe.'

'He isn't the problem,' I said.

'I am a bit,' Bane admitted.

My eyes caught his and he nodded, giving me permission to explain.

'Tim, aside from … traditional reasons, we can't sleep together yet because I'm pretty much, well, guaranteed to fall pregnant if we do. It's a Cherub thing.' Strangely, I could feel my cheeks starting to heat even though I didn't actually feel at all embarrassed. It was as if my brain was as unfussed as any Edenite, while my body was still trying to react like I would have a few years ago.

The reactions from around the room were varied. Mick looked unsurprised, which was unsurprising, Tim looked devastated on our behalf, and Dallmin looked like someone had slapped him in the face.

'And before you ask where the rest of my rabbit-warren-sized extended family is, let me clarify that once the next Cherub is born, this hyper-fertility of ours shuts down. I can't lie. I'm somewhat looking forward to that phase,' I said.

Tim glanced over at Bane, then back at me, confused. 'I still think you should give Bane a little more credit. He'd never do anything you don't want,' he muttered.

'That's the problem,' I whimpered. 'What I want. He's aligned to it a bit too well.' Straightening my shoulders, I took a determined breath and tried to explain. 'Let me put it to you this way. Dallmin is physically changing to become more like the humans on this side of the boundary, and Bane and I are built to be more like the humans in Eden.'

By the confused look on his face, I realised I was going to have to be even more blunt. Thankfully Bane intervened.

'What she's trying to say is that we could have easily gone for seven hundred years without the slightest urge to have sex until we met the right partner. I don't know what it's like for you when you meet some-one, Tim, but back when Lainie and I first started to connect emotion-ally … let's just say it was a revelation for me to realise what it was I wanted. Or in fact that I wanted anything at all. I can't tell you how many cold showers I've taken since she's been back.'

Even the Eden part of my brain recognised how astounding it was for Bane to be so openly honest. He'd certainly come a long way since high school, when half his time had been spent staring down at his shoes. Apparently, the change had been recent too, judging by the expression on Tim's face. He looked both stunned and proud, almost like he wanted to hug him. He chose not to, sadly.

'Well,' he said instead. 'I guess there's one obvious solution. I'll have to sleep in here.'

A knife flipped into Bane's hand from nowhere, held toward Tim in clear warning. I may have been the only person who noticed his flicker of a smile; everyone else's attention was on the blade.

'And *there's* the guy I've come to know and love over the last three years,' he continued. 'I knew it was only a matter of time until you reap-peared, my grouchy friend.'

In the corner by the door, I could see Mick standing with his arms crossed, trying to hide a grin as Tim backed up a step, despite his air of confidence. Good to know the policeman could read the situation properly. Bane was teasing, in his own twisted, threat-of-violence way.

Unfortunately, Tim wasn't.

'All I meant was that the obvious solution is the old-fashioned one. You two need a chaperone.'

My evil sidekick literally rubbed his hands together in anticipation of his self-imposed duty.

An hour later I stared at the ceiling, trying to recall the lullaby my mother had sung to me.

'Bane?' I whispered, peering over to where he was stretched out on the floor on the other side of our sleeping supervisor. As expected, he was wide awake too, flipping one of Jake's coins around his knuckles. He knew exactly what those coins signified and was clearly preoccupied with thinking through every possible scenario Jake could use to get to me.

'Yeah?'

'Why didn't you tell me Jake could sense where I am?'

The coin fell from his fingers and he didn't answer.

'You didn't want to frighten me,' I guessed, answering my own question.

He turned to me, grey eyes turning charcoal in the dim light. 'I would have told you straight away if I thought it might frighten you. Nothing seems to frighten you, which makes you reckless.'

'What have I done that's reckless?' I asked, leaning up on one elbow to glare at him.

He glared right back. 'You've just spent a week pursuing the man who shot you, poisoned you, and is compelled to keep going until he kills you. Again.'

'So what have we been doing all week if you knew he would keep running away from me?'

Silence.

'You think I'm safer while we keep him running,' I realised.

'Keep the enemy too busy to plan an attack. Keep him off balance and guessing while we give Mick time to investigate.'

'That was your plan? Why do you get to be the one to plan?'

'I don't. You said you felt the need to go after Jake, so we've been following your lead. I trust your instincts. My thing was more of a back-up tactic.'

'You still could have just told me that.'

'I was planning to. I just ...'

It was tricky to see in the dark, but I knew his body language pretty well.

'You're jealous!' I realised, and then lowered my voice back to a whisper as Tim stirred. 'You're jealous that Jake can sense me. First Noah, now Jake.'

'I'm not jealous of Noah,' he blurted. Then he sighed. 'Yeah. I am a bit. This link I have to you, it's intimate. That Jake can feel you the way I do … I can't even think about it without wanting to hit something.'

I thought about that for a while. I could feel other Cherubim, and Bane was right; it was intimate, like a comforting presence always in the back of my mind. Noah was currently a long way behind me and to my left. Subtle and reassuring. I had to concentrate to feel Nathaniel, but he was there too. I wished I could feel Bane's presence the same way.

'Bane?'

'What now? You should get some sleep.' He still sounded like he wanted to hit something.

'I like that you're jealous. It feels nice.'

He let out an almost-laugh and I knew I had him. 'That doesn't sound very Eden-like.'

'No, it doesn't,' I agreed.

'Go to sleep.'

I really tried to, but a couple of minutes later we were still both lying there, staring at each other.

'Bane?' I whispered again. 'Run through the reasons why curing Tim's snoring is essential to protecting Eden,' I begged. 'Please?'

Delicious icy water embraced my body as I hit the surface of the river. My breath longed to escape as laughter, but I dutifully held it in while I let the current tug my lethargy away downstream. Yet even without breathing, I felt as if the last week of suffocation had suddenly ended. Bane knew I needed the river badly and so he'd stopped by the bridge in Nalong without me even asking. Mick had waved goodbye to us out of his car window as he continued on to the police station.

Songs of life echoed all around me and I revelled in the energy and healing that coursed through my system as I floated gently to the surface again. Tangled folds of my dress pulled at my legs, pleading with me to let it go and play on its own. I started to shed the annoying fabric before remembering I shouldn't. So many stupid rules.

A sudden wave engulfed me when Tim dive-bombed in off the bridge. Hypocrite. Laughing, I splashed and then dunked him before looking around for Bane. He was still standing on the bridge, holding an umbrella and saying something to Dallmin with a stern look on his face. Dallmin nodded obediently, took the umbrella, and sat down with his legs dangling over the edge, looking a little bit wistful.

'Did I do it again?' I asked Tim as he swam in lazy circles around me.

'Yes, but we all knew it was coming, and it's kind of handy the way Bane can sense if it's a safe spot to jump in. Don't worry about it.'

'I made sure the car was completely stopped, I'm sure of it.'

He laughed. 'Yes, you did. Just. He didn't even have to use the child locks.'

'So why isn't he swimming?'

'Because,' he said in an exaggeratedly deep voice, using his best Christopher Lee impersonation, 'your chaperone forbade it!'

I dunked him again for that.

By the time I decided I'd swallowed enough of the life-sustaining muddy elixir to ease the worst of my cravings, Tim was shivering on the bank where Bane was waiting for me with a towel. A minor fight broke out between them over who should help to dry me off, so I crept behind them and nicked the other towel lying on the grass, flicking Tim across the buttocks before Bane looped his towel around me and tugged me into his arms. I should have known I could never sneak up on him.

'Hey, not fair!' Tim protested as he pulled me away. I stomped on his foot before Bane accidentally hurt him. Despite his soft smile, I knew my Guardian was a mere hair's breadth away from violence if anyone was foolish enough to try to manhandle me. Anyone but himself, at least.

'It's okay, Bane, I can dry myself. I'm not a baby,' I said, stepping away and poking my tongue out at Tim for the sheer sake of irony. They both laughed.

'You sleep like one,' Tim commented, shrugging back into his shirt. 'Do you realise you both slept the entire four hours from Geelong? I only had Dallmin to talk to and he started feeling queasy from eating too many marshmallows an hour into the trip. I had to take them away from him and then he got bored and wouldn't stop with the questions.'

'Jake can't get to her when she's travelling that fast in a car,' Bane explained. 'Stony' didn't begin to describe his expression.

'Bane,' I scolded. 'Whenever Jake turns up, I'll deal with it. I'm not afraid of him anymore. Actually, I'm kind of in a hurry to get it over with,' I said, squeezing out my hair.

He looked ill. 'You're never afraid, Lainie. That's part of what worries me. I heard what you said to him, you know, while I was fumbling to get the stupid hotel door card to work.'

I winced. I was hoping he'd missed that. No wonder he'd been so angry.

'What did she say?' Tim asked, drying his ear with a corner of the towel.

'She challenged him to a sword fight,' he explained through gritted teeth.

'Get out of town!' Tim looked ecstatic.

I could practically feel Bane's growl rumbling under my bare feet.

Tim took a small step back. 'I mean … Lainie, how could you? That was a terrible idea.' Wisely, he chose not to comment any further and started to back away toward the car instead.

Grey eyes pinned me in silent accusation. He wasn't going to let it go.

'Fine. You can be my champion if you want. Try not to hurt him too badly.'

The eyes bulged in disbelief.

'I mean Jake. Not the demon. The demon needs to be banished, obviously. I think Noah and I have to do that part ourselves, though.'

Confusion coloured the irises.

'Jake is still in there somewhere, Bane. He's not like us. He's not a demon that has been born into a human body. Rabisu's possessed him. It's wrong and unnatural, but it gives us the advantage.'

He crossed his arms. Crossly. And blinked rain out of his eyes. 'What advantage?'

'I'm still working on that.'

He rubbed his temples. 'You said you had another weapon to use against his kind. An amulet?'

'Yeah.' My mind tapped its fingertips together in glee. *Aamuuulet.*

A hand waved in front of my eyes, bringing my attention back.

'Right, sorry. I only pretended to know anything about it.'

'Well, then we have a problem.'

It was my turn to look confused.

'How can I be your champion when I can't touch him and have no weapon I can use against him?' he asked, putting his hands in his back pockets, looking unusually vulnerable. 'I charged at him pretty hard and it did absolutely nothing.'

'Except make Jake nearly pee himself.'

A small gratified gleam lit his eyes. 'So I guess Rabisu is still limited by Jake's pathetic cowardice,' he construed.

'Whereas you aren't limited at all by mine,' I happily pointed out.

Before he could unravel my logic, I took full advantage of Tim's distance and threw my arms around Bane's neck, kissing him so thoroughly that by the time we finally drove away Bane wasn't the crankiest one in the car.

Our homecoming was overladen with hugs. Walking through the door was hampered somewhat by Aunt Lily throwing herself at me with so much enthusiasm Bane had to take a deep breath. It had only been a week since we'd left on our futile search, but I'd missed her more than I'd realised.

'Lainie, you look exhausted. Come into the kitchen. I have some upstream water for you and a fruit salad. Mostly local and definitely safe,' she added, glancing at Bane as he pulled off his muddy shoes at the doorstep.

I stumbled gratefully down the hallway.

'There are also some dry clothes for you in the cottage,' she called after me. 'You're sopping wet. It's not raining that hard ... you went swimming again, didn't you?'

There was no point answering her. Instead, I went straight to the glass of water waiting for me next to the sink, sculling it down before climbing up and stretching out on my back across the kitchen table. The familiar table meant home. And rest. And family. I shut my eyes in bliss.

Noah's voice intruded on my basking. 'Oh crap, she didn't die again, did she?'

I refused to be disturbed, so he took the opportunity to balance an apple between my eyes. All I needed was a glass coffin and a few dwarves.

Bane came in and woke me with his magical kiss before the evil witch had a chance to get his boots off at the front door. The nasty old crone took one look at us kissing as he entered the room and started pelting us with the marshmallows he'd confiscated from Dallmin earlier. I took no notice, but Noah ducked in front of us and caught one in his mouth.

'I've missed you, Tim! How'd the quest go?' he asked messily.

'Oh, you know. As expected. The heroine fell in love with the village boy, the elf charmed the peasants with his magic flute, the brave warrior went dress shopping, and the Nameless Sword of Great Power got put up for sale on eBay.'

'Village boy?' Bane grumbled, his warm lips still close to mine.

Suddenly I was giggling too hard to keep kissing so instead I jumped up, collected a few flying marshmallows, and began to juggle them. Just then Dallmin walked in, so I tossed him a few too. He looked at them in his hands for a few seconds, trying to decide if he wanted to eat them or juggle them. He chose juggling, so I tossed another one into his open mouth as a reward.

'Nameless sword?' Noah asked as he snatched my tiny flying pillows out of the air one by one simply to annoy me.

'Do you happen to know what its name is?' Tim asked hopefully.

The green-eyed Cherub shrugged one shoulder.

'I'm beginning to think "The Sword of Damocles" is becoming appropriate,' I grumbled, feeling my sense of fun melt away.

Tim made a sympathetic noise and tried to cheer me up again. 'Maybe it's a Vorpal Sword, like the one that killed the Jabberwocky. Does it go "snicker-snack"?'

'Not even a little bit, no,' Noah replied. 'It's a very quiet, well-behaved sword most of the time, even when it's spinning. It sang when Nathaniel was born though,' he said in a dreamy tone.

A vivid memory of the sword's crystal song cut through me like the cry of a bird on a winter's dawn. Crisp, pure notes that cleansed the cobwebs from my soul beckoned me to follow. How *joyful* it would be to follow that song. How had I ever been afraid of its power before? The sword was clean and pure and innocent. No wonder the demon was so desperate to destroy it. I had to get it back. I couldn't let him harm it, no matter what the cost. The sword was born of another realm, a place where everything was perfectly clean, and perfectly perfect. Even more so than Eden. Perhaps if I could follow its song, I could find where Jake had taken it. I closed my eyes and listened with my soul. A whisper from the north called to me, so I started to follow its thread until something tugged me back again.

A threat, lurking in the shadows.

Heavy intent. A malevolent spirit searching for a way past. Past what? I had no idea. I could feel it prowling. Hunting.

I opened my eyes with a gasp.

'Jake can't find his way to the cave while he's bodiless,' I declared to a quiet room. The truth of the revelation settled like a hand on my shoulder. 'Perhaps … Bane, what's wrong? Why are you holding me up?' His hand was gripping my shoulder and his other arm was wrapped around my waist. I turned to see him staring at me like I'd grown an extra head. There was sweat dripping down his temples.

'I'm holding you up because you fainted. Where have you been?' he asked, shaken.

'Been?'

'You went … I don't know. You disappeared.'

'I must have blacked out. I don't remember even feeling dizzy.'

Noah shook his head. 'He's right, Lainie. You didn't just faint, you also moved. Your body stayed here, but you went somewhere else.'

I stood up straight and took a step to the left so that when Bane turned to face me he wouldn't be able to see the ecstatic expression on Tim's face. That guy was going to get us both into so much trouble.

'How long was I gone?' I asked.

Bane took a shaky breath. 'Ages.'

Noah rolled his eyes. 'About fifteen seconds, tops.'

'I could still feel you, I just couldn't feel *where* you were,' Bane explained. 'Almost as disturbing as whenever you cross the boundary.'

Tim gave a low fake cough. 'Event horizon,' he mumbled, then coughed again.

I smiled. That's what I'd always wanted to call it.

'What exactly did you do?' Noah asked, popping another marshmallow in his mouth.

'Nothing! I thought I felt the sword, so I started to follow it. Like a scent. Then I felt the demon. It's hunting for the cave. I don't understand why it can't find it, given it's been there before.'

'Perhaps there's some ethereal complication,' Tim suggested. 'The world might not look the same on that plane as it does in real life.'

'Could you do it again?' Noah asked me. 'Follow the scent of the sword?'

All the colour disappeared from Bane's face. It looked like he had a storm of inappropriate vocabulary brewing, depending on my answer.

'Nope,' I lied. I needed time to think and Bane needed time to come to terms with the inevitable truth that I was going to at least try. We needed the sword back. It was that simple. 'I'm going to go and put my stuff away,' I said, and promptly bailed on the whole discussion.

Chapter 18

Later that afternoon I was snoozing on the sofa while Aunt Lily sat at the computer doing the accounts, cursing Noah's handwriting, when Jake made another attempt to breach our defences. This time, it wasn't a sneaky dream-walk or planned poisoning. This time he simply drove his stolen Barina up to our front gate, opened it, and sped off toward the state park before any of us realised what was going on. Bane and Noah had taken the ute down to the gully paddock to gas out a rabbit warren, much too far away for me to even consider waiting for them. Tim and Dallmin were playing carefully selected non-violent video games in the study and didn't even notice. By the time I reached the shed, Tessa was shoving her bare feet into her boots. Her shirt was unbuttoned so she'd probably cut poor Nathaniel off mid-feed when she heard me call out. I didn't have time to ask. I raced through the shed door only to find that the key to my dirt bike was missing. The keys to everything were missing. Of course. If Jake could move things, he could travel here and hide keys. I began to hunt around, hoping he'd had enough difficulty manipulating them that he hadn't moved them far. Then again, he could have hidden them under the concrete floor for all I knew of his abilities.

'Stop. Think. You have more tricks than he does,' Tessa reminded me. 'You don't even need keys.' She shoved a helmet over her wonky ponytail and fumbled closed a shirt button. Then she swung her leg over the seat of the little Honda, gripped the handlebars and looked at me expectantly.

I grinned.

Three silky Words later, both bikes roared to life. Mud and gravel spun through the air as we followed the fresh tracks up the hill. I even gave one of Bane's cameras a wave as I sped past. Of course Aunt Lily would be watching. The Barina had managed a decent head start, but Jake had completely missed our usual shortcut along the river. Instead, he was flying along the track through the state park and we only caught sight of him after the bridge. He must have noticed us because he sped up, sliding into the ruts and causing hideous scraping noises. He left the track so suddenly that Tessa almost overshot the turn, her back wheel sliding on a steep angle as she banked hard. The hill was covered in rocks big enough to slow us down and the poor Barina copped a few good dents as it bounced across the rough terrain. I wove between obstacles, trying to come up with a safe way to stop the chase. Stopping the car would be simple. Blow out the tyres. Choke the fuel line. What then? What if he'd brought a weapon? Trying to use Words to protect myself or anyone else had never worked. Was this his plan all along? Lure me out here and then change his intent from wanting to reach the cave to trying to kill me? It didn't change what I had to do. He was heading straight for the one place I could never allow him to get to. I squinted at his right front tyre. A Word flipped from my chest to my tongue. I opened my mouth to speak … and then the world jolted and the bike disappeared from under me. I kept moving though, flying. Falling. Landing. Something hit me, pain sheeting like electricity through my head and across my shoulder. I realised I was rolling. Rocks hit my helmet like hailstones.

And everything went black.

Jake was still moving. I couldn't see him, but I could feel him drilling into my soul with every metre he moved closer to the cave. I tried to open my mouth to speak the Word that would blow out his tyres, only my face was numb. Stupid, cumbersome body. How was I supposed to do my job, tied down to this lump of flesh? I needed to see. Needed to speak. Needed to breathe. With supreme effort, I dragged in some air. It felt like a lungful even though I knew it wasn't. That was okay. I didn't need much. Just enough to exhale a single Word. All four tyres blew. I could feel it. Feel him stop moving. Feel when he got out of the car and started to run. Still northward. Still straining to reach Eden. Dimly, I heard Tessa shouting my name. She was lifting my wrist, checking for a pulse. She didn't need to because I had never felt so alive. Words sizzled behind my teeth. I had more tricks than Jake did. All I needed to do was think outside the box. Think outside my body. With my brain this numb it was actually very simple.

I watched him from above and tried not to get too excited about my first real out-of-body experience even though I wished I could video the whole thing for Tim. I tried to look at myself, hoping for something ghostly, but there was nothing to look at. I had top-down perspective only, and Jake was a little ant ready for me to squish. One Word and a large tree branch fell in front of him, missing him by inches. Another tripped phrase and the rocks beneath his feet began to roll. This was too easy. I felt like a conductor, commanding the elements to obey. With a smile, I remembered the rock art Tessa had discovered when we'd first started exploring the cave system all those years ago. The picture of the Cherubim standing on the top of a hill, arms stretched up, and a flock of birds descending on the intruders. Six more Words spun from my barely moving lips and squawking filled the air as hundreds of magpies answered. Not even a demon could withstand angry magpies. I watched as Jake bolted for the cover of the tree line, arms over his head as the creatures swooped and pecked and slashed at him. At my request they drove him on, steering him toward a huge manna gum that overlooked the river. As he squatted at its base, the birds fell silent. Eerily silent. Each one found a neighbouring tree to land in. Watching, waiting. The wind grew still. So still that the rustle from the branches above him made Jake flinch. He peered up from beneath his elbows. A grey paw flexed, stretching out its black talons. The beast shook itself awake, unimpressed at the disruption to its slumber. Thick fur shuddered along the creature's spine as it peered through the leaves at the meal so conveniently huddled below. A fluffy white ear twitched. Its pale muzzle drew back into a snarl, revealing fangs not found on its gentle leaf-chewing cousin. One talon tapped against the branch. Tap. Tap. Ta-tap-a-tap-tap.

That was its only warning. Jake didn't move fast enough. The drop bear roared and launched itself off the branch, its fangs skimming Jake's neck while its claws tore the shirt from his back. In all our years of PE together I'd never seen Jake run so fast. The very real, very carnivorous

Thylarctos plummetus took a couple of lumbering steps but didn't chase him. Damn. Jake must have had Vegemite for brekkie.

It wasn't until Jake had crossed over the river and was limping back along the road toward town that I was comfortable enough to stop supervising him. Problem was, as soon as I turned my attention from him the road disappeared. So did the entire state park. There was no sky or trees or river. There was no *me*. That was when I realised I had no idea how to get back to my body. I couldn't feel it, and I couldn't find it.

Chapter 19

Viridian eyes stared from a face that shimmered with a thousand shifting colours. The creature flying toward me was spectacular. Beauty, perfected in shape-shifting form. Iridescent wings the size of windsurfer sails rippled as they guided the creature through the misty haze to where I floated.

'Where are you going, Lainie? Bane is falling to pieces back there. What happened? Is Jake around somewhere?' Noah's voice emerged from the exotic creature's mouth and yet that somehow seemed entirely natural. He looked like a creature from a Barbie movie, which thankfully seemed to have escaped his notice. He scanned our hazy surroundings. 'And where the hell are we, anyway?'

Instead of answering, I threw myself at him, clutching at the familiar feel of his alien form. Without hesitation, he folded me into his arms and hugged me. We spun in the air-that-was-not-air while I wished I could answer even one of his questions.

'Can you take us back?' I asked.

'Easily. It's staying here that I'm struggling with. Tessa is shouting at me. I feel like I'm being stretched like a rubber band. Hold on, I get the feeling the spring-back will be a heck of a ride.'

∽

Tim's upside-down face met my snapped-open eyes. I could see straight up his nose, which made me laugh. The flight back to my body had been kind of fun. Turning my head away from the disturbing view, I looked around for Bane. He was sitting in the corner of the kitchen on the floor with his knees tucked up to his chest. Ashen grey eyes locked on mine. He had tears streaming down his face. I couldn't remember ever seeing him cry before and it broke my heart. What was going on?

'What am I doing up on the kitchen table?' I asked, confused. Memories of flying dissolved into a dream. 'Did I fall asleep?'

'For a little while,' Tim replied, his lips twitching. 'Better lie still until Bane makes sure you're okay.'

'She's fine now,' Bane rasped, staring at me with a hurt look.

Tim helped me to sit up. Dizziness ruled for a few seconds. My body felt so unfamiliar that I looked down to make certain I was in the right one. Fuzzy curls of brown hair stuck to my cheek. Yep. That was definitely mine. On the floor below me, Noah was lying with his head cradled in Tessa's lap. Dallmin was cuddling Nathaniel, humming a quiet tune, and Aunt Lily was standing by the phone as if about to make a call. She was giving me a worried frown. Rain beat against the kitchen window.

Tessa scowled at me. 'What happened, Lainie? Where did you go?'

Go? Oh, right. Jake's Hail Mary dash in the Barina. Oh, and that stack. No wonder Bane was upset.

'Aunt Lily, you should call Mick. Jake's walking toward town trying to scum a lift. Mick might get lucky and pick him up first.'

She nodded, but didn't move.

'Tessa. Tell me the truth. How's my bike?' I asked, jumping down with a wobble. Tim steadied me with a hand on my elbow.

'Totalled. You got the front tyre caught between two rocks and I don't think there's a single piece of it that isn't bent. It suits you perfectly,' she snapped.

'Well, listen. I've been riding these hills my whole life, but it isn't exactly easy trying to connect with sacred Words of power and negotiate a path through that sort of terrain at the same time, you know.' I sat down in the nearest vacant chair and looked around at the room full of narrowed eyes. They waited for more of an explanation.

'Why is everyone so mad? I did what I had to do. Jake was heading straight for the cave.'

'If you could just go into a trance and attack him with magpies, why did you need to chase him at all?' Noah asked. 'And why didn't you tell me we could do that?'

'I didn't know!'

'So you just, what, fell out of your body when you knocked yourself out?'

'Exactly.'

Even Tim looked disconcerted at that.

Dallmin stopped humming. 'It may be because you have died so often lately,' he suggested. 'Your stickiness to your body is not working properly. Like this clever stuff that keeps Nathaniel's bib together at the back.'

'Velcro?'

'Velcro.' Dallmin nodded, practising the new word. 'It gets fuzzy and won't stick.'

Tessa looked intrigued. 'And it probably doesn't help that a human body isn't a Cherub's natural form,' she added. 'Humans are welded to our bodies, while you only have Velcro.'

'And mine is full of fuzz because I died?' I glared back at Noah. 'If that's true, how did you find me so easily?'

'Easily? It took me over *two hours*. I could tap into a vision of Jake and I could feel you following him, only I didn't know how to get to you. Bane was that frantic, I suggested he knock me out to see if that would work. Which was when Tessa sat me down and we went through the breathing techniques we learned in antenatal classes. It's possible I fell asleep. Either way, it worked. I brought you back.'

'You did. Thanks, Noah. Wait, two hours? So Jake will be long gone. Damn.'

Tim pulled out a chair and sat on it backward. 'Tell me everything,' he begged. 'Astral projection could be a very handy skill, you know. What was it like?'

'It was confusing,' I said. 'You were right, everything looked different. As soon as I stopped focusing on Jake as a point of reference, everything familiar disappeared.' I looked at Noah, hoping he had something useful to add.

'It was colourful,' he supplied.

I grinned. 'You looked like a sugar plum fairy.'

His face paled. Noah wasn't built for supernatural shenanigans. Well, maybe he was, but he clearly wasn't comfortable with it. I understood completely.

Tim looked thoughtful. 'If you used Jake as a point of reference, do you think you could do a similar thing with the sword? Maybe you can track it down without even having to leave the safety of this room.'

Before I could answer, Bane got to his feet and left, slamming the front door on his way out.

'Give him a few minutes,' my aunt advised when I started to follow.

I turned back to Tim, who was wincing at his lack of tact once he remembered I'd died in this very room. Under his watch.

'I need a cup of tea,' I decided, clicking on the kettle and pulling out a few mugs from the cupboard. 'Who else wants something?'

Silence answered, so I turned back to see what the problem was. They were all watching me with varied expressions. Noah looked ill, Tim looked even more awed than usual, Aunt Lily looked like she wanted to cry, and Tessa still looked cross.

'Are you sure you're feeling okay?' Aunt Lily asked.

'Of course. Why wouldn't I be?'

'Because according to Bane you fractured your ribs, broke your wrist, and cracked two vertebrae in your neck. It's a little weird watching you make tea,' she replied.

I stood there dangling a teabag from my fingers, while my other hand reached behind my neck to feel for an injury that wasn't there. I tried to think of what to say. Some wisecrack that would relieve the tension in their eyes. I had nothing.

The rain had stopped, leaving only the sound of water gurgling into the tank by the time I plucked up the courage to look for my Guardian. I eventually found him sitting against an aged fruit tree in our orchard, staring at nothing. Very sternly. A few metres away I could see his knife embedded in an innocent pear tree. The poor thing had taken a few hits.

A light breeze played with my hair as I climbed up to the lower branches of the winter-bare apricot tree. I scooted along and leaned down over him. Then I carefully dropped my little gift down next to his feet.

'What is that?'

'An apology,' I answered, leaning out as far as I could along the branch. It bent a little, so I wisely backed up again. No point making things worse between us by falling out of a tree.

He picked up the tiny Cherub I'd made from twisted bark and chicken feathers and studied it grimly. 'It looks fragile,' he pointed out, smoothing out a feathered wing with the tip of his finger.

'It's tougher than it looks,' I insisted.

'It could fall apart at any moment. With absolutely no warning.'

'That's why it has this.' I dropped another little figurine down to him, hoping like crazy it would hold together. Otherwise, my analogy wouldn't look terribly comforting.

He picked up the tiny bark Guardian and frowned at it. I'd made it a little green shirt out of a leaf, and a tiny knife from a sliver of stone I'd found on the gravel driveway.

'Waste of time,' he dismissed. 'You should have made another Cherub instead.' He went back to examining the Cherub's wings.

Swinging down from the branch, I sat down in front of him with my legs crossed. Out of the corner of my eye, I could see Tim pretending to feed the chooks not far away, trying to look inconspicuous. I ignored him.

'Bane, please tell me you're not really jealous of Noah.'

'I *am* jealous,' he snapped, leaning away from me. Anger and pain clouded his eyes as he looked away.

'But we—'

'I know, Lainie,' he interrupted. 'I'm not jealous in that way. I'm just a little pissed off that he's so much better at my job than I am,' he explained, staring down at the toy in his hands.

'What do you mean?'

'I mean that each time I've failed you, he's picked up the pieces. You don't need me. You never have.'

'You just healed—'

'You'd be better off if I hadn't. At least, not all of it. Pain exists for a reason. A bit of pain might teach you to be more careful.'

That was probably true. Harsh, but true. 'So next time, leave a bit of pain behind. Enough to—'

'Never,' he snapped, offended at the suggestion even though he was the one who brought it up. He tried to straighten the wonky Cherub wings. One fell off. 'Do you know how often Tessa's healed Noah since this all started? Seven times. Just seven. They've actually been counting. And most of those were minor scrapes and bruises he picked up doing farm work during the years you were safe in Eden.'

I narrowed my eyes. Bloody male ego. 'So this isn't actually about me at all, then? This is all to do with winning. If I die again, you lose points, is that it?'

His head snapped up, eyes flashing. In all the years I'd known him, and after all the hideous and disrespectful things we'd ever said and done to each other, he'd never looked so hurt. At that moment I realised I couldn't have been more wrong. It was a good thing I was paying attention because a moment later the hurt was gone, replaced by cold indifference. He didn't speak. Almost as if he wanted me to believe I was right.

Fighting back a sob, I almost fled to the river. Almost. Eden had made me childlike, but I was not a child. With extreme effort, I gathered my tattered will together and made myself choose better. No melodramatic storming off in tears. No drama queen running away, hoping he would relent and come find me. That would be a reaction of my own ego, and I respected him far too much to simply react. The ice in my chest made it difficult to breathe, so I sat very still and tried to focus on how to fix things. All I could see were Bane's slumped shoulders because his head now hung so low that his dark hair hid his eyes.

'If it isn't that, then help me understand,' I begged.

He closed his eyes and bit his lower lip and I wondered if he was praying. When he opened them again, he looked desperate for answers. 'How is it that Tessa hasn't become some arrogant overprotective alpha-male bastard? How has she managed to avoid it? Would she be different if she'd had to watch Noah die?'

I sat up straighter. 'Are you kidding? She pulls the overprotective alpha crap on me *all the time.* Just last night she tried to ban me from watching that documentary about serial killers. I thought she would send me to my room.'

'And yet she somehow still manages not to be disrespectful toward Noah. Not often, anyhow.'

I raised my eyebrows at his implication, inviting him to elaborate.

'That day when Noah's mum … when you were compelled to stop her, I knew … I *knew* something bad would happen if you went into the cave. I tried to stop you, remember?'

I nodded.

'I respected your wishes and your authority, and I let you go.' A brisk breeze shook leftover rain down from the branches above us. 'I spent a long time regretting that decision.'

So many arguments tried to fight their way past my lips that I didn't know where to begin. Bane took hold of my wrist and hooked a finger under my bracelet. The word 'Shalom' had all but worn away.

'And yet, because of this, I knew I'd made the right one. All I'd wanted for you was peace and safety, and that was exactly what you had in Eden. I had to remind myself of that every single day. Remind myself that what you needed was far more important than what I wanted.'

Every argument I'd been about to launch fizzled away. 'And when I came back?'

'Since you've been back I feel as if I've been pushed into a role I don't understand. I trained hard for three years, learning to fight, learning to guard and defend. All so that if you ever returned I could keep you safe while you do whatever you need to do. Only none of my skills have helped us in the slightest. All it's done is turn me into exactly the type of person you used to accuse me of being back in school.'

'A broody-psychopathic-Baney-rabbit-dobber who spoils everyone's fun?'

'How is it you can't remember where your shoes are, but you can remember that entire name tag you wrote me for the Year Nine career info evening?'

'It took me five tries to get it all to fit on the sticker. It's etched into my brain now. And you aren't psychopathic.'

'You didn't see me when I was tied to that tree.'

I winced.

'I'm supposed to protect you, aren't I? I'm designed to be a fighter. When you disappeared today, I wanted to tear the world apart. I wanted to smash something. Anything. That violence, it wasn't … it wasn't who I want to be.'

There wasn't a single thing I could think of to say to that. My eyes drifted north toward the place where there was never any violence. To where everyone got to be who they wanted to be. 'What if we've been wrong this whole time?' I mused. 'What if your job isn't just to protect me from *physical* harm?'

He folded his arms. 'I can assure you that if I had any supernatural talent to protect you from spiritual harm, it would have been well and truly triggered by now. I healed you and it wasn't enough. I was useless back there, Lainie.'

No. You weren't. But I couldn't tell him because I was too busy staring at the hand he was holding out to me. An offer for me to see his point of view. Since my return, I'd deliberately avoided using my gift on him. Not only did it feel impolite, but I'd never felt the need to. Only now he was asking me to. Did I really want to know? I swallowed.

'You asked me to help you understand,' he reminded, fingers twitching.

I licked my lips and tried to stop my hand from shaking as I took up the challenge. His fingers were warm, as usual. His grip firm.

Bright images seared into my brain: the sight of my body crumpled on the rocky track. My wrist looked gruesome, bent that way. Bane had pulled off my helmet with hands that were on fire with the need to heal me, and he had, cradling my face between his hands and focusing his breathing to stop his own dizzy reaction. Then he'd searched for me.

'Don't go where I can't help you!' he begged, eyes closed, with his face turned up and to the west. 'Come back!' The cracked cry tore from his throat. A cyclone of fear and self-loathing ripped through him. Even the hollow loneliness of the past three years was better than facing the stark reality that I might be gone forever. All his thoughts were filled with one regret.

He should have made me return to Eden.

Slapped with the sheer manifest integrity of his emotions, I fell backward, breaking the contact. Mud slid between my fingers as I tried to stop the world from spinning so fast.

Bane's strained whisper fell. 'I can't do this anymore, Lainie. I quit. I just want to get on with my life.' Slackened fingers dropped the tiny Guardian toy, and he looked away.

'I don't believe you,' I countered. 'You think you're the only reason I'm here and not in Eden. And that if you push me away I'll go back there and be safe. Aren't you forgetting the whole obligation to protect Eden thing I have going on? You promised you'd help me with that. No backsies.'

'You don't need me. Even if Jake is stupid enough to come back, you're more than capable of dealing with him. You managed to boot him out of here while you were *unconscious*. One way or another you'll get the sword back and then return to Eden and I'll … be free from all this.' With a clenched jaw, he poured all his anger into his words, which left none for his body language. 'You were right from the beginning. I should have listened. I'm trapped here. I've sacrificed everything for you, but you don't need me, and I've had enough.'

The same wind that had blown through the valley for millions of years lifted my helmet-mussed hair, as if asking permission to play with it.

I blew him a raspberry. 'You used to do it better when we were at school. Back then when you pushed me away it was much more believable. You've gone rusty.'

He pressed his lips together and said nothing.

'I won't leave you,' I insisted.

Menacing eyes flashed. 'You already have. And it only took an instant.' He was clutching the toy Cherub like he wanted to tear it apart and couldn't quite bring himself to do it.

'It was an accident! I didn't know I was leaving. I don't want to leave you.' My voice cracked as I fought to contain my panic. I had no idea how to regain his trust.

'I don't … believe you,' he croaked. 'Higher things are calling you away from me. Things that I have no right to, and no place in.'

Pain gripped me as I heard the stark truth in his words, but I had even more truth than that. I drew his hand to my cheek, kissing the inside of his wrist. He still refused to look at me.

'I climbed a mountain to return to you,' I reminded him. 'I died. Repeatedly. Painfully. Not for Eden. For you.' He winced, and I mentally slapped my forehead. Probably not the smartest argument. 'I *want* to be with you. I won't leave you again.'

'You can't promise that,' he choked, silver tears falling on to the Cherub's wings. This was Bane. He *never* cried. I had hurt him deeply.

'Yes, I can. I can do things you can't imagine. I can tear the world apart if I need to.'

'It won't do you any good if you can't even stay in your own body,' he argued. Angry eyes stabbed like the steel of his knife.

I was undaunted. 'I have a plan for that,' I countered. 'If Dallmin's right about my soul's Velcro being too full of fuzz to work properly, then I think I know a way to make it stick better.'

He glanced at me with a hint of curiosity, which I took to mean he was willing to listen and not just sulk.

'Your soul is bound to my body,' I explained. 'So all we need to do is bind our souls together and I'll never get lost again.'

A moment passed and then another. And then, finally, golden hope melted the ice as he met my stubborn gaze.

I smiled. 'There's no escaping it, Bane. If you want me to stay safe, you'll have to marry me *now*.'

Chapter 20

Sun-warmed stone supported Annie's back as she sat on the grass and let her mind drift. She was no longer tired and yet in this place where the ancient monoliths towered over her like bodyguards, Annie had no trouble plunging herself recklessly into her dreams. Like an addiction, she defiantly craved her Guardian's presence and chose to ignore the punishing consequences. After all, it was only a memory, but it was *hers*, and she needed it.

'Let me carry it,' Lucas complained.

'No. And stop scratching. You've still got at least two weeks to go so you might as well get used to it,' she said, wobbling only slightly under the awkward weight of the hay bale. She tried very hard not to let Lucas see the way she slid in the mud the moment she stepped out of the shed. He was already grouchy enough.

She peered over the bale at her daughter, who had run ahead. 'Lainie, honey, please keep your gumboots on. There aren't enough socks on the entire planet to keep your feet dry when you insist on taking your shoes off every few minutes.'

Lucas scooped up the three-year-old with his good arm and fumbled to get her blue gumboot back over her sopping wet sock with the other. 'Two weeks? No way,' he said, giving it up as a hopeless job and placing the boot on her muddy hand instead. 'I can't do anything properly with this stupid thing on.' He knocked his plastered arm against a fence post as if trying to prove it didn't hurt.

'The doctor said five weeks, so anything under three would be unacceptable. Argue with him if you like.'

'It's perfectly fine. It was fine after two days.' Despite his frustration, he still smiled at the perplexed look on his daughter's face as she frowned at her misplaced footwear.

Annie heaved the bale up onto the tray of the ute and then glowered at him. 'Lucas, the whole town was at that footy match. You can't stay out of sight for a whole month. If anyone sees you without that cast too soon …'

'I'll stay here. On the farm. I'll hide if Dave comes over.'

The heavens opened again in one of the sudden violent squalls that had been pestering them all morning. Lainie laughed as hail bounced off her mess of curls and they scrambled to get into the shelter of the car.

'Lainie, sweetheart, stay still for a moment. Your hair is full of ice,' Lucas said. 'You look as bedraggled as a newborn lamb.'

'Like someone dipped a kitten in a bowl of rice pudding?' Annie asked, remembering when Lucas had assisted with his first lamb delivery.

Lucas laughed. 'Yes. She's a rice-pudding-kitten. That's your new name, baby girl.'

Lainie gave him a serious nod. Outside, the hail morphed into fat drops of rain that pounded at the windscreen.

'This weather is atrocious,' Annie said, turning the key and simultaneously flicking ice from Lucas's cast before it could melt and give him another excuse to try to remove it. As she waited for the engine to warm up, her eyes drifted north-ish to where she knew the weather was always perfect, even when it rained.

Lucas noticed and sighed. 'So I can't stay and hide. I'll need to do all the town errands while you two are gone.'

Sitting between them, Lainie sneezed in a perfectly timed passive argument.

Lucas kissed her forehead. 'But we were in the middle of reading *Snugglepot and Cuddlepie*. She'll forget and we'll have to start all over again.'

'Pie!' Lainie agreed.

'She won't forget. Children adjust better. And we'll only be gone for a few days. I only need to see if Pallano is back yet. He always returns for an eclipse and there's one due next week. He took Harry's rock with him when he left a couple of years ago. He said he knew someone who collects languages who might be able to translate it for us.'

'Only a few days. When have I heard that before?'

'We really do need to figure out what's written on the rock, Lucas. And why there's a picture of the gem on it.'

His face turned grim. 'I know. Maybe while you're gone I'll check up on the ruby to make sure it's still in the museum. We haven't been there for ages.' He grimaced as they hit a particularly bad series of potholes. 'Just make sure you're back by Thursday. Mum and Dad are coming up for the weekend, remember? You'll need a day or so to adjust, unless you want a repeat of the food fight incident.'

'That depends,' she replied. 'Will Lily be coming?'

He almost smiled. 'Good question. She promised me she'd bring her new man for us to meet, but it's still early days. A weekend away with the family might still be daunting for him.'

'Fair enough,' Annie agreed, easing the ute along the muddy trail that had, until that week, been a respectable gravel road.

'Annie?' He scratched idly at the edge of his plaster again. 'When you come back, take care near the river. It behaves differently now the drought has broken.'

'Lucas,' she admonished, 'the river would never hurt me. It comes from home.'

'Not all of it,' he mumbled.

Lainie nodded sagely, waving the blue gumboot on her fist.

Chapter 21

Deep orange sunlight turned the tops of the trees a burnished bronze. Dark clouds tricked the world into believing the night had already taken over, despite the streaks of glowing amber on the horizon. Birds flew everywhere, raucously fighting over the last of the sun's rays. In the lounge room of our sturdy farmhouse, two Cherubim, two Guardians, one farm manager, one dispossessed Edenite, one unemployed Army Reserve officer and a Senior Police Sergeant held a team meeting.

I was bored already.

Noah pestered me with questions. Yes, I could think of plenty of places where an amulet could be hidden, but I didn't particularly feel like searching out thousands of tree hollows. No, I was certain my mother would have mentioned it if she'd known anything. Yes, asking my mother about it anyway would have been a great idea except that *someone* had blocked off the cave *again*. It was his turn to tackle the cliff face if he thought it was worth it. Yes, I had heard the sword singing to me. No, I didn't know how I'd left my body—did he? Yes, I was certain it was somewhere to the north of us. No, I couldn't even begin to try to pinpoint its location on a map. Yes, I could probably find it. No, I wasn't going to try. I had made a promise.

Eventually, he sat back in the old rocking chair, cradling his son on his shoulder, lost deep in thought. Tessa was fidgety.

All eyes turned to me as if expecting me to outline some grand plan for what we were supposed to do next. It wasn't very fair.

'Our best lead so far,' Mick supplied, once it was clear I had nothing to say, 'suggests that Jake hitched a ride with a delivery driver to Mildura this afternoon. The driver remembers the guy had some nasty scratches on his face and wouldn't lean back in his seat. He must have picked up some fresh clothes from somewhere though, because there were no bloodstains. He said he had a job on a farm picking fruit. The driver dropped him in town, so we don't know which farm. Yet. We have an undercover agent trying to track him down. It's unlikely he's using his real name, but between his scratched up face and shoulder injury, someone will notice him.'

I thought about how painful it must be for him to pick oranges. The satisfaction I felt was very un-Eden-like.

'It's not good enough,' Noah said, standing up carefully so as not to disturb his sleeping son. Tiny arms flopped over his shoulder, and a squashed cheek made those adorable lips pucker in total relaxation. Noah picked up a blanket, a dummy, and a chuck cloth, and balanced them all in his free hand like a new juggling trick. 'I'm putting Nathaniel down. I'll be back in a minute. We need a proper plan. I can't live like this. Not knowing if I can even go to the shops without Jake making a dash for the cave. And if he hides the keys in the sump pit again I will find a way to stick a lightning bolt up his bum.'

I looked over at Tessa. She knew as well as I did what Noah was thinking and she was probably relying on me to talk him out of it. If he tried to travel bodiless to find the sword and got lost, how was I supposed to bring him home? It was far too risky.

'Tessa, what are these?' Dallmin asked, breaking the awkward silence. He was on her laptop, examining some images on the screen. At least there were other people around now to share the task of fielding his enquiries.

She leaned over his shoulder to have a closer look. 'Pictures of ancient manuscripts and tablets. Remember that Bible verse I found before Jake … before you went hang-gliding? The one that mentioned the people of Eden at Telassar? I was trying to find out more about it. I was hoping to find out if anyone else had crossed between worlds and if any had managed to get back. Unfortunately, most of the texts have been impossible to translate and almost as hard to date.'

He turned to her with an amused half-smile. 'One of these isn't text. It's a musical score. Lainie would recognise the tune,' he said. 'And this one is a poem. A sad one. It's about losing a dog. Strange, I never thought of such a thing as sad before, until I came here. I used to have a dog that followed me around until she disappeared one day and never returned. A friend of mine told me she'd followed him through a cave. He lost sight of her after she chased a furry creature through the trees. I wonder if it was the cave that led here?' he mused. 'Have you seen a yellow dog around anywhere?'

'How long ago was it, Dallmin?' I asked.

'Oh. Too long. Sorry, I forgot.'

'Never mind. Tell me more about the music,' I suggested before he could dwell on the passing of time or losing a canine companion. 'If you recognise the tune that must mean something, right?' I considered getting up to have a look, only Bane was playing with the ring on my finger and had that elusive smile I always craved, so instead I leaned back and let him rest his chin on my shoulder.

Instead of answering my question, Dallmin started typing madly. Something had piqued his interest. We left him to it, grateful for anything that would hold off the endless questions for a while.

Soft kisses feathered my neck. So, so, so glad I hadn't run away earlier. Flames crackled in the wood heater, logs popping and spitting out fire like angry dragons as we waited for Noah to return. I noticed my aunt watching Mick out of the corner of her eye. She watched him a lot, but not as much as he watched her when she wasn't looking. It made me smile in much the same way Bane was.

Noah returned quietly and sat on the floor in front of Tessa's armchair.

'Sorry to have to be blunt about this,' Tim said after clearing his throat, 'but I think we need to discuss what Lainie said to Jake the other night, and we also need to come up with a way for her to sleep safely that's better than driving her around in a car all night.'

He was right. I couldn't risk myself anymore, at least not unnecessarily.

Tessa sat up straighter. 'Be specific. How can Jake get to you, Lainie?'

As tempted as I was to play down the danger so as not to lose Bane's smile, she needed to know. 'When we spoke, I figured out a couple of things. Firstly, the demon—Rabisu—has memories that long pre-date Jake and knows things that the boy we went to school with couldn't possibly know.'

Aunt Lily nodded. 'So the demon has possessed Jake,' she clarified.

'He's not like you and Noah. Not born into a human body. He stole one. That poor boy.'

I knew she would think along the same lines as I had, but both Tessa and Bane glared at her. She wisely chose not to comment further.

'The second thing,' I told them, 'is that the demon still has to operate within the parameters of Jake's character. Jake isn't overly bright and can be pretty stubborn. He and the demon don't always seem to operate in perfect alignment. Hence the mood swings and the contradictions.'

'That's true,' Tim agreed. 'He wants to sell the sword and keep it hidden at the same time, and also destroy it. He can't seem to make up his mind.'

'I get the feeling that destroying it is the demon's first priority, but he can't do it easily.' A sour taste filled my mouth at the thought of the beautiful sword being harmed in any way, and yet a part of me still felt the revulsion and fear of it that had haunted me ever since I'd watched it incinerate Sarah Ashbree. That conflict would have to be dealt with at some point, maybe when I was less tired and could think more clearly.

'One more thing,' I continued. 'The demon is afraid of it and of us, but is also itching for a fight. I think it can be goaded into an attack if that's what we want.'

Arguments erupted then and I expected Bane to be in the middle of it all, throwing his broody leadership qualities around like a battle axe. Instead, he just continued to hold me against his chest, playing with my ring. He was muttering something about names. Lucas, Annie, Lainie. And then Beth. Annie. Bethany.

'Are you picking *baby names*?' I asked in a strangled whisper. 'Now?' He gave me the most smug smile I'd ever seen on him. 'Why aren't you arguing like everyone else? It worries me that you aren't arguing. You're supposed to be slamming the idea of initiating a fight, aren't you?'

'Hmm?' He nuzzled against my neck. 'You already promised I could be your champion. No backsies for you either. Besides, I want this over with as much as you do.' His warm fingers slipped under the hem of my t-shirt. My skin hummed where he stroked my waist. Tim was saying something to Noah in an impassioned voice, which I struggled to pay attention to, so I bit one of my knuckles as hard as I could to regain my concentration. Bane hissed, removing his hand from my stomach so he could heal me. I batted him away.

'Naughty boy. You deserved that. Stay focused,' I reprimanded.

'How do you expect me to focus when you're in pain?' he whined, but he was grinning.

'… so long as Bane agrees,' Mick insisted, snagging my attention back to where it should be. Guiltily we looked at him, trying to work out what he'd been saying.

Tim made an exasperated noise. 'I'll run through our options again,' he said, ticking them off on his fingers. 'One: we let the police track him down. Noah reckons that's too slow. Two: Noah and Lainie try to find him by doing whatever it was they did this afternoon, only Tessa vetoed that one out as way too dangerous and we all agreed. Or three: we entice him to come to us at a time of our choosing. For that we'll need more manpower.' He tilted his head at us. 'I suggested we invite the rest of our crew to visit and call Jake out while they're here.'

Seriously? It was hard enough to keep things inconspicuous as it was. If we needed to use real power, having more people around to watch would only complicate things.

'Great idea,' Bane said.

He still didn't get it, then. I could do *anything* to protect Eden and keep it secret, but revealing what I could do to outsiders would have exactly the opposite effect.

'Come on, Tim. You of all people should understand,' I grumbled. 'Every superhero has the same disadvantage against the villain—they're constrained by the need to keep the innocents safe while the villains aren't. Think about it.'

He smiled. 'But, my Lady Word-Binder, there's no evidence to suggest Jake has access to any superpowers. Not if he comes in person, and if he comes bodiless then he can't do much either.'

My eyes widened as I suddenly realised what he was doing. He was trying to play down the danger to me for Bane's sake. He didn't like seeing him suffer any more than I did. Seeing the effect my disastrous afternoon had had on his friend must have shaken him, too. He wanted to do whatever he could think of to set Bane's mind at ease, including finding an excuse to surround him with more people whom he trusted. I got it. Finally.

'Okay,' I acceded. 'If you think they can help, then go ahead. But I draw the line at having them share my room when I'm sleeping.'

Bane laughed. Actually laughed. 'Some of them snore even worse than Tim,' he agreed. 'And he takes up all the spare room as it is.'

'Wait,' Noah interrupted. 'I'm missing something here. Tim sleeps in your room?'

Bane replied before I could. 'Only since Jake became a threat. I won't leave her side for a second when she sleeps, Noah,' he declared, challenging anyone to disagree.

'Well, of course not, but—'

'They're horny. I volunteered to help,' Tim interrupted, as if saying it hastily would make it less awkward. 'As their chaperone, since … you know …'

Of all the reactions I had been apprehensively expecting, the one that threw me the most came from my aunt. She cracked up laughing and didn't stop even when I threw Nathaniel's fluffy toy penguin at her.

Noah looked at Tim with a horrified expression, which changed quickly to sympathy, and then finally amusement. 'You are a brave man, Tim. Truly brave,' he smirked, shaking his head. 'Don't worry, Lainie. I've got you covered. I sent off those forms I got you and Bane to sign. You can get married as soon as next month if you want.'

A sudden silence fell as everyone realised the implications. Tim, Tessa, Noah, and Mick all stared at me, as if trying to imagine me in a mothering role. Their expressions weren't very encouraging.

I lifted my chin. 'As a matter of fact, we do want to speed things up. Well, the wedding at least. We're still thinking about the timing of … the other stuff.' My cheeks were blazing, which probably meant I was readjusting to this world again if nothing else. 'How soon can we get things organised? We don't really care too much about the details.'

'I care a little,' Bane said. 'I want to do it right. I saw your notebooks, remember?'

Mortified, I buried my head in my arms, and Noah laughed.

'Actually, most of the details are pretty easy to arrange,' he advised. 'We did this not too long ago ourselves, remember? All you need to do is let me know what you want. The biggest problem will be getting all the guests to come on short notice.'

Guests? Annie. If only she could come. It would be impossible though. Even if she could somehow disguise herself from everyone who thought she was dead, she would never pluck up enough courage to leave Eden after all these years. The last two times she'd crossed the boundary had been violent and upsetting, and she hadn't even made it past the cave. Not to mention that the pathway was now completely blocked by Noah's landslide. I pushed the thought firmly from my mind.

'How soon do you think we can convince the rest of the crew to come down?' Bane asked Tim.

'Dunno. I'll make some calls,' he said. 'Do you want to invite—'

In the corner of the room, a chair toppled over as Dallmin stood up too quickly. His face was ashen and there were tears running down his cheeks. He looked straight at me, distraught.

'I've found a d … diary,' he stammered. 'Carved on stone, so it would last, although some has been broken off. It's written in the language of Siyyan city, with a few new words thrown in. Words for things I only now understand.' He stretched his long fingers toward the screen as if he could reach back in time to touch the author of the stone tablet. 'It's about a group of Edenites who strayed from home and couldn't return. It was meant as a warning to any of us who might follow.'

Utter despair resonated through every line of his body. 'It was written by my daughter.'

<h1 style="text-align:center">Chapter 22</h1>

'It's okay, Dallmin,' Tessa assured him. 'It can't have been written by anyone you know. That collection is over four thousand years old.'

'No mistake,' he insisted. 'This is my daughter's record of her time here.'

'Your *daughter*?' Noah spluttered.

'Four *thousand* years?' Mick asked.

But there was no point trying to ask him any questions until he'd calmed down. Sorrow had tied his tongue.

Looking around, I knew I wasn't the only one who felt like my head was about to explode from curiosity. Just how old was he? We made him a cup of tea, which he was too upset to drink. After a few minutes, he resolutely picked up a pencil and paper and began to translate what he'd found. In the half hour it took him to finish, none of us were willing to leave. As soon as he was done he handed it to Aunt Lily to read out, while he quietly slipped from the room.

… frightened to move across while we are so cursed, otherwise our choice would be simple. Some have taken the risk and stopped forever rather than face causing further harm, even though they are incomplete. Will their sadness remain unresolved forever? Others are so afraid of that fate, they have given themselves over to violence. Anything to avoid death. Know this—if there was a way to cleanse ourselves of this shame, not one of us would hesitate for a single second, even unto forever death. This land that so intrigued us on the first day now haunts us with its wretched pain. How we long for the River! Without it, we are becoming hollow. Each time our eyes behold fresh devastation, more of the River leaves us and drips into the dry soil. Such tears are common here, or so we've been told. I

don't see the point of them. They provide release, yet they do not heal nor sustain us. Soon we will have no more left and we will turn to dust and ashes, and forget our home.

We have commenced construction of a sanctuary to remind us of the city we have lost. Each of us remembers some precious fragrance of home, and although these walls are supposed to keep us safe, we have also tried to retain some of Siyyan's beauty. Over the years we have gifted knowledge and art to the curious locals. It is the least we can do for these people who struggle to even feed their children enough to grow to full stature. They see us as giants. They call us gods. In return for our gifts, they have aided our construction efforts. Sadly, they have no appreciation of fun, and over the decades we have come to accept that the city will never be as we remember it. We have, however, agreed on one thing. The tower is to remain as the centrepiece, not only as a symbol of hope that we might one day return to Siyyan, but also to protect us from unexpected attacks from the veiled ones. They were once our friends and it sickens me that we are learning the necessity of warfare, but we cannot risk being killed before we have found a way to free ourselves from this new burden of understanding. The evil of this world seeks to tear us further from our home and it cannot be overcome. It lurks in the doorway like a hunter after its prey.

Another page in Dallmin's neat writing and terrible spelling showed a separate diary entry. There were no dates; of course, why would there be?

I stand at the peak of the tower, observing my exiled friends below as they struggle and work to simply survive, and I remember. I remember the joy I felt the first time my father stood with me at the highest part of the tower back home and showed me how the eagles rode the east wind. Does he still expect me to return? Does my mother look to the hills and wonder why I never came home? My chest hurts when I remember them and yet I am grateful they never thought to follow. I can remain, and hold to who I am, so long as I know that they still play. I have named our new city after my papa. We are now all citizens of Dilmun.

I fear we will die here and will have to choose to either slip through to the next place or resist its pull as we have always done and hope that one day we'll be called back home. I cling to that hope. To be called home and wake up clean and whole, and this will all feel like a fading dream.

Yet how can that ever be? For we cannot un-know that which we now understand.

An ominous rumble invaded the dazed silence as Aunt Lily finished reading, and I leaped to the front window in time to see Noah's dirt bike skidding around the corner of the shed. Within seconds, Tessa had flicked her laptop from pictures of old pots and relics to show the images from the various cameras that had been installed around the farm. Sure enough, Dallmin was riding full pelt toward the bush gate, reckless as a puppy through the deepening dark. I felt sick.

Spinning toward the door, I began to bolt after him, but Bane was too fast for me. He stood in the doorway like a living brick wall.

'Bane, I have to go. He's going to hurt himself.'

'And he's just as likely to hurt you too if you try to stop him,' he countered. 'We need to take some precautions, not go pelting off in the dark.'

'She's right, we can't let him go like that,' Tim said, pushing past him.

'Tim, stay here,' Bane commanded.

'You aren't my commanding officer anymore, Bane.'

That brought us all up short, and by the time we recovered, Tim was gone.

Noah and I exchanged a glance. We both felt where Dallmin was heading. Nothing Bane could say would stop or delay us. Especially now that Tim had started up the only other functioning dirt bike and was heading there as well.

'Sorry, Bane. You know how this goes,' I said.

'I do, and it usually ends very badly.' He paused for a moment longer, then stood aside.

Noah tossed Tessa the keys to the ute and gave Bane one of his famous smiles. 'It'll be fine, mate. We won't let Lainie drive this time.'

I hated it when he picked on me for things I had no way to refute.

Soft rain dripped from the trees above as Tessa drove the paddock basher along the new path Noah had blasted through the bush, headlights bouncing in time with each rabbit hole. Darkness was slowing us to the point where I considered doing something Wordy to our headlights, but then we finally saw the two bikes, dumped on the ground under the drooping shelter of a willow on the riverbank.

Bane, Noah, Tessa, and I jumped out of the ute, slamming the doors and hurrying in the only direction that made sense. The river ahead roared in full angry defiance of the intruder who had already crossed in our little canoe. In the moon's dull glow I could see where Tim had stripped off his boots and jacket to follow.

Eyeing off the full winter flow of water with trepidation, I threw Bane a toothy grin and stripped off my shoes. He scowled, knowing better than to comment. Maybe we should have thought about investing in more than one canoe because swimming in the dark sounded way more sexy than it really was. It was also exhausting and we ended up much farther downstream than usual and had to fight our way back through dense scratchy bush in bare feet.

By the time we reached the cave, Dallmin was huddled against the wall of rock with his ankles crossed and his hands over his ears like a child. The feeble light from the lantern cast ominous shadows against the limestone.

'You don't know how she died in the end,' Tim entreated. 'She may have lived a long and happy life, with a family of her own. Try not to think the worst.'

'The worst?' Dallmin cried, looking up with accusing eyes. 'A long and happy life of what, a few hundred years at most? Only to die an old woman with the life stripped away from her until she became frail and old, with grey hair and misty eyes, limbs so bent she could no longer dance. What if she died in pain, leaving her children behind? *How is that not the worst?*' he yelled, leaping to his feet.

Behind me Bane stiffened, his hand sliding toward his knife. Thankfully Noah was faster.

'Dallmin, look at me,' he said. 'We can help you. You don't really want to hurt yourself.'

My heart leaped into my mouth as I saw the pocket knife Dallmin was holding. How on Earth had he ended up with that horrible thing again? If I could have found the Words to dissolve every knife on the planet at that moment I probably would have. I was completely sick to the stomach of them.

You know nothing of what I want, Dallmin signed back, glaring at me.

And I saw it. I saw the way his whole being *screamed.* How had I missed it before? He wanted to die, to move across, but he was scared. In a flash of understanding, I realised he hadn't signed a thing to me since the day we'd found him in the river. Signing meant communicating with so much more of himself than just words. It held no secrets. And now I saw what he'd been trying so hard to hide.

You want to move across? I asked, both with my words and my heart. I let him see all the sadness and regret his pain brought me as I reached for his hand.

'I am tainted by shame,' he snapped, our fingers barely brushing before he pulled away. 'What will become of me if I die with such a stained soul, Lainie?'

It was a foundational question that had probably gnawed at him since the day he'd first understood what shame was. The day he'd let Jake kill me. I'd only touched him for a moment, enough to read what I needed to: if he thought there was any chance for him to die clean of that shame, he would have left us in an instant. Death was nothing to him, and I understood perfectly. I opened my mouth to speak and then closed it again. I simply didn't have the answer he needed.

'I thought if I did everything I was told and followed all the rules of this place, that I might somehow become clean again.' He turned, tossing aside the small blade, and began to tear at the rocks, his elegant fingers casting them furiously out of his way. When Tim moved to stop him, Noah gripped his elbow. There was no danger of him making any significant dent in the barricade. The dark of the cave welled up behind us like a shroud as Dallmin scrambled with his bare hands to try to force his way back home. 'But I haven't even gained forgiveness for my first mistakes! They were too evil and too heavy to reconcile *no matter what I do.*' His eyes flicked across to Bane as he crumpled amid the debris, undone by the sheer impossibility of the mountainous task.

'We did forgive you. Remember? When you learned how to say sorry,' I said.

Dallmin turned his face to my Guardian. 'Bane never did,' he replied.

Noah and I turned to Bane for support. This was where he was supposed to assure us all that he had forgiven him and that Dallmin had been doing well.

My Guardian said nothing.

Dallmin's ancient brown eyes reflected real regret. 'I tried, Lainie. I really did.' His hoarse whisper sounded so tired. 'I ate when he told me to eat, even though I felt sick in my heart. I learned about your world so I could understand the rules better, even when the things I read about broke me into pieces.'

Fiercely impassioned words reflected the desperation I read in his body language as his frustration built. 'I chewed on meat that came from animals that had been slaughtered without their permission. I overcame my fear of the elderly as I saw in them my future.'

With each trial he listed his anger grew and he started tearing at the rock wall again, drawing blood from his fingers. Tim stepped toward him; again Noah held him back.

Dallmin kept ranting. 'I turned my eyes from women in case they stirred untrue feelings in my body. I remained imprisoned indoors when I wanted to roam, so you had no reason to worry about me. I lay unable to sleep each night for fear that the memories from home might overwhelm me and cause me to fail, again.'

All I could do was watch as my friend unleashed his fury on the unyielding stones.

'I ignored the wants of the people who were hurting because Bane told me they were strangers and could be dangerous. I smiled when you wanted me to smile and I played when you wanted me to play, but it wasn't enough, and never will be!' Finally his foot slipped on the mess of gravel under his feet and he fell painfully to his knees, hesitating in his tirade.

Torn between wanting to wrench him away from the boundary and wanting to hug him, I waited for Bane to say something comforting. When he remained silent I clamped my hand over my mouth to stifle my sobs. Cave-sheltered air felt suddenly too weak and cold to sustain the charged emotion the exiled Edenite was radiating.

'Please don't blame him, Lainie,' Dallmin continued, unable to summon the will to even lift himself from the stones where he kneeled. 'I understand why he's still so angry. You are his love partner, and you are

Shamar for the world that I hold more precious than anything, and I betrayed you. He *can't* forgive me for what I did to you.'

'No,' Bane murmured, swallowing a shuddering breath. 'No,' he said again, more firmly. His hand released mine as he stepped forward. 'You apologised for that and although what you did was … devastating to me, I did forgive you.' His voice trembled with contained fury. 'This was never about how obedient you can be. All of that means nothing to me. The rules were only supposed to make things easier for you. There is something else you *never* apologised for.' His gaze pinned Dallmin like a rabbit in a spotlight.

Dallmin looked up at him, dust and tears streaking his face in the dim lantern glow.

'You never apologised for not trusting me. I was your friend and you needed help, and instead of trusting me to help you, you chose to believe the lies of *the man who had kidnapped Tessa*. I know you didn't understand about deceit, but you never gave us a chance to give you the truth either. You went looking for Jake on your own. Even before you were lied to, before you even knew what a lie was, *you chose* not to trust me.'

Pure honesty cut through the oppressive burden of shame that had built up around Dallmin's soul as his face fell in acknowledged, tearful disgrace.

Chapter 23

'Her name was Nin,' I told the others later that evening once we'd changed into dry clothes and Mick had assured us Dallmin was actually sleeping. Aunt Lily had dosed him with some herbal sleeping tablets and Mick had stayed with him until he was well gone.

The fire in the lounge room had been loaded up by my fretting aunt until we were all roasting. No one complained. I'd spent some time alone with Dallmin in the cave once he'd calmed down, allowing him to speak freely without the presence of others tying his tongue in even more guilt. Now everyone wanted to hear the story behind the ancient tablet.

'She and a group of friends decided to explore the land on the other side of the cave. They wanted to find a new mountain to climb. The Cherubim at the time came up with all sorts of alternative ideas to distract them, but apparently Nin was well known for "expressing her wants" with so much passion that other people got caught up in her enthusiasm. They wanted whatever she wanted.'

'You mean she was as stubborn about exploring as her father is about flying,' Noah said.

'Or as stubborn as you are about hang-gliding, which is partly what got Dallmin into this mess,' I reminded him.

'I believe the word you're looking for is *charming*,' Noah argued. 'Not stubborn.'

A stern look from my aunt stymied my retort. 'Anyway,' I continued instead, 'when they couldn't be dissuaded from leaving, Dallmin and his wife gave them a wild party to send them off, knowing they would be gone for a long time.'

'He has a wife?' Mick asked. 'I didn't know marriage was a thing there.'

'Had a wife,' I corrected. 'And "wife" is possibly not the right word. When you find your partner in Eden, there's a massive celebration. A ceremony would be redundant because when you connect with someone like that everyone already knows you stay committed for a lifetime, and by lifetime I mean ...'

'Thousands of years,' Tessa said, exhaling.

'Dallmin and Jilana were together for a *very* long time.'

Tessa had that faraway sentimental look in her eyes as she imagined it, so I decided to move on quickly.

'After a few hundred years, Jilana began to look for them, but they'd disappeared. Despite the mystery, Dallmin still assumed the explorers would eventually return. After a couple of thousand years had passed, one of the Shamar admitted they had all moved acro—I mean, died. Jilana chose to ... die too, not long after that. Dallmin nearly followed her, only he couldn't quite bring himself to accept that *all* of them had chosen to leave their bodies forever. It was a puzzle he wanted to solve.'

Noah fidgeted in his seat. 'Perhaps that might explain why he was so eager to cross the boundary once he found out about this place from Annie. It would explain a lot.'

Including why he chose to remain in such an uncomfortable and unfriendly world and not just cross back after the first miserable hour, I realised. The thought lessened my guilty conscience a teeny bit.

Cradling a mug of hot chocolate, Tessa shook her head. 'I still can't believe the famous lost city of Dilmun was named after the guy who tried to cook a banana in our toaster this morning.'

'Lost city?' I asked.

'I wrote notes about it years ago, when I first started researching the children of Eden at Telassar.' She moved to the desk and pulled up a file on the laptop. 'The first written evidence of the city appeared in about 2300 BCE, although it could even have dated back to a thousand years before that. There are a lot of creation myths centred around it. One passage describes it as "the place where the sun rises". Another calls it "the Land of the Living".'

I could almost smell the intrigue in the atmosphere as we connected to the ancient myths.

'There are others that suggest the inhabitants were eternally young and suffered no illnesses,' she added, absently setting her mug down on the desk to scroll down further.

'Well, that makes sense,' Mick contributed. 'According to the Bible, Adam and his descendants lived for hundreds of years, at least until the flood. Maybe the longevity is more of a genetic trait than a result of eating the … the …' He swallowed and took a breath. 'The right foods.'

I had really tied his tongue in knots, poor guy.

'Or perhaps those "right foods" repair DNA so thoroughly that it has a long-term effect on lifespan and basic immunity,' Tessa suggested.

'Longer telomeres,' I agreed. Everyone stared at me. 'What? I was worried I'd forgotten everything from school, so I flipped through some of my old notes. Just because I've forgotten stuff doesn't mean I can't learn it again. Look it up yourself if you don't believe me.'

'You looked through your old school notes? How are you still such a nerd?' Noah asked.

My aunt, who knew perfectly well that my reply was likely to start a classic Noah-Lainie cushion fight, interrupted. 'I guess that bodes well for Dallmin. I was worried about the fact that he hasn't built up any immunity to common diseases,' she said.

I winced. He needed to survive the next few weeks first.

'What else have you found, Tess?' she asked. 'Anything about Nin?'

Tessa grinned. 'Listen to this little gem of a Sumerian myth. It refers to a goddess called Ninhursag, the Earth Mother, whose partner Enki made her this promise: "For Dilmun, the land of my lady's heart, I will create long waterways, rivers and canals, whereby water will flow to quench the thirst of all beings and bring abundance to all that lives." Of course, most of the Sumerian goddesses had names starting with "Nin". In Hebrew the name means "grace". It makes a certain kind of sense that they would have been seen as divine creatures by the people on this side of the boundary. Anyone who's been to Eden can hit you that way.' She batted her eyelashes at Noah, who grinned back at her.

My own protest died on the tip of my tongue as I thought about the star-struck way Tim still looked at Noah, Dallmin, and me when he thought we weren't paying attention. It was a little disturbing.

Noah leaned over Tessa's shoulder for a closer look at the screen.

'Nin mentioned something about unexpected attacks. Who would attack them if they were seen as giant gods?' he asked. 'Doesn't the Bible mention giants too?'

Tim literally tripped over himself as he jumped off the couch to peer over Tessa's other shoulder.

The next hour was spent researching all there was to know about references to giants throughout history, from skeleton hoaxes to Greek gods, and all the biblical references—including the pre-flood Nephilim whom most Christians believed to be men who fell away from righteousness, but whom most online gamers liked to think of as angel-human crossbreeds. There were also the post-flood Anakites, Amorites, Rephaites, and Emites. Needless to say, I drifted off into a haze. Noah seemed to tune out too. He did a lot of sighing and frowning in the direction of Dallmin's room and didn't even bother to answer when Tim asked him from which side of his family he'd inherited his height. Noah seemed to be as disturbed by Dallmin's breakdown as I was, and I knew why. We didn't feel like we could trust him. I couldn't even comprehend him. Not like I used to. I could always tell when people were lying to me, and from the moment Dallmin had used sign language again all I could see was conflict inside him. And something more. Something desperate and discordant. I caught Noah's eye and for a long moment he held my gaze, until I noticed Bane watching us. I blinked back a rogue tear and gave a muffled, fake laugh in response to a comment I hadn't been listening to. The last thing I needed was for Bane to think Dallmin was hiding something. Not when their relationship was finally beginning to heal.

Noah and I would keep a close eye on Dallmin. And we would untangle the mystery of the exiled Edenites. I tried to pay attention to the discussion, I really did, only the fire was so cosy and Bane's shoulder was so comfortable to lean on, and the safe scent of home eased some of my fear of sleeping. Quality sleep was probably out of the question, but I was surrounded by my friends and family, and I had to trust that Bane could wake me if my dreams became dangerous, or if the research uncovered anything worthwhile. It didn't.

Morning broke in an anticlimactic blaze of winter sunshine. Peeling back crusty eyelids, I was surprised to find myself alone in the lounge room. I had been laid out on the couch at some point and covered with multiple blankets, which I had mostly tossed off. Moving only my eyeballs, I double-checked to make certain I hadn't been mistaken. Nope, no Bane, no Tim, and no Jake. Only a crackling fire that someone had thoughtfully rejuvenated. So much for not letting me sleep alone for an instant; and yet, even as I thought it, a plate stacked high with hot pancakes entered the room followed by my ridiculously chirpy Guardian.

'Bonjour, fiancée,' he greeted me as I considered swallowing the whole stack at once, Scooby-Doo style. 'How are you feeling?' He passed me a glass of water, which I sculled down in one go.

'You tell me.'

'The question covers emotional health, not just physical,' he qualified.

'Fair enough. Well, I feel relieved that I made it through the night, and I'm hungry, and a bit stiff, and … oh my great grandmother. I'm getting married.'

Laughter like rain after a drought filled the room as Bane dumped the plate and threw himself headlong into my open arms. My whole body sang with his reflected joy as he buried his face into my tangled hair.

'Where's Tim?' I asked, feeling like we were about to be sprung by a teacher behind the shelter sheds at school.

'Out for a run,' he mumbled, breathing in deeply as if I'd washed my hair in strawberry shampoo.

I hoped my morning breath wasn't too gross. It hadn't ever been a problem in Eden, but I'd been back long enough to have to start considering such details again.

'Do you think we'll manage without him?' my sensible mouth asked, while my wayward fingertips traced the edge of his bicep. This somehow evoked a vision of him dressed in his army uniform doing chin-ups while being screamed at by a meaty-looking drill sergeant with a crewcut and scar down one side of his face. I had no idea if it was a true insight provided by my gift or simply a manifestation of what my hormones were doing to my brain; either way, it was extremely entertaining.

Shivering in response to my touch, he pulled away and smiled at me. 'I doubt it,' he admitted, grey eyes sparkling. 'Not unless I can distract you with something else.' His head tilted meaningfully toward the pancakes on the coffee table. There was maple syrup. His lips were softened in a smile. He was a whole different person when he smiled.

He gently pushed me away a moment later.

'You're going to get me into trouble, oh Mother of Memories,' he said, grinning.

'Too late,' came a gruff voice from the doorway. It wasn't Tim, but Noah was probably even worse. I sat up, crossed my legs, and tucked into my pancakes before he could nick any.

'Mother of Memories?' he asked Bane. '*So* not her. She can hardly remember her own birthday.'

'Well, maybe not so good with her own memories, but she's great with other people's,' he said.

A pancake battle ensued as Noah tried unsuccessfully to sneak past my guard. 'I could think of more appropriate titles for her,' he mumbled, stuffing a ripped remnant into his mouth before I could intercept it.

I deliberately wiped my syrupy fingers through his precious blond hair. 'So could I,' I said. 'Noah the Necromancer. Or is it Necro-woman-cer?'

'Lainie, Lady of Lawn Mowing,' he threw back, ducking away.

'Fabled Father of Fence-straining,' I responded.

'Guardian of Gumtree Gully.'

I laughed and stuffed some pancake in his mouth to shut him up. Then I took the sticky fork and touched each of his shoulders. 'I dub thee Reaper of Rogue Rabbits.'

Sensibly, Bane confiscated the plate of pancakes as well as the syrup and quietly waited for us to get it all out of our system. It only took a few minutes.

When we finally settled down again, Noah pushed his gummy hair behind his ears and reclined on the rocking chair with a pencil and notepad.

'Decision time,' he said, clearing his throat as if nothing had happened. 'You do realise June is the absolute worst time of year for a wedding, right? I'll run through a list of options for your big day and you pick the ones you like best. Firstly, location: one of the churches, the Memorial Park, Nalong Hotel, my folks' place, or here?'

I pouted at my remaining pancakes, but they stared back at me without any sympathy at all. It was going to be a long morning.

Days passed in a frenzy of wedding planning as we all pretended as best we could that things were normal. The more nights that went by without so much as a whiff of ghostly demon visitations, the less secure I felt. Bane's strategy of keeping Jake running from us to prevent him planning anything made too much sense. Now that we were leaving him alone, what evil scheme was he cooking up? No one slept alone anymore in case he decided to target someone else.

Mick took night-watch duty for Dallmin as often as he could, when he wasn't working, and Aunt Lily stayed with him the rest of the time. He was more zombie than elf, moping around the house. As if having to deal with the reality of his own exile wasn't enough, the knowledge that his beloved daughter had suffered the trials of this world and eventually succumbed to death in an unknown land was almost impossible for him to reconcile. Having a child was the most precious gift an Edenite could ever be blessed with and it was almost unheard of for a couple to have more than one. His daughter, therefore, had meant everything to him and it was clear he'd never really let her go.

Music still seemed to help, luckily, so we introduced him to Bane's mum and put them both in charge of organising the music for the wedding. It was good for him to keep busy, and after spending so long stuck in a car with us Dallmin was well aware of our individual music preferences and therefore fully qualified to oversee the entertainment. Beth was, of course, absolutely delighted.

'Can Lainie play the flute?' was the first thing she asked Bane when we sat down in the floral armchairs of her living room. Her short hair framed her face, and her stern grey eyes, so like her son's, took on a softer, wistful light as she looked at me in hope. The room was filled with instruments of all sorts. Dallmin inspected each one in turn.

'On her own wedding day?' Bane asked.

Her face took on a conflicted expression, like she was trying desperately to come up with an effective argument. 'I guess not,' she conceded a moment later, sounding so sulky I almost laughed. 'But we could have done a lovely mother-daughter duet.'

I blinked. Mother-daughter?

'No need to look so startled, Lainie,' she said. 'You might as well get used to it. I'm claiming you as the daughter I never had. We'll go shopping together, do each other's nails, you'll take me to the opera, I'll teach you how to cook … it'll be great!'

Bane stood up, ready to catch me if I tried to make a run for the door. He really had a lot to learn about body language.

'Will we get to talk about your son behind his back?' I asked.

'I'll give you a moment-by-moment dissection of his entire childhood while we eat cookies.'

Bane sat down again. Heavily.

'Or we could skip the pedicures and just watch telly a lot,' Beth remarked.

I smiled. If his mum had a sense of humour, there was at least a slim hope my Guardian had a comedy gene hiding *somewhere*. Or at least a comedy nucleotide. 'Can I call you "Mum"?' I asked. 'I haven't had anyone that felt right with before. I think I'd like it.'

She looked like she was about to cry as she nodded but was distracted by Dallmin, who was pulling her silver flute from its stand. Her expression went from 'aww, kittens' to 'if you don't put that down immediately I'm going to stick it up your nose' in about half a second. Just then Dallmin launched into a lively, tinkling tune and winked at me. I was grateful for his light-heartedness, no matter how temporary.

Then Beth really did cry. It took ages for her to let us leave.

The wedding was, after much painful negotiation, set for the end of June, giving us three weeks to prepare and entice people to come. Luckily, that part had been relatively simple, given that Bane had very little extended family and mine was all on the wrong side of a rockfall. Nearly all his army friends were coming, thanks to Tim's shameless emotional manipulations. I would have complained about his heavy-handed tactics if I hadn't understood how much Bane needed their support. It wasn't until they started turning up a whole week early that I realised how well he'd manipulated me as well.

'Well, you did insist on a large dance floor,' Tim defended as he helped the two part-time soldiers carry their gear to the smaller of our hay sheds. 'Hayden here is the best with explosives, and there are at least six tree stumps that need to be blasted if we want to turn the back paddock into a grand ballroom. Noah's already chucking berkos about how late we've left it.'

He wasn't wrong. My best friend had turned into the wedding planner from hell the minute we'd decided on the date. The same Noah who used to turn up late to almost every party, often wearing clothes smeared with drenching paste, was now insisting we pre-order canapés from Melbourne because the local ones were too 'noisy'. Whatever that meant. There was a fine line between charming and bullying, and the poor florist almost needed to be revived with smelling salts after Noah and his spooky green eyes had accosted her with his demands the previous week. I was all for keeping Noah pacified, but did we really need all these extra people underfoot?

'Tim, it's the middle of winter. You can't expect people to stay in the hay shed for a week.'

The look he gave me was almost condescending. 'We're army, Lainie. We sleep where we're told to and make the best of it. Besides, most of the hay's been moved to the other shed and it's quite cosy in there now. Kind of nativity-like. And we've arranged a power supply for some heating.'

'*We* sleep where we're told?' I challenged, grabbing a couple of sleeping bags from the boot and following him. 'Does that mean you're staying with them?'

He snorted. 'Nice try. I know where I'm needed most. I'm doing it for you, remember?'

'Right. And it has nothing to do with the fact that you'd rather be indoors in a real bed than out in a steel shed with a concrete floor?' Yet as soon as I entered through the little access door I realised how nicely it had been transformed. The remaining hay was stacked against two of the walls, which would act as decent insulators, leaving a good-sized area that had been swept clean and furnished. A roll of old carpet had been laid out, and five fold-out beds borrowed from goodness knows where. A table, some chairs, and an old kitchen cupboard meant they could set up pretty well with only a bit of camping gear. It looked like the world's best cubby house.

'Lukey! Hayden! Come up to the house and meet everyone,' Tim beckoned to the two athletic-looking guys dumping their bags on the floor. 'There's coffee,' he enticed. 'We'll set you up properly later.'

As he introduced me to his companions I decided I was glad they'd arrived early. It would give me a chance to spend time with people who knew the 'army' aspect of Bane's personality much better than I did.

Two days later, Luke, who was keeping a lazy eye on the computer monitor, suddenly cleared his throat and angled the screen away from me. Bane and Tim had set up even more security cameras in the past week and had told their friends about Tessa's abduction. It hadn't taken much persuading to get them to help watch the monitors while we all got on with wedding plans. A photo of Jake was sticky-taped up on the wall next to the computer, which was a bit creepy. Something in the way Luke's shoulders shifted told me he was hiding something. I could always tell.

'What have you seen, Luke?' I asked, tossing aside the bridal magazine I'd been flipping through.

'Nothing dangerous. All good.'

I was out of my chair in record time.

'Bane put a lot of cameras in,' Luke defended, trying to shield my view of the screen. 'He may not have been clear enough to everyone about where they all are.'

Peering closer at the corner of the screen, a dorky squeal escaped my lips as I watched my aunt lip-wrestle with Mick between the two water tanks. The next few minutes were spent prancing about the house like a My Little Pony on steroids, until I accidentally busted one of Noah's old cricket trophies. Totally worth it.

⚬

Stump blasting was kind of fun, not that Hayden let anyone else have a proper go. The part-time soldier, who was also a chemical engineer, seemed to delight in taking on the role of safety instructor, as he taught Nicole and me everything there was to know about Anfo explosives. My precocious neighbour had taken one look at the handsome new arrivals preparing to blow up the old stringy-bark stumps and practically moved in. Poor Tim was torn between trying to keep an eye on Bane and me and wanting to remind Nicole that Luke and Hayden weren't the only ones who could blow stuff up. So I generously sacrificed my time so I could let him do both at once. It also meant Bane could feel secure enough to leave my side, the poor thing. As much as we craved each other's company, there were things he needed to arrange that he knew would bore me to tears. Like Guardian meetings and sparring sessions with Tessa, and contacting his army personnel officer for a job reference to give to Mick, and shopping for wedding shoes. Yawn.

One by one the old stumps were blasted and dragged away to the next paddock, and by the time I'd finished with the grader blade on our tractor, the back paddock looked as smooth and flat as a dam on a windless day. Even Noah was satisfied. The minute I jumped down from the driver's seat though, he dragged me away to hound me about more wedding details. He'd long since stopped asking me pointless questions about what colour tablecloths I wanted and whether we should offer wine before the service began, but there were a few things I couldn't avoid.

'Let her check it one more time,' he begged as he prodded me toward the cottage.

'It fits perfectly, Noah. I promise.' And yet I wasn't really all that upset at the thought of trying on my dress again. It was pretty damn gorgeous. The morning after we'd picked the date, my aunt had pulled me aside to show me my mother's wedding dress. Apparently, Annie had asked her friends in Eden to design a dress for her and had then had one made on this side of the boundary to match it. The gown was simple and elegant, and woven from a delicate fabric softer than swan feathers and just as light. It was natural cream in colour, and the bodice was adorned with an assortment of tiny ornaments. Each time I examined it, I found another testament to a world that valued beauty in every minute detail—a part of a rock that glittered with mica, a feather speckled with deep purple mystery, a shell streaked with blue star-shine. How long had it taken Annie to find these tiny treasures? I could only imagine what their Eden counterparts must have been like.

As I slipped the dress over my shoulders for my aunt to check the fit, I revelled in the feel of my mother's presence and reflected that Tim's dress shopping advice hadn't been such a waste of time after all.

❧

'Noah, we need to talk,' I said the next afternoon, confiscating a whole bag of lollies he was using to make wedding favours. He'd already scoffed most of them anyway. Without a moment's hesitation, he shoved the rest of the little gift boxes across the table to Tim and then got up to follow me. Tim checked to see that none of his other army friends were watching before resigning himself to finishing the ridiculous task of filling the boxes with jelly beans.

The river giggled at us as Noah and I settled down on our favourite rocks a few minutes later, trying to remember how we used to find them in the least bit comfortable. These rocks were built for smaller bums than we had now. As I sat with my legs crossed I tried to pin down exactly what I needed to say, only now that I had him alone I was at a loss.

Noah always hated watching me fidget.

'Yes, it's the right thing to do,' he stated, answering my unformed question. 'You should go ahead with the wedding even though there's a demon on the loose trying to kill us both. And for the record, Dr Vertan and Bane's mum have been close friends for years. Bane insists he didn't add her to the guest list for medical back-up in case we're attacked.'

I raised an eyebrow at him.

'At least, not *just* for medical back-up,' he amended.

Tracing my fingers over the initials we'd carved into my rock years before, I grimaced at his bluntness. 'Mick said the cybercrime unit have hit a dead end trying to trace Jake's advert, and I did too good a job with the virus, so the whole thing crashed. There are no new leads. We're back to square one.'

Noah didn't look as annoyed at me as I wanted him to. I would have preferred him to tell me off for trying to be too clever. Instead, he stared off toward the northwest. To the place our hearts were always drawn to.

'Are you certain we won't be putting more people at risk?' I asked, drawing his attention back. 'This place is the eye of the storm, Noah. Always. And not to sound overly cliché about it, but there is a whopper of a storm brewing. Can't you feel it?'

He sat up straighter and gave me a stern look. 'I won't let you delay the wedding,' he declared.

'I know you've put a lot of work into it, but …'

'No, Lainie, you don't understand. I won't let you do that to Bane. Not again. It's not fair. Cut the poor guy a break.'

Taken aback by his angry tone, I baulked. I was trying to be self-sacrificing here; why was he so cross at me?

'You can't keep pulling away from him or sooner or later his heart will break beyond repair. He's more fragile than he looks, you know.'

'Pulling away? Who said anything about pulling away? I only want to wait until we can safely get married without military protection and a doctor in attendance. Is that so much to ask?'

'Yes, actually, it is. You didn't see him after you left. He was really messed up until your aunt sat him down and bullied him into getting on with his life. After that he struggled to come home even to visit.'

Wincing at the reminder, I tried to look away.

Noah refused to be ignored. 'And then, since you've been back he hasn't exactly been able to trust you,' he continued. 'Between having you go catatonic, dying repeatedly, and unexpectedly flying away from your body, I'm surprised he's even risking getting close to you again.'

A strangled protest gargled from my throat. That was *so* unfair. It wasn't my fault I died. He made it sound like I'd allowed Jake to poison me just to avoid commitment. Staring him down, I dared him to charm me out of my anger.

'How dare you imply that I'm not trustworthy?' I argued. 'He knows I want to be with him more than anything. I don't care what Jake threatens us with, I won't leave him again.'

His triumphant smile waited for me to mentally commit to what I had accidentally promised. Sneaky bastard.

Rolling up his shirt sleeves, Noah thrust his arms into the icy water and splashed his face and hair, washing away the tiredness brought on by the frenetic planning of the last few weeks. The invigorating freshness made him look vibrant and playful again, which made me smile despite my irritation.

'Lainie, you're my best friend. I know you better than anyone else does, including your overly zealous fiancé. Which means I know you aren't going to just sit around and wait for Jake to show up. We need to get the sword back, and to do that safely, apparently, you need to get married. I also know what you and I are both capable of, and although it scares the crap out of me when I think about it too much, I also know we can trust it. Whatever Jake tries to throw at us, we'll deal with it, somehow.'

'How, Noah? What exactly are we supposed to do? We can't kill him, but I don't want him to keep coming at us either. We need to stop him once and for all.'

'And we will. We just need to separate Jake from Rabisu somehow.'

Dubious eyes met his confident green ones. 'If we are so capable, why can't we figure out a way to fix everything, right here, right now?'

'You mean, say the right Words and summon the sword back to us, then banish Rabisu back to the pit of hell or wherever he came from so we can get on with our lives?'

'That sounds terrific. Let's do that,' I agreed, lying back with my hair trailing in the water.

Silence stretched for long minutes while we basked in the washed-out sunlight, totally devoid of anything remotely resembling a useful idea. No Words came. Not so much as a syllable. Concentrating as hard as I could on all the reasons I thought Rabisu was a threat to Eden, I waited impatiently for the slight dizziness that meant something was about to happen. My brain remained stubbornly steady. It seemed that if the demon wanted to get into Eden, he would have to act before we could react. Thinking about getting the sword back was even worse. The more I thought about it the more I worried that I might acciden-tally go after it again, until I found myself trying to think about not thinking. My brain began to hurt.

Beside me, Noah's breathing gradually deepened as he nodded off to sleep. At least that was one thing I could fix.

Pushing him a few inches to the left did the trick.

Chapter 24

A little before midday on the day of the wedding I was presented with the perfect opportunity to sneak past Luke and Hayden to the back paddock. Noah had instructed them to stop me from peeking past the back yard fence to where the marquee and dance floor had been set up. The tantalising sound of Dallmin and Beth running their soundcheck was making it hard to behave, so when the rest of Bane's crew arrived and greeted the two soldiers, I very nearly made a dash for the back gate. I changed my mind when I overheard Kate, Hayley, and Lachlan gossiping about their friend's unexpected nuptials.

'I bet she has light brown hair. He never even glanced at a girl unless she had brown hair. Did you ever notice that?' Kate was talking in hushed tones to the other two, while I busied myself raking leaves so I could blend in with the other helpers who were assisting us with setting up.

'Whoever she is, she must be something special to have cracked the Ice Man. Tim said Bane knew her in high school, but I never heard him mention her before. Doesn't anyone else find that strange?' Stocky and thick-muscled, Lachlan looked like he could have pulled our stumps out of the ground with his bare hands, although the way he was chattering along with the girls reflected a more laid-back temperament.

'You're only saying that because you're jealous, Lachie, admit it,' Hayley teased. He shrugged without denying anything.

I raked my way over a little closer.

'So long as she takes good care of our boy, I'm happy,' Kate said, as if subtly trying to remind the others to behave. 'I'm more worried about her. Do you think she knows about his obsession with knives? And does she realise how broody he can get? I can't imagine living with someone that intense for more than a few weeks. It would do my head in.'

Hayley drew her glossy dark hair over her shoulder in an unsubtle gesture. 'I, personally, would manage fine. I could handle sullen if only he didn't look at me as if I was his sister,' she grumbled. 'I tried really hard, too. He never even noticed. Did this girl blackmail him or something?'

I cringed, stood on the rake, and nearly poked myself in the eye with the handle. Did causing him gut-wrenching bouts of nausea when he left me count as blackmail?

'Maybe you should have dyed your hair,' Lachlan teased back, but then a scandalous look came over his face as he leaned in and whispered, 'Do you think maybe they were high school sweethearts and had a fight? Maybe she didn't like the idea of him joining the army. It would explain a lot if he's been heartbroken over her all this time.' He straightened. 'You know what? It shouldn't be too difficult to find out their back story.' Looking around, his eyes locked on mine.

To avoid his gaze I began to rake furiously until there were little gouges in the grass, but it was too late. 'Excuse me.' He smiled politely. 'Do you know either the bride or the groom very well?'

Pressing my lips together, I nodded, trying hard to look innocent.

'Did they go out together back in high school? Sorry if it seems a bit intrusive. We've known Bane pretty well for a while now, and we don't actually know how they met. Would you be able to fill us in a little? Were they always close?'

So much blood left my face that my lips began to tingle as all three of them watched me expectantly. Apparently, it hadn't occurred to them that the bride might be raking the back lawn when she should be locked inside having her crazy hair tamed by a team of industrial hair specialists.

'Uh, well, I ...' I cleared my throat and tried again. 'I don't know about *close*, but they've known each other since Prep.' I smiled and nodded.

They clearly wanted more.

Resigning myself to the inevitable, I tried to remember as much as I could. 'Okay, so in Year Seven when it was Lainie's turn to look after the class goldfish, he added blue dye to the water and left the little blue corpse in her lunchbox,' I admitted, remembering the look of horror on my girlfriends' faces that day at lunch. They never wanted me to eat with them after that. 'And then in Year Eight, he started a false rumour that the only reason she got selected for the netball team was because her aunt paid off the PE teacher, and so she basically sat on the bench all season and never got selected for any of the good games.'

Avid faces stared at me in open curiosity, wanting more. I had plenty more. For some reason, my memories of Bane were some of the clearest.

'That was the same year he set her locker on fire and got suspended from school for two weeks. Then a few months after that, he stole and read out her English poem in front of the whole class. It was supposed to be a sonnet. It wasn't very good. In Year Ten, he dobbed her in for borrowing equipment from the science lab, which she was only planning to use to make a foam explosion for her best friend. That one earned her a Saturday detention and made her miss the state showjumping finals. She couldn't convince them at the time that the equipment wasn't for something else. He also stole all her history notes, which meant she failed the next test and had to sit through one of those "If you could just learn to *apply* yourself, Lainie" lectures from the principal.'

Confused glances passed between my audience members. They probably hadn't expected quite such a mental-sounding version of their friend.

A warm hug collected me from behind as Bane's voice chimed in. 'In Year Eleven I swapped one of her maths assignments for mine and got an A-plus for the first time.' He kissed my neck in very belated gratitude. 'I also told everyone you had scurvy and that was why you ate so much fruit. Hacking into your emails was pretty easy too, so when everyone got all those annoying kitten pictures, they assumed it was from you.'

The scurvy rumour was actually pretty close to the truth in hindsight, but I hadn't known about that last one. It explained why Kiara had kept showing me pictures of her cat all year.

Hayley and Lachlan looked like they wanted to crawl into a hole and hide as they realised who I was. Kate laughed and kissed my cheek.

We were still catching up on stories of how everyone else had met when Noah lost patience and came to collect me. It wasn't as if I could hide from him, so I meekly let him drag me away as Kate stared after him with an all too familiar wistful expression.

As we left I heard Lachlan murmuring to the others, 'Who would have thought this backwater town would breed so many amazing human specimens? What on Earth do they put in the water here?'

I looked back at Bane who was struggling unsuccessfully to keep a straight face. When he caught my eye he laughed out loud. All his friends stared at him like they'd never heard the sound before.

As we walked down to the cottage, I thought I could smell something weird, like strongly scented flowers that were scorched by flame. What the hokey had Noah ordered from the caterers? Before I could ask, he bundled me through the door into the waiting arms of Aunt Lily and Tessa, who were both armed to the teeth with hair straighteners, brushes, and one almighty great big can of hairspray.

The wall of rock stared back at her in patient defiance as Annie tried once again to find the Words to shift it. There was a buzz at the base of her teeth that verified her conviction that she would be needed on the other side, so what was the problem? Nayn handed her a piece of flatbread, which she chewed on distractedly.

After weeks of scouring her memories for more clues, Annie had given up. It was as if the standing stones had been drained dry and had left the rest to her, only despite her best efforts, Annie still couldn't put the pieces together. Some vital clue was still missing, and she knew it had to do with the flat bit of stone that had been carved with a picture of a gem. Where had she seen it last? She'd brought it to Eden to have it translated, with limited success. So she'd taken it back to Nalong ... the rest was lost in a tangle of memories she really didn't want to unravel but had attempted to anyway. It was no use. No amount of sleeping or meditating had yielded any more hints. There was only one thing left to try. It was time to retrace her steps. Go back to where it had all happened. As if making that decision hadn't been difficult enough, she'd then been faced with the problem of the rock wall that blocked the cave. For a couple of days, she'd tried Lainie's method of scaling the rock face, until eventually she'd fallen and broken her hip. Nayn had silenced her pain with the sweet taste of Living Fruit. She refused to let that happen again, so Nayn suggested that he climb up instead and throw her down a rope, except no one in the village had one long enough and it would have taken them weeks to make one. So Annie had spent nearly three full days in the cave, staring at the rock face, trying to work out how to get past it.

And now her teeth were buzzing. There were two adult Cherubim on the other side. She shouldn't be needed there, and yet she wanted to bite something. Do something. Say something. Time was running out. She laid her hands against the cold stones and commanded them to move. Nothing happened.

❧

'Why does it have to be a boy's name?' Tessa asked as she yanked the brush through my hair. I was certain my scalp was bleeding. Bane would come bursting through the door any moment now to rescue me from her abuse. Any second now. Another firm tug nearly pulled me from the barstool.

Tim had joined us in the tiny cottage so he could make sure Bane didn't find an excuse to come and find me again, but really because he wanted to escape from Noah's tyrannical rule for a while. He insisted there were plenty of other people around to help set out chairs.

'I don't know of any magical swords that have girl's names. It's against the rules,' he replied as he passed me a bowl of chips he'd nicked from the kitchen.

'And I don't know of any others that are actually real, so I guess that means we can break whatever rules we want,' Tessa insisted.

I was sure I could smell my hair burning as she began to straighten it. The crazy thing was that she and my aunt were methodically putting each strand up into some sort of intricately organised design anyway, so why bother straightening it first? Aunt Lily frowned at me as if she knew what I was thinking. I tried to be patient.

'What we need is a name that reflects its purpose,' Tim suggested. 'That way it can be more like an adjective than a male or female name.'

He bit into an apple from the fruit bowl and winked at me as he tossed it to me to finish. I scowled at him in suspicion, certain now that Bane had sent him to make sure I ate something. Something not poisoned.

'Well then,' I supplied, 'it will have to have something to do with cleansing.' The apple tasted wonderful. I was hungrier than I'd realised. Pausing mid-bite, I realised the others were all staring at me in confusion. Tessa was the first one brave enough to ask.

'I don't mean to sound like I know what I'm talking about, because I really have no clue, but doesn't it sort of judge who can cross and who can't? I thought that was its purpose.' She put a few more bobby pins into my woven coiffure and I hoped quietly that the poor things might bravely find their way out again one day.

'That's the *reason* it's there, but that's not its purpose,' I explained, forcing myself to stop fidgeting. 'Its primary purpose is to clean. Unfortunately, it can't seem to do it without ...' I stopped chewing as I thought about Noah's mother, screaming as the flames engulfed her. Bile rose in my throat so I handed the apple back to Tim. To discipline my thoughts away from the painful memory, I tried to work out how I knew what it was the sword did.

The revelation that Dallmin's greatest fear was to die while he was tainted by shame had made me think. What if there was a way to become clean again, even if it killed you? Dallmin would take that option in a second if he could. A haunting memory of the bright innocent song of the sword convinced me there was a way, only I was afraid to think about it too much—for a couple of reasons. I didn't want to go back to that dark place where all I saw was Sarah in her last moments, nor did I want to take any more unplanned trips away from my body. The total purity of the sword was a power in and of itself, and no taint could touch it without being burned away. I was both encouraged and terrified by what that meant.

Tim waved his hand in front of my glazed eyes to make sure I was still on the planet. He breathed a sigh of relief when I blinked and smiled at him. 'So what do you think of the name Sadie?' he asked. 'You know, after "Sadie the Cleaning Lady"?'

Aunt Lily cracked up. 'That song was even before my time. My mum used to sing it to us in the car. It drove us nuts.'

Tessa glanced at her in confusion, looking absurd with a mouth full of bobby pins.

Groaning at the memory, I explained where Tim had come across it. 'Dallmin researched the history of the Australian music industry on the way to Nhill, when we were chasing Jake around the state.' We had all made a pact never to mention the hour spent singing John Farnham songs as loudly as we could at passing trucks. Secretly though, we'd all loved it.

Another four pins disappeared into the mysterious depths of my hairdo.

'Tim, you can't call it Sadie,' Tessa complained as she moved in front of me to inspect her handiwork. 'It's far too mundane. If you saw it you'd understand. Sadie is much too … sacrilegious.'

I wasn't certain if it was Tim's suggestion or my hair that was causing her to frown that way. Probably both.

'Well, it's just a nickname,' he said. 'I'm sure it has a real name that's in some unpronounceable holy language that us mere mortals are forbidden to utter.'

I threw a chip at him.

'Oh, that's right, I forgot. You don't like nicknames, do you?' he teased, throwing it straight back.

'What do you mean?' I asked.

'I mean you and Bane. I've never once heard either of you use a pet name for each other. It's not your thing, I get it.'

That made both Tessa and Aunt Lily nearly wet themselves laughing. 'Who do you think nicknamed him "Bane" in the first place?' Tessa asked, saving me the need to explain.

The poor guy reddened as the penny dropped. The name must have really taken hold if even Tim had forgotten that it wasn't his real one.

'That's not a nickname,' he justified petulantly. 'It's more like a sobriquet.'

'Stop trying to use big words to make yourself sound smarter,' Tessa admonished.

'I'll use whatever tricks I can think of to do that,' he countered.

'If you're really smart, you won't need tricks for people to see it.'

'Just like if the sword is really that special, then it won't need a fancy name for people to appreciate it,' he countered. 'I like "Sadie". It's friendly, feisty, and feminine.'

He bowed to us all elegantly and then, taking the chips with him, he retreated out the door before we could argue any further.

By two o'clock in the afternoon I had been buffed, polished, sprayed with perfume, dressed, and pep-talked. The fine early drizzle had worn off, and lemon sunlight glistened from the tip of every leaf. I breathed in the crisp winter air and hugged Aunt Lily one last time as I heard a clarinet begin to play. Every inch of my skin was buzzing in anticipation. It was time to get married.

She was supposed to give it to Bane, but she didn't want to. In her purse was a small wedding gift, and she needed to find him and give it to him. If she could catch him before the ceremony then she could admit once and for all how she felt about him, and it would finally be off her chest. Only, she was surrounded by strangers here and was worried that someone might overhear. She would be mortified if that happened. Besides, she was supposed to wait until the dancing. Perhaps that would be better. That would be a more appropriate time to give a gift, wouldn't it? Except Lainie would be with him then, and it would be better if she wasn't around. She could hardly be honest about how she felt if his new wife was standing right next to him. Confusion made her head hurt. What was it she wanted to do again?

Music began to play and everyone moved out of the back garden and into the brightly decorated back paddock where rows of chairs were set up to form a short aisle. Her mates were waiting for her in the back row, waving her over to come and sit with them.

She would just have to catch him on his own later somehow.

She didn't really want to.

At the sound of Annie's voice, the rock wall tore apart like cracking bones, and a cloud of gritty dust flew up with the violence of inverted hailstones. Concentrating hard on the crystalline structure of the rock surrounding the cave, Annie spoke soothing Words of healing to the strained granite above. Another Word, and the rubble cleared itself out of her way and landed in a tidy pile on the far side of the stream. She was tired of tripping over things whenever she came back. Honestly, those kids were so messy. As soon as she was convinced that the integrity of the cavern and surrounding tunnel would remain intact, she grabbed her cloth bag in one hand, Nayn's elbow with the other, and strode toward the far tunnel. They were needed *now*. That was why the Words had bubbled out of her so unexpectedly.

Fiery tears of joy threatened to undo an hour's worth of make-up artistry. The sound of a clarinet welcomed me into the floral vista that was once the muddy back paddock. Noah had outdone himself trying to replicate the feel of my shelter tree in my other home. Hundreds of purple and gold flowers adorned a fine mesh that stretched above the heads of the smiling guests. No wonder the florist had complained. Despite the glorious sight of such beauty, my attention was still captivated by Dallmin's heartfelt gift. As I walked down the aisle clutching Aunt Lily's arm like a strangled teddy bear, the haunting tune of my mother's lullaby enticed me forward like a comforting embrace.

Faces turned toward me with shining eyes, which one by one turned to awe as they noticed the unusual design of Annie's gown. A few faces showed blatant surprise, and Hayley looked almost twitchy as I passed by. I hardly spared any of them a thought as Bane captured all my attention with his dazzling grey eyes that brimmed with something suspiciously close to happy tears.

The ceremony passed in a blur as we were undone by the formal religious words delivered by the pastor from Horsham—whom Dallmin, of all people, had arranged for us. The simple phrases left me stunned as I heard them afresh in the context of what they meant for us. By the time Noah stepped forward to give the standard wedding Bible reading, I was reduced to a quivering ball of charged emotion. One more sniffle from Aunt Lily would have had me sobbing, for sure.

'First Corinthians chapter thirteen, verses one to thirteen,' Noah began, winking at me. 'If I speak in the tongues of men and of angels, but have not love, I am only a resounding gong or a clanging cymbal. If I have the gift of prophecy and can fathom all mysteries and all knowledge, and if I have a faith that can move mountains, but have not love, I am nothing. If I give all I possess to the poor and surrender my body to the flames, but have not love, I gain nothing.'

As he continued to quote the beautiful letter, written so long ago to a fledgling group of Christians in ancient Greece, I noticed Dallmin standing with his mouth open, avidly absorbing every syllable. Words of no less power than anything I'd ever uttered in defence of Eden caressed his soul with compassionate wisdom. The grace-given love Noah spoke about was undeniable proof that humans here still had the gifted ability to overcome flawed character. For the first time in far too long, Dallmin looked hopeful and sure of himself. Love had not been surrendered when his soul had lost its innocence. Neither had my own love been surrendered, even for a moment, since the day I'd returned from Eden to track down the hopeless tourist. I'd found what I wanted, and I was never going to let him go again. Every last fibre of my being was bound with Bane's. Bound and strengthened. That feeling was reflected in the eyes of my adoring husband as I leaned in to kiss him.

Touch ignited joy.

Bonded sensitivity forged fresh links as I surrendered to his innate integrity. Yearning permission was sought at the deepest level, unlocking moment by moment the rough ties that guarded his innermost sense of self. Respect and abiding honour flowed both ways as I melted into his steadfast presence.

And there was not a thing Tim could say to stop us.

Chapter 25

Another big rock bashed the side of the canoe as it slid mercilessly downstream. Nayn winced, throwing a concerned glance at Annie, who ignored him. The angry river was shouting at her to remember all she had lost here. If Nayn hadn't forced her to keep moving she never would have made it past the threshold of the tunnel into the stark winter landscape. One look at the river that had claimed the life of her Guardian had broken her down into a useless bundle of cowering limbs. The secret hidden in her bag had made it even harder to move. Her stomach churned with memories and guilt. No matter how long she hid from her past, it would always be there, waiting for her. Unchanged. Guilt from her present warred with guilt from her past. She would not lose Dallmin the way she'd lost Lucas, and yet making herself move forward was much harder than she'd anticipated. Eventually, Nayn had coaxed her to keep going, to climb into the little boat he'd gallantly retrieved from the other side of the raging water. He wrestled it through the rapids that would lead them to where they could feel the presence of the other Cherubim.

Pallid sunshine tried to comfort her shivering flesh, but the hollow atmosphere sucked all the warmth from senses that had grown accustomed to sweet fragrances and gentle touch. She huddled in the canoe with exquisitely sweet memories of Lucas slamming painfully one after another into her mind.

It wasn't until they started catching glimpses of open paddocks up on the hills that Annie began to really look around her. Like passing a car crash on a highway, it was impossible for her not to raise her face and *see*. That willow tree. That fallen log. That army of reeds standing guard like parade soldiers along the riverbank.

'We need to pull in,' she cried. 'Quickly! Before the next bend.'

Nayn heaved the canoe around and Annie leaped out as soon as it was shallow enough. The embankment was so steep that chunks of it had eroded into the river, leaving stark orange patches of clay woven through with naked tree roots. As her mind baulked at her intention, Annie scrambled up to the next flattish level, which revealed an overgrown trail. She marched along it with tears filling the back of her throat, choking her with the one memory even her dreams had refused to expose. The forgotten trail led over a narrow bluff before dropping back from the river, tricked by the sudden sharp bend in the watercourse.

Be careful, she signed back to Nayn, who was about to follow. *The river here behaves differently.* It was then that she caught sight of the broken sapling. Long since dead, its leaves missing, the young stump remained as a testament to the life cut short. Annie's tears choked out all sense of the present, and once again her memories cracked away from her tight control and took over.

'Lainie, sweetheart, not so fast. The ground is slippery here,' she'd cautioned her daughter, all those years ago.

'Daddy coming,' was the reply, which was enough of a reason for Lainie to ignore her and pelt headlong around the next bend.

'Yes, I noticed. Though why he would want to come out in this weather is beyond me. It's about to rain.' She took a moment to feel for her Guardian. He was even closer than she'd expected. 'You could have just waited at home and had hot Milo ready,' she called. 'And dry socks for Little Miss I-lost-my-boots-in-the-cave-again. Maybe we should set up emergency shoe supply stations along the riv—'

One look at Lucas's face was enough to cut her off. He had Lainie's shoulder in a death grip with one hand while the other, clad in plaster, seemed poised to clobber someone.

'I told you to be careful near the river,' he snapped. 'It's been raining almost solidly for three days. Do you realise how quickly she'd be swept away if she slipped?'

'I'm not a slipper,' Lainie assured him.

Annie started to laugh until Lucas glared at her. 'Sorry, Lucas. I had her walking sensibly until she felt you coming. She missed you.'

His face softened and he hoisted Lainie up onto his hip and kissed her forehead. 'I missed you both too. Sarah asked Harry to help her with their new stock delivery, and when he left I got fidgety. I hate being useless.' He stepped toward her, moving his broken arm as if to give her a hug before remembering he couldn't. 'This cast is driving me crazy. When I was at the museum this morning someone bumped into me and I came very close to spilling coffee over the cabinet with all those old stamps. I barely managed to catch the cup with this thing slowing me down.'

'They let you take your coffee in? Wait—more importantly, you caught the cup with your broken arm? Did anyone see you?'

Lucas scowled again.

'Right. Sorry. Not nagging. What did you find at the museum?'

'The ruby is right where it should be, on display. Still hanging from the same chain and everything. I don't know what I expected to find. The only surprise was seeing Mr Durante. Apparently, he got a job there after he closed his jewellery shop.'

Annie's heart sank at the reminder. The shop had closed a few weeks after she and Mr Durante had been held hostage and beaten by two members of an organised crime syndicate. The same men who murdered her mum.

'Annie, don't. I know that look. It wasn't your fault. If anything, he's the one … the one who …' Even the mere reminder of the danger she'd been in was enough to render him incapable of normal speech.

'Lucas, that's all in the past now.'

'Daddy cranky-pants,' Lainie said, wriggling out of Lucas's grip.

'Sorry, pudding,' Lucas said, letting her go. He turned to Annie and did a reasonable job of schooling his expression into something almost calm and pleasant. 'Did Pallano find someone to interpret the markings on the stone?'

Annie tasted the air around her, feeling for the emotions he was trying to tone down for her sake. The predominant one was relief but his temper felt sharp around the edges, which made her wonder how snippy he'd been before catching up to them. Something certainly felt off. Of course, she'd just stepped out of a place where no one ever felt cross, and she always became oversensitive to it when she returned.

'He did, but only partially. I guess languages must shift over there too, although that doesn't make sense because they all have perfect recall so even if the fashions change, they should still remember—'

Lucas stopped her rambling with a quick kiss. He looked impatient. 'What does it say?'

She gave a soft laugh. 'It says "Give it your best" something.'

'Your best something?'

'It's the "something" that they couldn't work out. The closest they came was the possibility it had something to do with a knee. Not sure how that helps.'

'Give it your best knee? Maybe you need to kneel to someone. Or someone should be kneeling to you.'

Annie shrugged. She reached into her bag to pull out the stone, as if looking at it again might somehow solve the puzzle. She still felt the tingle when she brushed her fingers over the diagram of the gem.

Lainie stomped past her in her wet socks. 'Tell me who is coming now,' she demanded as only a toddler could. 'Is it Aunty Lily?'

'Lainie, come back. You sit right here on this log,' Lucas instructed. 'Annie, is she right? Is someone coming?'

'Wow, she's pretty good at this. Yes, someone is heading this way and I think I know who it is. What I don't know is why. Did you leave your wallet behind at the museum or something?'

'I don't think so.'

'Well, Mr Durante has not only followed you home, he's followed you all the way out here in this freezing wind.'

Lucas drew her behind him as he peered down the track. 'Don't say a word to him, Annie. Let me do the talking. I know how hard it is for you to lie when you're this fresh out of the Garden.' He glanced back at his daughter perched on the fallen log, and Annie followed his gaze. Lainie's feet didn't touch the ground.

'She won't say anything. You know that,' Annie assured him. 'Shouldn't we keep walking? How are we going to explain why we're sitting by the river in wet clothes when it's about to rain again?' She started beckoning to Lainie, but Lucas grabbed her hand. He took the carved rock from her grasp and placed it behind the log, out of sight.

'We need to stay here where it's more open.'

'Oh, that does *not* sound good.'

Lucas set his jaw.

When Mr Durante came into view a few minutes later, Annie let out a tight breath. He was wearing his usual pale linen suit and carrying an umbrella, and was picking his way between puddles like they might be full of acid. Hardly the demeanour of a man looking for trouble. He was so busy looking down that he flinched when he finally noticed the three of them watching him.

'Oh, um, hello,' he said. 'Hello, little girl,' he squeaked to Lainie, who merely blinked at him. 'Lucas, isn't it? I saw you at the museum this morning.' He held his hand out to shake, but Lucas didn't move. Hardly surprising given he'd been offering to shake his broken arm. The man drew back awkwardly. 'When I saw you I, er, realised it had been a while since … well, since you lost your mother, Annie. I thought I'd pop round to see how you're both doing.'

A while? Almost six years. And in all that time he'd never so much as acknowledged her whenever they'd run into each other in town. Given the amount of guilt and rising panic she'd always felt from him, she wasn't offended. She'd negotiated for Fourby and Cruise to release him that day, and almost been killed by them soon after. She supposed that made for rather uncomfortable small talk at the shops. So why come all the way out here now?

'Mr Durante, why are you really here?' Lucas asked, taking a step toward him.

The man drew himself up. 'I'm looking for the truth about this.'

He reached into his jacket and drew out a necklace. The blood-red gem glinted in the dreary sunlight. How had he smuggled it out of the museum? Even as a staff member that couldn't have been easy.

'You know, when Geoff Doolan asked me to make a setting for this so he could gift it to his fiancée, he told me not to cut it. Only polish it up a bit,' Mr Durante said. 'He said he wanted to keep its natural imperfect heart shape. That it was flawed, and that's what made it the best the Earth had to offer. He said that his own flawed heart was all he could offer his new wife, so it was appropriate.'

Although he was speaking such sentimental words, all Annie felt from the man was desire and anticipation. As if he felt close to finding a long lost treasure.

'I guess that's one reason I never thought to question its nature,' he continued. 'Who would have suspected a blood-red gem to be a diamond until they tried to cut it? Geoff said it was a family heirloom, so naturally I assumed it had come from around here. Back then, no one had heard of red diamonds being mined anywhere in Australia. Of course, then they started digging up pinks at Argyle diamond mine up in north WA. Suddenly, this little beauty became very interesting.'

Annie's skin began to buzz.

'Mate, you've been getting sucked into someone's furphy. I remember the police reports as well as you do. They checked it pretty well. That's no diamond.'

'Of course it isn't. If I'd thought for one second that it was, I never would have encouraged Ruby Doolan to sell it. What she got for it was way beyond what a flawed ruby was worth, but nowhere near the price of a red diamond.'

Annie frowned. His words were accompanied by a heavy streak of doubt. Ugly grey, like a thunder cloud. She sat as still as the log she was sitting on, waiting to hear what else the jeweller had to say. He was pacing now, clutching at the necklace and no longer caring about the mud.

'When I received the second valuation report, I knew something was fishy. Insurance fraud. That's what the police decided, in the end. Only, the first valuer was adamant it was a diamond. Never backed down from his assessment. Went to jail over it, I heard.'

'He was mistaken,' Lucas declared in a dangerously quiet tone.

'No, he was lying. He must have been too afraid of the crime boss to admit he'd given a false assessment. Mr Rosa had it all set up. When the gem went missing I assumed he'd arranged a fake robbery for a fake diamond so he could claim the insurance money. Framed poor Geoff Doolan to take the fall for it. Ruby must have realised that. After Geoff died, they say she tried to break into Mr Rosa's office to try to prove he still had the gem, and jumped from the building when she couldn't.'

'They killed her,' Annie choked out. 'You know that.'

Lucas placed a soothing hand on her shoulder.

'I thought that would be the end of it,' Mr Durante asserted, like he was begging to be believed. 'Only, Mr Rosa kept on asking questions. Ruby and Geoff were gone, but the questions didn't stop. Had I heard any rumours? Local legends? Had I seen Kiah Langley do anything suspicious or unusual?'

Annie's heart flipped. Power sizzled on the tip of her tongue. He should not be asking such things about her mum.

The man's eyes bored into hers. 'Why was he searching for the necklace if he'd faked the theft in the first place?'

Lucas stepped between them. 'You need to leave now, Mr Durante. Get that damn necklace back to the museum before they report it stolen.'

'Stolen. Yes.' The man refused to move. He kept staring at Annie.

The air around them was charged with emotions and Annie fought to untangle them. Fresh out of Eden, she was finding it difficult. The man seemed so tenacious, and hostile—and also terrified. He had conflicting sentiments, like he was riding a horse with its head obediently turned right, but its legs moving left. His emotions were so incompatible that she even stretched out her senses to check if someone else was nearby. There was only him and his piercing eyes, hunting for answers.

Lainie kicked her wet socks against the log, getting impatient. The man's eyes locked on her before his gaze flinched away. He shivered and fidgeted.

'I tried to warn them,' he rasped. 'I saw Kiah and Anthony together in town one day, and I told Anthony about Mr Rosa's questions. I never told him his name, of course. No, I would never have risked that. If he'd found out I'd snitched, we would have all been silenced. I don't know if Anthony believed me. He seemed to listen, and then he died a few months later. Heart attack, they said. I was so worried that maybe Mr Rosa had somehow found out I'd said something. Surely not. How could he?'

Her dad, Anthony, had died trying to get into Eden. He'd wanted to hide them all away. Perhaps he *had* listened to Mr Durante's warning. Guardians could certainly overreact sometimes. And after losing Geoff and Ruby, it made perfect sense. So much death and loss and it all came back to the crime boss, Mr Rosa, searching for his stolen gem.

Lucas had obviously followed the same logic. 'Mr Rosa died in jail last year. The ruby is just a ruby, and there are no more questions to ask.' He began to shepherd the man back, but Mr Durante pushed past him and kneeled in front of Annie. The necklace hung from his fingers, the ruby dipped into the mud.

'It still has questions!' he hissed. 'It won't stop whispering them in my sleep. Is it you? The ruby tastes like you. It reaches for you like a lost child. Are you its mother?'

Words sizzled on the tip of Annie's tongue and the man's eyes lit up. She needed to stop this, and she had the authority to do whatever it took. One Word and this man could be made to leave. No, that wouldn't be enough. He had to stop asking questions. He needed the same embargo the rest of them had, or at least something similar.

The hunger in his eyes felt dangerous.

Annie opened her mouth to speak.

'No!' Lucas slammed into the man from the side, knocking him down. The sudden violence swept the Word from Annie's lips like a lost sneeze. 'Don't speak, Annie. Please!'

Too late. Maybe. She couldn't quite tell. All she knew was that Mr Durante was grinning at her, his face smeared with dirt. There was madness in his gaze, matched by the guttural laugh that morphed into a snarl. He hardly seemed like the same man, crouched in the mud like a dog poised to attack.

'It *is* you,' he spat. 'I waited and watched. I knew your monstrous nature would reveal itself eventually. You can't hide forever.' The man sprang up and latched his hands around her throat. A blur of movement, a grunt of pain, and then the hands were gone. As Annie fell backward she glimpsed Lucas swinging his plaster cast across Mr Durante's face. Lainie was screaming. Annie scrambled to scoop up her daughter as the two men brawled, throwing punches and grabbing at each other's clothes. The jeweller's moves were sluggish compared to the Guardian's swift reflexes, but he was implacable, taking every hit in apparent ignorance of the pain. Again and again he lunged toward her. Over and over, Lucas blocked his way, shoved him back, eventually clobbering him so hard with his cast that the man finally fell, breathing hard and staring at her, dazed. Lucas pinned him down with a knee on his chest.

'I know you now, monster,' the man said to her. It didn't sound like Mr Durante at all.

Annie lifted her chin. She was born to deal with this. This moment was hers to own. 'You will not speak of this to anyone,' she commanded, and then tripped out a prickly phrase of Words. 'If you try, all anyone will hear is a madman, talking to the wind.'

He gave an oily smile. 'Your command is bound to this flesh. I will simply take another and come for you. All of you.' His eyes darted toward Lainie before he let out a wail so full of despair that the clouds seemed to hear, and it started to rain.

Lucas caught Annie's eye. He had tears rolling down his face. There was no need for discussion. They would both do whatever it took to keep Lainie safe from this threat, whatever it was.

Annie put Lainie down and kneeled over the writhing man. Even with one arm locked in a cast, Lucas still had him solidly pinned. Annie placed a hand on either side of the man's face and looked him in the eye.

'Mr Durante, you will not allow any harm to come to my daughter. Do you understand?' Her words felt like waves crashing over a fragile shell. 'You will do whatever it takes to keep her safe.' Her Words felt right. Felt *necessary.*

Mr Durante stopped thrashing. His eyes were sad. 'He's afraid of the river,' he whispered. 'Let me go. I'll do what I can to stop him, but you need to hide better.'

Stop him? Who? There was something disturbing about all this and she didn't have enough information. And time was running out.

Lucas tightened his hold on the man's wrist. 'Annie, get back. I won't be able to hold him much longer. I can feel his intention to hurt you. You need to move.'

She stood, grabbed Lainie, and moved back into the trees. She could hear the river grumbling behind her as it curved around the bluff.

Mr Durante began to thrash around like a crazed boar, bulldozing his way out of Lucas's grip. He lunged toward them, enraged, roaring, and in the next moment he stopped so abruptly that Lucas almost flipped right over him. So her command to keep Lainie safe was holding. So far.

The air tasted like violence and jealousy, resin and rain. Mr Durante's emotions tasted like pure desperation. Annie watched as Lucas again leaped to stand between the attacker and his family, his Guardian reflexes unhindered by his pointless plaster cast.

Annie stepped backward, stumbling over the uneven ground until a small sapling blocked her retreat. She could hear the river below.

He was afraid of the river.

'Lucas, take Lainie,' she said as she tossed her daughter into his care.

An indignant toddler yell was her daughter's only response as Lucas barely managed to catch her with his one good arm. He somehow kept the flare of panic out of his voice. 'I've got you, Pudding-Kitten,' he soothed.

That child was never afraid of anything, and Annie was determined to keep her that way. She took a deep breath, clutching the sapling as Mr Durante narrowed his eyes at Lainie.

'Pudding-Kitten,' he snarled, and then wrenched his gaze away. That command *had* to hold. The man rushed at her again. Annie smiled and didn't move. He might be afraid of the river, but she wasn't. Not with Lucas nearby, able to find her no matter how far downstream she was swept.

She stepped behind the sapling, feeling the ground drop away under her heel. There was air behind her and now air below as well. She heard the snap-crash of breaking wood as Mr Durante slammed straight into the young tree, and then pain took over as her head snapped back, hit by a fist that was followed by the rest of the man's body. As they fell together she could hear Lucas cry out. She'd heard that sound before and had vowed never to cause it again. She was full of broken promises. Something hit her shoulder, tearing at the skin. A rock, or a branch— one of many that she bounced over as they plummeted down the river- bank. It was such a blessed relief to feel the icy water embrace her and pull her from the man's chokehold. She lost sight of him as they were swept downstream, and then she was too busy to care. The water was angry at her for breaking her promise. She was supposed to keep herself safe. She'd promised him. Still, all she had to do was to keep her head above water until it slowed enough for Lucas to help her out. Perhaps the river would take her all the way down to the open paddocks so she wouldn't have to walk so far to get home. Or perhaps not. She was really good at holding her breath, but that didn't mean her body didn't need oxygen. Where was the sky? Where was Lucas with a conveniently long branch? A moment later she felt her face break the surface and she sucked in a crisp breath. Rain pelted her cheeks. The next time she surfaced she felt something tug at her hair so she strained against the current and floundered around until she managed to grab onto it. A bunch of gum leaves, trailing in the water. She kicked upward, feeling them tear off as she fought to grip higher. The branch bent under her weight, but she'd played this game in Eden many times so she knew how to grip it until she could secure a firm hold further up. By the time she crawled up onto the riverbank, she was exhausted and freezing. Her nose was bleeding from the punch, and her ripped shoulder was stinging.

There was no sign of Mr Durante in the madness of the current, and for a minute she was torn between heading downstream to find him and going back. Searching for him alone would be stupid—and dangerous. She needed help, and Lucas couldn't do much with Lainie in tow, so she made her way upstream, rehearsing what she would say to appease Lucas for her recklessness. When he didn't explode from the thick bush to scold her she was grateful for the extra time to come up with an explanation for her actions. It had felt so necessary at the time. The look in Mr Durante's eyes …

Her gratitude turned to confusion when she made it all the way to where Lainie was waiting impatiently by the broken sapling. By then she was so cold she could barely feel her arms enough to hug her.

'Lainie, where's Daddy?' she asked through chattering teeth.

Lainie crossed her arms and made her grumpy face. 'Too cold for swimming today. N'long rules now, Mummy. And Daddy is not supposed to get his cast wet. Naughty Daddy.'

Annie turned back to the swirling water as horror rose in her throat. The river behaved differently now. And it looked furious about her dreadful miscalculation.

Chapter 26

'Annie,' Nayn whispered, kneeling down beside her and jangling her out of her dark reverie. *I am not certain this is best for you.*

'It *wasn't* entirely my fault,' she said in English. The revelation stung like antiseptic on an open wound. What a painful gift, living out memories. She could only imagine what it must be like to have her mother's or Lainie's natural gifting. They saw other people's memories all the time. These ones were her own and they were painful enough.

Nayn watched her with kind eyes.

I remember all of it now. I made a grave error here, and I remember why. There was a man. I think he may have been claimed by something … not alive. I did what was needed to keep him from finding out about us. I goaded him into the river. He was afraid of the river.

Nayn glanced down at the water below. *The river destroyed the veiled ones in Beltana's tale, so perhaps you made the wise choice,* he said.

Not so wise. Lucas followed us in, but he couldn't win against the current because his arm … that part was my fault. If only she'd let him take that stupid cast off.

I was wrong. This is best for you. Keep talking, Nayn encouraged.

Annie shifted over on the fallen log so Nayn could sit next to her. She swapped to the spoken language because it felt important to articulate what she remembered. 'I ran back downstream with Lainie, following the river the whole way, searching for him. Perhaps if I'd taken the usual path I might have been able to call for help sooner. It didn't matter. Lucas was already gone. They found the other man barely alive, caught in a tangle of branches. He never really recovered. They said he had … an illness caused by bad memories. I only saw him once after that, the following spring. He was broken. Broken by the creature's influence, and by my command not to hurt Lainie or speak of us to anyone. When he saw me he threw himself at a wall. I've never seen anything like it. His head hit the bricks over and over. It was clear the creature still held him—or perhaps he held it. He refused to look at me, but he kept telling me that the river had weakened it, and he would keep fighting to stop it from leaving. He was …' There was no word for terrified. 'I felt what he felt. He told me to keep away from him. That if I could hide from him then he might be able to hold on to it …'

The world dropped away as memories rose and crashed together.

'Nayn, that was why I had to leave! The whispering creature had marked me as prey. I needed it to think I was dead. If I'd stayed I would have triggered it to fight harder and Mr Durante wouldn't have been able to hold it. I'd commanded him to do whatever it took to protect Lainie, and he did. He wouldn't let it leave him. What did that cost him?'

One more strand of guilt to add to the rest.

Nayn gripped her hand.

'Any hint of supernatural occurrences—or even just my presence— could have tipped the balance. If it had changed hosts, the creature would have hunted me down and then it would have found Lainie. Found all of us. I *had* to leave.'

And that had been the strand that had tripped her over from guilt to shame. She'd left her own baby daughter. She'd had to. Lily had promised she would do what she could to prevent Lainie from attracting the wrong sort of attention. Harry would do his bit to keep people away. The biggest risk was her. She'd already been discovered. She'd had to leave.

She'd had no choice.

And she'd promised Lucas.

A stupid promise to do what she could to stay safe. A promise that she could claim and hold on to. She'd made mistakes and misjudgments and had plenty to feel guilty about, but she had no reason to feel ashamed. Because that was the one promise she'd kept.

Like antiseptic on an open wound, the revelation triggered new healing.

Chapter 27

Food and wine flowed freely as the afternoon sun lingered and our family and friends celebrated together. Tim, looking resplendent in his best man's formal suit, regaled us with tales of all the times Bane had managed to outwit and outfight his superior officers during his training for the Army Reserves. Then Noah, as my best man, proceeded to ruin my already dubious reputation by breaking more than one secret pact and spilling all sorts of secrets about the tricks we used to play when we were growing up. At least most of the stories condemned him as much as they did me. After all, I'd missed my chance to do the same to him when I'd chickened out of coming to his and Tessa's wedding. No matter how often he assured me that he understood my reasons, I would still never forgive myself for not being there for him on his big day.

'What are you staring at it so hard for?' Bane whispered as I scrutinised the wedding ring sitting on my bread plate. 'I promise it's real gold.'

'I know. I'm just trying to tweak it a little, to match yours.'

Much to Tim's delight I'd located my One Ruling Ring, but had been disappointed to discover it was way too big to fit Bane's finger—I'd made him shut his eyes while I tried it on him. That evening when I'd wistfully stared at it, thinking about how I was going to scrounge up enough money to get it resized and have the Mordor inscription removed, a more eloquent language had jumped from my lips. Glowing letters had appeared to replace Tolkien's clever poem. A single word, in a flowing script. *Guardian*. Other than when I'd spontaneously joined Dallmin's song for the people of Geelong, it was the first time I'd ever used Words of power to do something irrelevant to protecting Eden, and the graceful gift had left me breathless. Tim's face, when I'd shown him, had been satisfyingly awed. And of course the ring now fitted Bane perfectly.

Bane snatched my ring off the plate. 'Lainie! In front of everyone? Are you nuts?'

Lips curling in a whimsical smile, I reassured him. 'Of course I'm nuts. You figured that out in primary school and haven't once let me forget it. Stop fussing. It's already done.' Sure enough, the word *Shamar* was etched in matching letters on the inside of my ring, where only we would know about it.

As I slipped the band back onto my finger, I again noticed the strange smell of burnt flowers. It reminded me of something pleasant that had been ruined, like a mouldy apple.

'Is there more food coming?' I asked Noah, who was wiping baby slobber from his knee. Nathaniel was perched on his lap, staring at me with his fist in his mouth and a peevish expression on his adorable face, as if he could smell it too and didn't like it.

'Whatever it is, it doesn't smell very appetising,' I mumbled, hoping I didn't sound too rude.

'If it is the next course I'll be sending mine straight back,' Noah agreed, wrinkling his nose.

Bane tilted his head, about to ask a question, which was interrupted by the perfectly synchronised sounds of a keyboard and guitar. Dallmin and Bane's mum, Beth, had claimed the little stage. *Finally* it was time to dance.

Her black purse contained a secret. She wanted to look at it, but was too afraid. Part of her knew what it was. Her mind simply refused to think about it too much. Watching Bane dance with his new wife gave her mixed emotions. She was happy for them, wasn't she? Of course she was, which was why she needed to pass the gift on to them. It was imperative that she wait for exactly the right moment though. Soon. Very soon. Before she lost her nerve. Lainie had to leave the dance floor sometime. She only needed a moment.

Her limbs began to twitch in anticipation. They would be so happy to see what she had for them. She'd been assured of that fact repeatedly. They would like her gift. Wouldn't they? So why was she so nervous? Her head was pounding.

⸎

It must be nearby, Annie said, once her tears had subsided. *Lucas hid it behind the log somewhere.* She rummaged around in the dirt, prising away the angular stones that littered the surface. Ripping away the undergrowth, she searched until her hands bled in protest against the harsh world they had returned to.

Nayn watched her with gentle eyes.

Eventually, she let out a short cry of victory as her fingers closed around a smooth rock, slightly longer than her hand. It was carved on one side with something that she *felt* more than understood, and on the other side was an inexplicable message. Something about a leg-battle.

As she pulled it out, Nayn's eyebrows rose in astonished recognition. *I remember that rock. My father gave it to me. He said it was a letter for his grandson. Then he laughed and said his father had said the same thing. We decided it must be for* someone's *grandson. Didn't it have a picture of a gem on it?*

Annie handed it over. Nayn ran his fingers over the diagram and shivered. *Let's give it to Noah.* As he dropped it into her cloth bag, she winced, hoping it hadn't squashed what was in there too badly.

The gem may be here too, somewhere. Unless the man was still holding it when we fell into the river, she signed.

They both looked down the embankment into the torrent of winter runoff.

I don't like our chances of finding it in there, Nayn remarked, biting his lip.

That ruby had caused much grief over the years. Perhaps it was for the best. Only, why was it carved onto an ancient rock if it wasn't needed? Unless it was referring to the original Eden-sourced diamond she'd copied to make the ruby. Which would be unfortunate, given Harry had thrown that one off the top of a cliff.

She closed her eyes, remembering the last time she'd seen the ruby she'd made with her whispered Words. *It tastes like you,* Mr Durante had told her. *It calls to you like a lost child.*

Annie smiled. Her lost children were tenacious about tracking her down. She closed her eyes and spoke a Word, and the clouds above her broke apart. Sunlight lit the world again, sparkling the water and making the leaves glisten. Halfway down the riverbank, a flash of red caught her eye.

∾

Sexy muscled arms lifted me with every swirling leap, and I felt as if I could take off in flight at any moment. I hadn't danced like this since the night Nayn had arrived in our Garden. Memories of a sweet-looking man with sparkling blue eyes threw me off balance for a couple of seconds. The confusion of that night felt like a lifetime ago, and in some ways it was. I grinned at the deft way my Guardian led me around the dance floor. Unlike Pallano, Bane had no trouble keeping up with the steps. He was born to dance, and born to dance with me.

'Promise me we can dance together anytime we want to, now we're married,' I pleaded.

Pulling me closer, he swung me down into a gentle dip that was not at all part of the pattern I had taught him, but it still flowed seamlessly.

'I promise,' he said. 'I will dance with you anytime you ask, for as long as we both shall live,' he declared in a confident, sultry tone. He pressed his body even closer to mine. I could feel his heart pounding with an underlying pledge. Dancing wasn't the only thing he was promising. My bones resonated in irrefutable harmony. He chuckled and pulled me up, apparently aware of how weak my knees had suddenly become.

As our bridal waltz morphed into an even wilder version of an Eden celebratory frolic, others joined in. The music and vivacious steps were contagious, and the enthusiastic atmosphere fed on itself until I noticed even the caterers dancing along as they wove between the tables tidying up. Bane reluctantly let me go as the time came to swap partners and Liam took over, doing a wonderful job of keeping up with the complex movements. We spun, we laughed, we changed partners every couple of minutes until Dallmin finally took pity on us poor mortals and shifted into a slower tune. Noah sought me out and grabbed his chance to add to my dizziness as he swung me around, his formal jacket long since ditched and his shirt sleeves rolled up.

'You look stunning, Lainie, did anyone remember to tell you?' he asked as we tried to get our breathing under control.

'Once or twice. I don't mind hearing it again though. Just don't forget to tell Aunt Lily and Tessa how good you think I look. They put in all the hard work, after all.'

'Sure. I'll go up to my wife and tell her how amazing *you* look. And then I'll sleep on the couch for a month,' he said with a laugh.

'Tess won't hassle you so long as you stay away from Kate and Lachlan.'

'Kate *and* Lachlan?' he asked, glancing around to see where the soldiers were. They were both standing by the punch bowl with Hayley, watching us with wistful eyes. Noah blushed.

'Does that mean I'm allowed to dance with Hayley?'

'You could ask her, but I think she's too angry at me for stealing Bane away to want to dance.' It was true. She was staring at the floor, frowning.

'Who's angry at you?' Bane asked, having appeared from nowhere as he often did. He entwined his fingers with mine and neatly peeled me away from Noah's distracted grip. Graciously, my best man bowed out and went to look for Tessa before any of Bane's friends could get him into trouble.

'Your friend, Hayley. I hear she tried very hard to get your attention.'

He glanced over at her and scowled. 'She should have known better. I would never have dated anyone I trained with.'

Hayley caught Bane's dark expression and quickly looked away as if searching for someone.

'But you did date?' I asked, not quite knowing which answer I'd prefer. I hated that he'd been so miserable while I'd been flitting about Eden in ignorant bliss.

'A few times,' he admitted. 'Very badly. I tried, Lainie, because you asked me to, but it wasn't really fair on anyone.'

'Well, I promise I won't ask you to date anyone else ever again.'

I kissed him deeply in genuine apology, only breaking it off when Dallmin started playing 'Eagle Rock'. Some traditions were essential to uphold. Of course, it was impossible to de-pant when not wearing any pants, but my disappointment eased when I tripped Noah over and he fell right into the wedding cake. He made a spectacular mess.

The minute I sat down to slake my thirst with a cold glass of river water, I realised what had been making my spine tingle for the last half hour or so. Like a doorbell that had been drowned out by our wild partying, I had completely missed all the cues. Gasping, I looked across at Noah, who laughed and winked at me. It seemed he'd been waiting for me to pay attention. There were people nearby, and they'd come from the boundary. Not dangerous, or I would have noticed immediately no matter how distracting the dancing was. The newcomers were Cherubim, and familiar. I nearly choked on my excitement as I realised my mother must have overcome her terror of this world to attend my wedding. How had Noah managed to tell her about it? Did he throw paper planes off the cliff?

Spilling water everywhere, I forced myself to calm down and not bolt headlong into the darkening trees. My best man laughed at my clumsy haste. The words from the ceremony tumbled through my mind, a calming reminder.

Love is patient. Love is kind.

Annie and Nayn had both braved the reality of the rough transition into Nalong after years away from all forms of suffering. That was some serious love right there. As calmly as I could, I wandered back toward the house, forcing myself to appear casual by taking a moment to admire the wedding gifts piled on a table in the back yard. Tim had given us a pair of heritage grapevines from his family's estate. Not a surprising gift, after the amount of time he'd spent going on and on about what a great vineyard our farm would make. Lingering only long enough to smile politely at the guests nearby, I neatly made my escape at the first opportunity, ducking behind the shed and then sprinting into the trees past the orchard. Bane wasn't as subtle, making a beeline for me, his eyes blazing with curiosity. Noah and Tessa followed a minute later, with a sleeping Nathaniel draped over his mother's shoulder.

⁓

Somehow high heels and a strapless dress looked as natural on Nicole as her usual jeans and flannel shirt. Tim decided she was stunning in any setting.

'This wiring doesn't look right,' Hayley explained.

'Okay,' Tim agreed, pushing past her. He could see Nicole standing alone in the corner, bathed in the glow from all the fairy lights, waiting for someone to ask her to dance.

'Did you even hear me?' Hayley pestered.

'The wiring along the edge of the dance floor. I heard you. Everything's been taped down to avoid making a trip hazard. Maybe you should have come down earlier with Luke and Hayden to help set up. Complaining about it at this late stage is a bit pointless.'

When she kept arguing, he tuned her out. Something about the expression on Nicole's face was bothering him.

Both times when he'd asked Nicole to dance, she'd responded with 'maybe later'. Perhaps she was in pain. The heels weren't worth it if they were the reason she hadn't left the corner of the marquee all afternoon. He would simply have to convince her to take them off. When he drew closer to her though, his well-rehearsed glib phrases died on his lips.

'Nicole, what's the matter?'

In the few weeks he'd known her he'd never seen her act in the least bit scared of anything, yet she cringed away from him, clutching her hands to her chest. Sweat poured down her face and she looked like she was about to be sick.

'What is that thing you're holding?' he asked her. It looked an awful lot like something he was familiar with. No, it couldn't be.

'It needs to be now,' she sobbed, shaking her head slowly from side to side. 'I don't want to do it.' Her green eyes, when they locked on his, were full of terror.

⁓

My day was made complete in its joy as I threw myself into Annie's waiting arms.

'You came! How did you know? And *how* did you come? Noah blocked it off,' I said.

Instead of answering straight away she held on to me, trembling. With cold or nerves? I wished I'd thought to bring something warm for her to put on over her delicate shift. The sun had tried hard to warm our side of the planet, but was now giving it up as a bad job and slipping behind the ridge to try its luck elsewhere.

'Oh, I'm not here for you,' she said eventually. She had a wan smile, like she was working hard to keep it together. 'I heard Hunters & Collectors echoing around the hills and got sucked in.' Her smile faded. 'That song always made me cry. It always made me think of Sarah.'

'Noah said the same thing. That's why I asked Dallmin to play it.'

'My dress looks beautiful on you,' she commented after a few moments, clearly trying hard to remain composed as she tenderly brushed her fingers across the soft skirt. She cradled the brown and blue shell that had been given pride of place in the centre of the bodice.

My breath caught. As if coming here wasn't difficult enough already, now she was faced with the sight of me getting married in her own dress.

'I … I'm sorry, I should have asked you, or …'

She smiled. 'Hush, Lainie, I'm happy to see you wear it. My memories of the day I wore it are only beautiful ones. It's good to remember those.'

Love does not envy, it does not boast, it is not proud.

'Here,' she said, pulling something out of her bag. 'I have something for you.'

My eyes bulged at the sight of the blood-red gem dangling at the end of the chain. It was cradled by a pair of golden wings.

'Wow. You got me a wedding present? It's gorgeous!' I passed it to Bane and turned my back to him, lifting my hair out of the way.

Annie looked uncomfortable. 'Noah's grandmother was given an almost identical one for her wedding. It didn't work out so well for her. I'm hoping this one isn't cursed.'

Bane paused with it halfway around my neck.

'Just put it on. It isn't cursed,' I assured him. 'I was wondering if this would turn up soon.'

Tessa laughed. 'Of course. This must be the amulet. Amulets are supposed to protect you from evil, not curse you.'

Annie looked confused.

'Jake mentioned it in passing,' I explained to her.

'If it protects her, then it will be the best wedding gift of all. Thank you, Annie,' Bane said, taking her hand and lightly kissing the inside of her wrist in a formal Eden greeting. My man had been paying attention.

'By the way, you dance very well,' she told him as she hugged him. 'I'm glad I got to see it.'

Reaching over to pluck Nathaniel from Tessa's shoulder, Nayn beamed with grand-paternal pride.

'Tessa, this is Nayn,' Noah explained, scraping residual icing from his hair. 'He's my great-great something or other grandfather. He helped me … he helped us the day Nathaniel was born.'

The aged Cherub grinned at her, white teeth glowing against his dark skin. Nathaniel let out a decent burp and then settled contentedly in Nayn's arms.

I looked back across the paddock to see if anyone had noticed where we had all suddenly run off to. It would be awkward if anyone caught sight of my supposedly long-dead mother. Dallmin was saying something to Beth, who was reaching for her flute case. Tim was standing very close to Nicole off to one side of the dance floor, and Mick was pulling Aunt Lily by the hand, heading toward them. Trust him to have noticed where they were. The rest of the guests were heading back to the house, which seemed strange.

'Annie, how did you get past the landslide?' I asked again. Something wasn't right.

'I removed it. We needed to be here,' she said, frowning as she watched a pair of wood ducks waddle into the scrub. 'Did you get the sword back yet?'

'Not yet, no,' I said, glancing at Noah, who was deliberately looking down at his feet. Thanks for the support, mate.

'What have you been doing this whole time?' she complained.

'I've been working on it! We have a plan. First I had to get married.'

Annie crossed her arms. 'Your dad and I went out for almost two years before we got married and had you. You couldn't have held off long enough to go look for the sword? It's kind of important, you know.'

Nayn gestured awkwardly with one hand, trying not to disturb the baby. *I don't know the words you are using, Annie, but even I can tell they aren't kind. Lainie is celebrating a new love partnership. We will discuss the whispering voice later. Besides, I'm hungry. Surely there is food if it is a celebration.*

Whispering voice? I asked him. Mr D had mentioned something about a whispering voice, hadn't he? What did they know?

Food first, he insisted.

Noah shook his head. He could usually understand most of what we said in sign, but was still struggling to use the language himself. 'I'm sorry, Annie. Could you please tell him the food is all finished? Even the cheese platters have all been taken away. You missed them.'

My mother swung around to stare at him, her hand clutching at her throat. 'What did you say?'

'You missed the cheese ...'

Panicked shouts erupted from across the paddock and I turned just in time to see Tim throw himself at a familiar figure.

Moments later, the dance floor exploded in a hideous shower of wood, plastic, and torn flesh.

Chapter 28

Tim reacted instantly, shouting at Hayden to alert him to the danger. Nicole was holding a detonator, with her trembling finger hovering over the switch. A thin wire ran from it, behind a table and across to the edge of the dance floor, where it disappeared beyond reach, presumably connected to a hidden cache of Anfo explosive. Nicole must have connected the detonator while everyone was busy eating, he realised, because she hadn't moved from the corner of the dance floor since about then. Hayley had been onto something after all. He should have paid more attention.

The device was simple, and so very easy to disconnect, except that Nicole evidently could not fully control what she was doing. Tim knew enough to understand other forces were at work, and the slightest interference might well trigger an involuntary response from her. Still, she was bravely fighting whatever whammy Jake was trying to control her with.

'Hold on, Nic,' he said, locking his eyes on hers to try to hold her fragile attention. 'You do *not* want to flick that switch. I'll stay with you, and you will keep fighting,' he assured her, sending quick hand signals to his crewmates. Out of the corner of his eye, he could see them quietly ushering people toward the house, while Mick was dragging Lily away toward where Bane and the others had gone.

'I was supposed to wait until Noah and Lainie were both off the floor. He said it wouldn't work if they were in any danger. Why would they be in danger? I don't want anyone to be in danger. Do I?'

'No. We want everyone to be safe.'

'They're not here now, so I can't stop,' she gasped.

'And since when have you ever done what you were supposed to?' he asked, slowly placing his hands on her shoulders.

'Please, Tim, you have to run, he's too strong,' she cried, squeezing her eyes shut.

'No. Look at me, Nicole Ashbree. I'm not going anywhere. Not until you prove to me you can beat that little twerp. Just give it to me. That's all you have to do. He's nowhere near as tough as you are.'

Blinking through sweat and tears, she looked down at what she was holding. She made it look like it was the hardest thing she'd ever done, and maybe it was. Gritting her teeth, she opened her hand until the detonator was sitting balanced on her trembling palm. He slowly picked it up and placed it on the table next to them as she gasped in utter relief.

'I did it,' she sobbed.

'Yeah,' he said, letting out a pent up breath. 'Not bad for a farm chick.'

'And if I'd known you were going to be so bloody stubborn I would have picked someone else,' came Jake's snide voice from behind them. Tim spun and launched himself at the man whom he had last seen pinned to the wall of a shed by Bane's favourite knife—but he fell straight through the apparition and onto the floor.

The image of Jake snorted. 'Stupid human.'

'Run, Nic! Dallmin! RUN!' Tim bellowed, scrambling to find some part of Jake he could grasp. It was no use.

Curling his tongue in concentration, Jake carefully used one finger to click the tiny switch over.

Chapter 29

I had no breath to even scream. Bane's arms were locked around my waist so tightly that my feet barely touched the ground. I could only watch in horror as people moved about in confusion and terror. My eyes searched the crowd, ticking familiar faces off one by one—Mick holding my aunt back, probably worried about more explosions; Dallmin on his knees looking too terrified to move; Liam carrying Nicole, who was dangling limply in his arms; Hayden searching the surrounding area for any further signs of danger. Kate, Lachlan, and Hayley had automatically taken crowd control duty.

I couldn't see Tim.

'Let me go!' I gasped, struggling against arms like steel. A cry of pure agony cut through the space between us and I twisted just enough to see the look of anguish on Bane's face. I turned back to see what had caught his attention. Hayden was yelling something at Mick, who was on the phone most likely calling for emergency services. Kate left the other two to keep the crowd away and rushed back to help with whatever Hayden was doing. Tables were shifted away from a crumpled pile of blue cloth as they hurried to reach someone.

It was Beth.

'You can't help her, you can't help!' Bane cried, and I didn't know if he was talking to himself or to me. He was compelled to keep me away from danger, but this just wasn't fair, so I elbowed him as hard as I could in the gut. With a surprised grunt, his grip loosened enough for me to duck away from him as deftly as if we were still dancing. If he wanted to keep me safe then he'd have to catch me first. As soon as I had a slight lead I kicked off my shoes and bolted. Behind me, I could hear Tessa giving her best impersonation of a banshee as she shrieked at the other Cherubim to remain where they were. One Guardian protecting four Cherubim—she could have taught Bane's drill sergeant a thing or two about using a tone of authority.

As I streaked across the wet grass I passed Dallmin, still on his knees, looking up at me in fear and shock. It felt as if something else in him had just broken. Like he'd given in. Lost a battle.

'Come back and help, you coward!' I screamed as I kept running. After all the times I'd seen him jump recklessly off cliff tops, I had no patience for the fact that he was finally coming to terms with his mortality.

Love does not dishonour others, it is not self-seeking, it is not easily angered, it keeps no record of wrongs.

Well, it didn't say *never* angered. There were times when anger was entirely appropriate. And I would just have to deal with my dishonouring issues another time.

I skidded to a stop in front of the group of people who were crowded around my mother-in-law's bloodied form. Everything was wrong. Her limbs were twisted unnaturally and one arm was a mess of torn muscle and bone. Her skin was the wrong colour because she couldn't breathe properly around the massive wound in her chest, and yet she lay back, feeling with her good hand to check if she still had both her earrings.

Words. I needed Words. I loved, didn't I? Wasn't everything meant to revolve around love? Mumbling sputtered phrases, I tried to force the Words to come, only I was too angry. Eden needed her, didn't it? Surely she was important, she was Bane's mum. *My* mum. And yet that hadn't helped Harry, or Sarah, or my dad. Nothing was fair here. How come I could write stupid inscriptions on stupid rings and not have the Words to do this?

'Ben, honey,' Beth exhaled as she saw he was okay. 'This was aimed at your beautiful wife again, wasn't it? You should get her away from here, it isn't safe,' she scolded. We hadn't told her everything, but she knew at least as much as the Ashbrees did about the events of the last few weeks.

'Our place is with you right now … Mum,' I stated before Bane could reply.

'Oh, honey. I really messed that up. I'm so sorry. You were such a tiny little thing when Annie died. I remember … when I heard the news … I cuddled Ben so tightly he threw a tantrum. When you asked to call me Mum …' The rest of her sentence was lost in a fit of coughing, and Bane kneeled down and took her hand in his, kissing it gently.

I didn't know how to do this. I didn't know what to say. When a voice off to the left snagged my attention, I let it draw me away from the woman who was almost Mum.

'… have to stem the bleeding quickly or he'll have no chance.'

I pushed through the debris to where Tim lay unconscious. Blood seeped from numerous wounds where bits of glass, plastic, and other shrapnel were embedded across one side of his body. It took me a few moments to even notice that one of his legs was completely missing below the knee. I closed my eyes against the horror of it and focused on simply breathing. His friends were dealing with the situation as calmly as if it was just another training drill and they didn't need me to interfere. Feeling completely useless, I backed up again, while my brain shouted at me that this was not the same as Dallmin's antics back in Eden. There was no Fruit here. No healing for any except a lucky few who had done nothing to deserve it.

By the time I reached Beth again, Dallmin had crept his way in and was crooning to her. Bane had her head on his knees and was talking to her in a strained voice. The other helpers had backed away, knowing their efforts were futile.

'It was a lovely ceremony, my son. She is entirely right for you, and I'm happier than you can imagine that I got to see this day. You were lonely for so long.'

The voice that used to loudly scold inattentive piano students was now hoarse from the blood filling her lungs. 'The music was incredible,' she wheezed, looking up at Dallmin. 'Only three weeks of lessons and you were by far the best student I've ever had. Gold star for you, young man.' Blood dribbled down her chin. 'You have a rare gift, Dallmin. Your music touches the spirit. Whatever you do, promise me you won't waste it. You have a voice like an angel.'

'Better than some of them, actually,' he replied.

'Well, I'll just have to test that out for myself when I arrive. Those angels had better be ready to bring it if they want to score better than my prize student.'

He blinked furiously and hitched in a raw breath. 'When you meet an angel named T'iel, please tell …' He glanced at Bane. 'How do I speak of a person who is neither male or female?' he asked.

'Them,' Bane answered, looking somewhat awestruck despite his grief.

'Tell T'iel I miss them. Tell them to sing for you the song Dallmin wrote for them. I think you will like it, Beth.'

'You are a strange young man.' Her singing teacher's textured bellow was now reduced to the barest whisper, as her lungs lost their capacity to suck in air. 'Sing for me, one last time.'

He nodded, and as his voice rose in exultant celebration of a cherished friend who had decided to move across to hear the angels sing, Beth's face lit up with the joy of one who had seen and heard all her heart's desires fulfilled.

With trembling fingers, I fumbled with the clasp on my bracelet. The more I hurried, the harder it was to do it up. Tim's wrist was thicker than mine, but eventually I got the tiny clasp to hook on, just as Dr Vertan lost patience and ushered me away. The air ambulance was fast, but keeping Tim stable while we waited for it to arrive was crucial. I needed to back off and let the doctor do her thing.

And suddenly, I was done. I didn't have the heart to go on. No matter how much power I had access to, people still got hurt. Tim was gone, Beth was dead. My happiest day was also my worst. Life was so precious, so fragile, so easily discarded. How easy had it been for Beth to let go? To travel onward and leave us all behind? Too easy. Like following a playful breeze as it skittered across a wide ocean. I knew.

And Tim. Would he follow that breeze too, or would he fight with urgent greed to cling to life? Would he have the patience to hold his soul still, and slow, and wait for his body to heal? Or would he toss it aside like a broken toy? Too easy. But did he know how much he would be missed? Did he understand how selfishly I wanted him to stay?

'Was that the bracelet Bane carried everywhere?' The husky voice came from behind me. I turned to see Hayden's ashen face looking to me for support. He'd been brilliant as he'd dealt with the sudden disaster, and Tim wasn't the only one who owed him his life. Who knows how many others would have been killed if he hadn't acted so swiftly to move the guests away? Now things had settled down and the strain was beginning to filter through as he allowed himself time to think.

'Yeah,' I said. 'He bought it for me a few years ago, but I gave it back to him when he needed it more.'

Hayden nodded slowly. 'Shalom. I read it once, when he fell asleep with it in his fist. It's a Jewish word, right? For peace?'

'More than that. It means being safe and whole in mind, body, and spirit,' I added. 'The way we're all supposed to be.'

A soft sigh escaped his lips. 'Well, I guess Tim needs it too, then. Maybe someday he can give it back to you.'

'He can keep it. I have …' What did I have? I had a husband who cherished me and protected me, and I had access to paradise and the source of life itself, and I had limitless power with which to safeguard it. Not going on with what had to be done was simply not an option.

I smiled at Bane's serious friend. 'Thank you, Hayden, for everything. We all owe you so much. I'm sorry my wedding turned out to be … you know, but I'm still really glad you came. Without you—' His crushing embrace cut off my sentence.

'I'm so sorry this happened!' he cried, hot tears pressing onto my shoulder. 'I was sure I'd locked all the Anfo away, and we watched the monitors so carefully. I don't know how Jake managed to—'

'Oh, Hayden! It wasn't your fault. Please don't blame yourself. You did everything right, I promise. Jake probably set it up during the night and …' The horrified guilt on his face caught my attention, and my gift told me the rest. Jake would have needed help to get into the locked cupboard where the Anfo detonator was stored, and to set it up correctly. The demon had messed with Hayden's head and somehow charmed him into doing his dirty work, the same way he'd tried to charm Nicole. The last thing we needed was for him to spend too much time dwelling on how he'd let this happen.

'I had a bad dream, Lainie, that's all it was, a bad dream. How could it have been real?' he whispered, moving his hands around as if unsure of what to do with them.

Placing my hands on his shoulders, I brazenly searched his emotional memories to find out more. Hazy images swirled with sickening shame—memories of actions he had no more control over than a dream. So with an indignant Word I transformed the memories into a dream-like pattern. Mother of Memories. Too right. My mother's treatment of Alex Beckinsale had made it clear that deleting a person's memories was a terrible idea, but Hayden shouldn't have to live with this. Neither should Nicole. I glanced toward the house where she was recovering and whispered again, hoping she would remember only the part of the nightmare where her strength and bravery had won out.

'Hayden, you did nothing wrong,' I repeated, wishing I could charm him into believing it. 'Jake came during the night and set everything up. I'm sure if you were to check, you would find that the lock on the cupboard was broken with bolt cutters or something.' I closed my eyes for the brief second it took for me to whisper a command to the lock. 'You couldn't have prevented this.' With another soft Word I commanded the taped recordings from two of the cameras to exchange the images of Hayden creeping about at night for ones of Jake.

Looking slightly puzzled, Hayden gave his head a quick shake. 'Farmers blow up stumps with Anfo all the time. Jake was brought up here; he would have known exactly what to do.'

'Exactly.'

'We'll find him, Lainie. I promise.'

Puffing out a relieved breath as he left, I jogged back to where Tessa was pacing in front of the other Cherubim. She reminded me of a lioness guarding her cubs. She had passed Nathaniel to Noah, probably to remind him that his place was with his family, not the other guests.

'Nicole will be fine,' I assured them as Noah searched my face. 'She's awake, and I've made sure she won't remember her role in what happened. The ambos are on their way.' I swallowed hard. 'Beth … she …'

Noah nodded, wiping tears from his chin, and I knew they had seen Beth's body being covered with the clean white sheet Aunt Lily had brought out. 'Tim is not good. Dr Vertan says she's dealt with plenty of injuries from farm equipment over the years and assured me she knows what she's doing.' Of course, as she was saying that she'd been thinking of the other cases she'd had that didn't end well. I really didn't like my gift sometimes.

'The air ambulance is pretty quick,' Tessa said, placing a comforting hand on my elbow before taking her son from Noah's shaking hands. 'I assume they're sending a helicopter?'

I nodded. 'Kate has people helping her rearrange the lighting for it to land. At least the back paddock's nice and flat now.'

'Any other injuries?' Annie asked me.

'Bane's friends managed to get everyone else to safety in time,' I explained. If Beth hadn't delayed her evacuation to grab her prized flute, she might also have escaped with nothing more than a bruise or two, but there was no point in dwelling on such useless thoughts.

Wringing her hands together, Annie looked agitated. 'Lainie, the reason we came was to warn you of a terrible danger.'

Feeling my temper rising again, I glared at her. Some warning. Thanks very much.

'No, you don't understand,' she said. 'There's more to come. Can't you sense it?'

All I could sense was the overpowering stench of ammonia and burnt flowers, but hadn't I smelled something similar even before the Anfo ignited?

Annie took my hand in both of hers. 'Use your gift,' she said. 'See the memories I have. Some of them aren't mine, which is why they're so important.'

Scenes flickered through my mind, way too fast and jumbled to follow. My brain couldn't take it all in so I pulled away, shaking my head. I couldn't afford to get lost in someone else's point of view. Not right now.

'It's okay,' Annie said. 'I understand why it frightens you.'

A different hand grabbed mine. Full of healing and profound devotion. Bane had caught up with me already. 'You were supposed to wait for the coroner,' I told him as he pulled me close and tried to relax his breathing. Damn. I knew those signs. His skin was on fire again.

'Okay,' Noah said to us. 'Time to fill you both in. Annie's been busy getting answers for us, Lainie. The demon that's possessed Jake has been searching for Eden for a long time, using different hosts. It tracked Annie down because of the ruby you have around your neck. She made it, and the demon sniffed out the miracle.'

'Sorry, you what?' I asked Annie.

My mother shrugged. 'It felt necessary at the time. Sorry I snapped at you for not getting the sword back. It's just that we really need it. I believe it's the only thing that will actually destroy the demon. Killing Jake would only render it temporarily bodiless again, and would also leave us powerless.'

'What do you mean, powerless?' Noah asked, tensing.

'I mean that if the demon can't kill us, it will try to corrupt us instead, to tempt us to kill. That's why he attacked your friends and family. Without Cherubim or the sword guarding the boundary, the demon will enter and consume Eden.'

'Tempt us to kill?' Noah asked, glancing at Tessa. He looked haunted.

'That would surely strip you of your authority,' Annie explained.

'We can't kill humans,' I argued. 'So it's a stupid plan. He's targeting our family for nothing.'

Noah ran his hands through his hair. 'Lainie, I'm not so sure. I know Uncle tried to tell us he couldn't do it, but I think he meant he couldn't bring himself to, not that it was impossible. Maybe he knew what it would do to him.' He'd obviously been thinking about it before now, which was concerning.

Noah kicked a nearby tree so hard Tessa stumbled back half a step, gripping Nathaniel tightly. 'If only I'd left the sword where it belonged, none of this would have happened!' he blurted.

For once I wisely kept quiet. So did Tessa, though her eyes were full of sympathy.

Annie laid a hand on Noah's arm. 'What you did had precedent. It's been used as a weapon in the past.'

Noah glanced at me as if seeking my opinion. I shrugged. I'd been dead when he'd done it, so who was I to judge the situation?

'Noah, listen to me. I would have done exactly the same in your position,' Bane said. 'In fact, I would do it again in an instant. I have no authority that can be stripped away. Tessa and I can kill if we have to.'

Eerie silence greeted that statement. What were we supposed to say? His mum had just been killed by the guy who was trying to murder his ... wife. And everyone else. It wasn't as if we could laugh it off.

Bane put on his lance corporal voice again. 'So. If this demon has possessed different people over the years, it could try to move from

Jake to someone else. Right now Jake may well be around somewhere in person, and that means all our closest family and friends are at risk of both physical and spiritual attack. Is there anything else? Are we certain there's only one demon?'

Good question. Annie looked like she was going to be sick and didn't answer.

Bane continued, his voice battle-firm. 'So what's the first thing we tackle?'

'We need to draw him away from our families,' I growled. Noah and I exchanged quick glances. It was obvious to both of us that Tessa, Bane, and Nathaniel would be the first targets if the demon wanted to tempt us to kill, but how were we supposed to lead Jake away from the very people who were compelled to stick to us like glue?

'We also need to defend the cave,' Noah agreed. 'But if it's true he can sense where Lainie and I are, then by going there we'll be drawing him right to it.'

Tessa took hold of Noah's hand. 'After the magpie attack, Jake knows there's no point trying to get to the cave while you and Lainie are any-where nearby to protect it.'

'Magpie attack?' Annie interrupted.

'It felt necessary at the time,' I defended through gritted teeth.

Tessa continued to push past the awkward moment. 'Jake will want to take you both out so he can get to Eden. He doesn't know about Annie and Nayn, though.'

Even the hairs on my fingers bristled at that. 'Annie and Nayn have done their duty to Eden. I want them kept out of this.'

Tessa looked like she was about to argue until Bane interrupted. 'Then we'll lead Jake away from them. He'll expect us to head to the cave because that's what we always do. Maybe we should try something different this time.'

'You're married now,' Noah said, turning to me. 'Should you use your, ah, "power nap" option to search for the sword?'

I answered before Bane could get his undies in a twist. 'Not unless I have to. I was out of action for hours last time. I could miss everything. Besides, Jake might have the sword with him. And it will be harder to keep me safe when I'm catatonic.'

Bane looked way too doubtful about that last comment, so I shoved him with my elbow.

'We should split up,' Tessa proposed, sharing a quick glance with Bane. 'The four of us will take a stand up on the cliff, away from everyone else. Annie and Nayn will cross back to Eden where it's safe. Dallmin can stay in the cave to help if things really go south.'

'Again. They already went south once before,' Annie pointed out. 'I'll stay and guard the cave with Dallmin in case we need to, I don't know, send Eden north again or something.'

I saw Noah's shoulders relax the same way mine did. The thought of Dallmin guarding the cave alone had made my bones shiver. Annie knew him better than anyone. If anyone could untangle his conflicted emotions, she could. And she was Shamar. She would never let him get too close to where he shouldn't go.

'What about Nathaniel?' Noah asked, stroking his son's tiny fist. 'We can't risk leaving him here.'

Tessa breathed in deeply, kissed her baby on the top of his head, and then passed him to a startled-looking Nayn. 'You get him across that boundary as soon as you possibly can,' she commanded him.

The weathered old Cherub didn't need any English to understand her demand. He tucked Nathaniel into his shoulder and then turned to start walking until I grabbed his elbow.

There's a faster way, I said.

Five minutes later I winced as Annie ground the gears in the old paddock basher. The faithful vehicle nevertheless jumped forward, as a trusty Holden should. Biting my lip, I waved to Dallmin as he bumped around in the tray with the canoe, hoping Nayn, in the passenger seat, could keep Nathaniel's head from bouncing around too much as they made their way upstream to safety. Beside me, Aunt Lily was staring after my mother, full of regret at having come so close to finally having a chance to talk to her again. She'd been crying, of course, but as usual was holding herself together to be where she was needed. She handed me my work boots and some socks, and tucked her red jacket around my shoulders. I squeezed her hand.

'Are you certain we can't help?' Mick asked me as he handed Tessa her phone and his own jacket for her to put on. I was still feeling hot from an evening of first dancing and then panicking, but there was mist coming out of our mouths. The temperature was plummeting.

I shook my head. 'You know how this works, Mick. Our best strategy is to remove as many potential targets as possible. If Jake wants us to watch our families being attacked, then we need to make sure there's no family near us for him to abuse. Besides, we need you here to do your job and make sure the authorities only discover what they need to see out of this mess.' I glared at him meaningfully, my eyes darting to where my aunt was shivering, hoping he understood I was also relying on him to keep her from doing anything foolish, like send the entire town to follow us with torches and pitchforks, or send Bane's friends to follow us with their army-issued weapons, or follow us herself armed with nothing but our old cattle prod. He reflected my concerned gaze right back at me and nodded.

'Speaking of what people need to see, you need to clean up some of the footage on camera four,' Bane told me. 'Otherwise Mick might have a hard time explaining what Annie was doing here hiding in the trees.'

I kissed his fingers in unspoken sympathy. Despite his efforts, all the cameras in the world wouldn't have kept his mum and best friend safe, not with the way Jake operated.

It was absurdly easy for me to trip out a quick phrase to fix the problem, to protect our big secret. I even remembered to loop the footage with another part of the recording rather than leave it looking like someone had tampered with it. Crime shows were useful to watch sometimes after all.

'Mick, send Bane a text if you need me to do any more tweaking. I can erase a text, no problem.' He nodded, with only the slightest tightening around his eyes betraying how he felt about tampering with evidence.

'Stay safe,' I whispered to my aunt as I hugged her once more and sent her and Mick back to sort out the ragged remains of my tragic wedding day.

Chapter 30

The enormous winter moon smiled cheerfully in mockery of how I was feeling. Dew was settling on the tips of the grass, reflecting the glow from its deep orange dawning. Low on the horizon, its cold beauty was mesmerising and I wished I could distance myself from my fear and misery the same way it distanced itself from our petty earthly concerns. Grief clung to me as horribly as the mud splattered across my beautiful wedding gown. My attempts to keep my skirt bundled up during the dirt bike ride to the top of the ridge hadn't been successful.

Standing atop a weathered granite boulder, I braced myself against a false wind that buffeted me with ethereal force. I could sense the malevolence of a multitude of creatures, just out of sight. Out of reach. I could answer Bane's question now. There was more than one demon on the hunt tonight. It seemed Rabisu had gathered some friends. I tried to summon the Words to banish them, but their intent was hidden from me, and apparently believing they wanted to threaten Eden wasn't quite enough. I needed to *feel* it, and for the moment something seemed to be holding them back. They were not yet a direct threat to the Garden. Not yet. Loose strands of my hair hung down quietly around my face as if to remind me the wind wasn't really a wind, which was a pity because I probably could have done something about that.

Beside me, Bane stood like an exquisite bronze statue basking in the moonlight, except the statue was trembling every few seconds in response to the danger I was in. I could only imagine his pain, being compelled to protect me rather than take the time to grieve his mother.

A little farther away, Noah paced along the edge of the cliff and Tessa was removing her favourite pair of heels. With a look of resigned annoyance, she whacked them hard against the edge of a boulder to break the heels off and then used her jagged knife to slice open the bottom of her elegant gold dress on either side. Jake would have to answer for that too. Tossing the long knife from one hand to the other, she peered into the trees, impatient for action. I wondered if she'd somehow been wearing her knife while she was dancing. Surely not. It was a really slinky dress for someone who had just had a baby a month ago. Yet she looked fit enough to run a marathon. Her quick healing Guardian traits had come in very handy, yet again. Looking down at my muddy skirt, I was grateful it wasn't a tight fit because I could never have brought myself to damage it. It looked great with my Blunnies.

Bane's fingers were freezing, so I cupped them between mine and breathed on them, and then had a better idea and pinched the back of my hand hard. It worked, even if it made him grit his teeth and give me one of his classic disapproving frowns as the healing heat flowed between us.

'Any ideas?' I asked him, hoping he might have something, anything that even remotely resembled a plan.

'We get the sword back so I have a weapon that will work on demons,' he said without a trace of cynicism.

I bit my lower lip.

'What's that look for?' he asked. 'I know we joked about me being your champion, but this isn't an issue of feminism, Lainie. I have combat training. You don't. Tessa's been training hard too. She's more than capable of defending Noah.'

'I know. It isn't that.'

He waited while I figured out how to tell him.

'Even if Jake does bring the sword with him, we don't know for sure if you'll be able to fight with it,' I warned him.

'Why not? It's really just a big knife. I'm good with knives.' He spun his own evil-looking dagger around his fingers to prove it. It was huge and I could absolutely guarantee it had not been strapped anywhere during the dancing. He must have retrieved it from the house when he should have been taking the time to say his last goodbyes to his mum.

'No doubt about that. It's only that I'm not sure Sadie works that way. The form she takes, looking like a sword, is a bit like me looking like a human. It's not who she really is. She's been given a shape that serves as a warning people can relate to, that's all, and despite Annie's assurance that she's been used as one before, I'm still not certain how useful she'll be as a physical weapon.' I took the knife from him and put it back in its sheath to make my point. 'I want you to be prepared for the possibility this battle might not be much of a physical one.'

Looking annoyed, he considered the implications of what I was telling him. Then he frowned. 'Sadie? Really?'

'Tim named it when I told him its real purpose was to cleanse things.'

'That's terrible.'

'Which is why he likes it.'

Bane nodded in bleak acknowledgment of the fact that the reasoning was entirely Tim-like.

'Have you still got phone reception?' I asked him, shifting from one foot to another. Mick had promised he would text us as soon as he had news about Tim's condition. We'd heard the sound of the helicopter echo around the hills as we were riding up the trail, and heard it take off again not long after. The sound of it fading away somehow made me feel like the world was fading with it, leaving us alone in the dark.

'Yes, but it's still too soon.' He gave my hand a quick squeeze. 'The wait for news is driving me nuts too.'

The eerie not-wind whipped around the surrounding hills, its pace frenzied yet random. Like it was searching for a way in. With no physical form, it was impossible for me to track. Unlike Rabisu.

'Jake is still on his way,' I said.

'I know. I can feel him coming for you. He's probably on foot, so it will take him a while yet.' Closing his eyes, he concentrated hard, tilting his head as if straining to hear something. 'You would think I'd sense the demon spirits too, but I don't. Does that mean they can't harm you?'

'I hope so. I can certainly feel them though, so they're a potential threat to Eden at least. I guess we'll just have to deal with things as they happen.'

He scowled at that. His war-craft training should have prepared him for dealing with the unexpected. That didn't mean he had to like it.

A whole hour passed, which was a very long time to stand around waiting. I could still feel Jake heading up the hill toward us, which was a relief. I was so much on edge that if he'd taken a single step toward the cave, I felt like I could have torn a tunnel through the rock under my feet to beat him there. Instead, he was approaching slower than a kelpie who knew it was in trouble. I couldn't help feeling bored. There were plenty of entertaining things I could have filled the time with, but none of them were appropriate. Of all the imagined scenarios I'd had of what my wedding night would be like, this one was way out of line. Frost made the grass crunchy under our feet and part of me wished I could ride down the hill and give Rabisu a lift. I did not think he would accept my help, since we were only waiting around to kill him.

'Hello,' I whispered to myself. 'My name is Lainie Gracewood. You killed my mother-in-law. Prepare to die,' I practised, trying to stay alert. My inappropriate humour left a bad taste in my mouth. Then I realised I'd just got my own name wrong. Maybe. Should I change from Gracewood to Millard? Was that old-fashioned now? And why was I even thinking about that while standing on the top of a cliff at night waiting for demons to attack me? I was overtired. If we weren't at Threat-con Delta, I might have considered taking a short nap.

'Lainie?' Bane asked, helpfully distracting me from running through the entire *Princess Bride* script in my head. 'Tell me about Eden. Anything. Any little thing at all. I know you can't say much, but you do let things slip sometimes.' He pulled the lapels of my aunt's fitted red blazer closer together in a vain attempt to warm me up.

Full of compassion, I watched him try hard to sound casual. I'd known this day would come and he'd done really well to delay it for this long.

'You're jealous,' I stated. There was no judgment in my tone, only stark truth.

'Of course I am. That place has captured your heart and soul, and you've captured mine. My world revolves around a place I can never see, and can barely imagine. Eden has cost me so much … Please, tell me something that will remind me what it is we're fighting for. Anything at all, no matter how trivial.'

His silver eyes shone the moon back at me, piercing my soul as if I was a window he could look through to see Eden. If I could have made myself into a clear piece of glass and shown him paradise, I would have. But what words did I have? A million, and none.

'Would telling you make things better? Could Eden ever justify losing your mum?'

He put one finger under my chin and lifted it to meet his gaze. 'Yes,' he said. 'To both questions.'

Choked by fresh grief, I scrambled around my tired brain, trying to think of something I could tell him that would help him understand he was right.

'Life doesn't revolve around a fear of death there,' I breathed, 'which changes everything. Love is the foundation of everyone's motivations. People in Eden can still choose to die, and it's a happy occasion when they do because they all understand that death is simply another journey at the end of a *very* long and full life. Here it's become a twisted thing ruled by fear, but the truth is only the ones left behind suffer. In Eden people only move across because they want to, and because they are … *complete,* and those left behind want whatever they want, so no one is sad.'

Mist curled around the trees below us as he stood silently letting that sink in. I had said far more than I thought I would be able to, and something about that worried me, yet it was one fleeting anxious thought among many, and the others were far more pressing.

'So am I selfish to want her back?' he asked, honest in his sorrow as tension knotted his jaw.

'Of course not. It's different here. Life is far too short already. You know how Dallmin regards us all as children—even your mum. Losing anyone here is like losing a child. It isn't okay at all. Ever.' I wrapped him in my arms and held him while he cried and I felt incredibly grateful and honoured that for once I could give him what he so desperately needed. Silent minutes passed. In far too short a time he pulled himself together and smiled at me, and I knew he was beginning to understand.

'It must be nice to be untainted and not have such conflicted feelings.'

'Sadly, even us Shamar with our sparkly clean souls still get conflicted.'

'True, although you don't let it ruin your fun for long.' He kissed the corner of my jaw as if trying to prove he could do the same. 'Tell me something fun,' he entreated.

Tiny electric shivers ran down my spine at his touch and I smiled back, then I put my lips close to his ear and whispered. 'There are dragons.' He looked dubious, so I added quickly, 'Tiny ones. Lizards with wings. They have them here too, in Indonesia. I looked them up on Dallmin's tablet. The ones here aren't as brightly coloured.'

He looked only slightly less dubious.

'I'm serious! I tried to convince three of them to hang around with me so I could play at being Mother of Dragons, only they got bored too easily.'

The conversation got sillier after that. All four of us were so tired that we did whatever we could to stay alert. We even bounced little rocks off our feet, competing to see who could keep them off the ground the longest. Noah won, but Tessa insisted that was only because she was hindered by her broken shoes. Yet despite their attempt at frivolity, the Guardians were becoming more edgy by the minute and eventually our time ran out. We all stood frozen and nervous as we felt Jake finally approach.

Placing his hands firmly on my shoulders, Bane pulled me around to look him directly in the eyes. 'Lainie, if the demons attack and there's no other way to fight them, you'll have to do whatever it takes. I really do understand that. Just promise you'll keep trying to come back to me.' His smoky gaze locked on mine with relentless determination. 'I won't let you go. No matter what happens I will keep calling your name until you find your way back. We're bonded now, which means we're in this together. Wherever you go a part of me will be with you. Feel for it if you get lost, and I'll bring you home.'

I tried to keep my voice light to reassure him. 'I'll try to stay as close as I can, although I bet you're regretting your second helping of the prawn appetiser now, aren't you?'

A furious shout from Noah saved him from answering. We spun around to see Jake stepping leisurely out of the trees, stripping off his shirt as if trying to show off his wiry tattooed arms. When he threw it onto the ground, Bane hissed.

'You all got that?' Tessa asked us quietly.

Noah nodded. 'The shirt disappeared. He isn't really here, although I'm guessing he wants us to think he is.'

'He really is a moron,' Tessa said, but she looked even more worried than before.

Then where exactly was Jake's body? Close, surely. Bane had the same train of thought.

'Could it be a decoy?' he asked. 'Could the real Jake be doing something else?'

'Not likely,' Noah said, 'given what happened to our bodies when Lainie took me sightseeing in the spirit world. Maybe we—'

'Well hello, old collegians!' Jake called out as he approached. 'So this is the spot you've picked for our little high school reunion? Nice view, I suppose, although it seems a bit rude of you all to have left the cleaning up from your party to everyone else.'

He looked me up and down, admiring my wedding dress, and then spoke to Bane.

'I can't believe you two are actually *married*. You do know she's put some sort of spell on you, right? I tried to free you from it, but now look what you've done. You married the weirdo who glued all the pages of your English novel together. Did you ever give me back my copy of *Animal Farm*?'

No one was in the mood to reply, let alone come up with any cleverly worded threats. Tessa shoved at Noah to make him step across closer to where Bane and I were standing. Two targets, two defenders, one opponent. She was planning tactics like a battle commander. Crouching slightly, knives held steady, the Guardians looked ready for anything as Jake swaggered closer. We had our backs to the edge of the cliff, presumably so no one could sneak up behind us. It made me a little uncomfortable.

'No weapon, Jake? What are you going to do, bite us?' Tessa asked, sounding as if she was delving for a way to fight back properly for a change.

Jake laughed. 'Trying to make me tell you where the sword is, are you? Don't bother. I didn't bring it. Lainie did say she'd fight me with or without a weapon, didn't you, sweetie?'

I hated it when people called me that.

'The truth is,' I retorted, 'you couldn't use the sword even if you wanted to. You can't even touch it anywhere except its hilt, right?

And even that must be excruciating. Moving it while bodiless would be impossible for you. It would simply burn you away like bleach on mould.'

That did it. All pretence that the person in front of us was still our friend from Nalong College disappeared as the demon roared in fury. I had just proven that I knew its weakness and it wasn't pleased. No, not *it*. He. Rabisu was a sentient being with his own spiritual awareness and intent. It would not be wise to treat him like some mindless monster. Although, as we watched in horror, the image of the man we knew started to grow into exactly that. It made me wonder whether trolls really did exist. Or perhaps the demon had watched as much TV as we had and wanted to frighten us. It roared again, then laughed, and then morphed into the form of a woman. She looked like the sort of warrior who could shoot you full of arrows from three villages away.

'Come and play, Shamar,' she said. 'Or have you truly forgotten how to shift? I used to envy your kind for this.'

It shimmered again, this time into a male form stunning enough to make the Hemsworth brothers cry. We all stared at it uselessly. How could we fight something so magnificent? So drool-worthy? A tiny whimper threatened to escape as the demon smiled sensuously at me, so I shut my mouth with a little pop.

Shifting did look kind of fun.

Love does not delight in evil but rejoices with the truth.

'A spirit does not have flesh and bones,' Bane whispered. 'It can't hurt us.'

Was he *crazy*? Rabisu was massive. And confident. I was certainly feeling intimidated enough. Besides, had Bane forgotten the way bodiless Jake had showered me with glass and set off a bomb? Oh … he still hadn't actually touched me himself. So far he'd only managed to manipulate inanimate objects. Damn. Those knives could become a massive liability.

'Bane, I know you won't like what I'm about to ask you to do, but I really think you should get rid of the knife,' I whispered.

The giant's expression changed in a flash as its gaze fell on the weapon. Apparently, demons had excellent hearing. Before Bane could even respond, Rabisu lunged toward him, intent on stealing it from his grasp. Bane twisted, slicing at the creature's stomach, and Rabisu laughed as the blade passed right through. Stupid ghost rules. I could have written a whole physics thesis on how this worked if I understood it better. Or at all.

'Go for his wrists!' I suggested. 'If he can touch things, then his hands must be at least partially corporeal.'

By then Tessa had joined in, and both of them slashed at the demon's ridiculously elegant fingers. A snarl told us we were on the right track, but it wasn't enough. Passing his long hands straight through Bane's fist, the demon gritted his teeth, concentrated, and yanked. Sheer giant strength forced the knife from Bane's grip and sent it spinning. Pompously, the evil hunk of fake muscles grabbed it out of the air and slashed at Tessa, who ducked beautifully.

Rabisu grinned again and lifted his head to the night sky, howling like a cross between a zombified wolf and a Nazgul with a sore throat. It was terrifying. The unnatural wind buffeted my soul in frenetic eddies.

'Your protection field is failing. You have not maintained it very well. Soon my friends will find a way in,' the creature said.

Noah turned to me. 'We have a protection field?'

'Go us,' I said.

Rabisu sneered. 'Cherubim have fallen a long way since we last fought. You have hidden for so long you now lack the strength of your predecessors. And their wisdom. I will destroy you, finally.' The giant lunged again and Tessa barely managed to avoid his stolen blade. He slashed and she spun away while Bane drew me behind him, unable to do a thing to help her. Noah looked at me, panic-stricken. The Guardians had no way of defending us or themselves without Sadie.

'Time to fly,' I told him, shooting an apologetic glance at Bane.

'Remember what you promised,' my Guardian said, leaping onto a boulder so he could reach the giant's hands more easily. The creature swung the knife at Tessa once again.

'I'll be back as soon as I can,' I said.

The hardest part was making myself lie down while a demon was slashing at my friends with a knife only a few paces away. I trusted Bane, and I trusted Tessa. I closed my eyes and focused on my memories of the sword, as I had the last time. It only took a second for me to let go of my fragile flesh, the same way I'd kicked off my shoes earlier. Beside me was a disturbing sight as Noah struggled to leave his body behind. It twitched on the ground in an unseemly manner, making Tessa look ill while his spirit form strained to break free.

'Let it go, Noah. Tess will look after it for you.'

The second he looked at me, he sprang from the ground like an elastic band had snapped. Startled, he began to flap his wings like a budgie and I had to laugh.

'Just do what I do,' I suggested, trying not to sound superior. I knew how testy he could get if he thought I was showing off.

Streaking up into the sky, I revelled in the look of sheer surprise on the demon's face as he abandoned the fight and tried to follow us, only he wasn't made of the same stuff we were and was far too slow. By possessing Jake, he'd given himself a way to exist in the physical world again, but it came at a cost. Travelling far seemed awkward for him while he still had to keep such a tight rein on his stolen flesh.

'What's the matter? Cumbersome flesh slowing you down?' I teased as I flipped forms into something with even larger wings.

The giant couldn't resist peering back over his shoulder through the trees to where I could now see Jake's real body lying unconscious on the ground nearby, thrashing around like a cat on a leash. It looked gratifyingly painful.

Noah growled, streaking back past the demon, clearly tempted to finish Jake off while his weak flesh lay undefended. Rabisu sprang back in defence, just as I deflected Noah's trajectory and hauled him away by his ghostly elbow.

'Leave him to the others. Besides, killing Jake wouldn't hurt the demon one little bit, even if we could do it,' I reminded him as we flew higher. Rabisu watched us, snarling, but didn't pursue.

'Lainie, Jake kidnapped Tessa. He *murdered* you. How can anyone expect me to let that go?'

I stared him down as if I could charm him. 'You know you can't kill Jake. You'd lose your authority to act in defence of Eden, and your baby son would have to pick up the slack. Imagine not being able to come with us whenever Nathaniel and I visit the Garden?'

His whole glorious glowing form went slack as he absorbed that. There wasn't much he could say in reply.

For want of a better direction, we soared straight up, high above the bright landscape, passing through a tingly wall of light that tasted like rock and nectar and a hint of eucalyptus. It felt so good to fly that it took a while for me to notice my surroundings. The ethereal wind was less of a brisk breeze here, and more of a stinky hurricane of malice. The stench of burnt flowers would have made me hurl if I'd had a stomach to do it with. I could now clearly see the other demons, cranky and all floaty, and I figured they had the opposite problem to Rabisu. They could drift freely around in this plane but were unable to physically harm anyone. They hadn't noticed us yet; they seemed preoccupied. Searching for something? There were maybe thirty of them, difficult to count as they writhed around like eels in the bottom of a drying dam. It took a few moments to control my revulsion enough to focus on what I was supposed to be doing. The sword. We were supposed to be looking for the sword. Then deal with the demons.

Where to start? North? Which way was north? The ridge faced west, but the landscape far below had now disappeared in a haze of … something. Instead of seeing trees and hills and the river below me, all I could see was a misty field, overloaded with wild and vivid bursts of energy. The landscape hadn't vanished so much as been made redundant in the sudden array of extra sensory input I was now receiving from all the living energy. No wonder I had so easily lost my body the last time.

'Noah, look at that,' I said, pointing to a translucent blue dome below us. 'That must be the wall of light we passed through.'

The structure was huge enough to cover the hills and valleys for miles around, and possibly the township as well. We'd flown a lot higher than I'd realised.

'Do you think that's the protection field we're supposed to have maintained?'

He leaned to one side, carving a graceful arc through the ether as easily as if he was back in his hang glider. 'It does look damaged. Incomplete. See where the gaps are?'

He was right. On closer inspection, I could see what looked like anchor points for the arcane field. Bright pillars of streaming energy, unfolding into tendrils of light that crossed over each other to power the dome. I counted four of them, but three more were missing, leaving multiple holes in the structure that seemed to attract unwelcome attention from far too many of the repulsive spirits.

'That'd be right,' Noah sighed. 'Even as higher beings we're still stuck with repairing the bloody fences. Why aren't they getting through the gaps?'

I spiralled in closer. 'I don't think they can see it like we do. It's like watching Poida trying to graze.'

Poida was an old ewe Nicole had raised as a poddy and refused to part with. She was blind and would be right about to reach a patch of new grass before wandering off on a tangent at the last second, oblivious to how close she'd come to what she was seeking. These spirit eels seemed to be doing something similar. I decided to test it out, shadowing the flight of one of the smaller spirits as it drifted straight for the dome. A little way out from it, the ghostly creature changed direction, yet kept exactly the same speed. A second later I felt it—a gentle nudge, like a subtle deflection. The dome wasn't only a force field; it was a really cool cloaking device. The spirits didn't even seem to realise they were being deflected … except for the places where the dome was failing. They were milling around those gaps. Curiously.

'Trees!' Noah announced from right behind me, giving me the fright of my life. 'Those pillars are trees. The light patterns look like they're being drawn in through the roots, up the trunk, and spread out through the branches. Like transpiration.'

Of all the surprising things to have happened to me in the last few hours, this one shouldn't have rocked me, but it still did. 'Did you really just use the word "transpiration"?'

'I know what it means, Lainie. I am about to finish a degree in agriculture, remember?'

He was officially better educated than I was now. Ouch. 'And do any of your textbooks happen to mention magic trees that deflect evil spirits?'

Noah grinned. 'No, but Uncle's old stories did. Remember the carved tree in the park he was so passionate about?'

We both glanced over to our right at exactly the same time. 'It's that one,' I said, and gasped when I realised he was pointing to the same blazing beacon. We could both feel it, like a familiar friend.

'Those Kolsom bulldozers have a lot to answer for,' Noah muttered, turning to the gap to the southwest.

'So do the McKenzies,' I added, pointing north. 'I knew something felt wrong when they cleared their southern gully a few years ago. I had the weirdest nightmares for weeks.'

'It's only a matter of time until they find a way in,' Noah said. 'I'll see what I can do to distract them, and maybe fix this thing while you go for the sword.'

Before I could advise against it, Noah let out a cry, not unlike the sound he used to make when he was about to go in for a rough footy tackle, and charged straight for the demons. First 'transpiration' and now this? When had my friend gone and grown up on me? I felt so proud of him right then, even if I did want to slap him for being so reckless.

'Noah!' I called after him. 'We're shape-shifters. Try to visualise a form that will help you fight,' I suggested as I watched the demons turn to him and hiss. The look of concentration on his face was almost comical. It was even funnier when he clenched his fists and silver blades burst out of his knuckles, Wolverine-style.

'Seriously? *That's* the first thing that comes to mind?'

He grinned at me.

Within seconds, however, his smile slipped as the demons pressed in to attack. He slashed at one in a way that should have cut it in half. The creature was deflected but seemed unhurt. It flipped around and came at him again. Noah was right. We needed Sadie.

'Noah, make yourself faster and stronger and keep them busy!' I called, hoping he could hold on for long enough. I tried to focus. Ringing in my ears was the pure sound of innocence, summoning me like a lost lamb calling for its mother. Spinning myself into a more streamlined form, I powered through the sky like a living rocket, leaving a trail of frantic spirits behind me. It was time to get the sword back.

Chapter 31

The sweet smell of oranges pervaded everything. Sadie's song had led me to a row of portable housing units on an orange farm. Although the harvest was over, there was still enough of the reject fruit around to infuse even the itinerant worker's cabins with citrus scent. The world looked like I was seeing it through a kaleidoscope filter, yet the smell of oranges had metaphorically and literally grounded me.

My prize was poorly hidden in the back corner of an old cupboard, wrapped in an old blanket and tied with hay band. Downright miracle it hadn't been stolen by someone else. Actually, it probably was some sort of 'miracle'. Jake might well have used some version of his charm to dissuade anyone from going near his stuff.

Concentrating as hard as I could, I tried to grab the tattered woollen blanket, but my fingers kept passing straight through it. Fine then. I'd just have to do it another way. The sword was needed, badly—and immediately—because Eden was now very much under threat from the demon intruders and this was the only weapon we could use against them. So I tripped a quick phrase from my mouth and felt my fingers become sticky. I pulled the massive bundle out and laid it across the lower bunk bed in the corner of the room. It was lighter than I'd expected. Using the loose end of some of the hay band, I sawed through each of the ties until they fell away. All I needed to do now was to unwrap it, grab the hilt, and find my way back to my body.

With my ghostly teeth gritted, I stared at the wrapped bundle on the mattress, waiting impatiently for me to get on with it.

My spirit-flesh crawled and my brain tried really hard to shut down. Blood, fire, Sarah … No.

Come on, Lainie. What Would Buffy Do?

Tim would have laughed at that. It didn't help me much.

Tim.

The memory of him throwing himself selflessly at Jake overlaid my older pain. He hadn't hesitated for even a split second before choosing to fight instead of running. He hadn't given himself the opportunity to think about it. He did what he'd been trained to do, and what his compassionate heart had given him the strength to do.

I was not trained to fight. But I was born to defend.

No more thinking.

⚬

'Please, Dallmin, talk to me. If not in sign, then in English. Give me something,' Annie begged.

The small lantern filled the cavern with shadows that stretched high across the walls. Dallmin had stopped just shy of entering the chamber. He pressed his back against the cold rock like he was afraid to come any closer.

'There is nothing more I can say to you, Annie. I ruined us with my selfish desires. It was my choice to come across the Skin of the World, and we both paid the price. And so have the others. My ignorance and pride got Lainie killed, and it's my fault Beth—'

'Ssshh … no, don't say that. You can't blame yourself for everything that goes wrong here. People make their own choices.'

'No, they don't. Don't you see? In this place we are *not* free to choose. Did Beth choose to die? Did Tim choose to live the rest of his life unable to dance, or even walk? Did Jake choose to be turned into a toy for a demon to play with? Has even *one person* I have met here lived a life they have chosen?' Fists that for thousands of years had not known anger were clenched in bitter rage. 'Everyone here is a product of the things that happen to them. That are *done* to them. They have no choice about who they are. I hate this place and what it's done to me!'

Annie took a timid step toward him, her simple dress wet and muddy, and her long hair tangled. 'I'm sorry. I'm so sorry I didn't find a way to stop you or to warn you better. I knew what this world was like, and yet I let you go. I'm so sorry.' Sobbing, she reached for his hand.

He shook her off so forcefully that she stumbled and nearly fell. 'Sorry doesn't always help, Annie. I want more. I want to go home. My heart and my body are tainted and it sickens me. Dallmin is dead, and I am all that's left of him, and I hate myself. This world has made me an evil man now, a man who causes only pain and grief. Why shouldn't I accept it, and take what I can get? I tried to follow the rules. They don't work. I'm still perverted, still shaped by the things I see and the things that happen to me. Today I saw violence, and now I want only more violence so I can punish Jake for what he's done. What does that make me? Tainted? Evil? Or just human?'

She reached for the words to comfort him and found none. He was so different to the man she'd known.

Dallmin wasn't finished. 'Bane speaks of the rules he follows in the army so that the work he does can cultivate peace, but who is he to judge who should live and who should die? Every single person here acts according to what has been done to them, according to what they think is the right thing to do, and none of it means anything because all of their desires are twisted by self-preservation!' He took a step into the cavern, and then another. His eyes were fixed on the far side of the chamber, where no rocks and no sword barred the way. 'And I am no longer the exception.'

The sword felt lighter than air, which was lucky because I needed to fly. I needed to find my way back as soon as possible, and I'd wasted time not only plucking up the courage to even look at it but also drowning in its exquisite song and pristine beauty for … far longer than I should have. The trick to it, I'd discovered, was to let the blade trail behind me where I couldn't get distracted by its perfect white sheen. Problem was, I still had no idea where I was going. Bane had promised he would keep calling me, only how was I supposed to hear him with all these noisy distractions?

Names. So many names echoed around this place, calling to the souls that travelled through. *David. He passed this morning, I have let Aunty Anne know, and she said she would inform the cousins. Emily …*

her mother has been so upset and still refuses to eat. Should we take her to see someone or give her more time? Mr Simpson … his wife passed away a few months ago. We see that often where couples have been together for so long. Mrs Millard, did you hear?

Whipping my head around, I scudded through the mist to follow the thread before it could get lost in the cacophony of untethered identities. Having never scudded anywhere before, I was rather proud of how quickly I moved. Mrs Millard. Was Beth here somewhere? Was she one of the glowing specks of beauty, shining as they whizzed past on their way to the next realm?

'Beth?' I called. 'Mrs Millard? Please, if you're here somewhere, I really need your help!' Who would have been speaking about her? Perhaps news of the explosion had already spread around the tight-knit Nalong community. If I found the speaker, would I then be close enough to my body to find it?

Mrs Millard … The echo was so faint.

The guttural shake in my voice betrayed my panic. 'Beth, please, if you're here I need to find you!' Opening my eyes, I tried to see where she was, but all I got was an influx of confusing images. I hurriedly closed them again so I wouldn't lose the fragile connection I was following.

'Beth … Mum, I …' What was I supposed to say to her, exactly? Sorry you were violently killed on your son's wedding day in a war you knew nothing about. In an attack aimed at me.

Remorse tore at my tangled focus. I was not enough. Not smart enough, not strong enough, flawed in character despite being 'untainted', whatever that even really meant. Unlimited power at my disposal and supreme authority to command the skies themselves, and yet I couldn't protect the ones I loved the most. And now Bane and Tessa were fighting for their lives, Noah was … somewhere, facing down a bunch of demons on his own, and I was wasting time trying to find someone who I knew in my heart was long gone from this realm.

'Mrs Millard. Did you hear me? Don't forget you have a new name now, if you want it. We are together. One flesh. Remember …' Bane's smooth voice rippled through the fabric of my overloaded senses, comforting and assuring.

Lainie, you bloody moron.

Chapter 32

I didn't need to look for him. He was already with me, reminding me of who I was. All I needed to do was let him pull me.

'Come on, girl, even if you can't find me, you can always find Noah,' Bane reminded with only the slightest hint of jealousy. *'Although I would prefer you to come back here if you can, because who knows where Noah is now?'*

A little way off to the left, or at least what passed for 'left' in this place. Now that he'd provided me with a connection, I could feel my panic subside and reaching out to find Noah became quite simple. The sense of relief I felt was incredible. How could I ever really get lost with so many people bonded to me? What had I been so worried about? Feeling for my friend the same way I always had, I zipped through the ether as quickly as I could. Before I reached him I began to choke on the sickly burnt scent of the demons.

'Noah? Need some assistance?' I called as I approached, hoping I wouldn't distract him too much if he was still fighting.

'Yeah, you could say that,' a tired voice replied. Fear laced his tone. The only other time I'd heard him sound so afraid had been when Tessa was abducted. Zooming in to where he was, I could see why. The demons had him trapped between them, tearing at the fabric of his form, which was looking ragged and flimsy. Whenever he tried to move or even flinch, the demons would snarl and bite at him until he forced himself to remain still again. He looked like he was in an incredible amount of pain.

'Wolverine didn't work out so well, then?'

'They almost found their way into the dome, but I managed to repair it. I don't know how long it will hold because the trees I had to use aren't very old, and they know the shape of it now. They've been trying to force me to dismantle it.'

I turned toward the streaming life force that arced up from the circle of carved trees. More demons were milling about it while others watched on, as if trying to detect a pattern from the way their companions were being deflected. Quite a few were gathered around a point that seemed less bright. It would only be a matter of time.

Suffused with a sense of justice, I swung the holy sword at the tangle of demon forms who blocked my way to Noah. I felt powerful and strong. I had a *magic sword*. Grrr … argghh. Sadie's white-hot flames seared away the filth as one demon shrieked and dissolved into mist, and then became nothing. It had taken the barest touch to destroy it, as if the demon could not exist in the same elemental space as the sword's sanctifying power. The others darted away like they'd touched an electric fence. I flew a quick sweep around the shimmering dome, scattering the demons from my path before returning to my friend.

Noah stared at me in outright awe. Which was great, because I felt pretty awesome. My body felt ghostly, yet still somehow natural, and wielding the sword filled me with purposeful clarity. We were not only allowed to kill these abominations, we were *supposed* to. I wanted to hunt them down, each and every last one, before they could come for me or my family again. I was faster than they were. I could catch them. They were fleeing, but I could hunt …

'Now that was fun to watch,' Noah croaked. He was hurting.

Wistfully I watched the last of the evil spirits flit away into the bright mist. Deep breath—not that I needed to breathe, but I did need to control the arrogant urge I had to hunt and destroy. It was so tempting with all that power at my disposal … No chasing, no hunting. There was no time.

The sword drooped as I turned back to Noah. 'Uncle always said it was about having the right tools for the right job. Are you okay?'

'Not really. I feel as though I've been slowly eaten alive for the last hour. What took you so long? Those things went troppo on me and there wasn't a thing I could do about it. Even though I made myself bigger than they were, they really stung when they nipped at me all at once. It was like being attacked by an army of bodybuilders and fire ants all at once.'

'An hour? Surely not ...'

He didn't answer. He drifted tiredly into my arms and everything about him felt fragile, which was so unlike my friend that the overwhelming sense of power I had experienced was slapped rudely back down to where it should be. Neither of us were cut out for fighting, Cherubim souls or not. We were still just us.

I clutched at him as if I could squish him back into shape. 'It's done now, Noah. We can go back. You did well to hold on. I think the best thing we can do now is to get Sadie back where she belongs. Let's hope your handiwork holds until then.'

'My handiwork always holds,' Noah said with a ghost of a smile.

'Sure it does. Like that water pump you repaired ... how many times?'

'Do you have any idea how old that thing was?' he defended.

We turned back to the glowing deflector shield that had stood in silent defence of Eden over the years. *Thousands* of years.

'We'd better hurry,' we said in unison.

My human mouth opened with a silent puff of mist. Eyelids followed, blinking against the stark silver brightness of the almost full moon. The first thing I noticed was that it was now high above us, no longer staring so closely at every step I took. At least it was still night-time. Not even midnight yet by the look of it, which was a relief. Time had a habit of sliding away from me when I least expected it.

The second thing I noticed was that Sadie the Sword of Awesome Hygienic Power was really uncomfortable to lie on.

'You did it! You brought it back with you. What an amazing creature you are,' came a tired, reverential whisper.

'How long?' I breathed, stumbling unexpectedly around the words. Something was very wrong. I was in my body, only I couldn't feel it properly. Everything was numb.

Suddenly a flood of heat washed through my fingers, stinging like I'd been splashed with boiling water. Snatching my hand away, my painful yelp came out as a mild croak. Agony shot up my arm as the fire flowed through my veins and into my shoulder.

'Bane, I can't move,' I panicked, struggling to get my numb lips to obey me. He was going to be cross if the reason my body was out of batteries was because I'd left something important behind in the soupy netherworld.

'It's okay, Lainie, you're just cold. Give me a minute … I'll see what I can do.'

He sounded dreadful. I stiffly turned my head to where he was crouched beside me, supposedly ready to do battle with anyone who came too close, except it looked like Jake could have probably toppled him over with his pinkie finger. Shivering madly, his face had about as much colour as the moon above us. A relieved smile softened his features as he reached for my fingers again. I batted his hand away.

'Oh no, you don't. You don't have enough heat to spare. I know what happens when you heal me.' Basic physics. Miraculous or not, his healing heat had to come from somewhere, and if he lost any more of his own body heat he might just shatter into a thousand pieces when Jake did come to push him over. That he didn't argue was testament to how bad things were. He simply watched me with a strange expression as I tried to wiggle my fingers. He seemed regretful, as if he wished he could think of some other way to help me, but there was something else there too.

'What about Noah? Did he make it back okay?' I asked as I checked that all my fingers were still attached.

'Yeah, I think so. I can hear Tessa telling him off. She hasn't stopped pacing for the last couple of hours so she's a bit warmer than I am.' He didn't need to tell me that the reason he hadn't done the same was because he'd been too sick. I'd travelled much farther away than Noah had.

'A couple of hours? It seriously felt like about ten minutes to me. I went as fast as I could.' I sat up with about as much grace as a zombie bride. 'Have you heard from Mick yet?' My stomach clenched in anticipation of bad news.

'Tim's stable. Long surgery ahead, and he'll be in ICU for a while, but for now he's … stable. His family are on their way to see him.'

Brave heart, loyal friend, whose future in the army had been torn from him. Would he have to depend on his family's money now? No. He would hate that. He'd find a way.

'He wanted to serve his country, and now he won't even be able to walk, let alone fight for a cause,' I said, feeling deeply saddened.

'I doubt he'll see it that way, Lainie. The cause he fought for might never be recognised by the Defence Force, but it was worth his sacrifice.'

Kneeling up was excruciating as blood began to flow back into my frozen muscles. Hypothermia was a real danger that wouldn't get any better by staying on the wet grass. Why on Earth hadn't he moved me somewhere warmer? Even back under the tree line would have helped a little.

As I glanced down I noticed something disturbing. The bodice of my dress had a massive tear in it and was streaked with blood. Lots of blood. Panicked fingers searched for a wound and found nothing, so my half-hitched breath sought answers from Bane's pallid face.

'It turns out you were right about our knives,' he said. 'I was too slow to realise it. Tessa was quicker, and threw them both over the edge of the cliff as soon as … as soon as she could.' In other words, as soon as they had pulled Bane's knife from my belly. No wonder he looked so ill.

'I never felt a thing. I'm so sorry! I didn't die again, did I?'

An impatient sigh escaped his frozen lips. 'Firstly, being stabbed while you're unconscious isn't something you should ever apologise for.' He paused, swallowed, and took a moment to breathe away the memory before continuing. 'And secondly, I find it disturbing that you actually have to ask if you died. I would hope you'd have noticed if that had happened, no matter where your soul was at the time.'

Right. Both good points.

'What happened to Rabisu?' I asked, extending my frozen senses to search for him. Everything was sluggish and heavy.

'Not sure. He ran away once the knives were gone. He must have realised his only other option would have been to start piffing pebbles at us. I know we were supposed to keep him busy up here, but we weren't prepared to leave you both lying here unguarded to chase after him. Can you feel for where he is now? And what about the other demons?'

I tested to see if my toes could wiggle before trying to stand on them.

'I destroyed one. There are plenty more. They're bodiless, so the difficulty I had with finding things in that place goes for them too. Without a point of reference—some beacon to guide them—they can't navigate.'

'What sort of beacon? Like you and Noah? Can they sense you the way Rabisu can?' He looked ready to hit something.

'If not, they can certainly sense Rabisu. You heard him call to them. In fact, they could probably sense the sword too, except there's a sort of cloaking device over this whole area, hiding us all from them. Unfortunately, it has weak points. I'm not sure what will happen if it doesn't hold.'

He sat back on his heels. 'I never even considered that Eden could be found on a spiritual level.'

'Me either. And trust me, Sadie makes a very bright beacon. Good thing my ancestors were so clever. Only problem is, we haven't been maintaining our camouflage very well. They are close, and on the hunt.'

'And this spiritual camouflage has kept Eden hidden from the demon spirits all these years?'

I nodded. 'They've had to possess people to search on the physical plane for clues to it. There are too many ways for stories to be shared now. That hasn't been a good thing for us.'

'And now that Rabisu's found us?' Bane asked.

'He must have called the others of his kind here, the same way you called to me. Of course, now that he's under our glowy-camo-dome they can't see him anymore.'

Bane expelled a misty breath. 'So they'll need to come the rest of the way on the physical plane. They won't be able to find the cave unless they possess other humans. That's good. I can fight humans.'

Good? Not the word I would use.

'Jake's down there somewhere, Bane, I can sense it. Hiding up here was a waste of time.'

'Not if it gave Nayn a chance to get Nathaniel to safety, and gave you a chance to get the sword back.'

I conceded that with a nod, but everything in me was resenting the choices that had left us stuck up on the ridge instead of being where we were needed.

'Of course, if Noah and I go down there now, any demons in physical form can track us there too.'

He swore under his breath in a very ungentlemanly way and his jealousy no longer felt so nice. It made me scared for him.

We heaved ourselves ungracefully to our feet, stomping around to make our numb feet take our weight. I shook my arms out, wondering if I had enough feeling in them to pick up the sword without dropping it and slicing off my own foot. Not that I'd feel it.

'Whether we draw them there or not, we have to get to the cave before Rabisu. And we *really* need to get down off this cliff and warm up.'

Just then I felt something disappear, like an unnoticed background noise that suddenly went silent. As I tilted my head to try to work out what it was, I felt myself being scooped up into Bane's arms. What was he planning to do? Carry me all the way to the cave? After separation nausea and healing me of a major stomach wound, he was in a much worse state than I was. Pointing back toward the sword, I tried to remind him we needed it, but as he walked toward the edge of the cliff something else clicked into place. Noah was gone. His presence had cut off suddenly, which was what I'd felt.

'You're right of course, Lainie. We do need to get off this cliff, and you're going first.'

As he pitched me headlong over the edge into the frozen darkness, my numb limbs barely even tried to scramble. There was absolutely nothing to grab. He'd picked a good spot. The cliff was undercut slightly so there was nothing but empty blackness all around me to absorb my petulant yell.

As I plummeted, wingless, through the boundary, I had only one ridiculous thought left. *Oh, no. Not again.*

Chapter 33

Frost glittered diamond-bright in the starlight, as Rabisu lurked by the entrance to the cave tunnel. Hours had passed since the Shamar had escaped, cheating as they flew to safety, leaving others to guard their useless flesh. If they travelled to where the sword was hidden, their next step would be to return it to its resting place, and once it was there he would have very little chance of getting past it. He needed to act now.

It had taken a ridiculous amount of time to climb down the ridge and find the cave Dallmin had led them to weeks earlier. Although the moon was bright, Jake's terrible sense of direction and slow body had hampered their progress. As they'd scrambled through the dark, Rabisu had strained constantly to catch the scent of the Shamar, convinced they would return at any moment and either beat him to the cave or find some new horror to block his way. So far the night had been crisp and too quiet, the sacred valley seemingly guarded only by the scurrying night creatures who watched from the trees. Each rustle had sent Jake cowering under his elbows, expecting claws and teeth, beaks and talons. Then the hated river had nearly killed them both. The stupid child had known how to swim but was weak, almost getting swept away while Rabisu had been overcome by the exquisite pain of its song. Frozen to the point of delirium, they had emerged from the water a long way downstream, and it had taken almost another full hour to recover and crawl through the thick scrub in the bitter dark. Still shuddering, Rabisu vowed to never again possess anyone in any danger of drowning. Drowning once was more than enough. He would rather infest the body of a dog. Again.

The cave entrance looked nothing like it had in the last battle he'd fought. Such a mundane gap between the rocks, bordered by a fallen slab of stone that cast shadows across the entrance. Shadows that were swallowed by deeper shadows. No hint of the glory hidden within. Voices danced in cracked echoes from the depths of the tunnel. When Dallmin had first brought them here they'd been faced with a Shamar in female form. She'd been angry at what he'd done to her daughter, and bursting with so much power his weakling host had wasted his chance and run away. The sentinels must be cheating because there were supposed to only be two. He remembered from previous wars. Two Cherubim in human form, guarding the entrance to paradise. And the holy sword. If only he had found a way to destroy it. Jake had fought him on that—his greed had sabotaged every attempt to pass it to someone who could help, and now it was too late.

Rabisu was determined to get into Eden before the ancient weapon was returned. How long did he have? Perhaps Noah and Lainie were lost in that maelstrom of wandering spirits. Perhaps the temptation to fly and to shift was too much for the Cherubim after being bound into human form for so long, and they'd decided to abandon their duty. Or maybe the other demons had found a way to defeat them.

Rabisu knew full well he could never be that lucky.

The voices smelled like chalk and grief as they rode up from the deep air currents. At least two people were down there, and he was convinced one of them was the female Cherub they had faced last time. They should attack her now before Noah and Lainie returned.

Pitch black embraced him and he scraped his bare frozen feet on rocks with nearly every step, but it was easy to ignore pain in a body that wasn't really his. Slipping in and out of pools of icy water, he crept through the labyrinth, straining to hear what was happening ahead of him. When he reached the final twist, Rabisu forced himself to wait and to watch.

Curled in a tightly shivering ball, the Cherub dressed as a woman sobbed like a lost child. She shook her head slowly from side to side as if trying to deny the truth of what the other person was saying.

'There is always a choice, *always* a choice,' she sobbed, over and over.

Although the man she was talking to had his back to the entrance, Rabisu knew who he was as soon as he spoke. Who else would speak in such an ancient and familiar accent?

Dallmin scowled at the Shamar. 'That's a lie, Annie. If there was a choice I wouldn't be here. Even you aren't free to choose. You couldn't even move across when you lost your Guardian. You had to stay until Lainie was old enough to take over your role, didn't you? You don't even have a choice now,' he sneered, striding toward the boundary.

Wailing, Annie hid under her hands and then spat out a sharp Word, and a small stalactite fell, glancing off Dallmin's shoulder before clattering at his feet. He wiped blood from his face as he turned back to her, horrified. 'You hurt me. Was that your *choice?*'

'They're coming,' Annie whispered as grief-torn tears flowed down her cheeks. 'The Guardians are here.'

The tunnel was narrow enough that Rabisu would only have to fight them one at a time, and the lack of light worked in his favour. Crouched in a hidden niche right before the final bend, he heard two people hurry down the uneven passageway, and all it took was a well-aimed kick to bring the first tired Guardian down—Bane, by the sound of the surprised grunt as he hit the floor. He followed up by slamming Bane's head hard against the rocks beneath. Jake's possessed hands grabbed the hilt of the dropped sword just as Tessa leaped at him. A tiny nick was enough for her to stumble back in agony.

'It's just a scratch, Tess, stop being such a girl. Or could it be that you're tainted too? The sword would know, apparently,' Jake taunted, swinging the weapon around to admire the feel of its perfect balance.

She seemed unfazed. 'Of course I'm tainted, you creep. All of us humans are. It's hardly news to me given I feel like ripping your head from your shoulders.'

Without hesitating further, Rabisu lunged forward to silence the girl once and for all, but she was too fast. Ducking under his reach, she somehow flipped around so she had more space to move while he was trapped between two jagged boulders. Fighting in this tiny body was tricky. Its muscles were weak and wiry and his possession had given it terrible coordination. And it had been a long time since he'd fought with a sword. How was this Guardian able to move so nimbly in the dark? It was obvious she and Bane had also swum the freezing river because their clothes were wet and they were both shivering, yet somehow they still looked like they were in better shape than he was.

Aiming a vicious slash at Tessa's head, he managed only to hit the wall as she ducked, causing the weapon to ring like a bell. Searing light flooded the tunnel, blinding them all as Words of power shook his bones. Something primal inside him screamed in reply. Aching with longing for something long lost, and yet at the same time deeply frightened, he turned to face the detested creature that had spoken.

'What have you done to Bane?' Annie's angry voice challenged. She seemed ready to join the dance.

Rabisu laughed. 'You can't protect him, can you? Otherwise, I wouldn't have been able to take Tessa last time. The Guardians can heal you, but you can't do a thing to help them other than turn up the lighting a bit.'

The look of abject horror on her face made him laugh even more until pain exploded in his side. Bane had somehow regained his feet and punched him savagely from behind. Ignoring the feel of his cracked ribs, he simply stepped away. There was no more time to waste on the human Guardians. All his deadly hate became focused on the Cherub standing before him.

I was lost, which felt quite nice. Searching for my body was futile. And boring. There was so much else to explore. Was that an imploding universe over near the misty sea? I could check it out if only Noah would stop yelling at me about unfinished business. Pretty sure that was how ghosts got trapped between worlds, wasn't it? Unfinished business. As if leaving the stove on was worth missing out on all this. Perhaps they were simply scared of the unknown. Or too attached to their flawed bodies to let go. Attached with Velcro. Or something. I couldn't remember. It didn't matter.

Except that Noah was crying. He sounded frightened. Perhaps I could give him a quick hug to let him know I was fine and then be on my way. He wasn't that far away …

Perky moonlight made my eyelids tingle in delicious welcome, and a flavour that was the very definition of ambrosial lingered on my tongue. Warm air, fragranced with honey, played across my face and enticed me to wake up.

Someone was watching me, wanting … something. Cracking open one eyelid, I giggled at the relieved look on Noah's face as he stared at me, his face mere inches from my own. Above us, feathered fronds danced on the placid night breeze.

'Finally!' he gasped. 'I nearly left without you. You got lost again, didn't you? I nearly did and it was my first time, not that I remember much. How many times has it been for you now, Lainie? It can't be healthy to do this too often.'

What nonsense was he going on about now? And what had I done to make him sound so snippy?

'You look very clean,' I told him as I brushed a damp lock of hair away from his eyes. 'Have you been swimming?'

'Oh boy. I forgot about this.' He pulled me to my feet, brushed me off, and handed me a wooden cup of water. 'I'm clean because Beltana kindly washed all the blood and icing off me while she waited for me to wake up.'

Beltana was standing nearby, cuddling my honorary nephew who was watching me with a stern expression on his tiny face.

'She's been minding Nathaniel for a few hours now, and would probably like to get some sleep, but I can't take him until we've finished what we're supposed to be doing,' Noah said. 'So if you could please hurry up, we can get on with it. How much can you remember?'

I blinked at him. 'Your son has green eyes, like you. Tessa worked really hard when she was pregnant, making sure everyone knew he would probably have green eyes. She figured if that was what everyone expected him to have, then he would. It worked. I told her she should have lobbied for purple just to see what would happen.'

'Beltana?' he asked, looking back over his shoulder. 'Is it normal that she sounds drunk or did her piece of Fruit get fermented?'

Although Beltana didn't speak English, she still laughed.

'Lainie, you're even flakier than I was. Please, try to concentrate. Why are you wearing that dress?' Noah asked.

I looked down at the torn gown, its soft white skirt glowing in the moonlight. It had been beautiful once. Now it was slashed with blood stains and its pretty ornaments hung from the bodice as if they were clinging on for dear life. I had tried to cling for dear life, but there had been nothing to cling to. His face had looked so regretful … Shaking my head, I let the strange dream slip away. It was too disturbing for such a beautiful place. Breathing in the scent of the night-blooming flowers, I stretched my arms out and wiggled my fingers, because it felt good. Casting shadows all around us, the pearlescent moon sent its mercurial rays down to see if anyone was still awake to play with.

'It's got to be getting close to midnight by now. Or have I missed an entire day? What day is it, anyway?' I asked Noah. 'And why is Nathaniel still awake at this hour?'

'That's not unusual for him, sadly,' he replied. 'And Nayn fed him Living Fruit juice. I think my son is on a bit of a high. Again. He's barely a month old and he's tasted it twice already. Does that make me a bad parent or a good one?'

'The Tree of Knowledge of Good and Evil isn't here any longer. I checked. So you'll just have to take my word for it. You're a good parent, Noah.'

Beltana signed to me with her free arm. *The baby pestered Nayn until I offered to take him to see what he wanted,* she explained cryptically. *I assume that means finding you both couldn't have waited until morning.*

Can I hold him? I asked her. *I have a song for him. My mother used to sing it to me when I was a baby.*

I began to hum the tune playing in my head until Beltana signalled for me to stop, wanting me to concentrate on something else.

Noah looked annoyed. 'Lainie, you walked down the aisle to that tune a few hours ago. You're still wearing your wedding dress, or at least what's left of it. Don't you remember?' He was pleading with me now, as if his remembering game was really important to him. He took my hands in his and looked me directly in the eyes. 'I'm sorry, Lainie, we don't have time for this to be gentle.' His green eyes glowed like polished emeralds, entrancing me and holding all my capricious attention. 'You married Bane. Then there was an explosion. Bane's mother was killed and Tim was badly injured. The demons attacked us and you scared them off by retrieving the sword. We returned to our bodies, but then—'

'Bane murdered me!' I finished in horror. 'He's been possessed by a demon, Noah. I thought he would be immune because he's a Guardian. He wasn't. He pushed me off the cliff!' Pure dismay washed through me like I had been dunked into a dam full of leeches, as all the hideous memories came flooding back. Bane, trapped by a demon spirit and compelled to destroy me, his own free will snatched brutally from him. The thought of such an intimate violation made me feel sick to the core. 'Why are *you* here? You disappeared right before I fell,' I remembered. 'Tessa too? *No.*' I tried to see up to the top of the cliff in the hazy moonlight, which was pointless.

'Woah! Settle down. They weren't possessed. They're fine. As far as I know, they're fine,' he assured me, pulling me around to look at him again. His comforting gaze was so easy to trust.

'Bane threw me. It wasn't an accident,' I insisted.

'They planned it all along. They even scouted out the best place to do it, that day when they had their secret Guardian meeting, remember?'

I could barely remember the last few hours, let alone a particular meeting they might have had weeks ago. Still, I trusted my friend. 'You're saying they pushed us off a cliff to our deaths *on purpose*?'

He looked up, as if trying to see what was going on at the top of the cliff across the Skin of the World. 'Once we passed through the boundary they wouldn't have suffered the feel of our deaths. It would have been excruciating to force themselves to do it, but I suppose it was the best way they could come up with to keep us safe. Ironic, much?'

'Safe?' I echoed.

'They know that nothing short of death could keep us from where we need to be.'

Sitting down with a clumsy bump, I took a few moments to wrap my head around what they'd done. I had no idea what time it was when they had forced us out of the action. All I knew was I'd been dead for far too long. Despair filtered through the inherent peace Eden had blanketed me with.

'Noah, what if we've missed everything? Bane and Tess could be—'

'Don't say it! I won't accept that. Besides, I can still feel the danger, can't you? We would know if Jake or any of the other demons crossed into here, and I can feel Nayn on this side keeping watch. Whatever's going on, it's not finished yet. Chances are, Tessa and Bane headed down to the cave as soon as they could, but even with the dirt bikes that would have taken at least half an hour. Longer, given how dark it is.'

An infantile wail interrupted our bickering. Nathaniel was making his wants heard.

I know, precious one. I woke them up as soon as I could. They did stop, you know. Give them time to adjust. Honestly, all you young ones are so impatient.

The baby watched Beltana speaking as if he understood every word and waved his tiny fist around as if arguing back.

She turned back to me, frowning. *I have learned to listen when Shamar children speak,* she said. *My son once predicted a dawn attack that would have destroyed our food stores if it had succeeded. We should get moving.*

My brain was pretty messed up, so I looked at Noah to see if he knew what she was going on about. Of course, his understanding of sign language was a bit hit and miss. He looked as confused as I was.

I will explain as we go, Beltana continued, pulling me up and shoving me forward. The shock of Beltana using even that small amount of physical coercion made me trip over a torn piece of my skirt. *The cave is not that close, remember. Get moving,* she commanded more firmly.

The speed she set through the dimly lit glade made me wince, given she was also carrying an infant and signing with her free hand. Yet she didn't take a single misstep. Of course not. She was Beltana. She had reflexes to rival a Guardian.

I stumbled to a halt.

Can you repeat what you just said? I asked.

She turned back, looking cross. 'I said, only story piece I not tell Annie was about final war. My son not allowed to come home,' she said in almost perfect English. 'Dallmin teach languages so much it got tiring to avoid,' she added, and then shoved me forward again. 'Shamar, keep moving!'

⌒

The light in the cavern dimmed as Jake tripped over the lantern to lunge at Annie again, but the light she had spoken into existence still allowed him to see enough. The enraged Guardians were systematically swooping in to attack him, wary of his holy blade. He'd given Bane a tiny nick, who had screamed as if he'd been gutted. He was almost glad they'd stolen it back. It was a very effective weapon.

'Where are the alien beasts?' he spat, fury rising as he stabbed again at Annie's huddled form. In his mind he felt the tip of the weapon slice through her hated flesh in a frenzy of blood lust, but in reality she was yet to even flinch, and then the female Guardian's fist knocked him off balance as she targeted his previous shoulder injury again.

'Dead. And beyond your reach,' Bane replied, crouching in front of the only remaining Cherub as a living shield. 'You can't feel them any-more, can you?'

Jake paused, blue eyes narrowed. 'Are you suggesting this place is now unguarded, except for this pathetic child, who apparently doesn't have a Guardian of her own?'

'Hey! I remember when you were born, Jacob Evans,' Annie protested. Even she looked surprised by the bewildering return of the long-forgotten memory.

At the sound of his name, in a voice that sounded so familiar in its maternal scolding, Jake hesitated. It was enough for Bane to dodge under his inept guard, tackling him with swift brutality until he was pinned against the uneven wall. Rabisu fumed at Jake's limitations and could do nothing to prevent the quick jab of agony to Jake's broken ribs, which was followed up by a solid knee to the stomach. Breath whooshed out of his lungs. Both his wrist and the sword were slammed with bleak finality against the rock, sending the blade clattering away.

Punches rolled as the two of them brawled. Tessa stayed out of their way, the look on her face suggesting she was impatient for her turn. Within the space of a minute, however, the demon realised that wouldn't be necessary. Without the sword, Jake's body was no match for the Guardian's trained reflexes and strength. It didn't take long for his tattooed arms to fall limp as his head flopped uselessly to one side. Conscious awareness fell to dark failure.

Annie huddled against a shell-pink stalagmite and watched Bane as he stepped away from his fallen enemy, chest heaving, trembling with

barely controlled rage. So much pain, and loss, and nothing left to fight. No outlet for his anger or wild adrenaline. In stark reflection of a similar scene long ago, after her own Guardian had dragged her from her burning home, Annie watched as he gasped with ragged aftershock, relief slowly easing his bearing as some of the danger to his bonded charge dissipated.

No one spoke.

Eventually, she walked over and pulled Bane into a gentle hug. Blood spread across her dress. As she led him to the tiny streamlet that flowed like gathered silk between the rocks, the dim light flickered briefly. With tender affection she washed his wounds. None of them looked too serious except for the lump on the back of his head. He winced when she made him lie back and soak it in the icy water.

Her worried eyes turned on him. 'Lainie and Noah, are they really dead?'

'All will be well, Annie. They're safe,' he assured her. 'Can you tell me about the demons? Lainie said they can't find their way past the protection dome, although she wasn't confident it would hold.'

'We have a protection dome? Cool.' She splashed water over her face and blood-stained shoulder.

'Annie, I think you should put the sword back in its place,' Tessa suggested, righting the toppled lantern.

They turned to Dallmin, who was pulling it out of a rim pool. The white blade looked like bleached bone. He lifted it up, inspecting the inscriptions along its length.

Annie hissed as his intent wrapped icy fingers of dread around her heart.

'Actually,' he said, 'I think I like it where it is.'

Standing on the threshold to Eden, Dallmin stood serenely tall, brandishing the magnificent weapon like it was a shiny new toy.

Chapter 34

Beltana ran through the trees like a gazelle, cradling Nathaniel securely to her chest. She didn't sound even the least bit out of breath as she told her story to Noah and me in broken English.

'Long after the flood removed all the veiled ones, a leader of men unbuilt a town called Telassar, where the children of those who left Eden lived. The leader hurt them, trying to make them tell where the cave was. The Shamar, Zyndel and my Tahuma, did not know until all were killed. Later, the son of the son of that leader unbuilt the island city of Dilmun, searching for writing clues. He still could not find.'

I forced my feet to keep moving. It was a lot to take in. Sweet Beltana, telling me about people being tortured? 'The ones who left Eden. You mean Nin? Dallmin's daughter?'

'Nin. Yes. My friend. She died many seasons before this piece of story. Bad leader killed her children's children.'

'And this bad leader's grandson, was it King Sennacherib of Assyria?'

Beltana stumbled to a halt, her eyes wide. 'Have his actions been so loud you have heard of him even as far as big southern land?'

I shrugged. Way too hard to explain.

Beltana frowned. 'I think he had a … lost person inside his head. I don't know right word.'

'Demon,' Noah supplied.

She nodded and started running again. 'Demon king look for writings in Jerusalem next. Shamar stop him. This was last war.'

'War?'

'Annie teach word when I tell her the story of the veiled ones. Eden's fallen children who were ended by the great water. In my first language, war is *tahazu*.'

I ran faster to get a bit closer. Surely I wasn't hearing her correctly. What did she mean, her first language? How did she know all this?

She kept up the narrative as she ducked neatly under a branch. 'My son, Tahuma. His Guardian was killed. Zyndel tell me Tahuma then became … one-person-war, and no more Eden for him. Zyndel not tell me more, even though I ask many times.'

Realisation slammed into me. The war she was talking about was when King Sennacherib laid siege to Jerusalem. It hadn't been an angel after all. This Cherub, Tahuma, had destroyed one hundred and eighty-five thousand soldiers in the night …

Zyndel was right. Beltana could never know what her son had done. My mind was spinning as we ran along the base of the cliffs toward the cave. If only I had more time to think through everything she was telling me. Beltana had a son who was Shamar. Her first language had the word 'war' in it. Which meant she was not born in Eden.

The path became rockier as we approached the cave, forcing us to slow to a walk.

'Zyndel move Eden. Important you understand this. She move it not for people of Eden. She move it to stop human war. Shamar power opens for human help, not just Eden help.'

Noah pieced it all together first. 'You're a Guardian? How are you here?'

Beltana didn't answer because we had reached the cave. Nayn was standing by the entrance, arms crossed, two dogs sitting by his feet. His expression was as grim as that of a nightclub bouncer. When he saw us, he gave a satisfied nod.

'Go,' Beltana said, pushing Noah into the tunnel. 'Be Shamar. I care for baby while you stop *tahazu*.'

⌒

'This pretty blade is the key to everything, isn't it, Annie?' Dallmin breathed, studying the weapon as if he could read the Words that shone along the white metal. She wondered if he really could. He loved collecting languages.

'There is nothing in either world as pure as it is. It is not burning now. Perhaps that means if I'm the one holding it, it will not hurt me.' He edged closer to the threshold.

Despair unbound Annie's last shred of composure. Driven to act, raw light exploded in the cavern like a white blistering firestorm, blinding everyone to a stinging retreat as white-hot destruction charged the boundary with hissing sparks of defensive energy. Backlash made her stumble, her knees hitting rock before gentle darkness returned, broken only by the shimmering pulses from the boundary wall and the steadfast glow of the little lantern.

Spun to dizzying confusion, she watched Dallmin stagger recklessly toward the threshold *yet again*, intent on grasping at his last shred of hope for resolution.

'Dallmin, wait!' Bane's cry made him pause. 'Don't make her do this.'

Faced with the truth of the full consequence of his rebellion, Dallmin turned toward her. A look of compassion broke his arrogant demeanour.

'Annie, you must act, or not, according to your want,' he said, blinking against his burnt vision. 'I told you before, I have no choice. *I can't stay here.*'

'You are so wrong, Dallmin,' Bane cried. One hand was pressed against his head wound as he tried to stand, blinking furiously. 'The choice is *entirely* yours. Along with every other choice you've made. Don't you dare presume for one instant that you're the victim here.' The tenacious soldier began to stagger toward where Annie was huddled.

She felt frail. Something was very wrong with the way she was breathing, uneven and hitched. Blood oozed from her shoulder, but the remaining light was too dim for her to see the extent of her own injuries. Everything hurt.

'Please, Dallmin,' Bane begged. 'You know she'll have to stop you. Please don't force her to do that. The harder you push to get through, the harder she'll have to push you away. If you push too hard—'

'I am not afraid to die!' he screamed, furious. 'I would rather die than stay in this place.'

'Dallmin, if she kills you—'

'I don't care. She can make her own choice. If that's what you believe, then it goes for her too.'

Crushed by bleak desolation, Annie lifted her face to meet Bane's caring gaze. Then she took his hand and kissed it on the inside of his wrist in wholehearted gratitude for what she was asking of him. If she could have done it herself she would have, regardless of the consequences, but Dallmin was a new creature, born of fight and fear. And she was too broken.

She opened her hand to give him a forbidden glimpse of the sacred gift she'd struggled so hard to bring across the threshold. It had made her feel so nauseated and dizzy she'd barely made it out of the cave, even with Nayn's help. She was prepared to pay the full price of her rebellion if it meant Dallmin had even a slim chance of coming home, even if it hadn't worked for her own father.

As she hid the gift back in her bag, she whispered an answer to Bane's confusion. 'Dallmin has died many times. He's well practised at lingering here until he is called back and healed. I have to believe that will make a difference. If not, then I'll follow him.' She clutched her old cloth bag to her chest again. She loved Dallmin, and although that acknowledgment had come far too late, she still felt relief. It made it easier to decide. Especially now she had help.

As her almost-lover stepped across the illicit threshold, she watched him sadly and did absolutely nothing.

Chapter 35

Shrieking agony reverberated from the cavern walls as I set my shoulder and rammed Dallmin back toward the charged Event Horizon. I'd never been very good at rugby, but at least I was tall. And committed. And I'd certainly caught him off-guard. Beside me, Noah bellowed with rage and pain as he, too, felt the unholy violation like a stab at his soul. Between us we shoved and dragged Dallmin back the way he'd come. Indescribable pain shot through me as the desecration carved into my innermost identity, easing only when I saw Dallmin's body launched back into invisibility on the other side of the boundary. Striding past the silky threshold, I watched him roll to stand up again and I held my hands up as a warning. I wasn't sure what I would do with them, exactly, only that I had the power ready to do whatever was required. The sound of metal bouncing on rock caught my attention. The terrible sword was lying at my feet. It was only then that my brain caught up with my reflexes enough to realise Dallmin had been holding Sadie the whole time. He must have dropped it when we bowled him over. Good thing we hadn't let him watch any movies with sword fighting in them.

'I knew it! I knew you wouldn't stay dead,' he roared as he tried to lunge at me. Luckily, something tripped him into a stumble, because his threatening attitude surprised me so much that all I managed was to stagger back a step. Steadying hands gripped my shoulders as Noah backed me up.

'Dallmin, what on Earth are you doing? You know we can't let you cross!' I flustered. The transition between worlds was making it difficult to assess the situation. Violence and sorrow resonated in the chill air, and the flickering shadows in the cave felt like they were suffocating me. I glanced around, trying to take stock of what was going on. Tessa was crouched in a fighting stance next to Dallmin, ready to intervene again in an instant. My mother's bloodless face peeked out at me from behind a boulder. Jake looked like roadkill, and the burning stench of charred flowers pervaded everything. On the other side of Dallmin, Bane was watching me as if waiting for me to give the okay to take Dallmin down. At least I hoped that was what he was doing. I was too afraid to really look at him. What if Noah was wrong? What if he really had been possessed by a demon?

'Either let me pass or kill me,' Dallmin challenged, stumbling forward again.

In horror I watched as he lunged for the sword that lay between us, unable to believe he would betray us again—not now that he understood what he was doing. Tessa shoved him back and Bane made a grab for the weapon before I could even move, hissing as his fingers touched the hilt too high up before he adjusted his grip.

Dallmin flinched away from the elegant blade and paused.

'So now you can all finally take your revenge on me.' Ancient eyes burned with newborn anger.

Bane didn't move.

'Go on. Do it,' he cried, his voice torn. 'I'm unarmed, but I can still hurt her.'

Like a cat, he jumped at me, his dancer's grace lending him power as he tried to hit me with his outstretched fist. Bane's elbow connected with his jaw and his head snapped back sickeningly as he fell. Lying at our feet, Dallmin groaned, locking his eyes on Bane's face as if inviting him to finish it. Once again my Guardian paused, unblinking, the giant white sword held steady—mere centimetres from Dallmin's throat. Everything in Bane's body language told me he was ready to kill. Ready to do whatever it took to keep me safe. He was poised on the edge of a blade every bit as sharp as the sword he was holding. Would he fall on the side of violence, or on the side of his compassionate heart? Or would he be cut in two?

This was what I'd seen coming ever since Sarah Ashbree had held a knife to my throat. I'd chosen death, and chosen to leave him rather than force him to ever have to make this decision. It hadn't helped. This moment had always been coming.

'Bane, no,' I begged, my eyes searching for help from someone. Any-one. Annie caught my eye and shuddered, and I knew she could feel my despair. She stood up and took a few stumbling steps closer before clutching at her shoulder, breathing hard.

Bane refused to look at me. 'This is what I'm here for, Lainie. To sacrifice this part of myself so you don't have to.'

'I know.' A quick glance showed me Annie was still approaching. Step by shambling step. Surely she knew how to help Dallmin with-out Bane having to kill him. She needed more time. Unfortunately, my Guardian was not going to wait around and give Dallmin a chance to attack me again.

'I know what you went through after the sword killed Noah's mum,' he said. 'I won't let you blame yourself for other people's choices again. This time it's my choice, and I take full responsibility.'

'Oh, like the way you chose to throw me off a cliff? Do you take full responsibility for killing me, too? Noah, why did you let me marry a homicidal maniac?'

'You know him better than anyone, Lainie. Don't blame me,' came Noah's defensive mumble.

Arguing with me was still enough of an ingrained reflex that it dis-tracted Bane from his intense self-sacrificing focus. If he hadn't been holding a six-foot-long sword, I was sure he would have crossed his arms and glared at me. I still copped the glare.

'I wasn't trying to murder you. I was giving you a shortcut that was supposed to get you here in less time and in better health. What took you so long?'

'Mur … der … rer,' I hissed. 'He murdered us, my precioussss, nasty Guardians murdered usss …'

He clenched his jaw and worked very hard not to roll his eyes at me. 'Whatever. I was called to serve, and I gladly gave my oath that I would. I have no right to enter that sacred place anyway. This isn't costing me anything,' he said, raising the sword again.

'You and I both know that isn't true.'

Real tears escaped his control and broke my heart. Then he

shuddered—the unrelenting reaction to the danger I was still in. 'Dallmin won't stop. He'll keep pushing until he hurts you or you hurt him.'

'I can't stay here,' came Dallmin's tired, anguished whisper. 'I've failed everyone. Failed myself. I *can't* remain here where I am not free to choose anything other than failure.'

'You're free to choose not to repeat your failures,' Bane objected. 'You can choose to trust me this time.'

'How can I trust you when you have hardened your heart against me?' he countered, tendons straining in his neck as he yearned for release.

Silence stretched in breathless appeal.

'*Look* at me,' Bane said with enough accompanying sign language to capture the man's attention. Body language could not easily deceive. He let the tip of the sword fall away. 'Can't you see I've forgiven you?' Hot tears sizzled onto the blade as Bane exposed all of his carefully guarded feelings. Open and entirely vulnerable, despite the giant weapon he was holding, he allowed all his compassion to show through.

Dallmin saw.

I saw.

And we both understood. Integrity and loyalty to rival even the purest of characters shone through him, rendering him *entirely* worthy of trust.

Like a wounded animal seeking assistance from higher beings, Dallmin inhaled deeply, stretching wide the arms that had propelled his body through the River of Life for countless centuries. He lay on the cold rock and locked his ancient brown eyes on Bane's face.

'Then … mate, I choose …' he swallowed. Took a breath. 'I choose to trust you to help me.'

The world froze as Bane drew back, ready to strike.

I couldn't watch.

I couldn't turn away.

This was not right. Not natural. Not fair. I couldn't let him do this.

I couldn't do it for him.

The sword glinted with the promise of holy death as it swung … and jarred to a stop when Annie caught hold of Bane's elbow. She tugged the weapon from his grip and Bane stepped aside, shaking his head in silent appeal to change her mind. Yet he had no authority over the Shamar.

My heart screamed as Annie plunged the white-hot sword straight into Dallmin's unflinching chest. Bright writing flared to life along Sadie's blade, dazzling Dallmin's fading eyes with her glorious cleansing beauty. A cry of pristine agony tore from him—a sound that sliced through to the heart of terror. Stretched to an eternity of crystallised suffering, his scream held all of the world's pain, funnelled into a moment's sliced flesh. Unendurable. Inescapable. Diabolical. Utterly inconsolable. Such intense agony was never meant to exist, and it felt like it would never end until finally I saw two malicious shadows twisting away from his lips as the remnants of his demon captors unravelled with tortured rage, rent from his body, and were dissolved from our realm.

In horror, I realised how sickeningly violated my friend had been by the evil spirits that had greedily trapped his body and mind. Even then, after the demons had been banished, Dallmin's tainted flesh continued to burn as the sword's fire ripped through him, burning deeper into his soul than any ordinary fire could.

Even blood refused to sully Sadie's perfection as my mother pulled her free with one hand, while her left hand drew a priceless gift from her cloth bag. A somewhat squashed, sticky gift. As Dallmin bled out before our eyes, Annie thwarted his mortal scream with a golden, juicy piece of Living Fruit.

Chapter 36

Blood flowed languidly onto the stony ground, leaching into hungry cracks in the rock. So much blood had been spilled in that spot it was incredible that it wasn't stained permanently red. A trickle of sanguine fluid snaked its way toward the body that twitched and convulsed on the floor as it miraculously healed, blending with the sticky pool of blood already there. Twin rivers of blood, joining life and death together until just ten short breaths later, Dallmin woke refreshed and whole again. He bounced to his feet like a child waking up on Christmas morning.

Sadie slipped from Annie's grip and Bane only barely grabbed the hilt in time as Dallmin gathered her into a tight hug.

'What have you done?' I sobbed, hugging them both. Somehow I refrained from knocking their heads together.

'I made a choice,' Annie said, looping the strap of her cloth bag over my head. It was heavy enough to dislodge me from the group hug with a stumble.

'All will be well,' she told Dallmin as he buried his face into her neck.

'I'm so sorry, I'm sorry! The things I said, that's not who I am. I don't know who I am, but that's not who I want to be. I'm sorry!'

I was astounded he could even remember what had happened so quickly. Perhaps after thousands of years of countless resurrections, he didn't suffer from the same disorientation I always did.

My mother held him like she wanted to squeeze out every last drop of his sorrow. 'Shhh … I know, Dallmin. The demons were playing with you. They're gone now. All will be well,' she repeated. Something about the way she said it caught my attention. That intensity and focus— so different from the carefree and innocent way she usually acted. I watched a series of rapid-fire emotions run across her face. I almost reached out to touch her, to find out what had triggered her distress, but she closed her eyes, inhaled deeply, and the emotions were gone. As if she'd swallowed them down like a giant pill.

Looking down, I examined the fresh blood on the front of my dress, and then glanced at Jake's listless, tangled limbs sprawled across the floor. The stench of burnt flowers had not yet disappeared. In fact, I could feel more demons approaching like cunning little beasts. And where was Rabisu? Was he locked in Jake's unconscious body or floating around like a bad smell?

'You should have told me Jake injured you when he attacked,' Dallmin murmured, stroking Annie's hair. The truth stung. If Dallmin had been her Guardian, he would not have needed to be told.

'You were a little busy,' she remarked, leaning on him with her right arm hanging limply by her side. Blood dripped like crimson bullets from her fingertips. There was a second flower of blood blossoming under her ribcage.

Noah stepped forward, trying to peer down the tunnel. 'They're coming,' he confirmed. 'The rest of the demons have found us.'

Four people were approaching the cave and their intentions were not peaceful. And there was more. I couldn't quite catch the full nature of the threat other than those greedy little eyes, cunning, quietly trying to sneak past us. Whatever they were, they were right on top of us. My eyes searched the cave. The walls, the shadows above. It was too dark to see up there properly. Or perhaps they were bodiless and invisible.

'Bane, give me the sword,' I said. 'I need to—'

A small creature scurried past me, dashing straight for the boundary faster than I could react. More followed, bounding past my feet and making me yelp. Tessa lunged for them, but even Guardian reflexes were no match for darting rabbits.

Demon-possessed rabbits? Seriously?

In the time it took me to draw a breath, Noah had already acted, speaking out a glistening Word. I almost barked out a laugh as a roll of chain mesh unravelled its way across the cavern, forming a buckled and warped fence that curved around the stalagmites. Most of the rabbits bounced off it as they ran full pelt for the boundary. A couple of them squeezed under where the ground was uneven. Noah swore and trilled a few new Words to fill in the gaps.

Behind me, I heard a cold voice and spun to see Rabisu in his ghostly form. He was gloating. 'You gave me the idea, Cherub-filth. You and those vicious magpies.'

I ran to the fence, trying to catch sight of the couple that had snuck through. They were so quick. It was already too late. As I readied myself to jump the fence and hunt them down, two streaks of fur came bounding out from the Eden end of the cavern. Bungee and Wendy each had hold of a rabbit and were shaking the evil right out of them. Wendy threw hers aside and stalked something hiding behind a rock. She caught that one within seconds and killed it too. I stretched out my senses to check. No more rabbits had made it past the fence. It had been a silly, yet effective tactic. The demons had found physical form so they could follow Rabisu's direction to the cave without interference from the deflection dome. They were all here now. And not all wearing rabbits. I turned back to the entrance tunnel where I could sense five more demons approach.

No light came from the tunnel behind them, so it was only as they stepped into the lantern's weak glow that I could see their faces. Luke, Hayley, Lachlan, Kate, and Hayden spread out in silence. Each of them holding an army-issued knife. None of them smiling.

For a moment I wondered if Aunt Lily really had sent them here to help us, until Rabisu filled the cave with his bone-chilling whisper.

They are here to kill you, Shamar.

Chapter 37

The look on Bane's face broke my heart. These were his friends. Crewmates. They had each other's backs. And yet he could feel their intention to kill me.

'Don't worry,' I assured him. 'Even Jake showed moments of reason. They can fight this.'

Rabisu laughed. 'I usually allow my hosts to retain some pretence of control. Otherwise, they tend to end up in medical facilities where they are of little use to me. These ones will have finished their task long before that can happen.'

'If your evil minions harm them in any way …' My threat was pointless, and Rabisu knew it. Whether the demons harmed them or not, I was still going to do everything in my power to destroy them all.

'How about this for a deal: the sooner you die, the sooner these toy soldiers can enter Eden and be healed,' he countered.

I shuddered at the thought just as Kate stepped forward, crouching like she was about to pounce.

Tessa stepped in front of Noah, a living shield, ready for the fight of her life despite the fact she was unarmed.

'Hi, Kate.' I waved cheerily at her. She hissed back. 'How was the swim across the river, Kate? Kate, you must be freezing.'

The girl literally growled, while Noah and Bane both glared at me.

'Look, it works in all the stories. She's in there somewhere. I thought saying her name might help bring her out again.'

Demon-Kate screeched, the sound echoing from the cavern walls in a way that made me somewhat less appreciative of the incredible acoustics. Then all I saw was her knife as she ran at me, her boots pounding on the rocky floor. A blur of white and clang of metal responded as Bane used Sadie to try to knock the blade from her hand. Kate cried out in pain, yet managed to roll with the movement so she could keep hold of her weapon. She spun and struck out at her friend, again and again. Each time, Bane blocked her. Her small blade moved like the wind, stabbing, slicing. Sadie had a longer reach, only Bane was trying to disarm her without hurting her. I took a few steps backward to give them space, but as soon as I did Lachlan and Hayley ducked past the two fighters on either side, reaching for me.

Bane spun and leaped to crouch in front of me again.

'No, Lainie. You need to stay close.'

His three friends didn't pause. All of them lunged at us, and I let out a very un-Cherub-like yip. Sadie danced, her white glow leaving streaks in my vision like sparklers on New Year's Eve as Bane parried every swing. Man, he was *fast*. Problem was, they weren't aiming to defeat him; they only wanted to get past him to get to me. And he was still trying not to hurt them. How could he engage them properly when they used every free moment to step around him? I considered lifting the dogs over the fence so they could round up the possessed soldiers and keep them together, except they were too busy snapping at the crazed rabbits still bouncing off the chain mesh. I needed them to stay on guard in case any more of them made it through.

A resounding clash of steel on … whatever it was Sadie was forged from, and Kate's knife spun through the air and landed at my feet. I snatched it up and looked at it, feeling utterly pathetic about my lack of fighting skills. In my hands it was guaranteed to be more of a hindrance than help, so I tossed it over the fence where it disappeared into the other world. I had better ways to fight. Surely now more than ever, I would have access to my authority. Only, what was I supposed to do with it, precisely?

'Demons, I banish you!' I commanded, searching for the matching Words. None came. I turned to Noah for help. He was striding with clenched fists toward Hayden, who had a reverse grip on his knife as he slashed at Tessa. She deflected the knife's trajectory and stepped in close to him, locking her arm around his elbow and using sheer strength to prevent him from using his blade. He threw her off much like Wendy had tossed aside the rabbit. She leaped for him again, a whirling storm of limbs. There was no waiting for him to strike first. Hayden doubled over as she got in a decent kick to his stomach. In the next instant, I gasped as Tessa backhanded Noah out of the way. She'd *hit* him. Noah stumbled back in shock. I don't know why we were both so surprised. She'd already thrown him off a cliff tonight.

For someone with only the training from Bane's sparring sessions and Nalong's Taekwondo club, Tessa left no doubt that she was still more than a match for a very fit Army Reserve officer. Guardian reflexes. Hayden grunted as she landed a kick to his knee.

'Where's Luke?' Tessa panted as she ducked Hayden's next strike.

I'd forgotten all about Luke.

Until I felt a knife at my throat.

Memory crashed into reality. Blood. Fire. Sarah. It was happening again. Perhaps the real Luke still had a snippet of control left, because I felt the blade bite into my skin and then pause. I didn't waste his hesitation. It was more a reflex than anything else. How could it not be, after all the times Bane had drilled me over the last couple of weeks? He'd told me over and over again that if Jake got to me, he wasn't likely to hold still and demand I hand over my wallet. He would kill me. I reached my right arm back, poking my fingers toward where I guessed Luke's eyes would be, grabbed the wrist holding the knife and yanked it down against my chest. Then I bit down on his wrist really, really hard—a tactic Bane had used even before he knew he was a Guardian. As Luke wrenched his arm free, I felt the edge of the blade slice across my ribs. Not deep, but it stung like crazy. I jumped away, becoming unbalanced by Annie's bag that I'd forgotten I was carrying, and promptly tripped over a rabbit. Was there not one single ninja warrior gene available when I was given this human body? Not even one?

I tested the first cut he'd made along my throat. That one was deeper than I thought. Half a second more and Luke's knife would have ended me. It still might. I cowered, expecting a knife in my back at any moment, but when I peeked up from under my elbow I saw Dallmin and Annie launch themselves at Luke, tangling up his legs and arms to unbalance him. Annie cried out as the blade caught her near her hip. That did it for Dallmin. He shoved Luke away from her and then performed a series of manoeuvres I could barely follow. They involved a spin, a foot hooking around an ankle, blowing in Luke's eyes, and a poke to his armpit—all happening while his other hand nimbly snatched the knife away. He spun it once around his thumb before flicking it across the boundary to join Kate's weapon. I hoped Nayn wasn't being tempted to come back, not with all these knives being flung down the passageway.

The punch Luke threw in retaliation sent Dallmin sprawling across the flowstone.

A snarl erupted from behind me and I twisted to see Bane holding the point of the sacred sword to Lachlan's throat while his other arm gripped Hayley in a headlock. Neither of them were holding their weapons. That wasn't where the snarl had come from, though.

Bane shouted a pointless warning as Rabisu's spirit form used his sufficiently real hands to shove me straight at Luke like a living battering ram. The demon grabbed hold of the bag around my neck and whacked it straight into Luke's jaw, nearly choking me with the strap in the process. Luke fell in a heap and didn't move. The demon turned to me with an oily smile.

'You are mine now, Shamar.'

'Really?' I rasped. 'You're claiming killing rights now? Then why the hokey did you even call them here?' I complained, unslinging the cloth bag before Rabisu could garrotte me with it again.

The demon didn't answer. Instead, he flew at me so fast I had no time to flinch. Pain smashed and all the air was forced from my lungs with the jarring impact. Slamming into me like a road train, Rabisu tried to force his way into my body using sheer strength, almost bouncing me straight out of it at the same time.

A few things clicked into place in my mind.

This had been the demon's plan all along: tempting me to leave my body and weaken my already tenuous link to it. Until Rabisu had shown me it was possible, I never would have been able to do such a thing. He didn't simply want to possess me. He wanted to steal my Ferrari.

Jagged pain made it impossible to think more about it as my body reflexively snapped away from the intruding violation. After so many out-of-body episodes, I struggled to hold on to the sanctity of my own flesh. Velcro ripped, too easily, and agony sliced through my skull as we flew through the air. Wanting to scream, but having no breath, I savagely wrestled with the malicious presence for the right to my own physical substance, only the creature was everywhere, all at once, as impossible to evict as poison—and I had already lost that battle once before.

As always, my Guardian broke my fall with a grunt as we hit the unyielding rocky floor. The second we touched, the demon shrank away, unable to compete with our freshly forged bond. Piercing agony shattered thought as my mind once again claimed ownership of my abused body. The world spun sickeningly. My body had been yanked around like a Mr Potato Head in the hands of two fighting children, and it felt as if my bones had been pulled out and used to punch holes in my soul and then put back again in all the wrong places. Despite the scruffiness of my previous memories of death, I was absolutely certain I had never felt anything this excruciating before. The pain went way beyond mere injury. I had been violently ripped from my own flesh and it had torn something … fundamental. Possibly in my central nervous system.

That was very bad.

Corrosive pain beyond measure. Beyond my brain's ability to even locate. Pain was all of me, and all of me was shattered into millions of tiny glass shards.

My scream found air … and was cut off with a gasp as miraculous soothing warmth melted the glass, aligning each fragment back into skin and muscle and blood and bones and lungs. Acid-burnt nerve endings unravelled and healed as Bane ran his fingertips down my spine and across my neck wound.

Relief pushed coherent thought aside for a few precious seconds, until it returned with the bitter truth about the nature of what we were facing.

And then I cried.

All I wanted to do was bury my face in Bane's shoulder and keep crying until the world made sense again. He didn't let me. Strong arms lifted me to my feet and he gripped my shoulders and looked me in the eye. He didn't need to say a word. He was Bane, and I was me, and we had always, *always* sparked the fight in each other. Together we turned to see what we would face next.

Chapter 38

In his haste to catch me, Bane had dropped the sword. Hayden, Kate, Lachlan, and Hayley were now fighting each other for it, snarling like beasts. Luke was still out cold and Rabisu was nowhere to be seen. Tessa was tossing yet another hard-won knife past the Event Horizon, hindered by Noah, who was binding up a nasty gash on her other arm with his shirt, begging her to keep still.

Over by the stream, Jake was still unconscious, and I was fairly confident he wasn't faking it given there were rabbits using him as a mini-tramp to try to reach the top of the mesh. Bungee and Wendy were still patrolling the fence line, snapping their teeth at the feral creatures.

While Bane attempted to figure out how to retrieve the sword again, I stumbled to where Dallmin was cradling Annie in his lap, pressing his hand against her bleeding shoulder.

She looked up at me with frightened eyes. 'Was that the demon inside Jake? Where did it go?' Her voice was weak.

'Into hiding, as usual. Rabisu likes to remain veiled until ready to strike,' I replied.

'Veiled?'

I felt for the gem around my neck. Miraculously, it was still there. 'Tell me more about this necklace, Annie. How is it supposed to help?'

She shrugged, wincing as it opened her shoulder wound. 'No idea,' she gasped. 'All I know is that gems and rocks are good for holding memories. Nayn said they're like the planet's own consciousness.'

Mmm, that sounded pretty, but wasn't all that helpful. I stroked my thumb across the ruby, wishing the planet's consciousness could give me a hint about what to do. Unfortunately, before it could bestow its wisdom, my attention was diverted by Bane's painful yell. Hayden had got hold of Sadie and blood now flowed down the side of Bane's leg. Hayden struck again before my Guardian could force his injured limb to move, and another cut opened up along Bane's ribs. Suddenly I was running. I grabbed up Annie's cloth bag and swung it at Hayden. I didn't miss, and whatever was inside was heavy enough to send him flying. No sooner had the sword clattered to the ground than the other three soldiers all made a lunge for it.

A single Word cracked across the shadowed chamber, and with a metallic scrape Sadie slid along the flowstone and then up, straight to Noah's waiting hand. As soon as he grasped it, the blade rejoiced into flame. My jaw dropped as my partner Cherub brandished the sacred weapon, his pale curls and emerald eyes enhancing his majestic expression. Sweat glistened on his bare chest as he brought the blade to a stop with vertical precision. It was a perfect moment, until he caught my eye and quirked his lips as if to say *see, I told you I'd figure it out eventually.*

Denied the option of claiming the sword, and unwilling to risk attacking the charming show-off holding it, Kate, Hayley, and Lachlan started laying into my injured Guardian again. Hayley had reclaimed her knife, and Bane only just managed to roll out of its way as she went straight for his throat.

'I trusted you,' Bane gasped out. 'We're supposed to have each other's backs.'

'Poor judgment will kill you quicker than any weapon,' Lachlan quoted as he kicked Bane in the small of his back, a savage, despicable move that had him grunting and coughing. Tessa's fist struck hard and then Lachlan was reeling backward, holding his bleeding nose.

'Don't you dare quote your captain back to him.' She snatched up the cloth bag and swung it at Hayley's knees, sweeping her legs out from under her. Who would have expected Annie to have brought along the most useful weapon? Whatever was in that bag had so far felled more people than Sadie.

Kate turned her gaze to me, assessing her chances of taking me out while Bane was down. I struck first, ramming my shoulder into hers in the sort of footy tackle that used to have me banned from games for at least a couple of weeks.

It was the worst mistake of all my lives.

I gasped as Bane leaped to his feet to reach me, compelled to defend me despite the knife Hayley was aiming his way. She struck twice in quick succession, first slicing across the front of his shoulder and then stabbing the blade solidly into his chest. He staggered, still straining to get between me and Kate until we all froze, staring at the blood that gushed from between his ribs. Even Kate. Hayley let the knife slip from her fingers, her mouth moving like she wanted to speak and had forgotten how. A flash of confusion lit her eyes for a moment before her expression reverted to its prior disdainful look.

Bane clutched at his ribs and gave me a guilty look. As if he should have done better. As if somehow he was to blame for the blood now seeping between his fingers.

There were plenty of people to blame. He was not one of them.

All the fear and rage I'd had under such tight control exploded from me in a molten phrase of ferocious Words. Below us, the ground shook hard enough to make both Hayley and Bane fall to their hands and knees. Blood dripped from Bane's mouth.

No.

Another bitten Word tripped from my lips, and a stalactite fell with a crash of ancient brittle tears. These people had invaded the sanctity of the cave, possessed by demons that were literally hell-bent on destroying paradise.

It would be so simple. Start a fire. Sweep them away in a flood. Surround them with an airless bubble. There were so many ways. It only took a short phrase for the three remaining soldiers to start gulping for air, eyes bulging.

Bane had trusted them, and they'd betrayed him. They had no *idea* how much it cost us to defend this place. Ignorant humans. All of them. How could Jake have allowed himself to become so weak-willed? And he wasn't the only one, not by a long shot. All these humans were weak. I should remove them all … remove the threat once and for all.

The demons couldn't steal host bodies if there were none left to steal.

They were all dead anyway. I could make it quick. Poison the air. Shift the tectonic plates. Alter the planet's magnetic fields, or its gravity. Move it a smidge closer to the sun, or a bit farther away. It would be easy. Words rolled from the air in my lungs, unfolding and melting on my tongue like rice paper. So simple. Power blossomed and with it came the knowledge I needed. The Earth and the stars were mine to command. Just a tiny change …

The ground trembled, and I held the lit match to the paper of the planet. The world would burn because the atmosphere contained a lot of flammable gases, and I held the spark on the tip of my tongue.

With my eyes glazed over, I didn't notice Noah approach until I was hit with the familiar feel of him slapping me across the back of my head. Hard enough that I stumbled and tripped over the hem of my torn wedding dress.

The stinging clarity of the slap cracked my trapped senses to flinching horror at what I was doing, but the Words were already forming and felt as unstoppable as the blood spreading down Bane's chest. A dominant part of me wanted to retreat into that place where shame ruled my mind and pain became so intrinsic it almost didn't hurt anymore. I had already been caught in that trap once, and it hadn't helped anyone, so instead I stayed on my hands and knees, scrambling for control over my senses and my mind. The Words were so alive and vibrant, deliciously ready to release … Could I limit the destruction to just the invaders in the cave?

'Lainie, no. Stop,' Noah begged. 'Let them go.'

I can't. Only I couldn't tell him that because if I opened my mouth to speak, atoms would split, shatter, smash, scorch.

Noah kneeled in front of me and took my face in his hands. Eyes of burning copper snagged my attention away from the taste of the stars. 'What you're doing now, this isn't us,' he entreated. 'It isn't for the likes of us, Lainie. We've been given all this power without the wisdom to go with it. We can't even be trusted to run a sausage sizzle at the Sunday market, remember?'

With his touch, I remembered, because he remembered. We'd been banned after the Great Tomato Sauce War. I never did get the stains out of my socks. A Word splattered from my tongue, and the Earth's magnetic field resonated in my chest like harp strings ready to be caressed. What a tune I could play …

'The stall next to ours was selling coffee and scones, and Dr Bala was running it. He told me I was overdue to get my teeth checked and you forced me to apologise to him for being such a difficult patient, do you remember?'

A part of me knew he was trying to charm me away from what I was doing. The Words were so ready. Those people deserved …

'While I had him distracted, you snuck over and put a whole lot of our chopped onions into the coffee urn. He's never sent me any reminders since.'

He was offering me a way out, and I wanted to clutch it like a lifeline. I wanted to stop. I didn't want to stop. What *did* I want? Was it right to do what I wanted? Or was I supposed to play by the rules? He kept babbling on. Something about spitting his filling out when he'd bitten into his first piece of Living Fruit and dental appointments being a waste of time anyway.

Noah's arguments became increasingly desperate and they bounced around my head like renegade echoes, easy to ignore as I focused my attention on the large and the small, the mega and the micro. A sucked in breath, and I could taste each element in the air. Nitrogen. Colourless, odourless, tasteless to human senses—like iocane powder—and yet to me it tasted like a volcano. Oxygen. Millions of plants burping and spitting it out. Each atom was a tiny unstoppable force as well as being part of the crushing entirety of the atmosphere. My mind drank in the feel of the planet-wide airbag that sizzled with electromagnetic storms, and the tiny electromagnetic pulses that stimulated the movements of the beetle crawling toward me. Small forces. Massive biological consequences. Teeny-tiny beetle. Diabolical flow-on effects. Pretty beetle.

A Christmas beetle, waddling around a cave in June, because Eden bugs didn't need the same seasonal restrictions to survive …

The insect lifted one tiny leg and then paused, as if enjoying the sight of its own iridescent reflection in the puddle it was passing. Eden beetles. The best the Earth has to offer …

When it all becomes too much to handle, I ground myself with the things of the Earth. The small things. The scent of the dirt, the feel of the rocks, the dance of the insects. Harry had smiled and placed the beetle on my shoulder. Such a long time ago. No time at all. *We belong to the Earth. We were sent here in human form for a reason. If you don't know what to do, then just be human.*

Beltana had said that Shamar power was available for human help, not just Eden help. *We belong to the Earth.* Sent to protect all humans. Not just Edenites. No wonder we weren't allowed to kill.

Words dissolved and left a tingly sting. Unspoken. Breathless. Gasping.

Gasping, like Bane's friends were gasping. I could hear them sucking in deep breaths as I gave them back their air. Still alive.

Still a threat.

And Bane was still dying.

Chapter 39

If only Zyndel had been close by to hit Beltana's son, Tahuma, across the back of the head like Noah had done for me. One hundred and eighty thousand Assyrian soldiers killed in response to the death of his beloved Guardian. I now realised he'd done well to restrict it to only that many. My face stayed buried in Noah's shoulder so I didn't have to look at anyone. My best friend was still kneeling with me. Always there for me. On the ground next to us, Sadie's white blade glowed as if showing off how pure and innocent she was. Yet Sadie had killed Noah's mum. I'd played my part in that too. Was true innocence even real?

I could feel Rabisu studying me, scrutinising my emotions and savouring my guilt. *Empathising* with it. Bile rose in my throat.

'Lachlan, don't even think about it,' Tessa growled. I glanced up to see her standing over the three gasping soldiers with the cloth bag clutched in her fist, ready to clobber anyone who moved. They looked terrified, yet their eyes still flashed with hate and desperation. Luke and Hayden remained unmoving where they'd fallen.

Those rotten demons. How was I supposed to destroy them without harming Bane's friends? I felt again for the winged ruby and pulled the chain over my head. If it was an amulet, perhaps it would protect the wearer from possession. Of course, there were a few problems with that. Firstly, the soldiers were already possessed. Secondly, they couldn't all wear it at once. Thirdly, the amulet hadn't given me the slightest bit of assistance when Rabisu had tried to hijack my Ferrari.

Noah helped me up. He gave my hand a final squeeze before picking up Sadie and moving to stand next to Tessa. Kate hissed as the tip of the blade stopped in front of her face.

'Tess, can you do anything for Bane?' Noah asked. 'I promise I've got this.'

She looked torn for a moment, and then nodded, jaw clenched. She slid to Bane's side and shook the cloth bag empty so she could ball it up to press against his ribs. I looked at what had fallen out. It was a flattish rock, a bit bigger than my hand. No wonder it had knocked people out. Bane picked it up, his hand shaking. He examined it and then showed it to Tessa, mumbling something I couldn't catch. Then he pointed to me.

Tessa glanced from the rock to me and nodded. No. Not me. She was looking at the ruby I was holding. She flipped the rock over and peered at something on the other side.

'Dallmin,' she called out. 'Can you read these markings? They look like the ones on that stone tablet your daughter wrote.' She tossed the rock over to where Dallmin was sitting with his back against a stalagmite, cradling Annie's head in his lap.

He caught it easily and narrowed his eyes to read in the dim light. 'Give it your best ...' He hesitated as Annie coughed and tried to sit up.

'Keep going,' my mother encouraged in a too-weak voice.

'Your best ... something ... knee.'

Annie's face fell.

Dallmin looked heartbroken that he couldn't help. 'I'm sorry, Annie. I have no context for the missing word. If I sound it out, it reads *tahazu*.'

'War!' Noah called over his shoulder. 'Beltana told us it means war.'

'War knee, then,' Dallmin advised. 'There was no such thing as war when I spoke this language.'

Everyone else seemed as shocked as I was.

'You're making that up,' Tessa insisted.

'Well, I was more innocent back then ...'

That isn't what she means, Dallmin, I signed. 'Tess, he can't be making it up. He doesn't even know what cricket is,' I reminded her.

My mother's eyes turned to me. She looked so sad, and I knew why. One of us had to tell him. We needed his help.

'The ruby can hold memories,' Annie reminded me. 'What are memories, if not the echoes of a person's soul?'

And if a soul was lost, afraid to move across when the body died ...

Edenites were so well practised at holding their spirits back until someone called them by name, assisting them to return to their healed bodies. Only, when their bodies were drowned and not healed, these ones would have had nowhere to go.

The ruby shone, reflecting Sadie's flames. It looked like blood was pulsing through its heart. I spoke a brittle Word, and the bronze wings broke off and tumbled to the floor, leaving the flawed heart-shaped ruby sitting naked in my palm.

'Give it to me, Lainie. I think I need to do this,' Annie said.

I passed her the gem. 'Beltana told me we have the authority to do what it takes to protect humans on both sides of the boundary. To stop a war.'

'You do,' she agreed, taking Dallmin's hand and clasping it over the gem with her own. 'Dallmin, you need to call them home, now. All of them. Close your eyes and remember their names.'

Dallmin shook his head in denial of what he now knew to be true.

'Please, Dallmin. They're so lost,' I begged. 'I can see their emotional memories. They remember you, and at the same time they're afraid to remember you. All they ever wanted was to go home. They've just seen you relive your most shameful memories at Sadie's touch. You were in such agony, and you've only been here for a few months. No wonder they're terrified. The things they've done …'

'They can never return to Eden,' he gasped. 'Never.'

'No. They can't,' Annie agreed, pressing her hand down over his, and that was the moment it really dawned on me. Annie could never return to Eden either. Not after plunging a sword through Dallmin's chest. She'd deliberately killed another human, albeit briefly. She may have retained her innate ability to read and assimilate other people's emotions, but her authority, her access to that sacred power was gone. She was no longer Shamar. She was lost to us.

'They can't go home,' Annie confirmed. 'But they can still be healed.'

Chapter 40

I laid a hand on Dallmin's shoulder, whispering to him in a language even he hadn't learned. That didn't matter. It was a language that spoke straight to the heart, not the head. As I shared with him the snippets of memories I was getting from the demons, he reflected them back to me as perfect re-enactments of the original events. His flawless recall reconstructed them in precise detail. That time when Edni had filled his wooden flute with tiny feathers. The first time Savina had danced with him. The underground thermal pool Ghinum and Dallmin had found together.

There were other memories too. Ones I refused to pass on to him. Of a stillborn child, and the loss of a friend when a home had caught fire, and countless fights and angry retaliations. I tried to tell myself they were no worse than what I used to watch on telly, only these memories were real. These children of Eden had become tyrants. Twisted by fear. Powerful in their rage.

It was those shameful memories that I passed to Annie to deal with.

Her whole body shook as she drew in all the fear, all the pain, all the lust, and the anger and despair. It was too much. Far too much to keep hold of for long.

All around us was silence. The three soldiers were watching us with wide eyes. Even the rabbits had gone still and were staring. Which was seriously creepy.

'Noah, tell them we have a place where they can rest. They're so tired,' I said. 'They need to trust us.'

Kate, Hayley, and Lachlan looked wary and didn't move. The rabbits looked ready to bolt.

Noah licked his lips and cleared his throat. 'Okay, um, she's right. We only want what's best for you all,' he said to Bane's friends. He couldn't seem to bring himself to talk to the rabbits. 'You know you can't keep doing this forever. If I were you I'd do whatever she says.'

Lachlan laughed at him. Kate actually growled, and the look I got from Noah was classic *I told you so.* With his head turned toward me, he didn't see Hayley move. She lunged for her knife and just grabbed hold of it as Tessa slammed into her, seemingly from nowhere. The two women grunted as they wrestled for control of the weapon, until Hayley pinned the Guardian long enough to draw back the knife, ready to strike at Tessa's throat. It was in that frozen moment that Dallmin's voice rang out, amplified by the superb acoustics.

'Savina!'

The cherished name of an unforgotten friend. The knife slipped from Hayley's grasp and clattered onto the floor.

'Savina, my friend,' Dallmin called out again, infusing the name with all the happy memories that belonged with it. Noah echoed the name like a prayer, enticing the exile to listen, to remember.

'Dallmin?' Hayley burst into tears, and then passed out. An unnatural breeze brushed past my face as the spirit was drawn to the jewel, drawn to the place where its sweetest memories were held, and none of the bad ones. Dallmin looked down at the ruby in his palm and then smiled up at me as I spoke a sacred Word to bind Savina in place. Then he called out another name. And another. One by one the demons were reined in by his appeal. Crushed by fear and shame, they'd resisted the instinct to move across when they died, instead hoping in vain for a friend to call them back to their bodies. It had been a long wait, but Dallmin had never forgotten them.

My heart was still racing with the urge to fight and defend, twitching with the need to hurry so we could deal with Bane's and Annie's injuries. Luckily Dallmin was still blessed with the patience of the Garden's peace as he called each spirit by name and reminded them of who they were. He even sang snippets of songs to a few of them. Others needed a little more convincing, so he made references to things they'd seen and done together.

I counted them off impatiently. Thirty-two lost souls gave themselves over to the ruby created by a Sentinel of Eden. Annie drew on their emotions and reassigned them to the crystalline matrix, while I did the same with their memories. Dallmin and Noah used compassion and charm to get them to follow. The ruby held onto them with unyielding strength.

Lastly, Dallmin called Rabisu's name. Nothing happened. He had no memories of the demon to lure him with—at least, no happy ones. Again he called, but the name echoed around the chamber, elusive as a shadow. He shook his head. 'I'm sorry, Lainie. It is not a name I know. I can't help.'

'Perhaps Rabisu was never one of the exiles,' Noah suggested. 'Perhaps he was something else.'

'So where is he?' Tessa asked.

I let out a tense breath. 'Who knows? That horrid demon floral stench is gone now though, so perhaps that means he decided to get out of here while he still could.'

And where would I go?

Anywhere but here, I told the whisper that had been hiding in the corner of my mind. *Or you'll share the same fate.*

Is this how you repay me for revealing the truth about my friends?

I already knew the truth. Now be quiet or our deal is off.

Thirty-two souls had passed into the gem's keeping. And one hadn't. I glanced around at all the unconscious people left over. Luke, Hayden, Kate, Lachlan, Hayley, and Jake lay like clothes left on the floordrobe. And all the rabbits had fainted. Noah stood holding Sadie with slightly bent elbows, as if ready to strike at any stragglers. And as if he'd been fighting with swords all his life.

'Dallmin, how many of your friends left Eden with Nin?' I asked, feeling the staleness of the ordinary words.

'Forty-six. Which means many of them escaped this fate.' He let out a shaky breath. 'And you showed me no memories of Nin. She did not become one of these fallen spirits.'

The relief I felt was almost enough to make my legs buckle. His faith in her was absolute, and I wasn't inclined to argue. Nin's diary had mentioned they were being attacked by the veiled ones who were once their friends. So not all the exiles had given up on doing the right thing. She'd also said some had chosen to die rather than cause further harm. My heart went out to those poor souls who couldn't see any other way out of their despair. At least, perhaps, they'd found peace.

Peace and resolution. A reckoning, for better or worse. Not a single soul could escape it in the end. *Not even yours. Not even mine,* I whispered.

I know, Rabisu whispered back.

I swallowed tears as I looked Dallmin in the eye. 'I'm sorry, friend. You know I need to do this.'

'I understand,' he said. 'They made their choices. They can't escape the consequences forever.' Closing his eyes briefly, he gave the ruby a farewell kiss before dropping it into my palm. I could feel the demons writhing inside, trying to escape. Now that Annie had stopped drawing away their negative emotions, their fear was taking over again. Problem was, the ruby was Annie's. A part of her. If it broke, would she break too? I looked at her face, at the trauma of all the emotions she was still holding, and realised that by doing so she'd taken on the greatest sacrifice of the night. So much blood was pooled around her, soaking Dallmin's shirt.

There was no more time. 'Noah,' I called. 'Think fast!'

I rubbed the gem against my knee, as if polishing one side of it to make it swing. Then I took as good a run-up as the uneven floor would allow and bowled the ruby as accurately as I could, giving it my best Warnie, as instructed by the ancient stone relic. 'Hit it for six!'

In the entire history of Cherub-kind, I was certain only Noah could have had the right reflexive response. He swung the holy paradigm of virtue like an oversized cricket bat. On Sadie's blade was a line of glyphs, tingling, sizzling like molten glass on snow as the ruby and blade kissed. As the jewel exploded into glittering dust, the lost spirits were unveiled, reconciled, and finally released into the next world.

⌒

'Annie,' I whispered into the leftover silence. She didn't react. Her eyes were glazed, and she rocked back and forth like she needed the rhythm to keep breathing. 'Annie, you can let go now. They're gone.' Still nothing. I squeezed her hand and remembered the first time I'd seen her in Eden, underwater, with laughter in her eyes and bubbles streaming from her nose. She'd looked so innocent then. 'Mum. It's done.'

She looked up at me with eyes full of stolen pain.

'Let it go,' I said again. 'You don't need to hold it in anymore.'

'It doesn't work that way,' she mumbled. 'But it's okay. All will be well.' She smiled, and her smile was full of want, for those of us able to see.

Tessa was the first to regroup, readjusting the cloth bag to press even harder against Bane's chest wound. It was completely blood-soaked. He looked like he was struggling to stay awake. Tessa shook his good shoulder and reminded him to try.

'Rabisu?' he mumbled, glazed eyes searching for the secrets in mine.

'Gone,' I lied, knowing he could tell. Perhaps it would make him fight harder to stay awake.

Tessa threw a glance my way. 'Don't leave it too long to get Annie back home,' she advised. 'And it looks like you're still bleeding too, so the sooner you take a bite of that Fruit, the easier things will be for Bane. Noah and I have things covered here. I assume Dallmin can go home now,' she surmised. 'Is that what Sadie really does? But that scream … I'm not sure anything is worth that.'

Noah crouched next to her, explaining softly so I wouldn't have to. 'Annie doesn't want to be healed. She's had enough. And even if she did, that isn't an option anymore.'

'Surely now that Dallmin can go back with her …' Tessa's voice dwindled away as Noah shook his head, and she realised what none of us wanted to articulate.

'She can't enter the Garden? Because she killed someone? That isn't fair. He was only dead for a few moments. Can't we do the same to her, or something? There has to be a way.'

Not for the likes of us. Not for what Annie did, regardless of her reasons. Unwilling to watch Tessa cry, I turned my face to the affectionate smile that lingered on my mother's face. She was barely breathing now.

'Lainie,' Dallmin rasped. 'May I have that?' He pointed to the little shell with the blue stripe that clung by a loose thread from the centre of my bodice. I plucked it off and tossed it to him.

He caught it with one hand. Then he grabbed and kissed Annie's fingertips, and wrapped them around the little ornament. 'I want to take you home and live with you there until the stars stop shining, but I can't, can I?'

Light from his newly untainted soul reflected from his loving eyes and shone like a tiny spark in each fallen teardrop.

'I would have shown you everything, Annie. Taken you everywhere. There is so much more we would have done. New places, new games, new dances, and more friends to meet. I would have shared eternity with you. From the depths of the glittering ocean to the peaks of the highest silver mountains, from the playful River to the pearly moon, I would have loved you forever.'

Softly then, his farewell kiss touched her lips, full of the promise of what might have been.

Annie smiled. 'And I would have loved you back, and we would have sung the stars to sleep,' she whispered. 'But I made my choice, and I made it freely.' Her rapt gaze was intense as she made her wishes known as clearly as she could, while blood poured unchecked from under her collarbone. 'My feet have found the sand. Finally. I do not ... *want* ... to live forever, and my grief and shame never belonged in the Garden.'

'And I don't want to live there without you!' he begged, undone.

'Your choices are your own again,' she affirmed. 'All will be well.'

He smoothed a tear from her cheek, as one of his own splashed down to replace it.

'You are the most beautiful liar,' he whispered, kissing her forehead as her shuddering body went still and darkness fell like a shroud.

Chapter 41

For a few long seconds, Sadie's flames dimmed and shadows stretched as if trying to snatch us away to a place where death was the only thing that mattered. I saw Noah wipe his eyes and set his jaw. He drew back and threw Sadie right at the boundary, where she stopped mid-air, her remaining momentum causing her to spin instead. Her fire blazed again, a beacon of hope. A call to ultimate healing. A warning of what it would cost to pass her challenge and level up.

It sings to you, Rabisu whispered. *It is yours to command. Will you stand by our deal even in your grief?*

Of course, I replied.

Noah pushed his shoulders back. 'So that's it, then. We should be safe now.' He spoke with such confidence, but when his eyes flicked my way, I knew that he knew. I had made a deal with a devil. Rabisu was still a threat and Noah could feel it. He was playing along, though. We really did make a great team when things called for sneakiness.

'Safe,' I agreed, and started humming under my breath. There wasn't much time left. Bane was gasping against a collapsed lung and his eyes, so captivating, were fading from quicksilver to diminished grey. Would I ever see that elusive laughter in them again? Despite the pressure Tessa was putting on it, blood still oozed from the deep wound in his chest. There was so much blood soaking his legs I could no longer tell which laceration it came from. Those army knives were far too long. His injuries were much more severe than Annie's had been, and she'd slipped away so easily. 'Hold on, Bane. I need you to hold on,' I entreated.

He gave a single nod, so I turned from him and faced the boundary to finish my remaining tasks while I still could. I wished there was a way to avoid a repeat of this tragedy. How could I lock a whole race of people away safely without affecting their free will? I had to restrict their access to the rest of the world without totally imprisoning them. They needed to be left with a way out of Eden if they really wanted it; there was something foundational in that which I didn't question.

I had unlimited power to play with, and I wanted to do it right. Single-handedly I could protect an entire world of people so long as I was clever enough. A stray thought made me glance over at the ancient discarded rock with its ridiculous message, and I could have kicked myself when I realised how obvious the answer was. Then I gathered my focus and began to whisper stirring Words, shaped to tune the boundary into exactly what I wanted.

It was easy. Insanely easy. I had to be careful.

'Tessa, do you remember anything from that biology assignment we did on Australian megafauna?' I asked.

She blinked at me.

'When did they die out? Tell me as much as you can remember.'

'The data keeps changing,' she said, sounding impatient at my seemingly pointless question. 'They reckon extinctions peaked about forty-two thousand years ago. All I remember is that First Nations people were either always here, or arrived here from the north around sixty-five thousand years ago. Whichever you believe, they co-existed with the megafauna for at least twenty thousand years, which makes it unlikely that humans were to blame for the extinctions … that time.' She glowered at the rabbits, at the ecological disaster they represented, for which human ignorance was totally to blame. Noah was in for a serious lecture when Tessa realised he could have just as easily relocated every feral rabbit in Australia to the middle of Sydney Harbour if he'd thought of it in time. Instead, he'd built a fence they would now have to take down.

'Those giant emus sound scary,' Noah said quickly to distract her, possibly having just realised the same thing.

'Exactly,' I said. 'Which is why I want to make sure I keep it to a time *after* they died out.' More than anything, I wished Tim could see what I was doing; he would have loved it. Bane watched me with compassionate awareness as Tessa helped him to sit up against a boulder so he could breathe more easily. Like a comforting embrace I could feel his glassy gaze trying to catch hold of me, encouraging me to finish things, and be brilliant, and so I was.

Shimmery haze turned the Event Horizon into a numinous pink wall for a few seconds before it began to fade. Interesting. I hadn't expected it to be pink.

Noah made a choked gasping sort of noise as he felt what I was doing.

'When?' he asked, awestruck.

'I'm hoping forty thousand years should be survivable,' I replied. 'I'm sure the local farmers will help them if they need it. It's what farmers do.'

'For everyone?' he asked with a worried frown.

'Except Cherubim.'

'Nice,' he approved.

Tessa looked from me to him with narrowed eyes. 'What's she done, Noah?'

Bane tried to laugh, coughing up more blood as he slumped crookedly. 'Time-lock?' he guessed. 'Tim wouldn't shut up about … his ideas.'

'He wore me down and I got curious. Had to try.'

Tessa put her hands on her hips, ready to argue. 'Are you saying you made some sort of time portal … thingy?'

'Only for Edenites wanting to leave,' I explained. 'They can freely move into the Late Pleistocene epoch. The continent was less arid then, but it still wouldn't have compared with the luxury of the Garden, so they probably won't want to hang around for long. So long as nothing goes wrong they'll be able to cross back and the right amount of time will have passed in Eden. They'll never know they time-travelled.'

'And if something goes wrong?'

'There are no guarantees. All I can do is ensure there are no demons around to make things worse. If somehow they do become corrupted, Sadie will still be there to guard the boundary.'

Dallmin smiled up at me in awed gratitude, while Tessa pressed her lips together, dubious about me messing with time.

I turned to my Cherub partner. 'Noah, we can't block it off anymore. No more rockfalls, and certainly nothing more permanent.'

The best the Earth has to offer.

Noah looked intrigued. 'You know something,' he prompted.

'No, I *realised* something. Eden doesn't really need us. God could have simply sealed it off completely when Adam and Eve were exiled. Instead, Cherubim were sent to become Shamar to guard its entrance. We don't belong to Eden, Noah, we belong to the Earth.'

Everyone was looking at me expectantly so I tried to put into mundane words the profound truth I'd gained from, well, from the shiny beetle.

'Uncle once told me Eden was made up of the best that the Earth had to offer, which seems pretty obvious. What he didn't mention was that it's not done yet. I totally had the wrong perspective about time.'

Dallmin blinked at me with an unspoken *well, duh*.

'The human race has been gestating for millions of years and this window of time that we're in now, these past hundred thousand years, it's like humanity has just taken its first real breath after being born. All healthy babies cry at that point. Still learning how to *live*. Still learning how to dream. The best of humanity is still to come, and our job is to persevere until the human race is redeemed.'

Love always protects, always trusts, always hopes, always perseveres.

That helped Tessa's expression. A bit.

Having sensed the change in the Event Horizon, two more Cherubim boldly entered the cavern. At least one of them was hungry, and the other was permanently looking for food whether he was hungry or not. Nayn stumbled to a halt in front of Noah's fence. He raised his eyebrows as he looked from one end of it to the other, then raised them further as he noticed the unconscious bodies and the pile of rabbits. Then he looked at me.

That felt weird. What did you do, child? Everything went shifty, and the baby is getting restless again. He wants his mother. Nayn handed the crying infant over the fence to a relieved and teary Tessa and then froze, staring at Annie's broken body.

'Don't we all,' I choked.

In recognition of what Nayn was, my rebellious tenant snarled with such sudden savagery it took all my willpower to keep my face passive. *How many more of you are there? You breed more than the rabbits.*

If only that were true. I would have loved having a sister. *Your end of the deal was to remain hidden and let me do what I have to do without interfering,* I reminded Rabisu. Luckily the others were distracted from noticing my inward struggle by Dallmin, who grabbed at Nayn's hand, his eyes pleading.

Will you take her body back home, my friend? 'Please?' he begged in English, turning to Noah. 'The people there will want to sing her across, even if it is a little late.'

Nayn looked uncomfortable. Noah opened his mouth to speak, and then closed it again, looking to me to explain.

'I'm sorry, Dallmin. Even now, we can't take her back to Eden. She gave up her ticket for you.'

Noah tilted his head with a gleam in his eyes. 'That's right. You can still go and sing for her yourself. You're clean again. That was the whole point of what she and Bane did, remember?' His smile danced for the one good outcome from the unrelenting series of tragic events. 'You can go home.'

Undone by hope and grief, the ancient child of Eden stood up shakily, climbed over the mesh fence, and walked toward Sadie.

She stayed tranquil, her flames flickering softly.

He stopped, very close, and his unsullied brown eyes looked lovingly into the fading pink glow of the Event Horizon for a long quiet moment. No one moved. Untainted tears fell like rain, proving he still understood what it meant to experience loss, and grief, and pain, as he stood poised at the threshold between worlds—clean, yet still partially broken. I hoped the Fruit would turn the last few weeks into a fading nightmare. A mere smudge in his long, long life full of sweet memories.

'Eden,' he breathed in reverence. 'Starlight and glistening dew. Blessed horizons of gold …' Awed delight reflected from his face. 'My true home, where wild flights of birds spiral endlessly through glistening raindrops. Where loving embraces are freely gifted from companions who have shared their whole character with me without restraint for thousands of years.' Slender fingers reached forward to caress the boundary as if he could feel its welcoming invitation, then paused, balanced on a keenly suspended moment.

He looked at me, and deep understanding dawned in his eyes. 'This world is not symmetrical, Lainie. A part of Eden is here too, and it throws everything off balance.'

I remembered the conversation we'd had in the park.

'I could never balance out the terrible things I did to you all, and yet you still forgave me,' he explained with a wry smile. 'You acted kindly toward me, always, and gave me food and clothing and music, and I never had the chance to balance any of it.' He sighed, and new wisdom blossomed with the sound. 'You are wrong, Noah,' he continued, still staring toward his beloved home. 'The whole point of what Annie and Bane did was to give me a free choice. A thoroughly undeserved gift.'

His replenished soul unfurled, straining toward the path ahead in eager longing. 'I can choose to overcome the darkness. I can choose to become the man I want to be …' Poised on a hair's breadth, he lingered. 'But across the endless reaches of eternity I can't ever return to the man I *used* to be.'

My breath caught in my throat at his words and I choked back a despairing cry.

He turned to face us, glorious determination drowning the harsh sorrow that had haunted him for so long. 'I choose to remain here.'

His fateful words etched the air with ineffable mourning, and inside my chest something broke.

'I can help ease the burdens of souls lost to shame—I can remind them that they still have the power to choose. I can uphold hope. How could I know the pain that is here and yet choose to live as I did before?'

Stunned silence filled the chamber. There were a thousand things I wanted to say to him, to make him change his mind, but that was not the Eden way.

'Gold star for me,' he whispered as he courageously and shamelessly walked out of the cavern to embrace his new chosen home.

As I watched him go, I choked out a pallid Word and sent my mother's body to a coffin that had been buried decades earlier in the Nalong Cemetery, under a gravestone with her name on it. Right next to my father's.

Chapter 42

Dallmin's decision sent Rabisu into shocked silence. Not even a whisper of that voice echoed in my head. I took the opportunity to think about what else needed to be done as I watched Nayn pick up the discarded rock Dallmin had translated.

So is this done with now? he signed. *I wondered why we had to keep it for so long, and why it had to remain on this side of the Skin. Did it help you?*

I am so confused, Nayn.

You're confused? You're the one who did the whole time-shifty thing. Don't blame me if you've created an impossibility.

My head hurt. *Are you suggesting someone will carve this thing sometime in the future and send it back through the time-lock I just made?*

It has been a sacred relic in my family for a very long time. We were never even supposed to let anyone else see it.

Oh. Pragmatically, I figured it would be best for it to not exist twice in the same time period, so I held out my hand for it, rather impatiently. I didn't have time for this. Bane was my only priority now. Nayn seemed only slightly regretful as he laid it in my palm. My skin tingled as I ran my fingertip over the diagram, and then a Word was on my tongue, and then it wasn't, and the rock was no longer in my hand either. It was gone.

Tessa cleared her throat. 'Noah, if anyone happens across this cave, what will they think of this ridiculous fence?' she asked.

'Oh. Righto,' he said. A second later it dissolved, along with the echo of his spoken command.

Tessa was really getting the hang of this.

I divvied up the rest. 'Noah, you can deliver Jake to the holding cell at the police station. Put enough alcohol in his system so he won't be surprised that he can't remember Mick arresting him. Don't forget to text Mick to let him know.'

'What … about my friends?' Bane rasped. 'I don't think I can ever trust them again. Not like … like I used to.' His breath was so laboured.

I tripped out a phrase and they disappeared.

'They're going to wake up in their beds and not remember a thing about the crazy dreams they had tonight. Although right now they're dreaming about a place that has to be believed to be seen. I suppose I'll have to give them back their knives so they don't ask questions. Hopefully, they'll be busy enough sorting out the aftermath of Jake's bomb that they won't notice any details I've missed. I've repaired a couple of tears in their clothes. And they're all in pyjamas except for Luke. He doesn't seem to have any.'

'Woah, Lainie, relax. I'll keep an eye on them,' Noah assured me.

My agitation was not entirely my own. The whisper filled my mind with frenetic razor-sharp thoughts. *Do something.*

No.

The fury I felt from the demon took my breath away. It was enough to trigger a memory of a scene, ancient and yet as clear as if I was there. Watching, bodiless and unable to do a thing to help the families being rounded up by the invading army.

You never act! You could have done something then, and you could do something now. You call us demons, yet your kind stood by and let my children be tortured. Do something, Shamar!

My mind reeled at the implication. The children of Eden at Telassar were tortured. And the Shamar stood by and did nothing? They may not have had a choice, if the army was hunting for Eden. No wonder Rabisu hated us so much.

Go after him.

No. It isn't my—

'I don't suppose Nathaniel and I can hitch a lift back with Bane?' Tessa asked, interrupting the internal argument and thankfully dispelling the vision of the ancient tragedy. She'd wrapped her son in Noah's dinner jacket and had him cradled against her shoulder. She stood next to Bane, legs braced like she was ready to be beamed up to the *Enterprise*. 'I don't mind if we end up at the hospital with him.'

I tried, but nothing happened. Beside me, Noah had his eyes screwed shut, looking like he wanted to stomp his foot. Neither of us could justify how transporting the Guardians would make any difference to keeping Eden secret. If anything, having them appear out of nowhere at the hospital in the state they were in would raise even more questions. We couldn't use our authority to protect ourselves or them.

Tessa nodded, taking it in her stride. The resilience she'd grown into since high school suited her. 'I'd better get moving then. I'll call Mick as soon as I get reception. He'll have kept an ambulance close by.' She made a valiant effort to sound confident as she turned to me. 'Bane will be fine. Guardian healing, remember? He'll be fine.'

He won't, came the whisper. *Deal's off unless you call him back. Make him come back, Shamar.*

It isn't my place to make him do anything. And you have no authority over me.

Don't I?

'Be quick,' I told Tessa, who was watching me suspiciously. She nodded, picked up the lantern and strode from the cavern with her son tucked securely against her chest. Noah followed her partway down the tunnel, full of suggestions as to what to say to everyone when she got back to the farm.

Nayn tilted his head to me as he passed back into the passageway to the Garden in silent acknowledgment of my loss. Moments later he was gone too, and then there was only Bane left.

I was too afraid to walk the few steps it would take to go to him.

This was always going to be the way it ended.

Rabisu was right. Why even bother to fight it?

Still slumped awkwardly against the boulder, Bane threw me an apologetic smile.

'You were amazing, as usual,' he slurred. 'Trust you to come up with such … a crazy solution for protecting the Edenites. I should have known you'd … find a way. You always do.'

There was even less time than I'd anticipated. His eyes were glazed and there was blood dripping from his chin. It had dribbled down from the corner of his perfect mouth. His breath was shallow and wet and I knew his airways were filling up quickly. It was a miracle he could talk at all.

I entwined my fingers in his. For once I had no words. This wasn't supposed to have happened and I didn't know what to do, so I just kneeled there, shaking.

'Oh, so *now* you're scared? You are … human then, after all,' he teased. 'Come on, it's not so bad. In fact, I was going to ask you … for a dance. I've been waiting a … long time for my turn.'

'Stop it, Bane. This isn't funny. You're dying. I've had enough experience to know.'

Untethered by my reaction, he turned his face away from me, but I could still see tears mingle with his blood. 'I'm not ready to leave you yet, Lainie,' he whispered. 'I need more time … just a little more.'

Anguish hung in the air between us for a long, quiet moment.

Hollow regret finally forced me to speak as I tucked myself in against his good shoulder like a child. 'I should have—'

'No! Don't say it,' he croaked. 'You made … all the right choices.'

'If I'd unlocked that power sooner I might have stopped them before this happened,' I said, pointing to the wound in his chest.

'By killing them. They're … innocent, Lainie.'

'But you're hurting so much. And I don't want you to go. I only just found you again …' I clutched at his torn shirt. My need for him was stronger than ever and it was selfish, and greedy. I didn't care.

With quivering fingers, he lifted his good hand to brush a wayward curl from my eyes, his touch lingering on the curve of my jaw. 'Too short a time,' he agreed. 'And so much of it wasted. I'm so sorry. I wish I'd …' His lips twitched in a shyness I hadn't seen for years and he blinked. 'I wish I'd had more time to dance with you,' he said, not fooling either of us as to what he really meant. Was the hunger in his eyes reflected as clearly in my own?

Suddenly I was tired of being hungry. Beltana was a Guardian. Beltana had been given all the time in the world.

There was a precedent. And I was not letting Rabisu break our deal.

'Fine, we *will* dance then. We don't need to worry about Jake anymore. We can get on with the fun stuff now, finally.' I gave him my most flirtatious smile as I sat up and cradled his limp hand. It had turned blue.

He shook his head. 'I would follow … you anywhere. Unfortunately, my legs are … being a little bit disobedient, so I think … rain-check on … dancing.'

Typical, he chose now to reveal his sense of humour.

'Not good enough, Guardian. You promised you'd dance with me whenever I wanted, remember?'

I craned my neck to look at Noah. I had felt him return, and he'd paused near the entrance to the cavern, giving us space. The reassuring light from the now quiescent sword reflected from his teary green eyes. My glare was fierce as I gave him the same look I'd always given him when I was about to do something a bit naughty and wanted him to back me up. Knowing me as well as he did, he gave me a worried frown but nodded anyway. He knew there was no point trying to argue. Then, taking Bane's cold hands, I placed them around my waist and then grabbed his face, forcing him to look me in the eye.

Love never fails.

'On your feet, soldier,' I commanded. 'I'm not letting you go anywhere without dancing with me first.'

Blood flavoured my fierce kiss. There was so little time left; he was struggling to breathe at all. Silently I cried for help, then, gripping him firmly around his injured chest, I yanked him brutally to his feet with every ounce of remaining strength I possessed. Valiantly he stood, swaying as he coughed up a crimson spray.

In a tremulous voice, I began to sing my mother's lullaby. The words were laced with regret.

Your want is my want, your love is my love,
Through every trial you're beside me
My pain is your pain that is healed from above
And your trust—it will never betray me

To hear the bright song of the River that flows
My heart will never misguide me
But listen, my love, to the wisdom that knows
You must double your pain to redeem me

Bane winced and clutched me tighter with his good arm, bravely taking steps that should have been impossible in his state. Strength flowed into him as he drew me into the muted dance, giving it his all and focusing everything on me. Sweat dripped from his hair, which made him look even more gorgeous. More real, somehow.

'If you tell me … to dance, I'll dance, even though … so cold. How do I … always end up doing … what you want?' His adorable smile melted my heart as he swung us around. I refused to acknowledge the metallic scent of approaching death.

'Because you are very strong,' I answered. 'And I am very stubborn.'

He drew my fingers to his lips and kissed them as we danced. Then he spun me around with false ease and drew me close again. His whole body was shaking; this couldn't last long.

'Best gift I've ever been given. One … final dance.'

A violent shudder rocked him so I gripped him even tighter. I was leading now and supporting nearly all his weight. He rested his cheek on my shoulder. 'Do you remember … our first dance?' he rasped. 'You bullied me into that one … too. I never thanked you.'

'I thought you were going to stand there the whole time letting me make an idiot of myself in front of everyone.'

'I … considered it,' he admitted, 'but, that gold dress, and you were *right there*, and I had to … hold you, finally. I *needed* to be touching you, just like … now.'

Fingers slick with blood traced delicate patterns on my wrist. His other arm hung down by his side, useless and cold. Our dance was more of a shuffle now, yet still painfully romantic in its morbidity. Although I wanted to savour every last moment of it, we were out of time.

'Are those flames from Sadie? Are you making … them bigger?' he mumbled.

'I guess I am. You did mention you were cold. Can you feel their heat?'

'No. Not at all.'

Rabisu could feel them though, and the demon wasn't happy about it. A cry of pure malice left my lips and I stumbled back. With a fierce grunt, Bane gripped my shoulder and pulled me forward again.

'Don't let me go!' I begged before Rabisu could clamp my mouth shut.

Bane looked me right in the eye, making certain he knew what I wanted, then nodded. 'I will protect … you with everything I have. Always. Besides … you promised me a … dance.' He hooked his good arm securely around my waist. Part of me quite enjoyed it, but my demon prisoner wasn't so impressed. In utter annoyance I watched my limbs thrash about, trying to break free from Bane's grip. I was powerless to stop myself. All my concentration was needed just to keep my will intact—I had none left for fighting for control of my muscles as well.

The look on my Guardian's face was unbearable. As if his own pain wasn't enough, what I was asking him to do for me went beyond dedication. He'd once described it to me as being 'as impossible as if I was trying to hammer my own thumb. Hard. On purpose.'

And Sadie's fire was worlds more painful than a blow from a hammer.

Within my mind, the demon began to shriek. *You broke your end of the bargain. The deal is off. Let me go!*

I never broke our deal. I said I'd let Dallmin go home, and I did. I have no authority to make his choices for him. Not anymore. And I kept your secret.

How can you leave him to rot here? You don't understand what it will do to him. Go after him, Shamar!

He can overcome the despair this world will throw at him. It won't be easy, but he has everything he needs to make the right choices. Have faith in him.

You still don't understand. I fought the veiled ones for so many years. So much pain. So much loss. And all I had left was the hope that one day I would find my way home. I clung to it so hard that when the time came I simply couldn't let go, and I became what I despised the most. My father should never have to face the things we faced.

He already has, thanks to you.

I didn't know! As soon as I saw him … everything I've done from that moment on has been for him. So he could go home. I even stood by and let others of my kind capture him and try to make him cross back. I would have torn down the sky to send him back to Eden.

Me too, I admitted in shared grief. Grief that weighed on me almost as much as Bane's broken body.

My Guardian coughed up more blood and gasped out his fear. 'You can't … feel the heat either, can you? The flames never burned Noah.'

'Sadie would never hurt me. I can't feel the fire at all,' I lied, simply to make him feel better. Would he even be able to tell the difference between his pain and mine? Because as the demon had so smugly guessed, Sadie would do exactly what I told her to do. Even kill me if I asked. With every shred of strength remaining, the demon was now trying to wrench free from my body.

She almost pulled free. Until I used the only card I had left to play.

'Nin! You are not free to leave!'

I didn't realise I'd yelled it out loud until I heard Noah sob from behind us.

Bane held me even tighter. 'Use your gift, Lainie.'

Apparently, he'd already figured it out, and he was right. I could use my gift to link her to me the same way I'd been linked to Dallmin right before Bane had proposed.

'Nin. We still have a deal,' I said. 'Your father need never know who you are, so long as you see this through.' If Mr D had managed to hold her all those years, then I could hold on for a few more moments, even if she was clawing at my mind like a frightened cat. The demon Rabisu, once known as Nin, screamed back at me, and Bane had to pin my elbow to my hip to stop me writhing.

You're killing me! Nin wailed. *Would you really suffer the same fate as your mother just to end me?*

'You are no longer human. You admitted that often enough. Turns out it's my *job* to end you, Nin.'

You said you would take me across!' she cried. *Why are we burning?*

And I am taking you, I thought back. *This is the only way in. Even I can't escape the process. I guess the only difference between us is how much will remain once Sadie has done her work. Will what remains of you be enough to even want to stay in this realm? Or will you choose to fly to somewhere new? You wanted to cross the Skin of the World, and who am I to deny a soul what it truly wants? So let's go!* I clenched my teeth together to hold back a scream. Once again I had forgotten how painful death could be.

Between one scorched breath and the next, Dallmin's daughter stopped fighting, and my disobedient limbs went meekly still.

'Is it done?' Bane asked, pressing his forehead against mine.

'Not quite,' I gasped. 'Thank you for trusting me.'

'I know you too well, Lainie. Rabisu … Nin, had no hope.' He smiled, ignoring the curls of smoke coming from his smouldering shirt. 'Remember Mrs … Armstrong?'

'Our Year Six teacher?' I was gasping now and struggling to stay focused. I hadn't done it this way before. It was brave of him to try to distract us both from the pain. Was he even thinking about retreating? But it was too late for him, and he would never risk leaving this unfinished.

'Sugar bowl …' was all he said before succumbing to another blood-filled cough.

'Sugar bowl? Oh, as in the time when I fooled her into believing it was the Year Nine class who filled the staff sugar bowl with salt?'

He nodded. 'She said …'

'She said I was a worse trickster than the devil himself.'

A sharp laugh escaped him. 'Turns out that was … a compliment.'

I wanted to laugh with him, only he was holding me so tightly with his one good arm that I could hardly breathe. Why had no one else in my family ever thought to do this? Were they all so afraid to die? Death was nothing.

'Bane, listen to me. I need you to stop healing me,' I gasped, my throat raw and my skin blistering everywhere at once. 'From what Nin told me when she suggested this, the timing is going to be important. I don't want you to leave me behind, even for a few seconds.'

'Since when do we … trust anything that demon has to say? Lainie, what are you doing? Why do I need … to heal you?'

His mind was beginning to shut down. I knew from experience that was a good thing. If he couldn't think, then he couldn't feel either.

'Because I'm coming with you, silly.'

He stopped dancing, scrambling for lucidity. 'No, Lainie. No way. You need … stay and … find someone else to … continue the line. Our link … broken soon, it will be okay.'

'Listen to me. There is *nothing* okay about our link being broken. Don't let me go!'

Bleeding fingers clutched at mine painfully.

Nin writhed, trying to escape. *I can't do this, Shamar. I'm scared!*
Your father did it. So can you.

'Lainie … I'm scared!' Bane sobbed in a heartrending echo of Nin's terror. 'You told me … human souls are pulled across … quickly. What if I can't find you?' Tears mingled with the blood on his face and his eyes were fading fast. Something sizzled in my left ear and I vaguely noticed my hair had caught fire.

'You can always find me, Bane. In fact, I'm relying on it. Promise me you'll stay with me. You'll feel a pull, but I need you to concentrate on *my* pull more. *Promise me!*' The pain was unbearable now and I fell, pulling him down with me. The fire was blinding and my eyes gave up trying to work at all.

It was then that something came loose inside my mind, as what was left of Nin ignited like flash paper. I could feel the last of her pain transform in exquisite resolution, leaving nothing behind but spiritual ash. It was done.

And only just beginning.

'Lainie, I can feel the flames now,' Bane cried. 'It hurts so much. It burns! Please make it stop. It's too much, I can't do it!'

I clutched his face with my blackening fingers. 'I know it hurts. I can't make it stop, but I'm here with you. I'm trusting my judgment the way you once told me to. Sadie is doing her job and burning off everything that's holding you back from embracing who you really are. It won't hurt for long, only a few short moments,' I promised, forcing the words from my scorched throat.

He didn't reply. Neither of us screamed as the fire consumed us.

If I speak in the tongues of men and of angels, but have not love, I am only a resounding gong or a clanging cymbal. If I have the gift of prophecy and can fathom all mysteries and all knowledge, and if I have a faith that can move mountains, but have not love, I am nothing. If I give all I possess to the poor and surrender my body to the flames, but have not love, I gain nothing.

Chapter 43

Warm purple mist embraced my new form as I struggled to acclimatise. Shrugging off my old form like a worn pair of jeans, I floundered a little as I tried to remember how to operate my limbs. This was nothing like travelling bodiless. This was another realm altogether and my body was solid and real and so was the ground, and so how I moved mattered. Different gravity—no worries. I couldn't see a thing through the mist, so I started to walk and then kangaroo hop like they did on the moon. Not bad, but also not enough. I needed to get above the fog and see what was going on. With that thought, something behind me quivered, and a pair of wings unfurled, large enough that they dragged on the ground until I figured out how to raise them. As soon as I did, a second pair unfolded, wrapping around my shoulders like a cloak. These ones were more like butterfly wings: dextrous, colourful, and rippling at the edges. Fascinated, I wasted no time worrying if I could control the stretchy things; instead, I launched myself into the air searching out the thermal currents. Probably a good thing Dallmin had rattled on for so long about flight dynamics.

It only took moments to break past the purple mist. Far above was a shimmering ceiling like a calm pond reflected onto the sky in a breathtaking reversal, and all around me I could see wisps of coloured energy rising toward the bright inverted surface, drawn like moths to a flame. Each bright tendril was a human soul that barely retained the echo of the form it had recently left behind. Using the same gift I had been given in human form, I could see their emotional memories shaping their new forms.

Bane had to be among them. Precious seconds had been lost when he'd come through first, and there were so many souls to search. It was like trying to find someone in a crowded street when everyone was running. The marriage bond that was supposed to help me apparently didn't extend beyond death. Even though 'until death do us part' had been removed from the wording of modern vows, that didn't change the truth. I was certain he could still find me, but would he remember to look?

Back and forth I flew, fighting off the lingering disorientation as I searched by colour, calling him by name over and over. Over there—a flash of gold? Someone shiny, drifting slower than the others as if lost. Streamlining my body, I streaked along, weaving my way through the crowd using both sets of wings for more intricate manoeuvrability. Yes, I would recognise that soul anywhere. Something about the way he appeared to be dancing, even when mostly formless. Bright gold and so beautiful, Bane was being drawn toward the sparkling white threshold that beckoned from above.

He was too far away.

'No, he's mine! We're not done!'

My wings strained against the riptide current, creating a wake that sent those pretty-coloured souls spinning. There were still so many of them between us. I needed to move faster. Needed to break free. It felt as if there was a fine tingly thread wrapped around my waist and the base of my wings, preventing me from using them to their full advantage. It felt delicate, like it had been worn away and yet it was still enough to slow me down.

Even as I stubbornly put on an extra burst of speed, I knew it wouldn't be enough. His face turned toward the shimmery ceiling, entranced by whatever it was he saw, and he began to drift faster.

'No. Please, Bane, wait for me!'

After everything we'd risked, I couldn't lose him now. He was my Guardian. Guardians always stayed with us, didn't they? More souls brushed past me, so intent on where they were going that I might as well have been invisible. Was their destination so enticing? Was it really so difficult to remember the world they'd just left? I knew the answer to that, because I had fought many times to retain my focus each time I'd crossed into Eden, or become bodiless, or died. It had taken practice. And help.

'Bane!'

He'd called to me each time—in one way or another—and I hadn't always listened. Now he was the one leaving me. I tore at the effervescent thread around my waist until it snapped and I surged forward so fast that the individual souls became a blurred rainbow in the corner of my vision. In despair, I glimpsed him ahead. He was stretching his fingers up to touch the glistening surface. His arm followed, and then his shoulder ... and I was too far away.

'Bane, *please!*'

He didn't even pause. All his attention was locked on whatever was past that shimmering curtain, and then he was gone, lost to infinite beauty ...

Chapter 44

Something bumped him from the other side and bounced him back down. It seemed rather rude. Not as rude as the way I bulldozed past the souls blocking my path, but given that he was in the process of making the transition into eternal life in heaven, it was awkward enough.

His golden spirit wobbled, off balance, and at that moment I finally reached him, sweeping him up in my arms and wings, and I hurriedly tried to figure out how my brakes worked as we tumbled end over end through the mystical air.

'Ahhhh, sorry about that,' I apologised as I got us more or less levelled out.

An ethereal laugh from beyond the shimmering membrane made my heart lurch in grief and gratitude. Annie. I could hear her singing the end of a Hunters & Collectors anthem in a jaunty goodbye as she moved along her journey—set free by her last gift to me. I blew her a grateful kiss before checking to see if Bane was okay.

'Lainie? What are you doing here? Did you go and die again? This is becoming a bad habit of yours, you know,' he chided, smiling at me. He seemed unhinged. I didn't blame him one bit.

'Says the man who pushed me off a cliff on our wedding day,' I countered, trying not to sound too miffed. He blinked at me, as if trying to piece together his hazy memories. For once I wasn't the only person who was disoriented. In fact, I felt quite at home here, at least now that I'd found him.

His face changed as he looked me over, drinking in my new form. 'Wow. You are *stunning*. I've never seen anything so beautiful. I thought you said you looked like a great big duck.'

'It felt that way in my dream. I do have wings.'

'You also glow like you're made from opals.'

I winced. 'Well, that's not embarrassing at all. Am I too weird now?'

'I'm used to weird when it comes to you,' he snorted. 'Nothing you do can surprise me anymore. Although I'm kind of glad you still only have one face.'

I couldn't help laughing at that. 'Haven't you figured it out yet? Why Cherubim are depicted as having four faces? Tessa said the Hebrews referred to us as a Tetramorph. Four elements in one unit.'

'Oh. I get it … Wait, which one am I? The man, the eagle, the lion, or the ox?'

My mouth stayed firmly shut.

'I think Tessa must be the lion, and surely you're the eagle?'

'Bane, try to think metaphorically. The "man" is simply the term for the humanistic qualities. I probably seem like the least human, but it turns out my humanity is the most important thing I have to offer. And Noah called dibs on the eagle,' I added reluctantly.

It only took him a second.

'Why do I have to be the ox?'

'I love you!' I laughed, because until then I hadn't realised a soul could pout. 'Oh, come on, Bane. Oxen are really strong. They symbolise strength. That's their thing.'

'I'd rather be the man.'

'Fine. You can choose to be whatever you want now. You be the man and I'll be a butterfly. I don't mind these wings.'

'They are large, aren't they? So soft. Are you sure I'm not hurting you?' He relaxed his grip a little but didn't let me go.

'I'm sure. These ones seem to be designed to cover things with. I can carry you easily. Besides, you aren't very heavy at the moment, just a bit … wobbly. I feel like if I don't enfold you completely you might dissolve and drift away. How did I ever manage with only two arms and two legs before?'

'I don't know. It did make it easier for dancing. I don't know how well I will be able to dance with you like this.'

Laughing again, I twirled us around in a complex three-dimensional spin, leading him in a flight of pure elation. He laughed with me, luxuriating in every precious moment we were given. After a minute or so he sobered.

'So, my beloved Shamar, what happens now? How long before you need to go back? Noah must be getting frantic.'

I slowed us to a lazy drift, listening for Noah's voice. 'I expect he's resorted to swearing at me by now. He thinks it made a difference that time when I was poisoned.'

'And did it?'

'Maybe a little. Not as much difference as the gift you were promising me though. I was more than a little bit intrigued by that.'

'I didn't know if you could hear me. I'm very glad you did.'

'Me too. It was an odd time to propose though, don't you think?'

'Fits right in with the way we seem to operate, Lainie. Everything we do is odd, in case you haven't noticed.'

'I like odd. And I like it here. This place is very odd. There is air here, and wind. I wonder what a physicist would say about it?'

His smile looked regretful. 'You should probably go. It'll get harder if you linger too long away from your body.' He moved a strand of glowing hair away from my face with comforting familiarity and his expression became very sombre. Very high-school-Bane-like. 'Lainie, I'm sorry I got so injured. I didn't want to leave you. I've been a pathetic excuse for a Guardian, I know. I don't think any other Guardian in history has allowed his charge to die this many times. I'll still miss it though. I love you and I always will no matter where I am.' He looked right into my eyes, full of longing. 'I'll wait for you. I won't mind if you have someone else by then …' A slight tightening of his lips gave him away. 'Okay, so that's not entirely true, but I'll still be grateful to him. I'll try to be nice, I promise. Just don't forget me.'

'Bane?'

'Yeah?'

'You're rambling.'

'Yes, I know. I should stop procrastinating. It's time for you to go back.' His words conflicted with the way he continued to clutch me around my waist. 'Goodbye, Lainie, I really will miss you. No matter what amazing things happen to me from here on, I'll still miss you.'

'Bane. Seriously. Shut up. I'm trying to concentrate on where Noah is.'

'Oh, right. Sorry. Let me go, then. I can feel the shiny thing pulling me. I'll be okay from here,' he said, looking back over his shoulder in the direction we'd come from.

It took all my effort not to start humming. That would have been a dead giveaway. And I didn't want to give away my dead husband. Of course, it wasn't my choice to make. 'Is that what you want? Do you want to move across it?'

He paused and then shook his head, as if he wanted to save my feelings by lying and telling me he did. He was clean of all traces of deception now though, so lying was impossible.

'No. I can't stand the thought of leaving you, even now, and I can still feel you pulling at me,' he said. 'It's stronger than the other pull. You're going to have to let me go or I won't be strong enough to break free from you at all.'

I looked him in the eye. 'Bane. What do you *want*?'

He smiled. 'The same thing I've always wanted. To experience all your humanness. All of it. Even the parts where you yell at me.'

'I was kind of hoping you'd say that because I've got Buckley's of finding my way back without you. It had to be your choice, though.'

Something in his demeanour snapped to attention. 'Are you saying you've lost your body again?'

'Nope,' I scoffed. 'Of course not *lost*.'

'You can't lie to me. Not here.'

I ducked away from his accusatory gaze. 'Not lost. Mislaid ...'

He began to look worried. Which was embarrassingly inappropriate for this realm. 'Even I can still feel my body,' he argued. 'It feels like a tingly thread coiled around my waist.'

'Oh. That thing. Oops. I may have busted mine.' Apparently, he hadn't lost that good old let's-blame-Lainie-for-everything look he'd perfected in Year Seven.

'How? Mine feels indestructible. I guess it must dissolve as we pass to the next stage. Wait, yours was already pretty weak, right?'

'Totally not my fault,' I agreed.

He made a sound that would have been a deep sigh if he'd had breath. 'So now what? Do we stay here forever?' He glanced around as if searching for the nearest place to buy coffee. Luckily I was pretty well-versed in how to proceed, even if I couldn't do it myself.

My lips brushed his ear as I whispered, sounding as seductive as I felt. He'd already made his free choice, so there was no manipulation in it. 'Can't you feel it?' I asked him. 'Feel the need to breathe?'

His eyes became unfocused, and he began to gasp. Perfect. Now all I had to do was follow my heart as it followed his.

'Hold on,' I told him. 'This part can feel a bit like getting struck by lightning, not that I've actually done that. Yet.'

'Where are we going?'

Was I this thick whenever I transitioned? Yeah. I was.

'I thought you might like to answer Noah's insults in person,' I explained. 'You can't always expect me to stand up for you, you know. Besides, I *really* hate it when he calls me lazy.'

He who has an ear, let him hear what the Spirit says to the churches. To him who overcomes I will give to eat from the tree of life, which is in the midst of the Paradise of God.

Revelations 2:7 NKJ

Chapter 45

With the faintest of touches, I brushed the iridescent blue feather across his perfect lips. They twitched in response and I grinned. It was so hard to be patient. Languidly, I traced it over each remembered scar: his forearms and wrists, his ribs and cheekbone. Not one of them remained now. I pulled his wedding ring gently from his finger to check if the inscription was still there. It was fine, not even warped, so I slid it back on, wondering if the words had glowed while we were in the fire.

The silky feather skimmed over all the places I wanted to kiss, which luckily filled in quite some time while Noah kept reminding me not to rush him. A flock of sparrows sang for us nearby, distracting me with their aerial antics as I related to their carefree flight. Laughing at their intricate sky dancing, I wondered how long it would be before I would fly like that again. There was no hurry. Other things held my interest more.

Noah had picked a good spot; it was secluded and indescribably pretty. He'd even adorned my new hair with some bright blue flowers he'd found before I'd woken up. I'd found yellow ones for his, and they looked terrific.

Finally I noticed Bane's eyelids flutter as he took a deep, relaxed breath. No subtle tremors shook his shoulders, and no tension pulled at his jaw. For the first time I could remember, he looked utterly peaceful. Like the river in the height of summer. Pale grey eyes opened, blinking, to a world they had never seen before, and his irises were even more beautiful than I remembered, backlit by the mercurial colour of his soul.

'Shalom, Bane,' I whispered, cherishing the smile on his face as he locked his eyes on mine.

'Shalom, Lainie,' his velvet voice replied.

Automatically making himself aware of his surroundings, it took all of three seconds for him to get his bearings, which surely had to be some sort of record for this place. Was that due to his soldier training or a Guardian trait?

'Where the hell are we?' he asked, sitting bolt upright.

Behind me, Noah cracked up laughing. Really laughing. So hard he snorted. I turned and glared at him. I was trying to have a 'moment', after all.

'I'm sorry, Lainie. I can't help it. Of all the words that could have come out of his mouth. I love it. Tell the world! Bane finally found his sense of humour.'

Turning my back on my mental Cherub partner, I tried to master my expression to look more appropriately serious. Bane looked at me in wonder, brushing my cheek with his fingertips.

'You are the most beautiful thing I've ever seen,' he whispered.

'Well, that's more like what a girl wants to hear. Although, I have to tell you, if that's true then you really haven't seen much. Look around you. Does this look like hell to you? Seriously, you can hardly blame Noah for reacting like that,' I admonished him.

Blinking rather stupidly, Bane looked around the meadow, taking in the difference in light and colour.

'It's ... it's ...'

Stern self-discipline kept me from laughing at his flustered expression.

'We're not ... You never said it was ... The air sparkles, and ... I never thought it would have such ...' His voice trailed off again in speechless wonder.

I waited for him to adjust to the idea.

He glared at me. 'How can *I* be here? What did you do?'

'I'm gonna tell it to you straight. There are no unicorns,' I disclosed, hoping he wouldn't be too disappointed.

He stared at me, dumbfounded.

'Welcome to Paradise, my love.' It was glorious to finally utter that phrase. Joy bubbled up inside me as I watched his features light up with understanding. Astounded, he started to ask at least three different questions, but didn't quite know where to begin, so I got in first. 'You did say that you wanted more time. I want what you want, remember? Besides, I happened to agree more than a little bit myself.'

'So you brought me to Eden?'

'Well, Noah brought your body and I brought your soul. Credit where it's due.'

Noah piped in. 'And for the record, I'd just like to say a great big "nope". Don't *ever* ask me to do that again. Three times I've had to drag your corpse over here now, Lainie. That's four corpses, if you count Bane. I'm done.'

'Oh, stop whining. You've done worse things on the farm over the years.'

'Worse than dragging my best friends' charred carcasses through a cave? Nope. Can't say that I have.'

'Point taken. I'll try to avoid it in the future.'

'That's exactly what you said last time,' he grumbled.

I turned back to Bane. 'Is it okay that I did this? It was what you wanted. You said so. You possibly don't remember that bit though, so you might have to just trust me. You wanted to stay with me.' It came out sounding a bit defensive.

'Of course I want to stay with you. How could you doubt that?'

'Well, the alternative is pretty good too, from what I hear.'

Not even bothering to respond in words, he pulled me down onto the soft grass with him and kissed me until my blood sang. I *knew* I'd done the right thing.

'When can we show him the slide? I'm getting hot,' Noah said, fanning his face with a giant leaf.

Ignoring him, I explored all the new sensations my freshly healed body was delighting in as Bane ran his fingers down my back.

'I'm serious,' he insisted. 'Tessa will want me to come back soon. I haven't waited all morning for Sleeping Beauty here to wake up only to stand around and watch you make out with him.'

Bane let me go and stood up, looking a little bit sheepish. 'Noah wants us to stop,' he said.

He was already adjusting to Eden-like instincts. His will was aligning itself with what he believed others wanted. Luckily I'd made the transition between worlds often enough to remember my own desires.

'Listen, Bane of my old life,' I murmured, stretching out on the grass sensuously. 'I have to apologise. I'm afraid our clothes didn't survive Sadie's fire.' My mother's wedding dress was gone, but it had served its purpose.

Bane eyes widened. He looked at Noah—who was still wearing his best man's suit—then down at himself, and then back to me. 'Oh. Well, okay. Um, I don't mind,' he flustered. A moment later his confidence returned with a smouldering look. 'Actually, I really don't mind.'

Neither did I. He was magnificent.

Noah cleared his throat and Bane glanced back at him, perplexed.

Chuckling at his understandable resurrection confusion, I said the words that would clear things up for him once and for all.

'I don't *want* to go to the slide yet. I *want* to keep kissing you.'

Noah threw his hands in the air and walked away.

My gorgeous retired Guardian didn't hesitate. He grabbed my hand and hoisted me up, laughing, and I led him to a place where we could begin a new life together.

'Lainie?' he asked, bemused, when we eventually tumbled down into the secluded soft meadow. Glitter bugs spun around us dizzily. 'Am I really here, or is this another dream?'

'Bane, for the first time in your life, you're finally awake,' I answered. 'Welcome home.'

Epilogue

Hundreds of people held their breath at the same time with their necks craned upward. For the last hour, they'd been treated to stunning displays of aerobatics, acrobatics, balancing acts, and trapeze catches. Just when they thought they couldn't be wowed any more, the masked man had appeared. Suspended from a split silken band, the man with the metallic blue hair had absolutely no fear. A perfect specimen of male physique, the performer's strong limbs held him easily through each swing, each twist, and each gravity-defying hold.

The old man smiled in appreciation.

'In my next life I want to come back as a piece of circus silk,' the young redhead in the seat next to him whispered to her friend. 'Look at the way it's wrapped around his thigh. I'm jealous. Of silk. Seriously.'

Her friend threw popcorn at her. Some of it landed in the old man's lap, but they didn't notice. They were too busy gasping at the sudden death plunge the artist had performed, their eyes bulging as they stared at him, hanging from his ankle with his nose brushing the floor.

'He's like a beautiful giant. I bet he's from northern Africa. Look at those muscles. Perhaps Wakanda is real after all. Does it say in the program where he's from?'

A few moments passed as they squinted at the program in the dim lighting. The old man smiled. Wakanda? Not quite.

'It doesn't say anything about him,' her friend replied. 'Not even his real name. They only refer to him as the Ancient Pilgrim. Weird stage name if you ask me. They should have called him Zeus, or Jupiter. Something god-like.'

'Sssshh!' came the inevitable protest from the row in front of them.

'There isn't even a photo of him without his mask on. Mysterious much?'

'That's show business for you. The more mysterious the better,' the redhead muttered. 'I don't mind. This way I can give him whatever face I want. He could even look like that DJ, what was his name? The one who spent all his money setting up the music school in Darwin.'

'Who, Daniel Goldstar?' the friend replied, hiding behind her carton of popcorn as if it would muffle the sound of their conversation. 'He was gorgeous, but that was years ago. He'd be in his late forties by now, wouldn't he? Eewww.'

The old man ran his fingers through his short grey hair as he was reminded of the real reason he'd come to watch the show.

'It's my fantasy, I can make him whatever age I want,' the young woman insisted as she curled a strand of hair around her finger. The man in the seat in front turned and glared at the two of them until they finally stopped talking.

As the performer held himself horizontally in the air by just one bulging muscular arm, the crowd cheered and applauded. The old man stood, picked up his bag containing the bottle of wine he'd snuck in as well as the photos his wife had discovered, and gruffly apologised to the people along the row as he shuffled his way past them. He hated pushing through crowds—he could never get used to them—and since he needed to get backstage he figured it would be easier if he went before the show was over. Somehow he would have to convince the bouncers to let him through. He was retired now, so he couldn't simply flash his badge the way he used to. Unfortunately, he didn't have Noah's charm either—or Bethany's precocious way of meddling with people's emotions. He wondered if there was a way he could get one of them to speak to Nathaniel over the phone if the bouncers proved to be as prickly as they should be. Nathaniel could get anyone to re-examine their morals. Just by smiling. Even on the other end of a phone connection.

The performer's security would be tight; he knew because there was a time when he'd been in charge of it. That had been years ago. It was imperative the paparazzi didn't get access to the performer when he was undisguised. Someone always managed it eventually though, and recently it had happened again. Someone had posted a photo on the net of the sought-after circus performer without his make-up on. It was a little blurry, and far away, but already there had been speculation. The man simply had too much talent in everything he tried his hand at. Too much fame. Far too much recognition, even when he tried to only work behind the scenes. He couldn't even sing publicly anymore without his voice being recognised, although he seemed content these days just to anonymously send his songs to emerging artists he liked. As varied as the styles were, it was still easy to pick which ones were his—invariably they were the ones that left you feeling like they were written specifically for you, and that you were meant for something … more. More than this mundane place.

Grimly schooling his features into an expression of authority the bouncers might respect, Mick knocked firmly on the backstage access door. He and Lily were supposed to be leaving for Nepal early the next morning to check on Dallmin's new orphanage, the business mentoring program, and the clean water management plan. After that—maybe by the end of the year—he was determined to get her on that cruise.

First, he had the regretful news to deliver. Tim had already called Dallmin numerous times, trying to break it to him gently, begging him to come home. Even tempting him with his latest batch of award-winning Merlot. Dallmin, as usual, had played down the risk. Mick understood why he stayed away from Nalong. Watching the people you love slowly age before your eyes while you stayed young couldn't be easy. Still, he couldn't keep performing here. Someone needed to tell him bluntly. In person. So Dallmin could read his body language and know it was serious this time.

When he finally made it through to the performer's well-guarded dressing room, Dallmin greeted him with an exuberant hug, which Mick had no qualms about returning.

'Shalom, my friend. Did you bring the wine?'

Mick handed over the bottle. 'Time to change careers again,' he stated firmly, looking Dallmin in the eye and preparing for an argument.

Instead, Dallmin leaned toward him with a mischievous grin. 'Want to see my designs for the next space shuttle?' He bundled Mick into the dressing room and shut the door, laughing at the startled look on Mick's face. 'Relax,' he said. 'Haven't you learned yet? All will be well.'

Acknowledgments

Really? You've hung around to read these? This isn't a Marvel movie, you know.

This is, however, a golden opportunity for me to thank you for your support. By reading these stories, you've blessed me in a way I never expected. I certainly never expected that lecture to my daughter ('Of course you can write a whole story. You can achieve anything you choose to put the work into. Let's write one together') to turn into a full-length novel (she got bored when I couldn't let go of the reins. Completely my fault.) I also never expected for the story to be accepted by a publisher (small press makes this world richer!). I definitely never expected this project to turn into four full-sized novels spanning two worlds, with someone as cool as you reading them. Yet here you are.

If this *was* a Marvel movie, then my beta readers/street team would be worthy of a catchy name. Something that would showcase each of their unique superpowers. From Alison's teacher-gift of digging down to the most accurate use of punctuation while still encouraging me to shine, to Alex's pernickety way of noticing a passing reference to a tree that shouldn't be flowering at that time of year—my crew are all superheroes. Perhaps I could make some sort of clever acronym pun from their names: Nickie, Alison, Kim, Addie, Maree, Paul, Alex, Brian, Pam, Vron, Colin, Zoe, Lily, Jenna. Nakampabpvczlj … or perhaps not. Never mind. They would never agree to wear the t-shirt anyway (except maybe Vron). Slick team names aside, I am genuinely grateful to each and every person who has assisted with this story, especially Sarah Endicott and Gillian Polack for their priceless editing support, and to the

YA Room in Melbourne for the relentless way they infect me with their enthusiasm for all things bookish.

Special thanks go to the First Nations readers who have generously given me feedback, encouragement, and assistance. I acknowledge that none of you could possibly be expected to speak for an entire continent of nations, but your input is still precious to me and always welcome. Thanks also to Michelle Lovi (Odyssey Books) for having enough of a soft spot for Eden to have put up with me for so long. And of course I need to thank Paul, Dania, Arden, Mum and Dad for helping me grow. It's what family does, apparently.

Lastly, thank you to the Creator who dreamed up a paradise for His children to enjoy. Thanks for letting me play in it. I look forward to seeing it for myself and laughing with you at all the ways my descriptions fell so short of its glory.

Oh, and it's not as if Marvel has a copyright on doing this sort of thing, you know …

About the Author

Carolyn lives on a farm on the outskirts of Melbourne. She has a science degree, far too many pets, and a fear of the ocean that makes her Mauritian mother roll her eyes. She enjoys writing spec-fiction novels, playing games with her horse, and frightening hairdressers with the concept of the forthcoming Singularity. As well as writing stories for *Aurealis* and *Andromeda Spaceways* magazines, Carolyn is also the author of the YA Australian fantasy series *The Sentinels of Eden*.

For teasers of Carolyn's other books, visit:
http://carolyndenman.com/books-and-publications/teasers/

www.ingramcontent.com/pod-product-compliance
Lightning Source LLC
Chambersburg PA
CBHW030709190726
48286CB00001B/238